Review

Through the Valley of Shadow is a powerful story that pulls you deep into its depths as Terr learns to accept what he is and what he has become, and the powers that work against him. The struggle that Terr faces and the political machinations that pulls the series together are brilliant. Stefan is a gifted writer with the ability to draw you into his world.

Millennium Science Fiction & Fantasy

I0592617

Books by Stefan Vučak

General Fiction:
Cry of Eagles
All the Evils
Towers of Darkness
Strike for Honor
Proportional Response
Legitimate Power
Autumn Leaves
All My Sunsets
F/X-26
28th Amendment
Night Sirens
Broken Rose

Shadow Gods Saga:
In the Shadow of Death
Against the Gods of Shadow
A Whisper from Shadow
Shadow Masters
Immortal in Shadow
With Shadow and Thunder
Through the Valley of Shadow
Guardians of Shadow

Science Fiction:
Fulfillment
Lifeliners

Non-Fiction:
Writing Tips for Authors

Contact at:
www.stefanvucak.com

THROUGH THE VALLEY OF SHADOW

By

Stefan Vučak

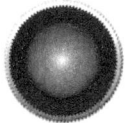

Note:

This is a work of fiction. All names, characters, places, and events are
the work of the author's imagination. Any resemblance to real per-
sons, places, or events is coincidental.

Stefan Vučak ©2000
ISBN-10: 064847318X
ISBN-13: 9780648473183

Dedication

To Helena…and her voyage of self-discovery

Acknowledgments

Orion Nebula – Credit: C.R. O'Dell (Rice University), and NASA.

Cover art by Laura Shinn.
http://laurashinn.yolasite.com

Map of the Serrll Combine

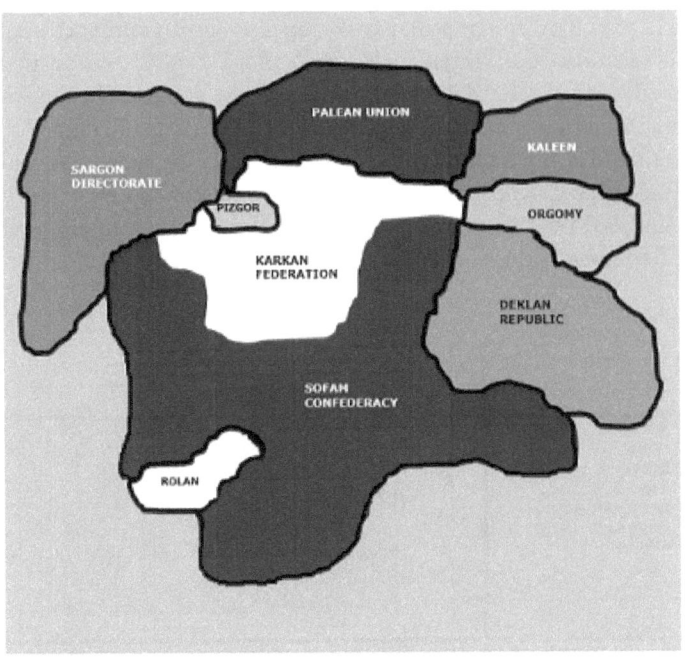

Composition of the Serrll Combine

The 247 star systems that make up the Serrll Combine is an association of six interstellar power blocks, split between two rival camps—the Servatory Party and the Revisionists. Each star system has a single representative in Captal's General Assembly from which members are elected to the ruling ten-seat Executive Council. Seats are based on a percentage of systems occupied by each power block in relation to the total number of systems in the Serrll Combine.

Name	No of Star Systems	Percentage of Total	Executive Council Seats
Sofam Confederacy	83	34	4
Deklan Republic	19	8	1
Palean Union	28	11	1
Karkan Federation	46	19	2
Sargon Directorate	32	12	1
Independents:		15	1
- Kaleen	8		
- Rolan	5		
- Orgomy	6		
- Pizgor	3		
- Other systems	17		
General Assembly	**247**	**100**	**10**
Outposts	40		
Protectorates	34		

Principal political blocks:

Revisionist Party:	Palean Union
	Deklan Republic
	Sofam Confederacy
Servatory Party:	Karkan Federation
	Sargon Directorate
	Nonaligned Independents

Composition of the Executive Council:

Security Council	Bureau of Colonial and Protectorate Affairs
	Bureau of Defense
	Bureau of Cultural Affairs
Administrative Council	Bureau of Administrative Affairs
	Bureau of Justice
Economics Council	Bureau of Economic Affairs
	Bureau of Technology and Development
Central Planning Council	Bureau of Central Planning and Development

Chapter One

"Teena!" Terr cried in torn agony, arms upraised as he reached toward a turbulent sky.

Jagged and stark, lightning touched the hills and made the dwellings along the skyline flare and dance with cold white fire. With a pealing crash, thunder ripped the heavens apart. The ground cringed and shuddered. Cold and biting, the rain came down in slanting sheets, pursued by the mournful thin wailing of the wind.

He stood there and allowed the power of the wind and the rain wash over him in a vain hope of replenishing something that had been drained, torn from his very soul. He lowered his arms and gripped the ramp railing until his fingers ached from the strain. A strangled sob escaped from somewhere deep within him. He buried his face in his hands and felt the hot wetness in his eyes leak between his fingers. He wasn't crying, just wiping the rain off his cheeks.

The hurt he felt was an agonizing throb deep inside him, of loss and betrayal and shattered faith. A feeling of being soiled, something the rain could not wash away. The pressure in his chest generated an exquisite sharp pain that probed and cut, threatening to burst through him. He clenched his fists and exhaled with a shudder. Mouth set in a rigid grimace, he tilted back his head.

"Nooooo!"

Defiance to hell sent with hate and forlorn longing. A cry of shattered innocence and lost dreams, but there was no one to hear his torment in the storm. Only the sound of rushing wind and hissing rain shared his anguish. He wrung his hands and swallowed. It went down lumpy and hard.

Shoulders hunched, he turned and stumbled back into the house. The door sighed shut behind him. His footsteps were heavy and loud in the empty corridor. Flat echoes surrounded him like a cloak, a reminder of all his yesterdays and of what might have been—fool's dreams. Now the echoes mocked him with each step he made. A wet rivulet slid down the back of his head and icy tendrils touched his neck. He leaned against a wall, weary and lost, wishing for oblivion and its peace.

Absently, he reached into his pocket and clutched her scarf, deriving a measure of comfort from its soft touch. The liquor bar lit up as he approached. He punched in something, not really caring what, simply to stop the hurt for a while. The frosted tumbler slid out and he held it with hands that shook with coiled tension. He drank the bitter mixture in hurried gulps. He breathed out the pungent fumes with a shuddering grunt.

"Anabb ought to try this," he mumbled and stared at the glass.

Rit!

Anger and hate boiled within him, burning with a consuming flame. That was one name he didn't care to think about. With a snarl of revulsion, he hurled the tumbler against the wall. The tinkle of broken crystal was a window into the fires of his mind, a glimpse into the chaos of his thoughts.

"Damn you," he whispered with hissing intensity. "Damn you to hell!"

Blinking rapidly, he stared at the scarf in his hand. He extended his arm and looked at the clinging material, hanging limp and lifeless. He opened his hand and tilted it slightly. The sheer piece of precious cloth slithered with a rush and fell without a sound to make an insignificant pile on the carpet. That's how easy it was to snuff out two lives. He regarded the material and his eyes misted.

"I'm sorry, Teena...sorry..."

He didn't know how much he drank, but it must have been a lot. His eyes felt gummy and his mouth dry, tasting like rotting lawn clippings. The Wall cycled through random color patterns and he could not remember having switched it on. He finally decided it didn't matter worth a damn.

He didn't remember getting into the cable-tube and the upper level. Clutching the walls, he staggered toward the bedroom. The door slid out of his way and he blinked as pale blue light touched the walls. The wide bed appeared in front of him. He fell across it with a heartfelt groan and the lights went out, leaving only the faint green safety strip along the bottom of the walls. Her smell lingered everywhere, on blankets, pillows, everything. The very air held her presence and he could not see her. Moaning, he clutched the sheets as something hot broke within him and flowed, cutting deep as it went.

"Teena," he sobbed brokenly and twisted with the pain, willing her to be there. Her form shimmered beside him, pale and transparent and he reached for her. He thought she smiled. Then she was gone, leaving behind her the heat and smell of burnt desert sands. He cursed feebly as darkness descended over him like a film of gossamer.

* * *

Darkness still reigned when he woke.

He lay with his hands clasped behind his head, fingers locked, staring into the dusky depths of the ceiling, thinking of black and evil things. Through the window screen, blinking points filled the eastern sky where the canopy of stars met the somber dark hills. No wind disturbed the quiet stillness as night held its breath. The storm had washed the land and gone, its rage and anger spent. Somewhere in the night, his anger and rage also washed away, leaving behind emptiness and a coldness that surprised him. Disturbingly, he felt a hunger to reach with his hand and see Death walk again.

The words came to him unbidden. His skin tingled and he tensed as Death came and he stood in its shadow. The sands were hot beneath his feet and the sun a white hole burning through an amber sky. His cape fluttered behind him and he held his arms high. Thunder echoed among the dunes. The power flowed through him and he became one with the desert and the sky. He tilted back his head and laughed with the echoes.

But his laughter was a hollow and empty thing, a mocking memory. He felt the weight of his transgressions and knew himself unworthy of the power washing through him, tingling in his hands. The towering buttresses of Athal Than rising out of the sands of the Saffal were sharp in his mind. Perhaps it was destiny the call should come to him now when he contemplated killing a brother. He didn't believe it. The gods do not beckon without reason. He figured that taking another life now wouldn't make much of a difference anyway.

The images faded, leaving him in the blackness of his turbid thoughts.

Small noises filled the night and the air smelled wet and cold. With the shadow of Death upon him, he tried to still the turbulence of his mind. To sleep meant to be at peace, and his soul knew no rest in the fires within which he burned. He wasn't feeling sorry for himself. That was someone else, someone in another life and another reality. Looking back, he could hardly believe how naive and stupid he'd been. The same questions tormented him over and over, but there were no new answers. A futile effort that only fanned the storm of hate raging within him. The peace he craved eluded him.

Among the murky shadows of political counterthrusts within which he and his brother worked, he could almost come to understand why Dhar may have wanted to eliminate him. Why didn't Dhar just kill him and be done with it instead of letting him crash on Earth? If he lived, Dhar must have known he would come after him. And Teena. Why take her? She had nothing to do with his missions. Was it because they were partners? That made sense, but why take her to Anar'on, of all places? He found the whole thing maddening.

Nightwings, my brother of the night...

Terr gave a heavy sigh and threw back the covers.

Rit!

Outside, stillness waited between his breaths, a silence he could feel: thick, heavy and comforting. The air crisp and invigorating, yet, as he walked toward the railing, he did not feel the cold. The moment had a timeless magical quality, and he remembered all the nights Teena and he spent beneath the veil of stars. Cloaked by their light, the two of them would sit and talk while the hills around them slept. A crazy madness where they used to explore and discover each other, becoming one. It seemed all so simple then.

My only love, to have you beside me now...

He turned and she stood there, a phosphorescent shadow that smiled at him. Her pale green eyes set slightly too far apart were big and soft, filled with compassion and love. Her small delicate mouth opened to reveal even white teeth. Long black hair stirred as in a wind. He could smell the desert sands around her.

"Teena," he murmured breathlessly and reached with a faltering hand to brush her face, aching for her touch. Her eyes never left his as she leaned against his hand. He felt the heat of her skin and his heart hammered loud in his ears.

'I love you,' she mouthed the words and her form began to blur.

"Don't go!" he moaned with tragic longing as she vanished, leaving behind but a burning memory.

He dropped his arm and stared at the spot where she faded, wishing her to be there. There was only silence and darkness to keep him company. His power can do a lot of things, but it cannot bring her to him. As he stared through the curtain of night, his thoughts wandered through the dusty corridors of his memories. Lost in another time and another world from which she was now gone. He leaned against the railing and gazed at the cold and cruel indifference of the stars.

Even now it all seemed almost unreal. He could hardly believe that his life could be ripped apart like this and so swiftly. Everything was gone at a stroke, a nightmare from which he longed to wake and find her beside him. He chuckled with bitter irony at the fates that led him down this road. What was really funny last night after all the things he said to Anabb, he couldn't even bring himself to kill the cold, scheming, evil old fart, him and his fancy speeches and world-saving missions. May the canal worm crap on him, his missions, the Orieli and anyone else who got in the way. Besides, what in the pits was so damned important about the Orieli or Earth worth being slugged, shot, hunted…being away from Teena. Because of the Krans? He had never even *seen* a Kran. Probably only a slick con job spun by the Orieli for the benefit of simpleminded locals.

Like the man said, it was all high politics stuff.

Anabb even said as much, cursed be his shadow. Terr could understand the twisted workings of that evil mind, the plots and counterplots hatched in some dark corner of Anabb's brain. That's how the Captal movers and shakers did business. It was a game played by the powerful everywhere. Terr was not so naive that he failed to recognize it. And for what? To save them all from the Karkan Federation and the bad old Servatory Party? By all the ten gods! Was the hand of the Revisionists any cleaner? If it meant his honor, pride and self-respect, they can all go and screw themselves.

It might have been a game, but the results were just as deadly.

But why you, Nightwings, my brother?

Could Dhar really be working for the Servatory Party and Terchran, and the Karkan was trying to get even because of the Gashkarali hit? He admitted knowing about the mission. Terr stiffened and a shiver ran down his spine. He felt the fine hairs on the back of his neck rise in faint alarm. He remembered as though it were yesterday. After the Salina conference, back on Taltair, Enllss invited both of them to a reception. An occasion to pour oil between the Servatory Party and Revisionist waters.

He cleared his mind and saw Dhar's face before him as they sat with Enllss in Anabb's office. His brother looked calm, but reproving, almost uncomfortable at the thought of meeting Terchran. A subtle reaction and anyone else would have missed it. Then again, Terr wasn't anyone. What was Terchran to him? If Dhar actively collaborated with the Servatory Party, Terr could not understand what possible motive his brother would have to get involved with them, and with Terchran, of all people. As Enllss said, the guy was a big cog in the Servatory Party wheel: a seat on the Executive Council and head of the Bureau of Technology and Development. A very heavy mover.

He simply could not believe that his brother would actually support the Servatory Party. He knew Nightwings better than that, or so he thought. He told himself that his brother was using the Servatory Party to gather intelligence for the Unified Independent Front. Dhar never made a secret of his clandestine work. If true, what threat did that pose to force him to engineer the dart crash? No, it had to be something more personal than mere intelligence gathering. Playing both ends against the middle?

In frustration, he abandoned that line of thought. It wasn't getting him anywhere. His facts were painfully skimpy and he needed to do some homework if he planned to mix it with the likes of Terchran.

In the end, he didn't care what Dhar's motive was. He only knew what he needed to do. On the way to Anar'on, he would make a small detour to Captal and check a few things out. Enllss was there and might be in a talkative mood, or open to persuasion, he mused grimly. He needed to remember that Enllss and Anabb were cast from the same scheming mold. A hell of an arrangement. Still, Enllss was family, not that it meant he trusted him. Then again, Karhide Zor-Ell would be there also, and he might have a few answers of his own.

The battle for dawn savage and short left the sky smeared with blood. With the dawn, he lost the last strands of innocence, trust and hope for any happiness. He did not know whether again a word or caress would ever heal his inner wounds, unless he walked the road of revenge. He knew the road he would walk was a dark shadow where Death lurked. It was also a trek of pain and misery. Each pebble a memory, each rock a word, a turning, a trial. At its end, Teena would be there waiting for him. She had to be there! If through the valley of shadow must he follow the path and face his brother with the horrors of his mind, so be it.

With a slash of a golden scimitar the sky parted. Fire splashed the hills and the shadows fled. He could feel the sun's heat and the silence of the dawn as it broke over him. Strung like crystal beads, dew hung from leaves, glistening with rainbow flashes. He watched a drop fall, almost pausing before it struck to shatter in a burst of diamond fire.

So he stood, his thoughts dark, colored with vengeance.

* * *

Terr slid the Service Special into the molded lining of his zip-jacket and brought the two ends together to seal it. Somehow, he had a feeling he would need it. In any case, the weapon was a comforting friend.

Earlier, he looked at a face and it was his. The firm features were tight and unsmiling. He brushed a hand through the slightly unruly brown-black hair, but the locks fell back into disorder. Worry lines creased his high flat forehead. The skin pale and drawn, somehow it wasn't him. Cold oval eyes mocked him above an aquiline nose. A faint scar ran down the left side of his temple above the eyebrow.

It took him a while to figure out what was wrong. The eyes, dark gray, remote and unforgiving, belonged to a stranger. Well, not quite. That part of him had been…sleeping. Now that it was awake, Terr decided the world from those eyes wasn't any damn different as seen from his. He pulled back his shoulders with a grimace and hoped that everyone better the hell be on the ball, for he was coming, ready or not.

The communal waited on the landing apron and he did not want to tarry. Somehow the rooms and the corridors felt cold and deserted, haunted with solitary memories lost in yesterday. Not a home anymore and he didn't belong now. He looked around one last time, not sure whether he would see his house again. On the rug lay Teena's scarf. Not knowing why, he reached for it and touched the flowing material. A feeling of warmth spread through him, comforting and soothing away some of the hurt. He tucked it into his pocket, set his mouth into a tight line and took the cable-tube to the lower level.

The door closed behind him with a smooth hiss and part of his life ended. He told the house to reset security and walked briskly to the landing ramp.

The driver stood beside the communal, its bubble open and inviting. When Terr walked up to him, the driver touched his head with the tips of his fingers and opened the door. Short and wiry, he stood there, staring through myopic steel eyes.

"Morning, sir," he growled, not caring. Just another fare to him. Well, that was all right with Terr also.

He looked through the driver, stepped in and settled himself into the upholstery. It smelled of cheap scent, unwashed bodies, and dirty socks, mixed with a hint of something sweet and tantalizingly familiar.

The communal rose smoothly. He glanced down where the house dwindled quickly, blending into the rolling landscape of the Tildera Estate. He kept his face pressed against the bubble and watched until the house vanished among the steep hills. The estates blurred together as the communal gained height, his residence becoming just one of many. Then he looked away. Hell, it was only a house.

"Tal Field, right?" The voice broke through his reverie and he looked at the back of the driver's head. Greased and stringy the hair hid a purple welt along the neck.

He thumbed the mike pad, thinking about things and nothing in particular.

"Yeah, military strip."

"Hey! You one of them Fleet guys, buddy?" The driver glanced at Terr in the front reflection strip, grinning hugely. The communal sagged to port as it swung past Barden toward the spaceport.

"Sort of," Terr said. At least he thought he was. He remembered Anabb saying something about resignation from the Diplomatic Branch. But then, a lot of things were said last night, and some of them might even have been true.

"Been there myself. Second Powerman on an M-4. Spent most of my time in the Palean Union. Ever cruised around there?" The communal steadied into a smooth flight. Terr could see others in the flight pattern.

"Mmm."

"Man, those Palean spotter chicks are the absolute end. Off the Wall." The driver shook his head and chuckled fondly. "Why, I—"

"Look, pal, I'm only paying for the trip, not a reunion tour. So let's cut the tourist crap. Copy that?"

"Just being sociable, buddy," the driver mumbled and his shoulders sagged.

Terr muttered something uncharitable and stared at the scenery. On his right, the city towers glittered in morning light as they pierced the sky. He could almost hear its cry of agony. The southeastern suburban sprawl merged into an olive haze of low, distant hills. Directly ahead the mixed industrial complexes appeared out of the surrounding parkland. He glanced at the thick neck before him and shrugged. It was the driver's bad luck to have picked him up this morning, is all.

The Field Administration building slowly reared itself

against the city's skyline and grew swiftly in size. The tower was a landmark feature of the terminus complex, a giant mushroom with two jutting flat platforms mounted a third of the way down. A flared base supported the round building. The lower larger platform served as a landing ramp for communals, combies, and cargo couriers. The upper level handled the business end of Taltair's SC&C control.

The traffic around them began to fill as they neared the inter-star terminus. The landing field lay spread in a pattern of work hangars, aprons, and approach ramps. Ships lay scattered around the docking rings. The traffic lines slowly merged into the control network, giving the Admin tower a wide berth. His pal up front kept glancing at him from time to time, muttering to himself. Maybe just checking that Terr hadn't walked out on him or something.

Tal Field was a busy place. In addition to civilian terminals the complex housed a major Scout Fleet service and refurbishment facility. The four civilian terminals, with their landing rings radiating out like spokes on a giant wheel were cluttered with all kinds of ships, from small scooters to giant Deklan passenger tubs. Connected by access tubes the ships looked like insects crowding the petals of a bright flower. Maintenance trolleys and cargo platforms sped across the apron in seemingly unordered confusion. In contrast the two somber-painted military complexes exuded a more subdued atmosphere.

A Sargon liner drifted down in slow majesty, a flattened glowing cylinder clad in an orange shimmer of its nav screen. Terr watched as it disappeared behind the building complex of the terminus and wondered where it came from. He didn't really care. Just idle curiosity. The communal swung into the service ring of the passenger terminal, then rocked wildly as a combie flashed before them and cut them off.

"Did you see that?" the driver screamed in outrage. "Bastard should have his permit revoked. I don't know what the hell this crapped-out place is coming to," he snarled and jerked the communal out of the ring and slid sharply onto the military strip.

Terr hardly paid attention, his thoughts far away.

Being in the Fleet, he would not have to clear customs or fight through the inevitable throng of wild-eyed civilian passengers with squalling brats and assorted luggage in tow. Their bored, vacant, anxious faces as they waited for their flights were pathetic and depressing. He hated civilian ports. He wasn't comfortable surrounded by cloying, noisy, undisciplined masses. A personal weakness.

A security point barred the entrance to the military terminal. A bouncer type MP, slick in parade grays, white gloves, and black boots, a phase rifle slung at port arms, waited to greet him. Terr looked him over. The MP was all solid slabs of muscle and carried himself in a manner designed to intimidate and discourage. He decided to forget the jokes this time. The guy looked mean, like he didn't care for any visitors messing up his floor polish. Especially some dirt-hugging civilian. The communal settled gently. The MP stood to attention as a matter of form and the rifle casually slid down his side.

The bubble slid away. The driver stepped out and opened the door. Terr climbed out and stood beside the communal. The driver looked wistfully around the landing area, and then climbed back into the communal. Terr waited as it rose quickly and watched it vanish in the curve of the military strip. Seeing the well-used rifle beside the MP, he recognized the smell in the communal—sagoran leather oil, used for the care and feeding of military boots. Was the driver one of Anabb's shadowing agents? He shook his head and chuckled, not caring.

"Ah, sir," the MP growled menacingly, fingering the rifle. "This is a restricted area. I'll have to ask you for some ID before I can let you go any farther."

Terr looked at him and nodded.

At the booth, he stuck his hand against the sensor plate. After a moment, it lit up, showing his rank and insignia of the

Diplomatic Branch. Then it flickered again and displayed a face he hardly recognized, a face that belonged to another time and another life. It was a younger version of himself, trusting and eager to right all the wrongs. He shook his head in wonder, bemused as he stared at the plate through his crusty shell of newly grown cynicism. Had he really been that naive?

A line at the bottom of the plate attracted his attention. It showed his status as 'Detached'. He shrugged with indifference. Okay, it might make a few things easier, but detached or not, he would find Dhar. Afterward, there would be plenty of time to add 'Permanent' to that notation.

The MP stood to, his face wooden, but his eyes were alive and full of questions. Terr barely glanced at him. Without a word, he headed for the cable-tube. It took him down to the landing area flight line.

Outside, he squinted at the sky, then looked quickly around the apron. Two M-4s towered like black cliffs beside him, but failed to dwarf the terminal despite their imposing size. Beneath their curved bellies, he could see part of an M-6 hovering on the far side of the field. On its right, three monstrous assembly hangars cast a black shadow across the daunting warship. Inside one of the open hangars, scaffolding enclosed part of an M-3. Bright floodlights glared against its exposed hull frames. Maintenance and Fleet personnel filled some of the empty spaces.

But he wasn't here for sightseeing. He took one of the parked sled-pads, punched in the landing bay number and the sled streaked across the apron.

His pulse quickened as the sled-pad neared the squat pebble shape of the M-1 scout. He felt mild anticipation at the prospect of getting away. In space, things were clean and simple, uncluttered by intrigue and deception. And right now, he needed to return to that basic simplicity. He needed a moment of peace and solitude to think things through. Rushing into danger and glory with projectors blazing might sound romantic.

That might have been enough when he thought it easy to tell right from wrong. Now, he wasn't so sure things were ever that simple. In that, he admitted grudgingly, Anabb could have been right. He was honest enough with himself to realize the threads making up the political tapestry held little interest for him, until now.

Like the guy said, it was all high politics stuff, sport.

The sled slowed and glided to a stop beneath *Sheeva's* curved hull. Terr jumped off, strode up the ramp and pressed his palm against the access plate. The plate stirred and the hatch slid open. Warm air spilled around him and brought with it machinery and lived-in smells. He walked in without a backward glance.

The tube brought him up one level to the command deck. The navigation bubble, running chest-high around the deck, cleared immediately. Sloping control panels hugged part of the curved hull. He lowered himself into the central couch and scanned the displays. A flight always made him feel renewed with zest and an eagerness to reach out and grasp the stars. This time, he felt nothing, only a desire to be off. Merely another body job like he'd done many times before.

It didn't take him long to preflight.

"Status?"

"Nominal," the computer responded.

"Secure for lift. Clear with SC&C for immediate departure and file a flight plan for Captal."

"Landing ramp retracted and all exterior connections secured." Terr felt a slight pressure surge when the hatch closed. "Navigation deflector grid activated."

Inactive panels began to glow soft amber and yellow in a mosaic of color-reactive contact pads.

"Surface Command and Control has cleared for lift. System check complete. Lift sequence enabled." The projected flight plan appeared as a bright line on the curve of the nav bubble above him. The main control plate before him glowed into life.

He was surprised that SC&C cleared him so quickly. Had he a suspicious and nasty nature, he might have suspected they were monitoring him. No matter. Out of habit, he scanned the status boards one more time.

"Proceed with lift."

"Lift sequence active. Confirm."

"Continue. Maximum boost."

"Caution. Maximum boost is in violation—"

"Disregard. Proceed," Terr said irritably.

Beneath the ship the landing skids retracted and *Sheeva* hovered. Free of an alien element, it lifted swiftly, accelerated and tore through the atmosphere. Thunder followed in its wake as air fell into a column of vacuum. He broke a stack of military and civilian regulations climbing out like this, but he simply didn't give a damn.

"I'm coming, Teena," he murmured as the sky turned black.

Chapter Two

Anabb picked up the frosted tumbler and took an absent sip. Ice clinked in the glass, a sound loud in the silence that hung around him like a heavy cloak. A bit early in the day for a drink, but he found the mere act of playing with the ice comforting. He sat back in the formchair and twirled the tumbler between his hands as he followed the merging patterns of outside traffic—fleeting lines of anonymous lives, appearing and disappearing, carried toward unknown destinations and destinies.

As seemingly was his.

He allowed his gaze to drift around his temporary office. His luckless First Assistant gave up the rooms with reluctant grace, office space at a premium at any time. The cramped place with its subdued décor made him grimace. Not at all in the style of his old luxurious chambers. Well, each to his own taste, he decided graciously. Anyway, he would only be here a few days.

He frowned as his eyes flickered toward the awkwardly placed window screen. The only thing he could see were the towers of the Center, linked by a web of tubeways and the city beyond. On a wall to his left hung a modernist impression relief. The colors were harsh and the angles sharp, a mountain terrain of eye-twisting shapes. He tried to keep his eyes from wandering to it. Blinking, he consoled himself with the thought that he would have to endure this optical torture for a couple of more days only.

When the cable-tube took him up that morning, he paused before his old office and looked in at the blackened walls, the splintered furniture and the charred hole where the window screen stood. The repair crew barely glanced at him. His skin crawled as he remembered yesterday. He didn't sleep well last night, reliving his encounter with Terr. Images of lightning tearing through him kept him awake, moaning, leaving him drenched in sweat. The boy's naked display of such awesome power had shaken him.

After washing, he stared at the reflection in the mirror and wondered at the change that had overtaken him. His hair looked more faded and the streaks of white were getting broader. The amber flecks in his brown, close-set eyes, hidden beneath ridges of untidy white eyebrows, turned muddy and lifeless. The high cheekbones, covered with an olive parchment-like skin, stood out sharply on the narrow chiseled face. The ragged blue-veined burn on his left cheek looked like a piece of dead fish. His thin white lips, pressed into a questioning line, were still firm and challenging. Well, it was something.

Being Director of the Diplomatic Branch had its rewards and pains. Not for the first time did he wonder whether the price of Serrll security was worth the coin of disillusionment and shattered lives. For the greater good, was that the current party line? When he left the Fleet seven years ago to enter the General Assembly, he promised himself he would not allow his Branch to get caught in the web of Captal intrigues. He moved the Branch to Taltair to make certain, among other things. Could his reasoning have been flawed, given the purpose of the Branch was covert operations and intelligence gathering? By being away from the center of power, did that limit his ability to exercise the Branch's charter? Something to ponder on.

As he sat behind the wide expanse of the borrowed desk, he looked down at his chest. Colored pins and stars—awards and orders—filled a red-bordered oval. Visible recognition of bravery, achievement and loyalty gained under fire, duplicity, and treachery. As an ex-Fleet flag officer, he ought to wear them with pride.

The Fleet had rewarded him well and also exacted its toll in the process. His duty postings often meant long periods away from his family. When he made the decision to leave the Fleet for the Assembly, it broke the relationship. His partner declared flatly she shared him with one career for forty years and looked forward to some quality time together. She was not prepared to share him with another, not on Taltair of all places, then threw his bag out the front door. When he happened to visit Captal, she declared, he could see her. And that's how it had been for the last seven years. His son was on an expedition somewhere near the galaxy's core. He might as well be dead as far as Anabb was concerned. Even with a subspace transition drive, those ships would not be returning for years to come, if at all.

He absently stroked the oval with the side of his thumb. Yeah, he had a lot to be proud of. Getting too old for this crap, he decided. Sentimental certainly.

By the beard of the canal worm!

The comms alert beeped and flashed for attention. He carefully laid down the tumbler and reached across the desk. He touched a pad in the inlaid control array and turned toward the Wall.

"He's gone, I presume?" he growled, watching the expressions fade and merge on the Tal Field Dispatcher's pinched face.

"Yes, sir. Just cleared the control net."

"What's his flight plan?"

"Captal, sir, as you indicated. I must point out that Master Scout Terrllss-rr committed several serious air violations with his unorthodox lift—"

"Thank you, Dispatcher," Anabb said and cut the connection, not really in the mood for the other's tirade of Terr's petty infringements. He had no time for such trivia. Let the dispatcher file a protest. The face wore a frustrated expression as it faded.

He touched another pad and the image of his personal aide swam into view. Her delicate high cheekbones accentuated the fragile beauty of full lips and long neck. Bald head narrow and oval, she looked delicate, which hid toughness that lay inside.

Dedicated and extremely competent, she could have her pick of corporate positions. For reasons he could not discern, she somehow tolerated his crusty and sometimes bullying behavior. She'd been with him since his time on Captal, and he could not imagine a day without her being there.

"Ariane, get me Commissioner Enllss-rr, will you?"

"Yes, sir," she said, her tight voice unable to hide the underlying tension and strain.

"You look terrible. Go home. You're no good to me all wrung out," he said gruffly, trying to hide genuine concern for his aide. It wouldn't do at all if his staff felt he actually *cared*.

Thunderation!

"I'm still capable of carrying out my duties, sir," she said sternly.

"So you say."

"Sir," she began reluctantly, wanting to share. "Terr…I mean, is he really a Wanderer?"

She always took Terr for granted. Everyone in the Branch did. He was what was known as a romantic figure. Despite dashing away to assignments in exotic locations, she suspected there was probably very little glamour in what he did, as Teena sometimes confided during their chats. Last night came as a rude shock and a sobering reminder of what he really was, or had become since his transformation on Anar'on. The image of Anabb's shattered door and Terr standing there, cloaked in some terrible power, left her weak. She did not sleep well and suspected that Anabb hadn't either.

"I don't know what he is, Ariane."

"Last night—"

"Try and forget it."

Her image dissolved into random color patterns and he frowned. That was a stupid thing to say. How could she forget what happened when his mind swirled with nothing else. He picked up the tumbler and stood up. The window screen cleared and the city glared at him. Two short steps brought him to the screen. The towers of the Center looked stark and alien, somehow cold and impersonal. He hated that view. What he needed was to get back into space. Things were uncluttered out there, the decisions different, something he understood well and felt comfortable with.

There was no going back, ever, and sinking into nostalgia would not get the job done.

The comms alert beeped. He strode back to his desk and sat down heavily. When the Wall cleared, it showed a face not unlike his own. A face used to intrigue, command, and manipulation. Studying the face, he could not help noticing the close family resemblance to Terr. They both had the same strong features and firm jawline above a thick, powerful neck. Enllss' unruly hair almost all white showed the years.

In the background, Captal glared in a blaze of light. The time differential with Taltair had always presented a problem with communication. Something he did deliberately. When setting up the Branch, he wanted to make sure Captal's bureaucrats would not be haranguing his staff unnecessarily. It served to filter out all but the most important messages.

Sometimes it worked.

"Took you long enough to call," Enllss commented dryly. "I'm about to pack it in for the day."

"Consider yourself fortunate that I called at all."

"Why the sarcasm? Had a bad day?"

"Bad night. Terr came to see me yesterday."

"Ah. Wish I could have been there."

"No, you don't."

"What happened?"

"He damn near killed me, that's what," Anabb snapped in exasperation. "You should see my office. It's totaled. I'm beginning to understand his dislike for some of my capers, as he puts it. In the same way, I don't like some of yours, Enllss."

"Any particular one in mind?"

"Yes, the one we're running right now. That *you're* running!"

"You'll get over it. Where is he now?"

"You just don't want to listen, do you?"

"I only want to know where he is, Anabb, not sit here having you pontificate on my policies or methods."

"Can't take it, eh? He left Tal Field a few minutes ago. You can expect him on Captal in five days."

"You're sure he's coming here?"

"Sure I'm not," Anabb said testily, his ill humor thinly veiled. "But that's the flight plan he filed."

"I'll be ready."

"What are you going to tell him?"

"I'll deal with it when he gets here."

"Deal with it now, or your office could end up like mine."

"I gather he must have been more than a little upset."

"Upset? Thunderation! How would you feel after returning from a mission which almost killed him, only to find your partner gone and a brother he thinks betrayed him gone with her?"

"Pissed, I guess," Enllss said and laughed. Anabb glared at him.

"I don't see anything particularly funny here. Your high-power plotting may have cost me two valuable agents." He felt smoldering anger at Enllss' callousness, obviously enjoying the situation at his expense. Then he realized Enllss only tried to relieve the situational tension.

"I shouldn't be snapping at you, but the boy was hurt and he hit back. I'm not particularly proud of what I had to do," he allowed to himself. He took a pull from the tumbler, only to find it empty. He banged the thing on the desk in irritation.

Enllss pursed his lips and thrust out his jaw. "It needed to be done and you know it."

"I wonder."

"You don't really mean that?"

"No, I guess not," Anabb said evenly, but felt the years on

his shoulders a real burden. "But they're both Wanderers and you've set forces in motion over which you may not have much control."

"Crap happens sometimes. The trick is not to be around when it does."

"Don't underestimate him, Enllss. Terr is smart, very smart. Should he find out that all this was done through your hand, he could take out more than your office."

"You think I don't know that? As I said. I'll deal with it when he gets here. Not to change the subject, is anything new on the Independent Representatives Conference?"

Anabb shook his head. "Marrakan isn't interfering with my agents, or Illeran's. I should pull them back for all the good they're doing. If someone wanted to disrupt the proceedings, I doubt they'll do it on Anar'on."

"Where then?"

"Salina."

"Salina? Now, that's an interesting thought. Why there? It's just a stopover."

"Exactly my point. All the delegates from the Rolan group and the surrounding nonaligned systems will gather there before proceeding to Anar'on. Each is either head of his respective system or some equivalent knob. Could be a perfect opportunity for Illeran to rid himself of irksome troublemakers. At least that's how he sees them."

"Not exactly a novel theory, Anabb. The Paleans tried that gag five years ago with the Naklanor Unified Independent Front plenary meeting, remember?"

"All too well, but it's more serious this time."

"Okay, let's kick it around a bit. Why would Illeran be looking for trouble this time around?"

"Illeran isn't going to implicate himself or the Servatory Party by doing anything directly to compromise the Unified Independent Front. He might not love them, but he's not a fool. However, there are plenty of other factions who'd be willing to do his bidding. Think of the consequences. If they succeed in silencing some of the delegates, it could disrupt the entire Conference. It could also delay the ratification of the Unified Independent Front, maybe beyond the coming General Assembly elections. The whole movement could founder, unlikely as that might be, and Illeran wouldn't mind it at all."

"You're right. He wouldn't mind it at all," Enllss said, pleased he never had cause to regret sponsoring Anabb into the Assembly or to his post as head of the Diplomatic Branch. It cost him some favors, but it had been worth it. As always, Anabb's analyses were sharp and dead center. "Did anybody ever tell you that you have a suspicious and distrusting nature?"

"After fighting Captal bureaucrats for twenty years, you'd also have a suspicious nature," Anabb remarked darkly.

Enllss chuckled. "Point taken. It strikes me, though, if you're going to start looking for plots, make sure you blame it on the right man."

"Oh?"

"It could be worth keeping an eye on our Sargon friend."

"Ed-Kani Takao? I haven't thought of him."

"Think of him now. My guess is that he would also sleep a lot better if something unpleasant were to happen to those delegates, even if he had to arrange the help. Just because five years ago their scheme to absorb Pizgor failed, it doesn't mean he or the AUP Provisional Committee have given up. This is mere speculation, mind you. A useful item at a cocktail party—"

"You would know all about that," Anabb said with a straight face. Enllss ignored him.

"All this is a lot of wishful thinking. Like Illeran, Ed-Kani wouldn't dare attack a diplomatic mission, no matter what the payoff. If the operation ever surfaced the resulting stink would mean Sargon's end. The Assembly would demand punitive action and get it. Ed-Kani's supporters and the Committee would not enjoy that kind of exposure."

"You'd never be able to trace it to them, Enllss. Nevertheless, I won't tempt them. I'll order an M-4 to provide the delegates with suitable transportation—"

"And protection?"

"I don't want any incidents. I've had enough already."

"Frankly, I think you're overreacting. After what happened at Italan, they'd be dumb to pull another stunt like that. I must admit the media aren't helping any either. They have blown this thing into endless rounds of analyses and dissections. The whole mess is giving me the craps."

"What did you expect? It isn't every day you get to see the formation of a new interstellar power block. And the Unified Independent Front is today's news."

"Maybe you're right. What about Marrakan? We would look damn foolish with our thumbs stuck up our asses watching everybody else while he got sanded."

Anabb waved his hand in dismissal. "I wouldn't worry about him. He seems well able to take care of his own."

Ever since Terr started working for the Diplomatic Branch, Anabb took it upon himself to study the Wanderers, the *Saftara*, and their enigmatic tribal leader in particular; Marrakan, Controller of Anar'on and Prime Director of the Kaleen group. His name meant Sword of the Wind. Sowing a swathe of confusion through Captal, the name was rather apt, he felt.

Steeped in the mysticism of the Discipline and the deserts of his world, Marrakan's was the life of every Wanderer on that desert planet. He also breathed life into the Unified Independent Front. As its most powerful advocate, Marrakan's personal magnetism convinced Orgomy to unite with Kaleen's group of systems to form what would become for some a very unwelcome new political force within the Serrll Combine.

"If we're covering everybody on the list, what about Tarim Alai Kamara? He's on Captal now, isn't he? Being Prime Director of the Orgomy group, he would be worth taking out of the picture."

"I doubt that," Anabb disagreed. "Orgomy is fully committed to the UIF, with or without Kamara. At any rate, Marrakan will see to it that Kamara gets old enough to enjoy his coming retirement. You know, of course, that sooner or later, Marrakan will notice the leaching of UIF operatives from sensitive Captal positions. It could be embarrassing."

"The government will not be implicated."

"What about you, my friend? If you're expecting a nomination to the Executive Council, an internal security scandal is the last thing you need."

"Your concern is laudable, Anabb, but unwarranted. I made sure I wouldn't be the one hanging on that proverbial limb. No matter what happens."

"Well, you're old enough to know how the game is played."

"Quite." Enllss cut contact.

Anabb gave a small smile. The day was looking up.

* * *

"Asshole," Enllss muttered, piqued at Anabb's flippant attitude.

The Wall faded. He reached across the desk and savagely tapped instructions into the inlaid console pad that shut down access to his office system.

What in blazes was wrong with everybody these days, anyway? Just because he openly declared his ambitions, everyone wanted to sand him down. Either because of political rivalry, jealousy, or revenge for pissing off some lobby group. Bastards, all of them, he decided in the end.

To hell with it. He'd had a long and weary day. Time to get out of the damn office. He stood and swept the office with one quick look. Satisfied, he strode briskly toward the milky translucent panels. They hissed as they slid out of his way.

His aide looked up, her delicate eyebrows arched in a questioning frown.

"Where is Tariq? He should have been waiting for me, his nose pressed against those doors," he grated, thumb hooked over his shoulder.

"The First Assistant is working on the Orieli brief you requested," she said primly, obviously upset with something. Right now, he had no time for office politics or handholding. Did they consider him a father figure? Let her talk to a mindbender.

"When he's through, remind him that I'll want his presentation first thing in the morning."

"He'll be spending most of the night—"

"Another thing," he said, not hearing her. "I'll want his update on our ecoforming operations in the Palean Union. He already slipped a day on that one. I better have that update on my desk as I walk in tomorrow or I'll get upset. He won't like it if I get upset so early in the day."

"I'll tell him."

"Anything else I should know?"

"Commissioner Sill-Anais from the Bureau of Cultural Affairs called a few moments ago," she said with a hint of disapproval. "He's waiting for you in the Executive Lounge."

"By damn! I forgot all about him. Call and tell him that I'm on my way up."

"Very well. Good night, sir."

Just because it was night, the Center and the rest of Captal hardly slowed down. As the political heart of the Serrll, Captal could not afford to sleep. For senior executives it sometimes made for a long working day—and night. Not all found the arrangement to their liking. Just one of the smaller prices they paid for power.

Enllss stepped into the cable-tube. The image of luxurious interior paneling immediately rippled and became transparent. The city around him blazed with light and activity. His gaze absent, he mulled over various issues he dealt with during the day or remained to be done. Some problems were personal, like

Terr's. Despite what he told Anabb, he didn't exactly relish the prospect of confronting the boy, but some things just had to be faced.

The cable-tube slowed and the outside scenery faded. The doors opened and slid into the walls. He paused before stepping out. Not crowded, the Executive Lounge had a sprinkle of faces he recognized. A pleasant buzz of subdued voices filled the plush dining room. Most of the tables around the edge of the softly lit dome were filled, which left an awkward emptiness in the middle. Everybody wanted a city view. High above the transparent dome, lines of commuter and commercial traffic, stacked at various levels, moved in orderly rows.

A discrete cough brought him back to reality.

"Mr. Commissioner?" The short waiter bowed, his bald head gleaming. Enllss smiled fondly at the frail bent figure, old when he was still a moist, fresh-caught Assembly representative.

"Mallaway, how are you tonight?"

"Tolerable. Thank you for asking, sir," Mallaway answered gravely. Wrinkled skin sagged on his sad, bony face.

"I understand your granddaughter will graduate from the Center for Political Studies soon."

Pleased that the commissioner remembered, Mallaway nodded. "With honors, sir," he said with obvious pride as they threaded their way between the tables. Faces turned and some smiled. Enllss nodded in acknowledgment.

"Don't forget my offer. If she wants to join any of the Bureaus, let me know."

"She's considering applying and I'll tell her. Your table, sir."

Sill looked up as Enllss approached. He waited until Mallaway seated him.

"Didn't mean to be late, Sill," Enllss said by way of an apology as he lowered himself into the yielding formchair.

"Ach! You've been avoiding me," Sill piped, his massive

barrel chest producing a surprisingly high voice.

Twin bands of dark gray streaked Sill's long white hair, worn in traditional Deklan fashion. Thin white eyebrows outlined large, liquid wide-set gray eyes. Pinched and dry beneath an olive complexion, the face had deep lines of responsibility. Most commissioners and executive directors had them. Tall and wiry, his movements were delicate and precisely measured.

"Hardly that," Enllss snorted.

Unobtrusively, Mallaway brought their favorite drinks and a tray of edible tidbits. They hardly noticed as he crept around the table. Mallaway prided himself on being unobtrusive. Enllss hated to think of all the plots and schemes the old waiter had overheard during his years of service in the Lounge.

"I wouldn't have to resort to secret dinners if you would condescend to see me during the day," Sill commented dryly.

"Secret dinners?" Enllss raised an eyebrow and looked around. "Seems crowded enough to me."

"Ach! You know what I mean."

"Relax, Sill," Enllss said and picked up a canapé. He scrutinized it for a moment, then popped it into his mouth. He chewed, swallowed and licked his lips. "The government won't fold because I didn't get around to seeing you."

"Ach! That's just it. It could."

"Oh?"

"Have you seen Illeran lately? It seems he's been keeping himself pretty busy. His office has more people coming and going than an inter-star terminus."

"I suspect he's positioning the Servatory Party to challenge the Sofam Confederacy's right to our fourth seat on the Executive," Enllss said casually, enjoying the look of surprise on Sill's face.

"Okay. How did you figure that?"

Enllss took a pull from his tumbler and nodded in appreciation. "Not bad. Must be new stock. Tried yours?"

"Ach! Who the crud cares—"

Through the Valley of Shadow

"Such language from a priest of the Path," Enllss admonished with an upraised finger.

"Damn the Path! This is serious."

Enllss laughed. "Take it easy, Sill. Leave the office closed for a change, will you?"

"Unfortunately, once you strap it on, it's for keeps."

"You've got that right. How is the family?"

"My partner is making a pilgrimage to Deklan."

"Ah, the Kalkoon festival," Enllss said and Sill shook his head sadly.

"It's the Kall-oon, you heretic."

"Whatever."

"Have you heard from Anabb?" Sill asked casually as he played with his tumbler. Enllss chuckled.

"As a matter of fact, I just spoke to him. He told me to expect Terr in five days. You can consider that part of the mission successfully concluded."

"Ach! Hardly the term I would use. You've not only compromised Dharaklin and the Servatory Party cell he ran on Taltair, you also alienated Agent Terr. Was that really necessary? As it is, I might lose both if there is a confrontation between them."

"Their ability to support the Unified Independent Front cause is neutralized," Enllss said flatly. "That's all that matters."

Sill stared at his friend in dismay. "I cannot believe you said that. Has your preoccupation with Sofam's political survival so clouded your judgment that individuals have become irrelevant? Your nephew—"

"Sill—"

"Ach! If either of them gets hurt, friend or not, I'll take you before the Bureau of Administrative Affairs. I mean it."

Enllss could see that Sill took this seriously, but was his indignation genuine or a twinge of a guilty conscience? He decided it might not be either.

"I wouldn't have thought it of you. Busy covering your ass

when so much is at stake."

"I warned you—"

"Let's leave it, okay? I'm hungry. You want to order?"

Mallaway appeared silently without being summoned, a minimum skill in the Executive Lounge. He waited for them to make their orders, then departed just as unobtrusively.

Sill appeared relieved by the distraction. "About Illeran—"

"Forget him, and I'm not understating the gravity of their challenge—"

"The difference this time is that they could pull it off."

"This time, we don't care," Enllss told him.

"Careful what you say, my friend. Ach! They lock people up for less than that. Your fourth Executive seat is vital if the Revisionists want to hold the government majority, you know that."

"Between you and me, Sill, I never did like this practice of sharing power based on a percentage of held systems. Executive policy tends to be colored by expansionist schemes of the participating power blocks."

"Or thoughts of conquest. Yes, I know. Consider Sargon and the Paleans."

"My point exactly. I console myself with the comforting fact that in two years' time they will all be gone. Illeran, Terchran, Ed-Kani Takao and their schemes with them."

"Ach! Only to be replaced by someone else with a new set of schemes," Sill pointed out and Enllss laughed.

"Of course. As for that fourth seat, we have it secured."

"By giving some protectorates independent status and getting them to join the Sofam Confederacy? It's the only way you can boost your percentage of held systems to warrant that fourth seat."

"That is *exactly* what we plan to do. And there is not a damn thing Illeran or the Servatory Party can do about it. By the way, we already have the systems and their agreements," Enllss said smugly, enjoying the stricken look on Sill's face.

"Ach! You've got to be kidding."

Enllss smiled and pointed at Sill's tumbler. "Drink up before your chin hits the table."

Sill ignored him. "When did Sofam manage to pull this off? Deklan never had any indication that you've taken such steps."

"I know. If your intelligence hasn't picked it up, then maybe Illeran's hasn't either. At any rate, it doesn't matter whether he knows or not. The agreement will be announced at the next Executive Council meeting."

"As coalition partners we should have been informed," Sill pointed out petulantly.

"What are you sore about, anyway? Because we didn't keep our nose pressed against the Ecumenical Synod's butt?"

"That's blasphemy!"

"You make me tired, Sill. Two years before the general elections, you come trotting in with dire warnings about that infernal fourth seat. What did you expect? That I would fall at your feet in gratitude for pointing out the obvious? If you were so concerned about the health of our coalition, I would like to know what in blazes the Synod was doing for the last seven years to help us solve the problem. I'll tell you. They were sitting on their hands practicing Deklan's particular version of coalition loyalty."

"Ach! That's unfair."

"Unfair? We've known each other a long time. So let's cut out the worm crap, okay? The Deklan Republic is feeling its religious muscle. The way you look at things, there isn't all that much to pick from between Sofam and the Karkans. Both are sinful, decadent, and lacking in moral fiber."

Sill sat back and chuckled, a high-pitched cackle. "Both of you *are* decadent. And your feeble attempt to provoke me will not work. We only want to bring the light of the Path—"

"Spare me! It's all about influence. Let's face it. It always has been. The difference with Deklan is that you disguise it as evangelism."

Sill stared hard at Enllss. "The Revisionists rule because of our support. Don't forget that, my irreverent friend."

"The unspoken threat being, should that support be withdrawn, Sofam would find itself in an unenviable position, right?"

"Ach! With Sargon wooing the Paleans, your dancing around the Unified Independent Front suddenly takes on another dimension, doesn't it? With two years to go before the next elections, Sofam cannot be certain that those independent systems you've signed on will keep their agreement."

"True. So?"

"You're actually worried, aren't you? You must know that Deklan would not withdraw its support."

"I know no such thing," Enllss said bluntly. Sill ignored him.

"However, if we were to consider it, hypothetically speaking, of course—"

"Of course."

"We would have you over that well-known barrel."

"Oh, I'm not worried about the UIF. They'll support us, all right," Enllss said comfortably.

Too shrewd to ask why Sofam was so confident, Sill figured they had something on the UIF, or Marrakan, or both.

"The problem with Deklan and the Synod," Enllss went on, "is that you have never forgiven us for blocking your attempt to annex the Kaleen group, have you?"

"It was our right! They are nothing but heathen savages."

"With delusions of godhood to boot," Enllss prompted and smiled broadly.

"Sacrilegious crap. Ach!"

"Not fit to hold an Executive seat at all, are they?"

"Exactly!" Sill snapped, then paled at the enormity of his blunder. "Ah, what I meant—"

"I know what you meant," Enllss said with dark satisfaction. "Converted into political coin, religious fervor can be a powerful influence. The rub is, you can only spend it once. If I had any influence with the Ecumenical Synod, Sill, I would tell them to do their shopping carefully. Changing allegiances might not turn out to be such a bargain after all."

Sill regarded Enllss for a long moment before raising his tumbler in a salute.

"Ach! You and your breed are indeed dangerous."

"Don't tempt us to prove it," Enllss said, his smile predatory and his threat clear. Sill reached across the table to touch Enllss' hand.

"My friend, the Deklan Republic has no intention of threatening the Revisionist coalition. Every now and then it is useful to remind your partner that you cannot be taken for granted."

"Sill, I never take *anything* for granted," Enllss said with a straight face and a cold shiver ran down Sill's spine.

It hadn't turned into one of his best evenings.

Chapter Three

The ship came out of subspace in a burst of scintillation.

It materialized; two oddly joined bulbous shapes, insect-like and unmistakably alien. One side of its forward section blackened, pitted with gaping burn holes that exposed the skeletal frames beneath. It paused, hesitating, then glided forward. Its leaking shields flickered with dull blue-green discharges along the force lines as they tried to stabilize.

Sensor scans probed the wedge slice of a white world glaring under the blaze of a main sequence yellow star. Emission signatures from high-powered antimatter plasma fusion reactors were unmistakable, as were the readings of refined metals and composites.

Long-range scans showed a small ship almost at the far edge of the system. Data flowed to the central nexus core deep within the stricken vessel as it evaluated its surroundings. The central nexus decided that the alien ship did not present an immediate threat. If the alien closed, it would be neutralized. Nothing would keep the central nexus from getting at the rich source of raw materials from the planet ahead, badly needed for the repair of its ship. Something like satisfaction seeped through its circuit matrix. Nevertheless, it issued a standard alert notice to the command cell on the control level.

Near the vessel's starboard quarter hung a gray half-moon. The ship changed course slightly, its shields flaring weakly in intermittent surges.

* * *

Ti Adi suppressed a yawn and blinked as the computer alert

34

flashed on the repeater plate. The nav bubble above him showed clear space. The stars were brittle points of light in the darkened command deck.

"Detecting an emission trace from an unidentified craft breaking normal, heading for an intercept on Devon 3-VL4's satellite," the computer announced. "Range, three point-eight-two billion talans. Contact in six hours, eighteen minutes, relative speed and status."

That was almost at the other side of the system, Ti Adi mused and pointed at the plate.

"I only got two hours to change of watch," he complained bitterly. "I don't want any complications. I just want to finish this watch without drama or excitement, everything nice and dull. This better not be some fool from Devon taking an unauthorized ride," he muttered darkly and turned to his Sargon watch officer. "You would think those dirt-hugging civilians on Devon would have the simple courtesy to notify us when one of them decided to take a joyride? It's not such a big thing to ask, now is it?"

His watch officer smiled in sympathy. It seemed they spent half their time shepherding would-be Scout Fleet drivers. A damned nuisance maintaining a patrol around these ecoforming systems. However, the bulging brains at Sector TACOPSCOM thought otherwise. With increased raider activity in the quadrant, command held a low view of some adventurous spirit practicing his flying skills around Devon.

"If that bucket is from Devon and he hasn't filed a flight plan, I'll ground the turd. I will!"

"I bet you would love to run up behind one of those guys and let him have a stern shot, wouldn't you?" the watch officer remarked dryly, relishing the resulting image.

"Hardly worth the effort." Ti Adi snorted.

"It would make the others keep their distance."

"Yeah, but I'd be filling out forms for a year. Now, if we had ourselves a raider…"

"That's no raider," a voice quipped. "It's a Sargon passenger tramp. And it's lost."

Someone else groaned in mock sympathy.

"We build fine tramps, thank you," the watch officer offered primly. "Not like your Palean tubs."

"Do you have an ident?" Ti Adi demanded.

Tactical data flowed on the main plate, repeated on the navigation bubble above them.

"Still searching. Weird looking hummer, whatever it is."

"Any comms?" Ti Adi asked, glancing at the tactical plate. The watch officer shook his head.

"Nothing on standard bands. Getting some energy surges, though. Could be leaking shields." The control crew had become grim professionals.

"Leaking shields? An engagement?"

"It's likely. Those energy levels are way over any commercial specs."

"Big son of a bitch whatever it is," Ti Adi muttered and frowned.

It didn't look like any ship he'd ever seen, and he'd seen some weird hulls. Take some of those Deklan liners. Better a survival blister than a Deklan deathtrap. It certainly didn't look like any joy orbiter from Devon either.

There goes my chance of an easy tour, he thought in disgust. And he only had eleven days to go. With accumulated leave, he and his friend Se Kinai, another M-3 driver, planned to take in some of the sights around the Orgomy group. The systems there were still quiet enough not to have been completely spoiled by overdevelopment. He especially wanted to go back to Tuleene, a world made to soothe away any spaceman's ills: warm seas, blue skies, plenty of fishing, and the women were very friendly. This sighting meant reports, debriefings, red tape, and official shits scrutinizing everything. It's not like they have been invaded or anything. Pits!

Could it be one of those Orieli Technic Union jobs out on

some excursion cruise? A possibility. He wondered what the Orieli would be doing around the Palean Union, and Devon 3-VL4 in particular. Nothing but an ecoforming station, about as far as someone could get and still be part of the Serrll Combine. Besides, the Orieli were supposed to come from somewhere above the Sargon Directorate.

Ti Adi hated it when things got complicated. He rubbed his chin and felt the rasp of stubble. He watched computer-generated images of the strange vessel rotate in various dimensions, trying to make sense of the data. The two bulbous sections were almost 1,200 katalans long. The trailing section a third larger than the leading pod, over seven hundred katalans in length.

Trajectory showed the alien coming from far above the general direction where the Orieli had their Line Tracking Net strung out. Could this be a Celi-Kran intruder? The thought chilled him. It didn't take him long to make his decision. He leaned over the color-reactive console set into the couch armrest and tapped a pad.

The comms plate glowed. After a long moment a face swam into view, eyes rimmed and still asleep.

"This better the hell be good, Ti Adi, or I'll have your ass!" the owner of the face growled, looking rumpled and disoriented.

"Sorry, friend Tetlas," Ti Adi said brightly, relishing the confusion on the dour image of his commander. "We picked up a visitor. Range, almost three billion talans."

"And you woke me—"

"The ship is alien. It could be an Orieli vessel, but it doesn't match any of the standard specs. Sensors show instability in what we read as a secondary shield grid. There are power surges in the primaries. Whatever it is, I would say it's seen action recently. Since we're not shooting up anybody that I know of, where did the thing get that kind of damage?"

Tetlas scowled. "Heading?"

"Devon's moon. I recommend we better get our act together snap quick."

"What in hell would an Orieli ship be doing way out here? It's crazy!" Tetlas growled in frustration. "They would notify us first, wouldn't they? Well?" They were avoiding the obvious and they both knew it. Tetlas winced in disgust and fixed Ti Adi with a hard stare.

"Assume standard intercept course and go to initial alert, in case it is a Kran prowler. Notify Controller Aill-Massai at Devon Center and…you know what to do. I'll be up when I clamp my face on."

Ti Adi nodded and the plate faded. He started humming a new tune, somewhat repetitive, but he couldn't get it out of his mind. He swept his gaze around the deck.

"Right, people, let's get it moving. Set initial alert. Give me twenty-two seconds at one-twentieth primary boost. We'll coast the rest of the way in on secondary drive. Comms…"

In the engineering spaces deep within the ship, almost directly above the phased array projector dome, the computer increased the level of energy management readiness. Stripped helium nuclei plasma powered the primary fusion chamber that fed the artificial antimatter convergence point and kept it from collapsing. The energy surge from particle annihilation was channeled through the containment field into separation wave-guides. Most of the generated power surge was directed into massive secondary bus nodes in the hull that formed tight lines of force

The primary shields enclosed the M-3 in a cocoon of energy extending six talans. The wave-guides allowed some of the energy to flow into a separate reaction chamber that flooded the single Koyami 9A generator. Coils fully powered up, the computer waited for the command to synchronize the firing pulses with the shield management system and the ship would be ready to engage.

After twenty-two seconds of boost from the main drive,

Through the Valley of Shadow

Valetta's distortion field depolarized and the M-3 dropped normal. Driving in at 6,960 talans per second, it did not take long for the ships to meet and for Ti Adi to confirm the visitor was not an Orieli vessel. Tetlas emerged out of the cable-tube hatchway. With a glance at the tactical plate, he slipped into the command couch. On tactical the alien ship's lines were odd, hard and hostile. He tried to swallow, his throat suddenly dry.

"Range, two point-four million talans," the computer announced quietly. "K-band ranging lock established. Effective firing solution in four point-nine minutes at maximum secondary boost."

Ti Adi turned from the command console. "Still no response from our comms, sir, and I cannot make out the crap they're sending out. It could be an interrogative." He stared at Tetlas, both of them reaching the same conclusion. Tetlas looked at the faces around him, reading in them his own unease.

"Very well. Maintain neutral status and prepare to go to primary alert. Notify Devon of our intentions and open a channel to Sector TACOPSCOM. Make sure that both are getting our TLM. I got a bad feeling about that thing."

"Devon Center notified and channel is open, sir," the watch officer said quietly. He might be a little nervous, but not anxious—yet.

The comms plate cleared and a bored face stared through. Arrays of monitor plates and display stations filled the background. "First Scout Tatllaa, Sector Tactical Operations Command."

"First Scout, this is Devon 3-VL4 picket, *Valetta*. We have an unidentified heavy asset closing on intercept with Devon's moon and I don't have a clue as to what it is. It doesn't look like an Orieli job, but it's too early to tell. I'm of the opinion that it's a Celi-Kran intruder. Plot shows it's carrying combat damage and there is a negative on all comms. It seems to be sending out something, but I cannot make zip out of the stuff. You guys got anything out here we should know about?"

Sofam Industries liked to conduct live fire runs with experimental ships in deserted parts of space. Fleet units sometimes ran into such an exercise. From a major security flap, this could turn out to be nothing more than an exchange of terse messages between Sofam Industries and COMPALOPS, Commander Palean Operations.

Tetlas hoped this was the case here.

The first scout looked blank, then turned to speak rapidly with someone in the background. He faced Tetlas and shook his head.

"Your comms telemetry is coming through now, *Valetta*, and it *does* look unusual. But this is definite. No authorized vessels in your sector. Suggest you—"

"Yeah, I'll keep it in mind. In the meantime, I got a ship to con," Tetlas said and cut contact. "Computer? Range profile."

"One hundred and ninety-four thousand talans," the computer responded evenly. "Target attempting to stabilize secondary shield grid. Have an interrogative on a possible target acquisition lock. Effective firing solution in twenty-eight seconds."

"Drop to quarter boost. Go to primary alert and prepare to take us out of here quick," Tetlas ordered as the bad feeling grew into a sense of inevitable certainty.

As *Valetta* increased its readiness status and extended its secondary shields, the alien's shield grid immediately flared and began to pulse from blue-green to orange. Ti Adi stared at the plate in disbelief and his face drained. Suddenly, the idea of a dull and boring patrol had a lot going for it.

"Pits!" he swore and his head jerked to see the startled expression of his commanding officer. "He's powering up for an attack!" Ti Adi frantically punched in a new shield configuration to strengthen *Valetta's* forward array.

"Computer! Immediate transition!" Tetlas roared.

The Sofam designated M-3/11 medium interceptor had the speed of an M-4 cruiser, matching its mission profile as a scout. Equipped with a single Koyami 9A phased array projector tucked into a dome beneath its belly, it could penetrate a twelve-cetalan thick polymer hull constructs with almost continuous traversing bursts of up to seventy-two TeV at an effective range of 64,000 talans.

The alien ship happened to be outside that envelope by more than two times.

A massive surge of high-energy flux, torn from a quantum point artificial singularity, flowed from the alien ship's power core and saturated the primary and secondary shield grids in a staggered cascade. The secondary shield overloaded and sent a searing track of pale orange ionization toward the M-3.

The impact ruptured the shield's delicate torus geometry precursor distortion field the computer attempted to form before *Valetta* could transit into subspace. The shields flared and pulsed wildly, then arced before dissolving in a spectacular discharge of flickering lightnings and backsurges.

Ti Adi felt the ship stagger and heard the frames groan. He turned his head and looked at Tetlas. It was awfully silent on the command deck. He hadn't planned on going this way, but...

Valetta reared under another impact. The polymer hull glowed and began to melt as it vainly tried to absorb the energy flux. Inside, display plate images strobed, then the panels burst under pressure, sending lethal fragments scything through the crew. Ti Adi watched in horror as Tetlas tried helplessly to pry a long sliver of polymer sandwich from a jagged gash in his face. Bright blood leaked between his fingers and caked his hands. The bulkhead beside him suddenly glowed and began to deform. Ti Adi threw up his hands and felt the heat scorch his hair. The air became hot and thick, and his lungs burned. Blue sparks coiled and jumped across the consoles from the near-field effect. Someone screamed and he wondered if it was him.

The alien ship drew closer and the orange track stabbed again. Weaker, but *Valetta's* shields were down and debris began to drift from the savaged ship. Deep within the M-3, safety circuits failed and the antimatter fusion torus flickered and dropped, shooting a power surge through the primary containment field. In a sudden flash of brilliance, *Valetta* vanished within a sphere of expanding radiance. The plasma cloud cooled quickly into an orange ball that glowed briefly dull red, then faded.

When the alien ship reached Devon 3-VL4's moon, it went into low orbit and glided slowly along the terminator. Then it stopped, its shields flickering erratically as it settled among the jagged cliffs. Devon glowed white above a torn horizon.

The central nexus integrated its sensor data. The short engagement with the small ship had drained badly needed power. With damage to its operations management system that controlled the quantum point singularity, energy reserves were approaching criticality. It issued instructions to the command cell and drone units became very busy.

* * *

Afternoon shadows cloaked the dunes beneath a painted sky. A bloated orange sun hovered above a broken desert, its outline twisted and shimmered as it sank. Softly keening the wind brushed the dune tops and drove the sands in long wavy patterns along the sharp crests. As the sun's waning light touched the horizon the wind died and silence began to steel over the dunes.

Dhar sat cross-legged, his hands rested on his knees as he watched the desert. Behind him, his shadow stretched sharp and black into the coming dusk. He opened his awareness and allowed his spirit to merge with the soft whisper of the sands. His body alert and aware of every sound, movement, and pattern of light flowing around him.

In the village behind him came the shriek of children at play. The women would be ready to serve the evening meal, always at sunset. He could hear the sharp snorts of oark being driven into the corrals for the night. Poultry cackled as they moved slowly into the coops. Lamps would be lit in the mud huts, sizzling in thick oark oil. The elderly, accompanied by the Rahtir, would drift out of the communal hut where they talked, sipping peelath tea or its fermented berry juice. The routine familiar and comforting, a point of sameness and stability. The images of his childhood came to him, clear and carefree. If only he could recapture that simplicity now.

Breathing slowly and deeply, he opened his mind to the desert. Free, his soul roamed the sands in peace despite the saddened at pain he felt at the prospect of confronting his brother. The path he trod lay strewn with thorns, but it had no turnings until he fulfilled his destiny. In this, his master was strangely unhelpful. He felt the burden of the gods heavy on his shoulders. It was unfair that they should seek to punish him like this. He immediately checked that emotion, ashamed. The gods *had* warned him. He had seen his brother's hands stretched toward him from the hospital bed where he lay wounded on Earth, lightnings blazing. Yet what choice did he have? Even with free will, one's life seemed almost preordained.

He didn't believe that for a moment.

A faint odor of cooking drifted past him.

The sun hung as an orange sliver of light above the dunes. It wavered and slipped beneath the sands, leaving a painted yellow-red sky where it had been. Behind him, the sand whispered as it shifted under awkward footsteps. He relaxed his body and his breathing quickened.

He heard a swirl of robes and a flurry of shifting sand. A small figure sat beside him and let out a long exhale. He could hear her labored panting slowing as her tension receded. He waited for her to relax completely before turning to look down at her. It would not be an infringement for her to be with him like this. After all, she was a friend and already paired. Her pale green eyes sparkled with vitality and she returned his gaze frankly, her cheeks flushed with health.

"This is a beautiful and magic land," Teena husked breathlessly, then sighed deeply and hugged her knees. "I never imagined it to be like this. So wild, savage, cruel and gentle all at once. Terr tried to explain it to me once and I cried at the pain and longing in his voice. I couldn't understand how he could be touched with such hunger for a burning desert. But being here, now…"

They sat in silence, aware of each other and the desert that held them together, content.

"It is indeed strange," Dhar said after a time, the rumble of his voice deep and resonant. Teena gazed at him intently and shivered.

He was so tall, thin and wiry, honed down by the needs of the desert, she unaccountably felt a flutter of fear. The power he held in check, almost palpable, held her fascinated. His yellow skin smooth, deep lines etched the corners of his mouth, adding character. The large orange eyes with their vertical red slits that could cut and probe with disturbing ease, stripped away her defenses, were kindly as they regarded her. The membranes that protected his eyes from abrasive sands were withdrawn.

"The affinity with the desert is strong within him," he said quietly as they watched the shadows deepen. The dusk cradled them and he continued. "I was born here in the village below. When the Rahtir selected me for training in the Discipline, it came to me easily. I took it for granted that one day I would walk in the shadow of Death. That is the way of the Saddish-aa and I never questioned it." He paused reflecting on a memory. "Only after I looked into Terr's mind that I saw the desert through his eyes and at last, I understood what I always took for granted. The gods have touched him and the Saffal is now a part of him. He may not know why, but strong is his love for this land, and here is where I must face him."

She reached with a slender hand and hesitated before

touching him. "Nightwings…" she murmured and felt him stiffen at the use of his warrior name. "Sorry. I should not have called you that." Terr told her once that only another Discipline initiate could call him by his warrior name, but Dhar appeared not to notice the infringement.

"You have a right…I fear the shadow of Death within which he walks," he said softly. "Though we are brothers, he might not be able to stay the hand of revenge, or want to."

Teena's eyes were troubled and uncertain. "Because of me?"

Above them the stars blinked in a profusion of light. The constellation of Amulran the Damned and the bent pattern of stars that was the Stalker were hard and white. Following his gaze, Dhar once told her that those stars always appeared first. When she asked him why, he refused to explain. Infuriating man! Behind them, Aribus began to push up from beneath the horizon, the small moon still bloody and stained from its struggle.

They sat in silence, lost in thought as darkness covered them gently with its cloak. He turned and smiled at her.

"Are you being treated well? The Rahtir will make allowances, but you will have to forgive them if they forget."

She giggled and placed a small hand over her mouth. "The other day, I inadvertently tried to enter their communal hut. Some of the children were playing outside. I was curious and wanted to see what was in there. As I climbed the steps, the kids just gaped at me. I didn't know why then and I actually made it to the entrance. One of your elders inside saw me. He was so startled that for a moment we simply stared at one other. Then he raised his arm and bellowed, 'Out woman!' and I fled. The children thought it hilarious."

Dhar chuckled.

"Later, he tried to apologize…" she trailed off, an impish smile still lighting her face. "The men seem to be held in greater respect—"

"Only the elders, senior initiates of the Discipline."

"The Rahtir, yes, but women run things, don't they?"

"Does that give you satisfaction?"

She sensed his amusement and laughed, a tinkle of music in the night. "It does."

"The Saffal does not offer all the comforts that you—"

"Good grief! Is that a sound of condescension?" she demanded mockingly.

"Just concern," he said gravely.

The women had accepted her more readily than she expected. At first, uncertain of her outworlder appearance and status, they treated her with formality. Only after she displayed part of her wardrobe to some of the younger girls the facade dropped. Of course, the garments were far too small for the tall native girls, but they all cooed with undisguised delight at the soft fabrics and their flowing colors. She gave them what they could use to make scarves, shawls, or pretty handkerchiefs. They accepted her gifts and they accepted her. It did not prevent the senior wives from making her work, though. It was all so stimulating. Her days may have been weary from unaccustomed labor, but her nights were spent in happy slumber.

"Are meals always such noisy affairs?" she asked on impulse, listening to the scampering of children below.

"Usually." Dhar nodded. "It is about the only opportunity in a busy and otherwise long day where noteworthy items and gossip can be exchanged."

"The elders seem to come in for their share of japes." She giggled again and Dhar smiled.

Absorbed in their sober talk the elders usually ignored the boisterous antics of the young, incurring good-natured chiding for being cubes.

As an honored guest, the matrons invited Teena to sit with them during the meals, but she declined, preferring the more informal and gregarious company of the younger women. She found the almost ritualistic behavior of the elderly too stifling and the conversation almost meaningless, lacking as she did the background and the nuances of the villagers' daily lives. When the matrons did talk to her, the conversation stilted and everyone felt the strain.

One thing did surprise her. They usually baked everything that needed cooking in the hot sands, containers wrapped in broad peelath leaves. Fire, they told her, was a luxury in absence of readily obtainable fuel, to be indulged in on special occasions only. The Wanderers were predominantly vegetarian, the high-protein legumes and carbohydrate-rich roots grown in the gardens, comprised the bulk of their diet. Foraging the Saffal and trade with nearby villages provided occasional variety. Dried meat was a rare delicacy when available. Without the oark and the milk, butter and cheeses they provided, life in the desert would not have been possible.

She found it a far cry from the conveniences of her autokitchen. Gazing at nothing, she stirred the sand with her toes.

"Dhar, can I ask you something? At night in one of the huts, I saw a blue glow. What was that?"

He cleared his throat, momentarily embarrassed. "Sankri will show you," he said after a moment.

She shook her head at his stubbornness. He could be so exasperating sometimes.

"What's really going on between you two?" she demanded at last, her patience exhausted. "I need to know. The whole thing is driving me mad."

"He will tell you soon enough," he said gruffly and she sensed sadness in his voice.

"Men!" She snorted in disgust, surprised at her outburst. "I have to sit here worrying myself to death while you two play games of honor and revenge with your lives, not knowing whether either of you will survive the encounter. Even if you do, what will be my price? All the way from Taltair, you refused to explain. I want to know!"

Suddenly, she sensed a charge of electricity around him and

felt real alarm. She had forgotten what he was. Afraid to move, she could hear her heart pounding.

"Nightwings…" Her courage deserted her, then. He looked at her.

"Do not fear, Teena," he said heavily. "It is just that your words have startled me."

She sagged weakly, her knees trembling. "Forgive me, I shouldn't—"

"No, you have a right to understand. I wronged Sankri, betraying the bond that binds us. I had no choice, or maybe I refused to make a harder one. It is complicated. The deed is done and it's too late to change things. Let me ask you this. What did you feel when you saw Taltair receding, knowing you would not be there when he returned?"

"I…sometimes, he calls me. It's like a waking dream, all shadows and silence. I can see him and touch him, but he doesn't hear my words. It's a link we share."

"Can you understand then what he must have felt when he found himself back on the Moon and I couldn't there with him to explain?"

Teena stared at him, her small mouth open. "By bringing me here, you're telling me that he believes you would harm me?"

"I don't know. It is possible. With everything that has happened—"

"But you rescued me from those Servatory Party kidnappers. How can he think—"

"It is not as simple as that."

"Heavens! You mean the dart crash?"

"Yes. We all have our duty. Sometimes the burden of duty can be a heavy one. You work for Anabb and you know how it is. In the end, I had to do what I did, but Sankri will see it as a betrayal. I fear that by bringing you here has only made matters worse."

The breeze, warm and gentle, whispered across the sands

around them. She didn't understand it at all.

"But you're brothers! No matter what happened on Earth, what you did was in the line of duty. He has to know that."

"The evening meal is waiting," he said simply.

Men! Just overgrown boys.

She shook her head in frustration and gave his arm a quick squeeze. She stood up, shot him a glance, then slid down the dune's face. Below, oil lamps hung from the straw roofs of the mud huts, the soft yellow light diffused by fine dust still hanging in the air. A group of children ran screaming among the huts, pursued by angry words from the women. A background murmur of voices drifted in the warm air. Youths and unpaired maidens were bringing food to the long tables.

Dhar watched as Teena disappeared among the shadows. After a moment, he turned to look at the last traces of a purple sky.

"I shall be waiting, my brother," he said with finality before following.

* * *

Terr woke to the unrelenting squawk of the alarm, feeling mean and nasty, ready to give someone a bad time. Mumbling improbable suggestions to himself, he lurched into the shower and howled as icy needles worked him over. After the initial shock, it wasn't so unpleasant. Drying off got some of the circulation going again. His skin glowed pleasantly and his mood mellowed. Life did not seem to be so bad after all.

That feeling changed quickly.

Watching tendrils of steam coil above the unlikely contents of his plate, he took a cautious sniff. His lips curled with distaste at the unappetizing mess, the stuff guaranteed to provide a balanced and nutritious meal. He hoped it wouldn't ruin the plumbing as he shoved the damned thing into the disposal chute, plate and all.

Definitely not one of his better mornings.

Rit!

The navigation bubble dark, disturbed only by the somber flicker of instrument lights from the color-reactive panels. Even the computer status reports sounded subdued. He sprawled on the command couch, clasped his hands behind his head and looked up through the bubble. Captal hung before him, a flattened greenish orb flanked by the muddy gray of its moon.

Passing slowly by, a huge Sofam Industries-built colony ship was a glittering jewel around which cargo vessels clustered like moths. He had only seen one other like it and wondered where this one was bound. It looked more like a small moon than a ship. His eyes wandered past it to the planet below. He stared at Captal with mixed emotions. So much of his past was down there. Torn with nostalgic longing to see Enllss and an eagerness to lock horns with whatever enemy waited for him there, he waited to land. He also felt fear lurking deep in the shadowy corridors of his mind. A fear he knew he would have to face somewhere in the sands of the Saffal. Ponderous forces shifted within him and he shivered. He trod a dangerous path and risked more than merely his life.

"SC&C link enabled. Ready to copy," the computer announced.

He could still change his mind...

"Approved."

The stars began to wheel as Surface Command and Control brought him in. He checked the main nav plate. It wouldn't be long now.

On the way down, he reflected on his yesterdays. They were dark and filled with cold memories. Taltair was an eternity away, a shadow of another reality. During the flight to Captal, he didn't remember the days as they went, letting time and space merge as the stars drifted past him.

He remembered spending long hours in the darkened command deck; thinking, staring at the twisted, barely visible strands of gravity waves stretching into infinity around him. He thought of his tomorrows, of wasted moments and Teena. He thought of hot blood that had now chilled, of flowing desert sands, burning winds, and amber skies. He thought of Dhar waiting for him when he came to seek him out. He didn't have it all figured out, but the picture turned out to be bigger once he removed the wrinkles.

He realized quickly that if he wanted to confront the face of his enemy, he had to deal with him on his own ground. Know your enemy, straight out of the Fleet Strategy and Tactics manual. Was Dhar really his enemy, or even the only one?

In the anonymous solitude of his cabin, with the Wall his only companion, he went back to basics. One of the first things he did was access the Bureau of Cultural Affairs virtual data bank on Captal. He needed to connect Dhar's activities over the last year into some pattern he could understand. He knew *how* his brother betrayed him. What he needed to know was why. After inputting basic search parameters, he allowed the powerful intelligence computers to sift through the mountains of information.

What he got back set him thinking along lines he didn't initially consider relevant. Ordinarily, he would not have attached much significance to the murky underworld of Captal's politics and the power byplays between the Servatory Party and the Revisionists. His interest stirred by recent events, certain that everything was connected and important, even if he could not see the links. Not yet, anyway.

At first glance, nothing spectacular jumped at him about the pattern of Dhar's assignments, handling the usual skungy jobs normally given to junior officers nobody else wanted to do. What struck him was that over the last year, Dhar had spent a lot of time in the Bureau of Colonial and Protectorate Affairs on detached duty. That meant Enllss. Terr knew Dhar moused around for the Unified Independent Front, and the Bureau of Cultural Affairs clearance would have given him unprecedented opportunity for information gathering. Dhar had never made a secret of his clandestine activities for the UIF. Terr suspected Enllss knew all about it and secretly approved. After all, the Revisionists wouldn't mind another Executive Council seat backing them, however uncertain that backing might be at the moment.

Chewing things over, he wondered if Enllss actually approved of Dhar's activities.

"Dump detailed profile of BCPA assignments. Same subject and run hard copy," Terr ordered the computer.

"Hard copy not authorized for your location."

"Okay, dump visual profile only."

The Wall swam and he scanned the data for patterns. All of Dhar's assignments had BueCult security blocks on them. Laundering money for some commissioner, eh? Terr grinned. Then he saw it.

"Page forward," he said with sudden interest and watched the images change. He let out a loud exhale and stood up as his eyes ran through the information. Absently, he touched the scar above his left eyebrow.

The last two entries were joint missions with the Diplomatic Branch. As with others, the assignment details were blocked; Commissioner eyes only—Sill-Anais, and by extension, Anabb. He stepped closer to the Wall and the image receded…the last mission still active. Still active? He stared at the mission start date and alarms clanged at the back of his head. He nodded with grudging admiration. The devious and murky ways with which Anabb ran things never ceased to amaze him.

Or was it Anabb?

"Dump personal profile. Summary only."

His missions were also blocked, but not to him. Not that he needed to check them. What interested him was his Trillian mission start date. He smiled grimly as he stared at the notation. The assignment roughly matched Dhar's date, coming a few days later. Somehow, Gashkarali, the Orieli, and Teena, were all part of the same comedy and still running.

Why would Dhar be involved with Gashkarali? Even with Terr's clearance, the data bank remained stubbornly unhelpful.

He should have asked another question. Why did Anabb insist to include Dhar in the Orieli formal Mission to Salina? Just to bring together two old buddies? Unlikely. Anabb simply was not that charitable. Trained experts from the Bureau of Colonial and Protectorate Affairs usually handled alien contacts. Dhar had spent an awful lot of time at the BCPA, Terr reminded himself. A connection clearly existed somewhere, but it lay beyond his unraveling. Thinking about it, perhaps he should have rephrased the question. Why had *he* been involved? Because he made the first contact with the Orieli? Flattering, but hardly a valid reason.

Anabb never did *anything* without a reason. Terr also remembered talking to Dhar how Anabb may have been ordered to include both of them on the Salina Mission. The only person able to issue such an order was Sill-Anais, Bureau of Cultural Affairs director…and Enllss who ran the Bureau of Colonial and Protectorate Affairs, responsible for ecoforming worlds, protectorates, outposts, including alien contacts, not that they've had many of those of late.

Something cold ran down Terr's back and he shivered, not daring to form the thought that teased him. He and Dhar were both Wanderers. Including them in the Salian mission may not have been designed to bring them together, but perhaps remove them? But remove them from what?

To figure out Dhar's motive and Anabb's possible involvement, he planned to expand his search.

Terr's Fleet Academy grounding in political and strategic studies were extensive, but his blood was hot then, and more interested in making history, or notoriety, more accurately, than studying it. Now, he needed to apply what he remembered of that theory into actual practice.

When he tried to sleep, his mind tumbled through the Ser-rll's tortuous chronicle and the formative ages of its interstellar power blocks. Figures of infamy and prominence served as convenient markers, pointing at turns in time that eventually coalesced into what today became rivalry between the Revisionists and the Servatory Party camps.

The faces of yesterday became the faces of today. Like all living things, political bodies exhibit character and inertia. As they became more ponderous, the more difficult it turned out to change, until brought to a nexus of time by a person or event.

Terr was interested in only one political body: Terchran and the Karkan Federation that dominated the Servatory Party coalition. If Dhar worked for them, he had found his real enemy. Unfortunately, that frame quickly became too narrow. He simply didn't know enough about Terchran to discern the Karkan's motives. Assigning him to the megalomania bin would be to underestimate a powerful adversary.

Was he focusing too closely on Terchran? What if another hand guided Dhar, guided them both? Even on Taltair, he somehow knew this wasn't Anabb's maneuvering, but buried the idea deep. He faced a cruel decision and the emotions warred within him.

From there, it was a natural step for him to turn his attention to the Sofam Confederacy, the power behind the Revisionist Party, and to Enllss.

What are you up to, Uncle?

A day out from Captal, he asked the Wall to re-dump some of the data on Anar'on and the Unified Independent Front. All the while images of rolling dunes beneath amber skies kept him company.

"When we meet, my brother," he whispered fiercely.

* * *

Sal Field was a hive of frantic activity with ships coming

and going in constant streams. Big and small, all shapes—a swarm of ships. The Serrll capital world always a busy place. Near the military terminus complex, flanked by patrolling APCs, Armored Personnel Carriers, hovered the stark and forbidding shape of the Orieli survey cruiser. A huge ship over eight hundred and fifty katalans long, almost twice the size of an M-4. Its auxiliary nav screen was barely visible, flickered dull orange, and made the hull outlines flow and blur.

Nothing overtly threatening about the alien vessel. The geometric simplicity of the smooth flowing lines of the dark rectangular slab with its drooping edges, belayed its awesome power and sophistication. A stark and chilling reminder of the gulf that lay between the Orieli Technic Union and Serrll cultures.

Terr wondered what must have gone through Anatol Keller's mind when his shield grid dropped and he stared at his main plate waiting for the fire that would have ended it all. If their paths crossed again, he would see Karhide Zor-Ell. There were questions that needed asking and Zor-Ell might have some of the answers.

Outside the terminus, the broad tree-lined Paulo Way Boulevard permanently packed with hurrying, strolling populace from all over the Serrll. Kiosks, bars, shopping complexes, amusement centers and other less savory inducements lined the Way. A major attraction, and at any other time, he would have loved to linger and peruse. Most of the Paulo District reflected the relaxed, opulent and sophisticated lifestyle of its residents.

He found himself in a gorgeous sunny day, warm and still, and a shame to waste it on business. Locals and tourists stood on the glidewalks, talking, staring, or just waiting to get to wherever they were going. Heavy clouds were massing in the east and he hoped they wouldn't ruin his day by dumping. He picked up a communal and asked to be taken to one of the strip hotels along Taiko Way circling the Center. After an indifferent glance from the driver, they made the short flight in silence.

Captal city and its Districts were a sprawl stretching into blue haze without end. Through the canopy of green, rose clusters of towers, business centers, residential complexes and tourist traps. Captal represented a curious mixture of baroque, contemporary, and the futuristic. A blend of many worlds, representing as it did the Serrll Combine. Consequently, its Districts were more a collection of enclaves than a homogenous expression of its native culture, to the lament of traditionalists.

The communal landed at one of the hotel's ramps and he took a tube down. The foyer cool and quiet. His footsteps echoed on the stone floor as he walked to the reception desk. The attendant looked bored as he made the booking and didn't bother hiding it. Terr got even by not giving him any gratuity.

The room obviously not the luxurious Ambassador, but he did not mind. He wasn't on an expense account this time. It had a comms board connection to the Wall and a bed. It would do for a day's stay. The window screen cleared as he walked to it to gaze at Celean Park a block away. The government Center complex occupied most of the Hiat District behind the park. The Security Council administration tower loomed against the treeline. He looked up at the massing clouds that smeared the greenish sky. Somewhere in the east, thunder rumbled and rolled across the heavens. After a lingering murmur, it faded and the clouds drifted in. With the sunshine went some of his original good humor. At the comms board, he punched in a selection and soft strands of music made the Wall shift and melt in patterns of color.

For what he had in mind, some of his more shady and unsavory contacts were better suited to giving someone a bone-crushing workout or a permanent change of health. Not that the crowd occupying the Executive Council were beneath such behavior. It would not do to be seen associating with one or two of his more questionable pals this early in the game. Since this was the political center of the Serrll and all, Captal's rarefied atmosphere deserved a touch of finesse and class. No need to appear uncouth and slovenly, an amateur.

He freshened up and went prowling.

Like the beltway of any inter-star terminus, bars, tourist dives, hotels and establishments of dubious reputation lined the main avenue of Taiko Way along Celean Park. He searched for a particular hole, if it hadn't been closed down. It had been a while since he cruised the bars here.

He found the establishment and pushed at the door. It creaked as it swung aside. He paused before stepping in. The subdued place made him blink, lit by pale orange light. Insects cruised around the light strips. A smell of stale booze, cheap perfume, and unwashed bodies lingered in the air. In the corner, the pairs ring stood empty, waiting for dusk to settle before the action started. Shadows were thick and the faces blurred. Still early and most of the tables were empty, cluttered with glasses half full or overturned with contents glistening in the gloom. Someone looked up, eyes puffed and features hanging like dirty washing as Terr picked his way toward the bar.

He leaned negligently against the woodwork and turned slightly to better see the door. It was that kind of a dive. A small portly figure ambled out of the shadows, grumbling as he brushed the top with a grimy rag. His huge round face mottled red and he wheezed as he walked.

"The usual, Kelso," Terr murmured, his eyes roving among the deserted tables.

"Why, if it isn't the hero!" the barman chortled and slapped a meaty hand against the top. "Been a long time. Heard you'd been cruising around."

"You've got long ears," Terr said and Kelso chuckled with pleasure as he filled a tumbler. "Razzo sends his love," he added casually.

"He can shove it," Kelso grunted, gave a belch and patted his sagging stomach. He slid the tumbler toward Terr and placed his elbows on the bar. "If Razzo was any kind of brother, he'd come visiting. Besides, he's a shithead like you. Well, runt?

What brings you to this hole? Lost your way, have you?"

"Catching up on old friends, is all," Terr said, eyeing the oily gray liquid with suspicion. "Last time I had this stuff, I woke up on a tramp to Salina." He screwed his eyes shut and took a quick gulp.

"Yeah, figures." Kelso chuckled, watching Terr kill himself. His cold blue eyes danced. "If you cannot cut the score, you shouldn't be in the game."

When the coughing stopped, Terr wiped his eyes. "The games are all fixed and so is your booze," he croaked, pointing accusingly at the tumbler.

"In your ass," Kelso said. "Been corked for years. Only the best on account you being a hero and all," he added with a smirk.

"Rit!"

Kelso looked around quickly, then leaned across the bar top. "I heard about your partner. Tough break."

"Yeah. I haven't stopped laughing."

"What I mean, runt, is that I know where she is."

"I know where she is. That's not why I'm here."

"Yeah?"

"Know something? Back on Earth, there was a moment when things got a bit sticky, if you know what I mean. I thought of your joint here, Kelso. I wanted one of your cold specials so bad…" His eyes unfocused in memory and the hot sands shimmered beneath a hard sky.

"Crap," Kelso said.

That's what Terr liked about him. He always knew where he stood with Kelso. He grinned and the tumbler clicked against the bar.

"Like that drink, I need your help now. What can you tell me about Terchran?"

"Punch any Wall."

"I don't mean any of that official groker shit. Besides, if I'm gonna punch anything, it's not likely to be a Wall. I'm after the juicy stuff."

Kelso tilted his head and squinted. "The dirt, eh? Not much that I *can* tell you. He's a high roller. Straight as far as I can tell—for a politician. On the outside, at least. They're all crooks basically. Dharaklin's been seen with him, you know. Tanking up, cruising around, that kind of stuff. Don't know if they're pals, but I wouldn't mess around with that guy, runt. He'll chew you up without spitting out the bones. More likely choke," Kelso chortled.

"Heh, heh. Very cute. Has Dhar been seen around any of the Servatory Party operatives?"

"Hah! Sure, he's been around. So?"

"Don't know."

"You think he's working for them?"

"Maybe. That's what I want to find out."

They admired the view and the silence for a while, then Kelso's eyes widened and he grinned.

"Just remembered something. He's been cruising around with your uncle quite a bit lately. Before this Orieli mess turned up, I mean."

"Enllss?"

"You got any others?"

"Sarcasm doesn't become you, Kelso. I'll check on that one. It's probably nothing, but thanks anyway. Keep your refrigerant cool." Terr pried himself loose from the bar and stretched.

"Hey, hero. I wouldn't want this to get around, see. I mean, it might not be healthy for me. On account I likes it here. Get my drift?"

"I just dropped in for a drink, Kelso. In case anyone asks."

"The thing is, runt," the barman began and looked around quickly to see if anyone watched them. "I don't know if it's true or not, and I don't particularly care, but I've heard it said that Dhar runs an SP cell on Taltair. Might be worm crap for all I know."

Terr looked at him closely, wanting to ask where he got his information, but knew better. Still, if true, it could explain a lot of things. If true.

"Interesting. Thanks."

"I hope you find her, hero," Kelso grunted and started polishing the bar again.

"I'll find her," Terr said. He threw some Serrll fivers on the bar top and walked out.

* * *

The cable-tube brought Terr within walking distance of the Security Council complex. He decided to make the short walk through Celean Park rather than take the tube straight in. Old gnarled trunks lined the path, their branches hanging over him in a whispering, swaying canopy. His footfalls crunched on loose gravel. Ahead, pale shafts of light came slanting down to splash against fallen leaves. He felt the strength of the ancient trees around him, their bulk almost comforting. Their permanence and mastery a solid presence that swept away petty doubts. They seemed above mere emotion and pain, indifferent to the frantic activity of mortals around them.

The Bureau of Colonial and Protectorate Affairs tower rose before him. Connected to other towers of the Center by tubeways, it was a slender needle of ceramic and reactive panels, indifferent to emotion and pain of the people below as were the trees in the park. The glidewalks were packed with locals, bureaucrats, and gawking tourists. Easy to tell the bureaucrats from the locals and the tourists. The bureaucrats invariably sported stiff, starched expressions of importance and worldly concern. And the locals, they laughed at everybody and everything.

With mixed feelings, he ambled up wide, creamy stone steps. He paused at the top. With an amused glance at the crowd behind him, he walked through the main entrance. His footsteps echoed in the dark vastness of the pale yellow marble hall. A sprinkling of visitors gaped at tapestries, murals, and paintings from far worlds that adorned the walls. Statues of heroes and dead politicians littered the floor. Hushed voices interrupted the cathedral-like atmosphere. Office workers walked briskly between the exits, ignoring the curiosity seekers. It was a long walk to the main reception area. For a while, he thought he wouldn't make it.

Very pretty and all alone behind a huge round desk console, Terr smiled broadly at the receptionist. Somewhere in his yesterdays, he would have enjoyed her company and more. That part of him was, well, resting, which was a damn shame. Still, she deserved some of his attention.

"Welcome to the Bureau of Colonial and Protectorate Affairs, sir," she said politely, her eyes cold. He could bet that she must have heard all the come-on lines ever invented at one time or another.

"Don't you get tired of that opener?" he asked her seriously.

She looked at him with frank curiosity. "I had my choice."

"Of what?"

"This or Cantor."

"Should have picked Cantor."

She shrugged prettily, a complex movement of small shoulders and body parts.

"Is there anything I can do for you, sir?" she repeated, cool and sophisticated.

He looked wistful. "I wish you had asked me some time back. Now…"

Her small nose crinkled as she flashed him a genuine smile. "Tough break."

Footsteps echoed behind him. "What's this? What's going on here?" the voice brusque and no-nonsense.

Officious pipsqueaks gave Terr a real pain and this item was no exception. He turned and scrutinized the apparition.

The Base Scout glowered at Terr, looking as though he owned the place.

"Mister," Terr said with feeling, "one month with me and you would either be a new man or dead, no matter how many Prima Scouts you had for a father."

"Now, who do you think—"

"You stand to order when addressing a superior officer!"

The Base Scout snapped to more in reflex than anything else. Terr walked around him, stopping to study a face that looked like a dish of stale minced meat.

"I could learn to hate you—bad. That wouldn't be very comfortable for you."

"I—"

"No one gave you permission to open your trap!" Terr hissed and the Base Scout gulped.

The youngster had gone pale and sweat began to bead on his forehead. He did not know who Terr was and he could not very well ask. Either way, things didn't look good.

"Now, Mister. What were you about to say?"

"Ah, I…Can the Bureau be of any assistance…sir?"

"It can. Master Scout Terrllss-rr to see the Commissioner."

"The Commissioner is a very…" the Base Scout started automatically, then his eyes flickered. "Ah, the Commissioner is expecting you, sir," he said weakly.

"I should damn well hope so."

The Base Scout turned to the amused receptionist. "Notify First Assistant Tariq that Master Scout Terrllss-rr is on his way up, will you?"

"Yes, sir," the girl said and gave Terr a conspiratorial look.

"Thanks, pal." Terr grinned sourly. "I'll remember you."

"I would be honored to escort the Master Scout."

"Don't bother, I won't get lost. Besides, I think I've had enough of your warm company to last me for quite a while. I wouldn't want to overdo it."

He left the youth gaping after him. The poor slob would

probably spend a week wondering if he would wake up on Cantor one day in charge of a guard detail. If nothing else, he thought savagely, it would keep the snot focused.

He picked one of the high-speed cable-tubes that went all the way to the executive offices. Bored faces waiting for lower level tubes hardly gave him a passing glance. His tube arrived and he stepped in. As the doors shut, an outside view replaced the paneled interior.

A waist-high rail formed, the image providing psychological protection only. The tube started up smoothly and the ground rapidly fell away. Celean Park spread before him, merging into the rest of the city. Beside him the wall of the building became a blur as the tube raced up the tower. He could even hear the soft hiss of air rushing past. For a moment, tempted to change the scenery program, he thought better of it.

When the tube stopped, the interior became solid again and the doors opened. All around, high clear window screens provided an unobstructed view of Captal. He stepped out and his feet sank pleasantly into a thick green-tinged rug, the dull yellow-orange crest of the Bureau woven into the pile. The reception area had softly contoured couches tastefully arranged between workstations. Potted plants provided discreet little pockets of intimacy. Finely textured Catlan moss panels lined the back wall. He hesitated to think what it cost to shape them like that and keep them alive; citizen's taxes at work. Background music filled the hollow spaces with muted unrecognizable sounds.

A mature executive type strode purposefully toward Terr, a worried frown creasing his face. Caused, no doubt, by being interrupted in the performance of his critically vital civic duties. After all, he was an Assembly rep, not some damn messenger boy.

"Master Scout, if you would come with me," he said politely, but coldly and turned, clearly intending Terr to follow.

"And you are?" Terr asked without moving.

Stefan Vučak

The other jerked to a stop and gaped, appalled that anyone would dare question him. "I am Tariq, the Commissioner's First Assistant."

"And I'm sure your assistance is appreciated. Lead on," Terr said with a wave of his hand.

Tariq's little button eyes glinted. If Terr had been anyone else, that would have been the end of the visit. As it was, he took it like a man, bit his lip and walked off.

In Enllss' private reception area the potted plants looked pretty much the same as Terr remembered. Behind a perfectly empty desk sat another provocative looking woman dressed to kill. She appeared to be studying an inlaid screen, tapping an occasional command into the console pad.

Tariq pointed at some loose couches.

"If you would wait here the Commissioner will be with you in a moment." He didn't bother waiting to see whether Terr liked it or not.

Watching his retreating back, Terr wondered why Enllss always seemed to pick the hard cases.

"Warm personality," he remarked to the woman. She looked up and flickered him a smile.

"Don't mind him. He's sore that his nomination for a second term in the Assembly didn't come through."

He doubted it. The guy was just cold. He chose one of the couches at random and sank into its cloying softness, letting his hand wander over the luxuriant material. The powerful apparently did well for themselves. It certainly beat an ordinary form-chair all hollow.

It didn't take long. After getting pleasantly drowsy, the translucent doors slid aside and a familiar figure walked out. He tensed, rose and stood to. Illeran flicked a glance at Terr, his pointed tongue flickering. Without looking back, the Karkan walked out. Terr was sure Illeran recognized him, wondering what the hell he was doing here. Well, let the bastard wonder.

"Terr, my boy!" Enllss boomed and spread his hands in

64

welcome as he emerged from behind the panels. "Well, don't just stand there. Come on in! No calls," he said and threw a glance at his personal aide. He stood aside and waited for Terr to walk into the office.

Terr took in the wide desk, its polished surface large enough to jog on. In one corner sat two cups and a teapot on a tray. Behind the desk, a floor-to-ceiling window screen showed Captal's sprawl. The Wall on his left cycled through a new pattern he hadn't seen before.

Enllss punched him on the shoulder and grinned broadly. "It's good to see you again, my boy. Really."

"Thanks, Uncle. It's been a while, I must admit."

"You're looking a bit thin," Enllss observed sternly and frowned beneath bushy brown eyebrows.

"Been on a diet," Terr said easily as he looked around the office.

"So I've heard." Enllss pointed at the antique padded chairs in a little alcove on their left. "Make yourself comfortable. Drink?"

"Sure. Why not?"

A dark bottle with matching crystal tumblers already waited on the low oval table. Terr got himself settled while ice tinkled and glasses clicked. He turned to Enllss and saw him through different eyes, wondering whether the images were the same. Stockier perhaps, face a bit more wrinkled and hair a little grayer with only a few flecks of brown showing. He toyed with the idea of looking like that in eighty or ninety years. Enllss was of average height and powerful. The bulge around his middle had shrunk somewhat. Terr fought back a smile at the thought of Enllss having to work out.

Enllss handed him a tall tumbler and raised his. "What shall we drink to?"

Terr shrugged indifferently, not really in the mood to play. "Rit! Let's just drink."

Enllss grinned as ice in the crystal tumbler tinkled. "To

your safe return."

Terr savored the mix and nodded in appreciation. "It's been some time since I tasted this kind of stuff," he remarked casually.

"Personal stock, my boy. Too good to waste on someone who would go and ruin it with a fizzer." Enllss leaned back, eyeing his nephew above the rim of his glass. "Had a good flight over?"

Terr couldn't help chuckling. "When I took off, I was mad as hell. Ready to be boiled. Now, I don't know. Wrung out, hollow, and uncertain."

"What was it like?"

"You mean crashing, being shot, starved, and chased by Earth's authorities?" Enllss didn't even blink. The years of making tough calls had built some armor around his conscience. "It's only a memory now. That part of me must have died somewhere back there."

Enllss placed his glass on the small table and smirked. "Into philosophy now, are you? Let me tell you something, boy. Granted that you've had a rough ride, but that's what you signed up for. Feeling sorry for yourself maybe?"

"Didn't anyone tell you that you're a heartless and manipulative bastard?"

"It's been mentioned once or twice."

"I'm not surprised. I don't know how Aunty puts up with you."

"We have an understanding," Enllss said with a grin.

Terr pointed at the cups on the desk. "Been entertaining?"

"By damn! My boy, if you ever decide to stop this pussy-footing with Anabb, let me know. You're wasted in the Diplomatic Branch. What's your interest in Illeran, anyway?"

"Just curious." Terr took another sip. "As Executive Director of your Bureau and a major mover in the Servatory Party, it must result in a curious relationship. I mean, one of the most important departments in the Security Council is run by the

Servatory Party."

"Let's say that power sharing can get complicated, okay? But that's how the system works, and works well most of the time. Honestly, my boy, I could use you here. Lots of opportunities outside the Fleet. Ever consider getting out?"

"Funny you should mention it. I've done just that."

"Done what?"

"Quit."

"Quit what?"

"The Diplomatic Branch. Maybe the Fleet."

"You aren't serious?" Enllss looked stricken.

Terr twirled the ice in his tumbler. "I've had a lot of time to think on my way from Taltair. About myself and other things, about what I was doing with my life. I decided that Anabb and his schemes don't fit into what I wanted from my life anymore. Teena was the only piece of sanity I held onto every time I went out on one of his crazy missions. Now she's gone and I wasn't even there when she needed me. Anabb took everything, everything I had, even my brother," he growled in outrage and took a long pull from the tumbler.

"Terr, you don't understand—"

"You're right. I don't understand. The funny part is that he sent Dhar, of all people, to find her." He chuckled at the irony. "Ironic, don't you think? You see my problem, Uncle? I need to find out why Dhar betrayed me and if he's working for the Servatory Party. If he is, you won't have to worry about him being a security risk when I catch up with him."

"Tell me what you're feeling."

"What I am feeling?" Terr grinned wryly and shook his head. "You cannot even begin to imagine what this has done to me. Dhar and I are closer than any blood brothers could ever be, and this is tearing me apart. I don't want to believe he deliberately sent me to my death, but I cannot ignore the facts. I almost died in that dart crash. Yet the whole thing doesn't make any sense. You know, if I didn't know better, I would swear that Anabb had something to do with it. It has his stamp and I can smell it from here."

"That's pretty wild. Even for you," Enllss murmured over the rim of his glass.

"Maybe. You wouldn't happen to know anything about this, would you?"

"Me? What would I know about one of Anabb's operations? That's Sill-Anais' department."

"I heard that Dhar's been seen hanging around your skirts. Before the Orieli mission, I mean. I also heard he runs a Servatory Party cell on Taltair."

"Who told you?"

Terr ignored the question. "Now, take his mission profiles. Very interesting if you know what to look for."

Enllss did not say anything. He sat there looking predatory. He'd been playing the politician too long and his facade had developed cracks. Or maybe Terr knew him better than most and could read the small signs.

"You have access to his mission profiles, Enllss, and the Wall is there," Terr said and pointed with an open hand.

Enllss gave him a wintry smile. "Dhar is part of the Bureau of Cultural Affairs. I have no authority there."

"Even though he is seconded to your Bureau? I guess I'll just have to do this the hard way."

The sound of ice in his tumbler became suddenly loud. He looked at Enllss with a heavy heart. He only had a suspicion on account of his seedier self, a hunch that fitted some of the facts. He desperately hoped he was wrong.

"How do I go about seeing Terchran?"

"You don't. And why would you want to see him?"

"If Dhar is working for the SP, Terchran could be his control." Terr felt the fires blaze in his eyes.

"As an Executive Director, Terchran wouldn't soil his hands by being involved in a field operation."

"Perhaps. Either way, he might tell me things, and I'm sure

I could persuade him to cooperate."

"Like you did with Anabb?"

Terr laughed without warmth or feeling. "What did he tell you?"

It was Enllss' turn to smile. "He called me a few days ago, saying you were on your way here. Then he added something about a mess in his office."

"I bet."

"Aren't you getting a bit out of your depth, my boy? You don't go barging into the office of an Executive Director and start throwing accusations. Bound to raise comment. Anyway, those tactics wouldn't work on Terchran, and you would be a fool to try it. If Dhar is working for him, your actions might precipitate events not in our interest. If he's not, you could be placing him at considerable risk by drawing attention to his activities. Either way, you don't have the facts to confront Terchran. Or anyone else, for that matter."

"Yeah, there is always that," Terr agreed glumly and stroked his scar. "Still, a nice thought."

Enllss muttered something, plucked the tumbler from Terr's hand and made a production of refilling it. Terr stood as Enllss held it out like a peace offering. He admitted grudgingly that Enllss was right. He allowed his emotional reactions get in the way of professional judgment. A bead of condensation slithered down the tumbler's cold side. It touched his finger and he suddenly shivered.

He turned to face the Wall and watched the patterns merge and flow with ponderous certainty. Insignificant whorls of color expanded and twisted into impossibly complex images, only to disappear in another wash of merging patterns.

Without turning, he said, "Before I came here to see you, I had some grand idea involving state secrets and you telling all. I planned to confront Terchran and wring the truth out of him." He shook his head and looked at Enllss. "At least that's how the matinee thrillers make them out."

"Why *did* you come here?"

"To find some answers. For help, I don't know. Things just don't add up. Nothing I can pin down, but the picture is all wrong. There are too many contradictions."

"Such as?"

Terr took a pull from his tumbler.

"Well, like me, you, Anabb and Dhar, to mention a few." He placed the tumbler on the small table and sat down. "That was complicated enough, but when I began adding in the Servatory Party, the coming General Assembly elections and the squabbling over who the Unified Independent Front would or won't support, I felt it was all beyond me. Do you understand what I'm getting at?"

Enllss lowered himself into the formchair and leaned back. "You have me interested, I'll give you that."

Terr grinned. "This reminds me of a story I told Karhide Zor-Ell once. He also thought my yarn worth a few chuckles. This situation is very similar and for the same reason."

"You going keep me in suspense?"

"Okay. Let's start with an easy one. What's the one thing in Captal that everyone is obsessed about?"

"I have never been too good at guessing games."

Terr smiled. "I'll tell you, then. Survival. Survival on an individual and party level, and you can pick which comes first." Enllss remained silent and watchful. "Survival implies a security apparatus, which in turn leads to a need for an intelligence-gathering organ, right? Now, what if your Bureau and the Bureau of Cultural Affairs, through the Diplomatic Branch, meaning Anabb, had an obsession about one particular aspect of survival, such as making sure the Revisionists continue to dominate the Captal government?"

"You wouldn't be thinking of the Unified Independent Front, would you?"

Terr gave him his innocent grin. "Not interested in guessing games, eh? But you're right. I *was* thinking of the UIF. It's the only thing I can see, not counting the Orieli and the Sargon/Palean merger plot that managed to get everyone in Captal hopping."

"Go on."

"The government must realize that the UIF will be sanctioned by the coming elections, despite the apparent maneuverings by everybody. It's a matter of simple arithmetic. Between them, Kaleen and Orgomy will hold more than five percent of all inhabited systems within the Serrll, which will automatically entitle them to a seat on the Executive Council, political halitosis notwithstanding."

"I didn't know your interests ran into formalist political structures."

"A recent hobby."

"What's your point?"

"My point is, the Unified Independent Front seat will be important, very important. To the Revisionists as well as the Servatory Party. Both of you want to see that seat in your camp, either to control it or woo its support to strengthen your own position. Then again, the UIF are a bunch of annoying independents and nobody wants to be too generous to them in case the whole deal falls through the cracks and the UIF never gets ratified. No one would shed a tear if that happened, I'm sure. In the meantime, something needed to be done. Such as removing all Wanderers from security-sensitive areas, perhaps?"

"It's one possibility," Enllss conceded, his face wooden. The boy was good, no doubting it.

"Looking at it that way, Dhar's mission profiles started to make a lot more sense. From a pattern of seemingly random assignments, emerges a singular examination of protectorates and their relationship with Captal. Or more accurately, with the Revisionist Party."

"That would suggest Dhar is spying for the Unified Independent Front," Enllss pointed out. "Being a Wanderer, we took steps."

"And that's why you would want to neutralize him," Terr said smugly. "Including all the other Wanderers who may be hanging around Captal. As many as possible anyway. There is no way you can remove all Anar'on Assembly rep staffers."

Enllss smiled with grudging admiration. A neat bit of reasoning, and Anabb warned him to be careful how he handled Terr.

"Left myself open there, but how do you tie him in with the Servatory Party?"

"I haven't figured it out, but it's only a matter of time, and it could all be part of the same deal. Spying, I mean. However, there is one thing you can tell me. Why would Dhar be interested in Gashkarali and my Trillian mission? It doesn't seem to have anything to do with the UIF and it's not something Anabb would cook up all by himself. It has the smell of high-powered Captal politics. Something you'd be involved with."

"You're letting your imagination run away with you, my boy."

"Probably. However, what happened to me on Earth is not imagination, Uncle. It was very real and revolves around two people: you and Anabb."

Enllss raised an eyebrow. "Me?"

"I know Dhar is on detached duty to your Bureau, maybe still is. More than that, he reported directly to you, which made me think. A lowly Second Scout in bed with a commissioner? Hard to figure, unless he handled something really important or really sneaky. The way I see it, you wanted Dhar out of the way so he couldn't spy for the Unified Independent Front anymore. Fine. What better way to do it than attach him to me and Anabb's Orieli Mission to Salina. At first, I couldn't figure out where I fit in. Then it hit me. You wanted to get rid of me as well on account that I'm also a Wanderer, and you were not sure of my loyalty. That showed subtlety and a degree of callousness, me being your nephew and all. But no one can accuse you of nepotism or being soft, Uncle, and that's why you exposed my Trillian operation to Terchran. When I figure out Dhar's role in this, I shall have it all."

Enllss was stunned. There were a lot of details missing, but essentially, it all lay there, his entire strategy and operation exposed.

"My boy…"

Terr stared into his uncle's eyes, but couldn't read anything in them. Not comfortable with what he was about to do, but he didn't have any choice. He never did. He said the words from the *Saftara* and waited for the touch of Death, then reached with his hand. Small blue sparks danced between his fingers.

Enllss' face drained, but he didn't move.

"I don't care much for your intrigues, Enllss. I told Anabb the same thing before I blasted his office. That's your world and both of you can keep it, shitty as it is. I have outgrown your games. I don't know if my suspicions about you are correct or not, and I don't particularly care. But I'll tell you this. If Teena gets hurt and I find out it was through your hand, the House of Llss-rr will have more of its blood spilled, and I will have broken a blood bond…Uncle. Thanks for the drink," Terr said, stood up, and headed for the doors.

"Wait!" Something in Enllss' voice stopped him and he turned. He could see the internal struggle in the old man's face before the hard resolve snapped back into place.

"Things look different when you step back and consider the big picture," Enllss said. It almost sounded like an apology.

"When I stepped back, you fell into that picture," Terr countered coldly.

"Governments sometimes have to use covert methods to achieve their ends, my boy. They are not always pleasant. Believe me when I say, I would never want to see you or your loved one hurt. I don't work that way."

Terr nodded. "Not deliberately, perhaps, but once set in motion, events get a will of their own and sometimes take off in unexpected directions."

"It's a risk we all take in order to get something done. I can tell you that I am involved, but I cannot tell you why without compromising my or the government's position."

"Even if it means Teena's life, or Dhar's, or mine?"

Enllss suddenly looked angry. "You're exaggerating the scope of the problem and your importance in it. No one is threatened here."

"I'll have to remember that when I face Nightwings."

"Damn you, boy! If you would just park yourself at my place for a few days, all this will blow over."

"I cannot do that, Uncle. You know I cannot."

Enllss sighed and his shoulders slumped. "I guess not. You have to charge in and do it your way, as always; like your father. In your position maybe, I would be doing the same thing. I don't know. Will you be at the General Assembly when the Ori-eli make their pitch?"

Terr hesitated. Ever since his father was killed, apparently on another senseless diplomatic mission, Enllss had been there for him as long as he could remember. A little sorry for what he had done, but he didn't want to maintain a facade simply for the sake of family. Not on these terms.

"Probably not. I still have some questions that need asking and I realized the answers are not with Karhide Zor-Ell. Not the important ones anyway."

"Where are you going then? Anar'on?"

Terr grinned and shook his head. "A good agent doesn't reveal his plans, or some crap like that."

"We'd love to have you come over tonight, you know, before you leave. Rhea will be very upset…" Enllss spread his hands in irritation. "Damn it, boy! Do you have to make this any more difficult?" he growled and thrust out his jaw.

"I'll be there." Terr nodded and gave him a lukewarm smile. "And you can tell Aunty I look forward to seeing her again."

"Terr…I…" Enllss took a step forward. "I'm sorry about Teena."

"Yeah. So am I…for a lot of things."

Stefan Vučak

Chapter Four

"Prime Director Kernami Asai Tainam is fighting a losing cause, friend Beanab," Ti Inai said, wearing an oily smile, enjoying Beanab's confusion. His hands twined, the long fingers twitching like coiling snakes. His delicate button nose glistened on a small, triangular face. Above a pointed chin, enormous morose black eyes protruded beneath a high rectangular forehead. Ti Inai was bulky for a Palean, testimony to his enjoyment of Captal's culinary attractions. That, however, in no way diminished his predatory skills.

"A losing cause? I don't see how," Beanab Kari Anam ventured uncertainly, confusion evident on his black face. He bore little love for the Palean, and Ti Inai's inference eluded him.

Bright outside, the window screens filtering out most of the glare. Ed-Kani Takao's office reflected the subdued opulence accorded a director in the Executive Council. As commissioner for the Bureau of Technology and Development, Ti Inai didn't do so badly himself. Still, he would not have minded changing the title to 'Director'. Getting Beanab onside would help. It would help all of them.

He smiled indulgently and glanced at Ed-Kani.

"Pizgor's support for the Unified Independent Front is an exercise in futility, friend Beanab, and a very expensive one," Ti Inai said smoothly, slowly maneuvering Beanab into a no-win position. "One that cannot be making the Pizgor Triumvirate very happy with Kernami's policies."

"They are not," Beanab said ponderously and nodded with self-importance. "Trade has fallen off and it's hurting our shipping carriers. I have been advising Kernami that by supporting the Unified Independent Front, he damaged Pizgor's interstellar interests, but he refuses to listen. Him and that lackey of his, Commissioner Hiraki."

"And Hiraki has ignored you, against the advice of his Ministry of Trade and Shipping. It must be galling to be sidelined like this." Ti Inai permitted himself a moment of ironic amusement, stopping short of underestimating a dangerous opponent. After all, appearances weren't everything.

He considered Beanab an opportunist and a fool, as did many in the Assembly. Nevertheless, as Secretary to the Executive Council Moderator, Beanab wielded real power. He ranked with a commissioner, and only in his second ten-year term in the General Assembly. To have risen to his position in such a short time was no mean feat. Beanab *couldn't* be as stupid as he acted.

Then again, who was he to say?

"Ti Inai is correct," Ed-Kani hissed and snapped his delicate jaws several times. "Your ambitions can further Pizgor's cause—"

"But only within the Alikan Union Party umbrella," Beanab allowed and raised a long finger to emphasize his point. "As much as I lament the misguided actions of my countrymen, I remember my history. Your AUP Provisional Committee's covert action five years ago to stifle our trade exploded in your face when the Fleet exposed our Lemos raider operation. You then tried to make a deal with the Rolan group for their systems. Unfortunately for you the Orieli showed up and the Fleet base went to the Paleans, which effectively scuttled the deal with Rolan. Mr. Director, I am not unaware of the fact that some of our current trade problems stem from the fact that Sargon and the Palean Union have been rerouting their carriers away from our traditional shipping corridors. You wouldn't be trying a back door approach for Pizgor again by going through me perhaps?"

Ed-Kani shifted and his formchair automatically remolded

itself around him. His icy blue-white eyes were blank windows set wide on a narrow, bony face. Completely hairless offset deep character lines around the eyes and mouth.

He looked hungrily at Beanab, his smile raptorial. So, there more lay behind that face than would first appear, and Beanab was right. Five lousy systems. That's all that stood between him and his ambition to create a Greater Sargon. At the next Executive meeting, the Central Planning Council would be announcing the allocation of independent systems that agreed to join one of the neighboring political blocks after the next general elections. That would bring the total number of aligned and nonaligned systems to 257. He knew that Sargon would be getting two and the Paleans one; not nearly enough to push their combined number of held systems over the required twenty-five percent to rate an additional Executive Council seat, even if Sargon and the Palean Union merged. He needed Pizgor to push them beyond that twenty-five percent mark. If he could sway Beanab, Pizgor would deliver its three systems and two outposts to him, willingly or unwillingly. Once Pizgor fell, it would be easy to persuade some of the wavering independents to abandon their nonaligned status and join Sargon or the Paleans. That would clear the way for the merger, and the Alikan Union Party would rule the Servatory Party. Greater Sargon would rule! He *had* to get those systems, and he had the perfect bait.

With Pizgor in his hand, Ti Inai would also be more tractable, he reminded himself. Despite all the hard work by the Committee and the growing support within the Palean Union, the merger by no means assured. The uncovering of the damned raider bases on Lemos and Italan were political disasters, which cost the Committee billions and years of effort. And Ti Inai's venture with Khiman-ra, certain that Ti Inai engineered it, hadn't helped the cause at all. As always, when it came to making hard choices the Paleans preferred to vacillate, waiting to see which way the wind blew before making a decision, seemingly unaware that they themselves were part of the problem. And Ti Inai was as bad as they got. It sometimes took all of Ed-Kani's considerable diplomatic skill to keep himself from raging at the Palean in frustration. Time enough to even the score once he consummated the merger, he reminded himself.

"After Lemos, trade became tight for everybody and Sargon had to regroup," Ed-Kani said smoothly. "It's unfortunate that Pizgor happened to get caught in the middle."

Beanab smiled with genuine amusement. "Mr. Director, I wasn't born behind a shed. Please don't patronize me. The Paravan Trading Association may have put the squeeze on you, but that was five years ago. Paravan is not our problem. You are, Mr. Director. The Triumvirate may not like what is happening to our trade balance, but it doesn't mean Pizgor will cede its systems to you. What do you have to offer to change our mind that we haven't heard before?"

"I will bring order to the Serrll Combine, Beanab."

"The Serrll is not at war."

"That's where you're wrong!" Ed-Kani hissed. "The Serrll is very much at war, a trade war. And it's a war being waged by the Sofam Confederacy and its cursed Paravan Trading Association against all of us, Pizgor included. Your ground and orbital cargo handling terminals are the best anywhere, but they wouldn't survive a day without massive Triumvirate subsidies. And the reason your government is forced into these subsidies is to head off Paravan's rapacious tactics. That's the cold reality, my friend, and no amount of posturing by the Triumvirate will change it. Once Sargon and the Paleans are united, Sofam will have to face us in battle. Win or die on a field of honor with the Code! They won't be hiding behind the skirts of traders and merchants then. When the Alikan Union Party sits in Captal, there will be real free trade. Monopolies like the Paravan will be obliterated, and Pizgor will be free to pour its investment into civic infrastructure and expansion."

Ti Inai glanced sharply at Ed-Kani. Code indeed! He wondered to what extent the general Sargon populace shared Ed-Kani's enthusiasm to revert to a martial footing. He supported the merger and the Alikan Union Party's Provisional Committee. The current plan to win over Pizgor had much merit, but it didn't mean he or the Palean Union were prepared to plunge the Serrll Combine into chaos merely to satisfy one individual's craving for power and a place in history. However, right now, he did not want to have an argument with Ed-Kani.

Beanab gave a fruity chuckle. "You're probably a very good campaigner, Mr. Director. Your rhetoric is passionate and I would be swayed if it were not so misguided. While you dream of a grand union, what of the Karkan Federation and your partnership in the Servatory Party coalition? I doubt that Illeran or Terchran will sit idly by while you weave your schemes."

Ed-Kani laughed in admiration, a thin prolonged hiss. His teeth glistened as he bared his mouth.

"Let's say that for the moment, Sargon's interests loosely coincide with those of the Karkan Federation. We both want to see Captal's bloated Revisionist bureaucracy dismantled. It doesn't necessarily mean that Sargon wants to see it replaced by a Karkan one. Without Sargon's support the Servatory Party is nothing. You also have to remember, Beanab, our ties with the Palean Union and the Alikan Union Party are ancient and still strong. Strong enough to want us freed from the Sofam overlords."

"Yes, listen to friend Ed-Kani." Ti Inai bobbed his head, fingers locked, twitching. "There are elements within the Palean Union who would see this vision of our future disrupted, preferring to suck up to the Revisionists. We must be strong and not be swayed from our common purpose."

"Like Tao Karam and his Sofam supporting faction?" Beanab suggested dryly.

"Exactly, friend. They have forgotten that independence can be lost through means other than expansionist conquest.

Political and economic domination is as real as a military one." Ti Inai's stern expression faded and he chuckled, suave and persuasive.

"That's not a revelation," Beanab pointed out. "Still, by ceding our systems to Sargon or the Palean Union, Pizgor would vanish as an entity."

"A matter of perspective, friend Beanab. Let us say that Pizgor would be contributing to a greater whole," Ti Inai said smoothly.

"Caught in a vice between the Paleans, the Karkan Federation, and Sargon, Pizgor has always been out on a limb," Beanab allowed softly.

Ed-Kani permitted himself a small shrug. "Face the inevitable. By blindly supporting the Unified Independent Front, Pizgor is risking becoming ostracized by the other independents. Not all of them like the idea of Kaleen and Orgomy going out on their own. They feel betrayed and see their positions weakened. If the UIF becomes a recognized political entity, they won't care about you or anyone else. Pizgor should start looking after itself and secure its future as a pivotal component in the new order instead of maintaining a misdirected loyalty." Ed-Kani closely watched Beanab's reaction.

"It is possible what you say is true," Beanab mused, thinking furiously, weighing up the situation. His term as Secretary to the Moderator will lapse in two years. The indications were that he would not gain a nomination for commissioner, solely because of Kernami's opposition. The thought of being stranded in the political backwater of the General Assembly was, how would he put it, distasteful. He saw himself destined for greater things. He wanted later generations to remember Pizgor and Beanab together.

Eyes lost in a glittering future, he stroked the side of his forehead and looked at Ti Inai.

"You must realize that Tao Karam is your single major obstacle. His faction is openly opposed to any merger with Sargon. Unfortunately for all of us, his faction also dominates the Palean Congress, and with it, the Palean vote in the Executive Council. For your plan to succeed, you will have to deal with him."

Ti Inai dismissed the matter with a characteristically agitated wave of his hand.

"The man is an old relic, friend Beanab, who should have retired long ago." He cleared his throat and replaced the oily smile firmly back into place. "The coming elections will see him and his guard swept aside, making way for younger blood who have the vigor to pursue their visions."

"And you would be at the forefront of that movement?" Beanab snickered and raised his hand in apology. "No offense intended."

"As you say, friend Beanab. I am prepared to reach for power just as you are. The Palean Union risks much in contemplating this merger. The Lemos failure cost us dearly."

"But it wasn't *your* cost." Beanab cackled slyly.

"Enough of this!" Ed-Kani hissed and pinned both of them with a hard stare. "There is more at stake here than ambition and personal power. It all comes down to cold numbers, as always. Beanab, if you can sway some of the undecided Triumvirate members that Pizgor's interests lie with the Alikan Union Party, we can all realize our ambitions."

"That's all very well for you, but it leaves me in an awkward position," Beanab said, looking anxious. "I may aspire for better things, but I will not risk Pizgor's independence to get it."

Ed-Kani exchanged a glance with Ti Inai. "Pizgor's sovereignty will be respected. We don't want to interfere with the internal workings of the Triumvirate or your economy. We just want your systems to boost our territorial numbers," Ed-Kani hissed with a touch of exasperated irony.

"I know what you want. It's a powerful motive indeed, but what do I get out of all this?"

Through the Valley of Shadow

"That third Executive seat? It could be Pizgor's, friend Beanab." Ti Inai grinned hugely and dangled the baited hook. "It could be yours, in recognition of Pizgor's contribution. Think of it!"

Beanab thought of it, all right, and the images were very pleasant. It would mean nomination to Executive Director and another ten-year term. The position would bring with it power, prestige, and respect. Everything he ever dreamed of, in fact. It never happened before that a group with only five star systems had held an Executive Council seat. He could be the first. His name would hold a prominent place in history for all time.

He looked straight into Ed-Kani's stony eyes. "You propose an intriguing option and dangle an inviting bait, Mr. Director. Mind you, Kernami will have to be dislodged before the Triumvirate would even consider your proposal. That will be very difficult. His policies are working and he's extremely popular with the electorate. However, with the current, ah, trade difficulties, there are people within the Triumvirate who would not be unsympathetic, if properly motivated. I'll have to make a few calls."

Ed-Kani snapped his jaws with satisfaction. His eyes smoldered as he watched the emotions fade into each other on Beanab's scheming face. Too bad that his other problems were not as tractable. Beanab might be a self-serving fool, but he was right about one thing. He needed to do something permanent to Prime Director Kernami, and soon, or the Committee would be facing another very expensive failure, one which could possibly cost him his head.

On the other hand, Pizgor might be taken out of the equation entirely if Sofam finesses itself and its motion to abolish the independent's Executive seat backfires and is actually passed. He knew that Sofam was pressing the Unified Independent Front to support the Revisionists. If the UIF refuses, they would suddenly find that all independent nonaligned systems were under threat of being absorbed by one or other major blocks. If the Paleans annexed Kaleen, the Provisional Committee would have more than enough systems to affect the merger and the Alikan Union Party would have its third Executive seat. Sofam must know that, surely.

The question, of course, would Sofam push it to a decision?

The other question that warranted serious consideration: would Anar'on and the Wanderers allow Kaleen to be annexed?

* * *

Sitting at one end of the long table, Terchran shifted uneasily in his seat. His eyes narrowed into a probing stare. "Fa'sure, I'm forever damned if I understand you, Illeran."

His cold fishy eyes were hard as he regarded his recalcitrant friend. Thin bony ridges kept Illeran's sunken eyes in perpetual shadow. The weight of almost thirty years serving Karkan and the Servatory Party's cause, handling the responsibility and internal infighting, keeping factions and Sargon at bay, must have become crushing. Terchran hoped to see weariness reflected in Illeran's face, but he was disappointed. He only saw unfailing resolve and determination. In a way, that made him glad. The next two years would probably be very trying for both of them.

The silence lay tense between them. They were seated in Illeran's executive guest room occupying a large portion of the floor's corner space. The transparent floor-to-ceiling window screens gave an unobstructed view of Celean Park and Captal's central downtown sprawl. One floor down and to one side protruded a flattened dome protecting Illeran's private landing ramp. As an Executive Director, he had precious little time to enjoy the superficial privileges of his position.

Lush greenery, hanging moss and potted plants thrived in the humidity of the room. It reminded every visitor of Karkan's jungles and swampy climate. Terchran didn't mind it. A Wall display station took up most of one wall, showing an oily sea lapping against a black sandy beach. The image blended well with the room's decor. A huge fish tank took up the other wall. In the gloomy interior, shadowy shapes glided or hovered with a myopic stare at the tableau in the room.

Illeran permitted himself a moment of distraction as his thin pointed tongue flicked quickly between dry lips. He hissed, looking searchingly at Terchran. He shook his head with a delicate and graceful twist of a long, slender neck. A reptilian gesture in the way his slightly flattened head moved from side to side. He allowed a rumbling growl of displeasure to tremble deep within his chest.

"I know that," he said. "You're looking for subtlety and hidden meanings when sometimes the obvious is staring you in the face. The Orieli Technic Union has given the Serrll a serious problem in the shape of the Celi-Kran. It's a problem I hope Karhide Zor-Ell will clarify when he makes his pitch to the Assembly. However, the Krans present a problem for you and me as well, my friend."

"I know what the Krans mean, Illeran."

"Of course you do." Illeran nodded and pried himself out of the formchair. He walked to the fish tank and peered in. A sand groker whipped quickly beneath a weed-covered rock and snapped at a passing morsel.

"Ed-Kani and his AUP Provisional Committee are using the Kran threat to accelerate the merger under the claim that it's a legitimate defensive posture, which is a load of groker shit, but they've put a good spin on it and the populace is swaying."

"I don't agree, Illeran. The Committee's move is premature. After what happened to Lemos and Khiman-ra, too many Palean Congressmen are still skittish and wary of declaring openly for the Alikan Union Party. As long as Tao Karam's faction remains in control, Ed-Kani will not succeed."

Illeran turned and raised a finger. "Tao Karam and his cronies will be swept away in the next elections. Don't forget that."

"Fa'sure, and so will Ed-Kani and the two of us."

"True. It doesn't remove the threat to Serrll stability, though, and we cannot risk being complacent. There is too much at stake. Even with Ed-Kani gone, the Provisional Committee would still be very much alive." After a brief struggle in the tank, a swirl of sand, everything became still again.

Terchran felt something of the other man's frustration. It only reflected his regret and disillusionment at seeing dreams crumble into dust after decades of struggle. He held Illeran in profound respect. To hold an Executive Council seat for the Bureau of Colonial and Protectorate Affairs after two commissioner posts was an achievement to be envied. He did not necessarily agree with all of Illeran's policies, which have recently tended to be reactionary rather than planned, confrontationist rather than conciliatory. Perhaps both of them should make way for new ideas and directions.

Or maybe he felt piqued at the intransigent position of the Kapu Maluran legislature on Karkan. The home government stubbornly refused to be guided by Illeran's advice, and his own, for that matter, when dealing with Sargon and the Paleans, insisting the merger was doomed to failure. Bah!

"The Committee may be actively pursuing the merger, but they still face the same intractable problem," Terchran said smoothly. Illeran smiled and nodded.

"They need systems, right. We cannot allow Pizgor to be swallowed up, you know that. But Pizgor is merely a symptom of our own malaise and complacency. The Kapu back home haven't helped either. I'm afraid we underestimated the resolve of the independents to maintain their self-determination and overestimated our contribution to allaying their economic and political fears. We should not have been surprised when Kaleen and Orgomy sought to form the Unified Independent Front. Instead of opposing them, we should have been supporting them, ensuring that in turn, they would exercise their Executive vote in support of the Servatory Party. It would have been a potent lever against Sargon's merger ambitions. As it is, the UIF vote will probably go to the Revisionists. We blew it, you know that, don't you?"

"Don't start feeling sorry for yourself," Terchran said harshly and saw Illeran stiffen. "I never questioned our analysis of UIF's intentions. They are a dangerous development and represent questionable policies."

"Questionable policies, yes. Only because they're not *our* policies. But a dangerous development?" Illeran grinned ruefully and shook his head. "Given our preoccupation with wresting power from the Revisionists, our loss of oversight became inevitable. Still, it's done. We'll have to take them into account as another variable to be dealt with."

"Not if Bakral's motion is passed," Terchran said softly, referring to the senior Sofam Executive Council director.

Illeran gave an amused hiss. "Not much chance that Sofam would abolish the independent's Executive seat. The move would set off a feeding frenzy by everyone to absorb the independents. That in itself would not necessarily be such a bad thing, but it would lead to instability, and that's not in Sofam's interest, or ours. They just want to send Prime Director Marrakan a message. Sofam will not stand in their way, provided the Unified Independent Front supports the Revisionist coalition."

Terchran's eyes sparkled. "But Sofam is relying on Deklan to defeat the motion. What if we were to offer Deklan something that would make it worth their while to vote *for* the motion? In politics as with everything else, you take your opportunities as they present themselves."

"Let them have Kaleen and Orgomy?"

"They've been after those systems for some time."

"As Revisionist coalition partners, Deklan would never vote for the Sofam motion. Mmm. If the motion were passed, it would mean the end of the Unified Independent Front and a second Executive seat in the independent's camp. Not bad, but you've forgotten the Paleans. They've been lusting after Kaleen themselves."

"Let them take Kaleen and Deklan takes Orgomy. Wait a minute! For this to work, we would have to convince one of the Sofam Executive Directors to defect and vote to pass the motion."

"That's right."

"Fa'sure. Have you discussed this with Ed-Kani Takao?"

"Sargon is a coalition partner. To vote for the motion, he needed to be consulted," Illeran said smoothly and carefully watched as Terchran's expression of smug satisfaction turn into consternation.

And Terchran *was* concerned. If the Paleans took Kaleen and several other independent systems, Pizgor would not be an issue anymore, and nothing would stand in the way of a Sargon/Palean merger and a third Executive seat. A nightmare out of the blackest swamp that would tear the Servatory Party apart, forever destroying Karkan's hope of gaining a governing majority. In itself, the merger wouldn't change the balance of power in Captal. Despite losing the Palean vote, the Revisionists would continue to dominate the government with their four damned seats—with Karkan's backing—because the Karkan Federation would never side with the Alikan Union Party to create a Greater Sargon.

"Even if we succeeded, we could end up screwing *ourselves*!" Illeran mused.

"Has Ed-Kani been lobbying the Deklans?" Terchran asked.

"What do you think?"

"Fa'sure. I would be." The idea represented a grim picture.

"Suddenly, it's not such a brilliant opportunity, is it?" Illeran allowed himself an amused chuckle as he followed Terchran's line of thought.

"Sofam must have explored this scenario before Bakral discussed the motion with you."

"Of course. In the unlikely event the motion is carried, they would take the Rolan group and their disputed fourth seat would be secure. That's all they care about. The Karkan Federation are the only ones who stand to lose from this in every way, no matter which way things go."

"Sofam slime! Don't they know that the Alikan Union Party could send the Serrll into open warfare?"

"Sofam would never risk Serrll's stability just to see the Unified Independent Front destroyed," Illeran said comfortably.

"Then why are we interested in pursuing this?"

"Because, my friend, this could still work in our favor. The Deklans *may* be persuaded. What is more, even if the Paleans do take Kaleen, I believe your initial assessment is correct. They are wary of Sargon and not quite ready to jump into bed with them, and we would have rid ourselves of the Unified Independent Front."

Terchran frowned heavily. "It's a very dangerous gambit just to send Marrakan a message."

Illeran bit his lip. "Oh, I don't know. I am sure that Marrakan has seen through Sofam's tactic. Besides, he would never allow Kaleen to fall into Palean or Deklan hands. And you know why."

Terchran did know. The Wanderers wielded Death in their hands, and one does not trifle with Death.

* * *

"Holy worm shit," Aill-Massai whispered in shock.

Eyes glued to the large tactical display plate, he watched the replay from the scanner trace where the M-3 was now nothing more than an expanding cloud of iron filings. In the background a pulsing blue dot moved steadily toward Devon 3-VL4.

"Is that the alien ship?" he demanded and shot a sharp glance at his executive assistant. Standing beside him, Mataeer pursed his thin lips and nodded.

Aill took a deep breath and felt his massive barrel chest expand, then exhaled noisily through flared nostrils. He heard an awkward shuffle of nervous feet around him. Someone coughed to break the suddenly stifling silence.

"Ach! I have seen enough," he managed a thin growl. Straightening his wiry frame, he waved at the plate. When it faded to a neutral pastel, he turned to face his staff.

Aill's hair light gray, streaked by a single black band along the right side of his head in normal Deklan fashion, indicated a young male early in his maturity. A darker gray band had started to show on his left side. Old age. It came to the best of them, he thought morosely, his reflection in the plate still vivid in his mind.

The Operations Center was deathly quiet. No one wanted to openly express the nervousness and tension written clearly on their faces. Showing weakness did not fit the image of a tough can-do planetary engineer. That might be, but he suspected that all of them would need the light of the Path before this day ended. What of his fears? He whispered the litany of guidance to sustain him in this moment of need.

Mataeer's quizzical look told him he wasn't fooling anyone. To the pit with it. He didn't have time to worry about his image now or wallow in self-indulgence. He ran this operation and these men wanted leadership from him and action.

"Where is the blasphemous thing now?" he piped in high treble, trying to sound confident and positive as he dragged the heavy thermal coat off his shoulders.

Out of one disaster into another. He did not usually get himself involved with field problems. That's why he had field managers, but failure of one air-warming reactor, caused by shoddy maintenance, forced him to visit the plant site some twelve hundred talans away. What he said didn't make the supervisor's day, or enhanced the individual's chances of getting his regular quarterly bonus.

"The alien vessel is parked somewhere on the far side of

the moon," Mataeer said quietly in a deep, steady voice, watching Aill closely.

Their lives could depend on how Aill handled himself in the next few hours. He recognized Aill as an able and capable administrator, and more than competent to hold this post. Still, Mataeer had never seen him perform under real pressure, not where lives were involved.

"They haven't responded to any of our signals. At least none that we can detect. Shortly after we ceased transmission the alien ship launched two small craft heading our way." He glanced at the display panels. "You can expect them in two-and-a-half hours. After what happened to the M-3 sweeper, I doubt this will be a social call."

"I agree. Less than three hours, eh? Ach! It doesn't give us much time to coordinate with the other outposts. Have those ships been scanning us?"

"Nav checks only and some stuff that's a lot like our K-band acquisition sweeps."

A burly chief atmospherics engineer pushed himself past two admin types.

"What the crap does it matter if those things are scanning us? We're engineers Aill, and administrators. Professionals, all of us. We're not the military." A growl of assent rippled behind him. Aill looked up at the stocky powerful man towering over him.

"What are you trying to say, Kadal?"

"I think I'm speaking for everybody here," Kadal said and looked around for support. Several men behind him nodded. "We signed up for a rough and dirty job in a hostile environment. But we knew the risks. Ach! Ecoforming a planet is adventure enough for me, for all of us. I have no desire to get involved in some cursed war. We've got enough trouble from raiders as it is. With *Valetta* gone, our asses are hanging out in that breeze, man. I want to know if we'll be around tomorrow. Will our families?"

Mataeer was a good exec and knew when to keep his mouth shut. The faces around him told the story. Hell, there were a few questions he wanted to ask himself. One look at Aill and his steely gaze and firm resolve, Mataeer decided in a flash the boss-man had the innate ability to capably handle this situation. What worried him more was the small twinge of anxiety lurking in his mind. He prayed to whatever gods were around not to let him screw up and to keep the faith.

"Ach! This is merely another crisis we must face, Kadal. Perhaps a bit more serious—"

"Serious? You aren't kidding," someone interjected, followed by a strained titter and jostling of elbows.

Aill frowned at them. "This project has seen us through some sticky situations before and we weathered them all. Let's not fly off the handle and panic. If we follow established emergency procedures, we should be safe enough until help gets here. I'm sure the Fleet is aware of our predicament and won't leave us out here holding our dicks."

"You hope," Kadal grunted without conviction. "What if those two ships decide to come after us? What do we do then? We're in no position to—"

"Instead of whining, you should be thinking about checking out the systems in the emergency shelter. We'll need heating, food, clothing, comms gear, and lots more."

"Those caves haven't been used since we started the atmosphere project."

"Ach! All the more reason to make sure they're still serviceable. Look, I have no time to debate this with you. Whatever needs to be done, we better do it quickly. We have less than three hours. Deep down, I think we all suspect the aliens are not coming here on a sightseeing tour. Provided that Sector TACOPSCOM is on the ball, we should be able to hold our own until support units get here." Aill looked hard at his engineer. "We don't have any other choice!" he snapped and walked toward the window screen covering one of the walls.

Through the Valley of Shadow

A quiet afternoon, Devon was a shimmering yellow globe painting the sullen gray clouds with ribbons of gold. Aill thought he could hear the thin keening of the wind outside, but that was only his imagination. Over five tetalans of armored panel sandwich lay between him and the frigid environment outside. In the distance, snow-covered peaks thrust their jagged points into a rusty, fading sky. The foothills were already deep in gray shadow where low clouds lay bunched in the steep valleys. A cold world, harsh and unforgiving, but it was his.

Two worlds, both in the Sargon Directorate, now bore his stamp. It would be decades yet before permanent settlers could begin to carve out a new existence there. Still, he saw both transformed from deadly poisonous hells into a promise of life. With Devon, he came with the job almost completed, to what was perhaps an even greater challenge.

Would there be a tomorrow? After two years the place had crept up on him and stolen his heart. With a pang of regret, he realized that now, alien terrors, creatures without the Path, were likely to turn everything they have worked for into slag. After the destruction of the patrolling scout, he did not doubt the aliens' hostile intentions.

Below him the crude makeshift buildings of the Center reflected the spirit of the outpost: young, alive and free. The other three outposts scattered across Devon 3-VL4 would be just as worried. He would need to talk to them. Could he hold it all together? The Operations Center and the outlying stations might be destroyed, but the work they have done would remain. Even without them, Devon would go on.

Aill squared his shoulders and turned to face Mataeer. "Any feedback from the other stations?"

"They are waiting for your word," Mataeer said.

"Anything from Sector TACOPSCOM or Commander Palean Operations?"

"Nothing. I would guess that Prima Scout In Tain is still evaluating the M-3's TLM."

"Ach! What the blazes does he need to evaluate? A body count?"

Mataeer refrained from answering and pointed at the blank display plate.

"You saw the damage, Aill. *Valetta* paid dearly for its information. Someone hit the alien and hit it hard. Probably the Orieli. There is no one else out here. Except—"

"Yeah."

Kadal blanched. "You're saying the thing is a Kran vessel?"

"Ach! We need to keep that possibility in mind," Aill said.

"If that *is* a Kran ship, what's it doing here?"

"Looking for a place to hole up, make repairs, and signal for assistance," Mataeer said.

"It doesn't explain those two craft coming our way, though."

"On the contrary." Aill smiled mirthlessly. "It makes perfect sense. You saw the damage to that ship." He clasped his hands behind his back to stop them from waving around.

"They plan to raid us for materials?"

"Ach! I would, but I'd take some precautions. My guess is that they'll hit us first and knock out our comms capability. Afterward, they'll move in and start stripping down the Center. Whether I'm right or not is not the issue. That ship is a Fleet problem and they're welcome to it. My responsibility is to see to it that all of us get out of this alive. Mataeer? I want you to notify all stations and atmosphere processors to begin immediate evacuation procedures, which includes everyone here. Get them moving. You and I will remain until the aliens' intentions become clear. They might not be heading for us."

Mataeer nodded. Aill might be worried, they all were, but they could handle a routine evacuation procedure no matter how grave the circumstances.

"This is gonna make shit out of our schedule," someone remarked. A ripple of edgy laughter broke some of the tension.

Through the Valley of Shadow

"I'll be asking the Bureau of Colonial and Protectorate Affairs to include this under extreme hazard pay," Aill remarked dryly to more nasty chuckles. He looked closely at his atmospherics engineer. "Kadal? Can you handle this?"

The burly man snorted, amused that Aill questioned his physical courage.

Instructions were issued quickly without the need to say much. Brief orders, a few curt words that hid the emotions beneath, a touch, a gesture, and it was enough. People got busy and quickly cleared the command complex. Alone, Aill and Mataeer waited. Small noises from computer and comms systems kept them company. Night descended quickly as Devon sank behind the austere peaks. Mist lay in thick bands along the valley, ghosts wandering along aimless treks.

"Our crusty atmospherics engineer may have a soft underbelly," Mataeer remarked softly.

"Kadal? Perhaps. Ach! He has a family. He isn't saying anything I wouldn't if I were in his place."

"You know Aill, if that thing out there is really a Kran ship, it could threaten all our ecoforming stations along the length of the Palean border."

"Ach! If it's a Kran ship, my friend, it will threaten much more."

Mataeer digested that in silence. What if after finishing off Devon, the alien headed for an inhabited planet? What if more of those infernal things showed up? His skin crawled at the thought.

"In that case, I hope the Orieli have their shit together, or we're crisps."

Aill glanced at the chronometer display and swore softly. "Call TACOPSCOM, will you? Those damned morons have forgotten all about us," he snapped and waited for the Wall to clear.

"First Scout Tatllaa, Sector Tactical Operations Command."

"First Scout, Devon 3-VL4 Center is about to get creamed and the mighty Serrll Scout Fleet has its collective finger up its ass," Aill observed, staring intently at the face before him. "By the Path! We're not equipped to handle a military engagement, Mister. Ach! You could have a lot of stiff bodies on your hands in a few hours. What are you doing about it?"

"Mr. Controller, I'm painfully aware of your predicament, sir, but we're not in a position to do much," Tatllaa answered slowly, relieved it wasn't *his* ass on the line. "At least not at the moment. We diverted *Kopan*, an M-3 sweeper, to your sector—"

"An M-3 sweeper?"

"Yes, sir."

"Ach! You've got to be kidding me."

"We need confirmation of the event before other units can interdict the area."

"Ach! What confirmation do you want? Isn't one scrapped M-3 enough for you people?"

"Sir—"

"How long before *Kopan* gets here?"

Tatllaa looked uncomfortable. "I'm afraid—"

"I'll worry about the fear department, son. How long?"

"At least eighteen hours."

"We'll all be dead by then." Aill gave a long sigh of weary resignation. "It's all right, Mister. Not your fault. We will keep automatic comms telemetry going for as long as possible, for what it's worth. And First Scout…"

"Sir?"

"I suggest you get something heavier than an M-3 moving our way. If that's a Kran vessel, you'll need it. Am I getting through?"

"We are already looking into it, sir."

"You don't know what a warm buzz that gives me, son," Aill growled and waved his hand. The Wall faded into a swirl of color patterns and he turned to Mataeer. "Holy worm shit!"

Through the Valley of Shadow

"You'd think the Fleet is working for the Krans." Mataeer chuckled and shook his head at the mysterious machinations of the military bureaucracy.

The computer alert suddenly flashed and the tactical screen cleared. "Warning. Unidentified craft entering low orbital insertion. Range, six hundred and thirty-two talans and closing. Contact in eight minutes, relative speed and status. Belligerency status indicated."

"Right!" Aill clenched his fists and glanced at the tactical display. "As I expected. They're heading our way. We might as well clear out."

The cable-tube took them quickly down to the landing ramp where a combie waited. With a surge of power, it lifted and streaked out the hangar toward the white peaks. Behind them, a high pitched whistle tore the atmosphere as two stubby bulbous craft swept above the darkened installation. They glowed dull orange as they circled. Lightning and thunder echoed through the valleys as the bombardment started.

Flames licked high into the night sky. The slender towers of the Center were quickly reduced to smoldering, twisted skeletons.

* * *

Anar'on hung above him, a bloated crescent smeared by fractal patterns of yellow and brown desert sands and broken escarpments. The planet's tilt hid the northern pole within a black chasm blotting out the stars. Azure tendrils cut into the desert from the small northern icecap and widened into shallow purple seas and patches of muddy greens as they worked themselves into the equatorial deserts. Streamers of brilliant white cirrus cloud shrouded the bottom of the world.

Terr sat in the darkened command bubble and watched the planet slip overhead. Small ship noises whispered into the silence. He felt a measure of peace and fulfillment steel through him like something warm that started from his middle and slowly spread out. A feeling akin to religious satisfaction. The place did it to him every time, a sign of welcome that seemed to come from the world itself. Absurdly pleasant, he allowed himself a few moments to savor the sensation.

With regret, he shook off the feeling and clamped his mouth. He could not afford to forget why he came here, or be swayed by his yesterdays, especially as he planned to kill a brother.

After fourteen days in space waiting for this moment, his resolve remained firm, but his feelings were torn. He extended his right hand and clenched his fist. Sweat beaded on his forehead as he watched the image firm before him of a tall hooded figure, cape fluttering behind him, outlined against an amber sky—a lord of the desert. He allowed himself a moment of shared memories before he dropped his hand and the image faded.

He moaned heavily at the fatal inevitability.

"Forgive me, my master. I am not a worthy disciple of the Discipline," he muttered and remembered another place and another world where he also spoke those words.

Rit!

SC&C brought him down smoothly. Small, Kanarath Field looked cramped, almost deserted. Checkered plots of green crowded the Field boundary and vanished into the heat haze hanging above the shallow sea far in the distance. The city itself crowded the spaceport, its slim towers swam and twisted in the hot roiling air. The landing skids extended and *Sheeva* touched down daintily.

He took the tube to the lower deck and waited for the ramp to descend. With the curve of the ship hanging over him, he looked around the field. Two M-3s stood parked near the terminus building. A small Sargon liner hovered above its landing ring. Odd maintenance sled-pads lay neatly arrayed near an open hangar. There didn't seem to be anyone about. Dust whorls chased each other across the deserted apron. The air shimmered and swayed in the heat. Still early in the morning, but already blistering hot. He could feel the dry, oven heat soak through his shirt even as he threw the zip-jacket over his shoulder. It had been a while since he felt it last and he'd forgotten. He walked down the ramp, looked up and stretched his arms, welcoming the heat and the desert smells. He fancied the sky itself glared at him. Was it disapproval?

He took a sled-pad to the terminus building. The immigration formalities were mercifully quick. Kanarath was not exactly on a tourist must-see list and his military clearance smoothed the way. When they recognized him as a Wanderer, the formalities were waived. The cable-tube's run downtown did not take long. He found it relatively cooler along the broad Avenue of Light in the central district lined with thick native brush. Tall peelath hovered protectively over the glidewalks. And there were, of course, the constant city noises: the shuffling of feet, the babble of conversation, shouting, and other things. Overhead, streams of communals, combies, and private sled-pads caused shadows to dance on the streets.

He slowed his walk and paused beneath broad peelath branches that drooped limp and weary. A hanging garden spanned the width of the street, making welcome shade for those below. He'd never been in one of those joints before, being strictly a tourist trap. Right now, he would have relished its coolness. There would be tinkling water fountains and soft music to fill the air for offworlder patrons. He licked his lips, undecided whether to give into temptation. Then he nodded and walked off. There would be time for that later.

Most of the people along the Avenue were using the glidewalks, rubbernecking at storefronts, or just being carried along for the hell of it. There seemed to be an unusual number of offworlders strolling about. Nothing definite at which he could point, only a growing unease as he watched the movement around him. The density and texture of the population did not fit into what he considered to be the norm, and he hadn't been away *that* long. Could all this activity be due to the upcoming Representatives Conference? Highly likely.

He took a turn into Morena Path, getting increasingly irritated and uncomfortable. The buildings here belonged to the Center and reflected a more official, subdued atmosphere. That wasn't what bothered him. It took him a while to figure it out. It was the background chatter of people around him and the constant movement of feet like receding surf. The faces were all the same; emotionless and indifferent, all hurrying toward aimless destinations. He didn't like to be pushed around, jostled, or shouted at. And he didn't like crowds. In a fit of paranoia, he felt sure that these masses of anonymous bodies must have waited for him to show up before descending to annoy him. Cities and ports, they were strictly for busybodies with briefcases.

He regretted not taking a combie from one of the Field rental dealers instead of venturing into the city, but he wanted to pick up something for Teena. Looking at the displays, nothing caught his imagination. He touched the softness of the scarf in his pocket and, avoiding the glidewalk, kept strolling on the walkway. Had he become so solitary that crowds irritated him now?

Two Wanderers dressed in traditional brown surtaf robes, one wearing a yellow, the other a red hood, were striding easily with their long, purposeful gliding gait. When they drew close, one of them hesitated and looked searchingly at Terr. The Wanderer's eyes were deep orange, the skin golden, slightly faded yellow.

"Our souls travel with you, my brother," he rumbled at length, the sound coming from deep within his chest.

Terr shivered and the hair on the back of his neck bristled. He knew it could not be Dhar, but the voice was hauntingly familiar and his emotions were churning.

"Tabe," he thanked him in a strained tone and momentarily

covered his eyes in respect. "May the gods always smile on you, my brothers."

The Wanderer nodded, satisfied, yet his eyes searched and probed.

"We feel your pain…" he began uncertainly.

"Tah, it's in the hands of the gods," Terr murmured, amazed at the Wanderer's perception.

"As you say, my brother. I wish you peace, then." The Wanderer bowed with a gentle movement of his long neck.

Terr watched them walk off, his feelings mixed. The crowd closed behind them, swallowing them in a sea of bodies and noise.

Out of the corner of one eye, the left one, he saw a fishy-eyed Karkan staring at him. The guy smirked and sauntered off. Terr could not have mistaken that flattened reptilian head covered with broad pale green scales, or the flickering of a thin pointed tongue. It reminded him too much of Illeran.

Walking on, he felt being followed, although he couldn't see anyone. Just a tingling at the back of his head, but too powerful to ignore. He'd had those feelings before and they were always reliable.

Playing it cool and debonair, he swaggered to one of the large store displays and pretended to admire an assortment of exotic female accessories. He spotted him then. Terr could see him in the reflection of the display panel, hands in pockets, walking loosely on the other side of the street. The guy was good, not glancing his way once and Terr grinned—his friend the Karkan wise-ass with the nasty smirk and fishy eyes.

Terr needed to do this quickly before the wise-ass became suspicious. He pulled a real beginner's trick. When he neared a building corner, he hurried, stepped around and pressed himself against the warm ceramic. He didn't have to wait long. The Karkan looked the wrong way as he walked by. Terr tsked and stepped in front of him. They stood eyeball to fishy black eyeball. He grabbed the guy's shirtfront and shook him a little, just to see the Karkan's eyeballs dance. He could almost hear them rattle.

"Now that you found me, pal," Terr said with pent-up relish and gave him a toothy grin. "Care to tell me why you've been following me?" He shook him some more, keeping him disoriented and flatfooted. "I know. You just wanted to explain that smirk at the Wanderers, right?"

"Hey, let go of me!" the wise-ass managed to squeak, full of hollow bluster, his thin tongue flashing quickly. A bystander glanced at Terr and his eyebrows climbed.

"Just dusting him off," Terr said with a shrug. The other grinned broadly and leaned back against the wall to admire the developing action.

"Now then…" With one hand, Terr quickly patted the Karkan along the sides of his body. The bulge looked familiar. When he dragged out the Service Special, it could have been his. He tossed it into the gutter and shook his head. "Naughty. Don't you know that you could get hurt playing with such toys?"

"If you don't—" The Karkan gasped as Terr slammed him against the wall and thought he heard the teeth click. He reached out and dug out the ID card. It held the insignia of the Bureau of Colonial and Protectorate Affairs. He frowned. What the hell were Enllss' thugs wandering around Kanarath? The Conference? Then he checked that thought, remembering that Illeran ran the BCPA. And Illeran was a Karkan. He threw the card after the gun and leaned close to the fishy face.

"I don't like sneaky little guys smirking at our hosts, and I don't like being followed. I don't know what laughs you had in mind by tailing me, but you'll have to think up something else. Get the picture, pal? If we were to meet again, I might not be so friendly, see? So tell me. What's the big idea?"

"I don't know what the pits you're talking about," the Karkan hissed and tried a funny with his knee. Terr blocked and leaned against him. The Karkan's face began to turn purple and his mouth worked like a landed groker.

"Pity," Terr said mildly and shook his head. "If I wasn't so pressed for time, we could've had a real nice long chat. Now, I guess I'll have to live with the disappointment. A word of advice. Don't hang around this place. It's not healthy for you. Especially with your fishy looks. Don't even pack. Just disappear. Preferably off-planet, or you could disappear under its sands. Understand me?" Terr pushed him a bit too hard, then. When he let go the guy moaned and slithered down the wall like a soggy Serrll fiver.

He looked down at him for a moment, his good humor restored, and walked off with a jaunty step. The man leaning against the wall grinned and nodded as Terr strolled past him.

A great day!

It didn't take him long to find what he wanted. With all the ad boards and signs, he could hardly miss it. He argued a bit over the price, but his heart wasn't really in it. He let the bored salesman think he got the better of the deal. After all, he only wanted to rent the heap, not buy it. The place had everything he wanted and the camping equipment didn't take much room.

The combie lifted with a sure surge of power and Kanarath quickly fell away beneath him. He punched in the nav points into the console and sat back, watching hungrily as the desert drew near. He could have spent the night at one of the hotels, but he was impatient for the silence and the healing solitude of the open sands.

"I'm coming, Teena," he whispered as the desert closed around him.

As the day waned, sharp black shadows stretched into the endless distance. They blanketed the dunes, making them ready for the coming of night. The combie lost height as he made a leisurely sweep over the rolling sands. It rocked gently a few tetalans above a clearing, then settled to a hovering stop. The bubble slid back with a hiss that drowned out the spooling power plant. Smells of burnt rock, sand, and tarad grass assailed the cabin. He breathed deeply of the hot, dry air, lifted his arms and felt the bones creak. It felt good and he grunted with pleasure.

Like pillars of cold fire, the great Athal Than escarpment swam and shimmered in the distance, its towering buttresses supporting a purple dusk. Behind him the sun hung low in the sky, a twisted flattened orb that played with the shadows. Slowly the fires died and the base of the escarpment turned dark, occasionally glinting bright red as a crevice caught the dying rays. The strangely flattened tops of some of the ramparts seemed to float, suspended between the fires of heaven and the creeping blackness of night. His shadow faded and merged with the desert.

Terr watched the escarpment. He didn't know why he decided to stop here. Was it to try and make the gods understand? To make excuses for what he intended to do? But the gods cared little for the ways of mortals, and he had no time for them right then. Let them damn him if they wanted. After a moment only the night remained. Beyond the escarpment lay the vast tract of the Saffal, the Keep of Death, the open desert girthing half the planet...home of the Saddish-aa Wanderers. Somewhere out there in a small village, he would meet his destiny.

He kept his camp simple: thermal blanket and zip-jacket for a pillow. Unless a sandstorm came up during the night, he didn't need additional shelter. It hardly ever rained in the Saffal and it promised to be a balmy night.

One hand locked behind his head, munching a sandwich wafer with the other, he listened to the soft whisper of the sands around him. Only the dunes moving in the still of night, the sand still warm beneath him. Above him, The Arch spread an impossibly thick band of stars cradling the sky. He stared into blackness where Athal Than slept. They said the gods learned to walk there, that thunder and lightning could be seen at night where there was no cloud. They said Death ruled in its shadow. Those touched by its hand died or went mad. They said that within the shadow of Athal Than the hand of Death had touched the people of the Saffal and they became the Wanderers—children of the capricious gods.

So they said.

He could not say one way or another, but the place was lousy with legend and mystery; like the one about some Sargon busybody archaeologist. He supposedly set out to debunk the superstitions of a primitive and backward people. According to reports this joker went into Athal Than amid a lot of fanfare and publicity and never came out. After a while they sent some Wanderers after him. They found him, stiff as a block of stone, for that's what he was, wearing a haunting look of surprise and terror.

He'd heard another one about a little offworlder girl. After being lost for two months, she emerged healthy and chipper, unchanged and looking like the day she disappeared. She had no idea how she survived, or that two months had passed. Perhaps the gods have compassion after all.

Even from here, he could feel it pulling at him, calling him. He walked once before within the shadow of its towering walls, twisting canyons, and dark crags. The hand of his master upon him the whole time, in spirit at least, for this, he had to do alone. After having his soul ripped apart and put together again, he stood within the shadow of Death, transformed. The parts hadn't quite been put back the same way. Had he known what waited for him there, he might not have been so eager. He had nothing to complain about. The gods have been more than fair. They returned his sanity and memory. His aspect came as a bonus. He figured he should be grateful.

The pull of the gods nagged his conscience.

"Soon," he muttered irritably and lay back to gaze at the blaze of stars winking in jumbled profusion above him. They crowded the black sky from horizon to horizon. A shiver ran through him.

He remembered when he emerged out of the escarpment

that first time. The sun hot and high overhead, his master said, "Twice more shall you walk within the shadow of Athal Than before you are complete." Sidhara turned to look down at him, his orange eyes burning and Terr could not look away. "Each time you take the trial, you must come to me."

"When will I know?" Terr asked, still uncertain what happened to him.

"You will know," Sidhara rumbled as he gazed into the desert, his hood covering his head. "Until then, nothing more will I teach you."

He never called Terr 'foolish creature' again. A small beginning.

It seemed like a lifetime ago, an eternity of time and experiences.

Beyond the escarpment, he still had some three hundred talans to go before he reached the village deep in the Saffal. A place of pea-gravel flats, rolling sands, and towering dunes, a harsh land; savage, wild, and compelling in its austere beauty. It was his land and he belonged here. He accepted the realization, but also a torment as he struggled to reconcile the pull between two different destinies.

With the shadows thick about him, he turned his head to where Aribus lit the desert with its blood. The moon loomed large, painfully bright, and smeared the stars. A thin white halo glittered in frosty silence around it, remote and aloof, indifferent to the problems of lesser creatures. The companion moon Rima still hidden by the veil of night. Soon, it too would spread its light across the sands, turning it into glittering, winking silver like a blanket of fallen snow.

A thin wind set up its moaning, sending wisps of sand trailing along the dunes. Getting cool, he breathed deeply of its freshness, wondering how he would face tomorrow and kill. A path on which he trod with unwavering finality. He relived his crash as though he were there. Earth grew before him, the atmosphere ripping in tortured agony before the survival blister plowed into the mountain. He felt the pain of the furrow in his side from a shot meant to do more than wound, and winced at the memory. There were images of burning desert sands, gnawing hunger, thunder and lightning, and fear. They all flashed before him.

He relived it all and remained untouched, cold and detached. It was only a memory, something that happened to someone else in another reality.

Still, he could not shake off the feeling that what he intended to do felt wrong somehow. He squirmed with nagging indecision and doubt. The cloak of righteous indignation beneath which he had conveniently hidden, now disquietingly showed a few ragged holes of uncertainty. He knew Dhar as well as he knew himself, or so he thought. They were one in mind and spirit. He could not imagine Dhar's bright flame of strength, courage, and integrity, tarnished with...what? Tarnished with the kind of backstabbing, gutter crawling, and low skullduggery *he* indulged in? It opened a novel way of thinking about it. After his crash in a survival blister when Dhar pulled him out of whatever hell he had sunk to, part of him remained with his brother. Just as Dhar's gentleness and strength had remained with him.

It opened up a hell of a lot of possibilities.

But he could not forget one salient thing. Teena was gone and Dhar took her. Now the pain of that loss may no longer be sharp and poignant, but still there, seething, throbbing, and with him always. Even though Teena seemed to be all right did not diminish the loss at all.

Rima crept up to touch the horizon. He lay there looking at it as the sand gently caressed his face.

Chapter Five

A soft chime interrupted Arlon Dee's train of thought.

"Karhide Dee?" the housekeeping computer inquired diffidently, the voice floating before him.

The lounge almost dark, lit only by the indirect amber glow coming off the soft pile covering the deck. It provided an anchor to reality from the image of naked space all about him. On his left, four softly contoured couches surrounded a low oval table. A coral flower, all red and orange, provided a distracting decoration. It was a gift from his first diplomatic mission deep within the galaxy's arm. When stared at long enough, small sparks of light could be seen dancing along its fragile branches. Looking at the coral now, he smiled. He had been very young and naive then. It seemed such a long time ago, he mused wistfully, a time of vigor and pride and energy. Some of that had also faded with time.

Hands folded across his chest, he watched lines of pale brown gravity waves twist and shimmer against the backdrop of stars. Nothing impeded his view as he stood alone in his private lounge, the ship carrying him in silence through the void. The virtual image surrounding him was perfect. Like being out there, but he derived little pleasure from the view.

He took a serious gamble rushing toward the extremities of the Serrll Combine. He risked a reprimand at best, and at worst, he could possibly upset a delicate and fledgling balance between the Orieli and the prickly Serrll. Captal had been maneuvered into accepting indirect intrusion into their space in the shape of a Line Tracking Net station in the Sol System with their attention diverted by the Kran gambit. Soon, someone would be asking the Orieli some pointed questions. Questions they would be pressed to answer without revealing information the Serrll were better off not knowing. Nevertheless, the Orieli's preoccupation with Earth would have to be disclosed sooner or later, severely compromising OSCOM's, Orieli Space Command, intelligence-gathering options.

Thankfully, that decision was not his to make.

But if this pursuit didn't come off, OSCOM would be asking *him* some pointed questions. Such as, why had the Kran cruiser been allowed to slip through the patrol net in the first place? It is not as though he was personally responsible, the LTN-5 commander would answer that one, but bureaucrats tended to view things in their particular obfuscating way. Compounding the problem, he entered Serrll space without permission. Well, if he managed to clean up the mess quickly and quietly the whole thing may be conveniently forgotten as being in the best interest of both sides. Irritated, his thin pale pink tongue ran around fleshy, black lips.

"Yes, what is it?" he rasped softly, responding to the computer. The air in the lounge crisp, colder than he liked, it nonetheless stimulated and helped him focus, to decide.

"Message from LTN-10, Karhide," the computer announced flatly. "Positive lock established on the Celi-Kran *Daktar*-class cruiser."

Arlon tensed with anticipation. This time, there would be no mistake.

"Are we within sensor range?"

"Not at the moment."

"Very well. Inform Opturkarh Tavac to meet me in Primary Flight Control."

After four days of searching, waiting, hunting, the prey had finally reared its head. It had only been a matter of time, and he needed time. After tracking the alien vessel all the way from LTN-6 on receiving an advisory from LTN-5, he closed on and attacked the much larger ship. The encounter brief as it was brutal. Sustaining major damage, the Kran vessel disengaged, dropping into normal space in an attempt to evade. Arlon's initial thrust had hit the Kran hard and he pressed his advantage, despite receiving significant hits himself. Sustaining additional damage the *Daktar* had fled rather than risk being totally disabled.

Forced to make repairs before being able to pursue at full boost, he spent his time fretting. Tavac worked as quickly as possible, but nothing could satisfy Arlon's desire to finish the engagement. The Kran ship should never have been allowed to get this close to Serrll space to begin with. LTN-5's commander and his pickets would have some awkward explaining to do.

The war with the Krans worried him from a different perspective. Space Command didn't have to say it, certainly not to those who served on this side of the Karina Shield, what the Serrll called the Moanar Nebula. The Orieli were facing their most serious strategic threat in twelve thousand years of space-faring. OSCOM wanted to set up another interdiction line, closer to the inner arm of the galaxy to protect vulnerable settlements. He could almost sympathize with the idea. It would be a monumental engineering feat, though, and a logistical nightmare. There was also the question of cost, always uppermost in the minds of policymakers on Zaron. Some in the Klanina Caucus were expressing even more extreme sentiments. Collapse the Karina breach, they argued, and shut down the transport portals. The Krans can have the Serrll and all the space in between. After all, the Orieli didn't owe them anything.

Damned bureaucrats!

Couldn't they realize that once the Krans held this side of the Karina, how long would they have to wait before Kran ships appeared on the Orieli side? Then what? The Orieli's position in this part of the galactic arm would become almost untenable. No, this needed to end right here. He could only hope OSCOM was listening to operational commanders such as Karhide Zor-Ell. If survey ships were going to be sent out to locate Celi-Kran home space, he wanted to be there. It was time to take the fight in their face.

"Opturkarh Tavac has acknowledged."

"Very well." He stepped into a little alcove set into the wall. "Initiate personal transport to PFC."

Materializing, he waited for a moment as the transceiver's after-effect tingle subsided. Tongue running over his lips, he glanced around the command level of Primary Flight Control. The single watchkeeping officer, sitting easily in her shape-hugging swivel-couch, looked up. He nodded to her in acknowledgment.

Tapal's PFC was an ellipsoid some six katalans high and fifteen katalans wide, split into two levels: Command and Operations. The command level stood out as a protruding platform curving along the long axis halfway up the chamber. A low contoured console hugged the bulkhead. Swivel-couches faced the holoview repeater readouts from the main operations stations below, projected along the length of the platform's edge; a wall of images for those not hooked into the VI. One of the displays constantly showed a multicolored cutout of the ship's critical areas. Using voice commands or touch-recognition backup pads, provided authorized access to all ship's functions, but the Cent Comp VI coupling served as the primary thought control system.

Operations was some three katalans below the command level. Like a bowl, its inner surface mounted one long backup contoured console, above which were projected three-katalan-high holoview images. They showed endlessly changing repeater displays from every part of the ship's internal and tactical operations.

One image displayed a contoured map of the Palean Union, where at its edge a blue dot pulsed steadily.

Six form-hugging swivel-couches, separated by curving touch consoles, faced the center of the bowl. In it hung a variable image holoview sphere almost three katalans in diameter. Each operator controlled a specific area of ship's duties, such as tactical, engineering or sciences, feedback provided through the VI coupling, repeated in the holoview sphere and the command level displays. At the moment, only two of the couches were manned.

"Plot," Arlon commanded and the computer hooked him into the Virtual Interface coupling. For him the external world faded, replaced by full-dimensional images from the tactical display projected by the central housekeeping computer directly into his visual cortex. By willing it, he could immerse himself totally into the ship's sensor arrays, or superimpose the PFC reality over the image.

Two wide swivel-couches were set against the curved bulkhead of the command platform. Simple color-coded pads covered the broad armrests. Already hooked up, Tavac waited in one of the seats until Arlon took in the tactical situation before standing up to walk to his commander.

"Talk to me, Tavac," Arlon growled without moving, still studying the mainframe plot, his pink tongue working around his lips. In the background, quiet voices registered normal operational status, interrupted by occasional computer readiness responses. Not everyone needed to be hooked into the VI.

Tavac allowed himself a brief smile, revealing a flash of white teeth. His skin a beautiful shade of blue, flowing into green, growing black around the eyes and mouth, betraying his ancestry from the Zaron equatorial belt. Large brown eyes glowed with intelligence and confidence. He spent almost three years with his Cetan commander, long enough to get used to all his quirky moods. The last year saw them on this side of the Karina Shield running Kran patrols. Then came the Serrll mission and the enigmatic Terrllss-rr. As with his friend Dharaklin, there was something compelling about Terr. Tavac pushed the thought away.

"They're coming on true to form, Da. Typical transmission. Long and complex, aimed in the general direction of Setlan Eleven." Setlan was one of the farthest Orieli outposts lying near the hub arm of the galaxy.

Arlon turned, his large orange eyes allowed little expression. They reminded Tavac of Dharaklin.

"Anything else?"

"We know where they are. Holed up on the edge of the Palean Union. An ecoforming planet, as far as we can tell. Captal has not been overly generous with their data packs."

"I don't blame them. Serrll Scout Fleet activity?"

"No detected power emissions. Our sensitivity will improve as we close. We're still some eight light-years from the target area. At present speed we won't reach the system for another eleven hours. We could be there in two hours at maximum boost."

Arlon pressed his lips and shook his head. "No. Maintain standard boost. They're bound to send in some units to investigate. For now, we'll leave the *Daktar* to them. It wouldn't do to come storming in and create a diplomatic incident. We're in enough trouble as it is. After all, it *is* their space."

Tavac looked searchingly at Arlon. "Karhide, that Kran *Daktar* had the system mapped out to the last decimal point as soon as it made its approach. They will be sending out scouts. I would hate to be down on that ecoforming planet when they arrive."

"You're assuming the Serrll have no patrols in the area."

"Whatever they have won't be enough. An ecoforming station would not warrant heavy support units. The *Daktar* will simply brush away whatever stands in its way."

"But it's damaged, remember?" Arlon said, then sighed with resignation. "Still, you're probably right. Nevertheless, we cannot just barge in, even if it costs lives. There are strategic considerations, which we cannot ignore. Tactically, what worries me more is what could happen once the Serrll sends someone looking. They will find us and reach a hasty, but incorrect conclusion. You follow me?"

Tavac's eyebrows climbed. "They might blame the Kran

attack on us?"

"It's possible. Trigger happy lot, that's what they are. Anyway, why would the *Daktar* go there? You know what I'm thinking, don't you?"

"I am reading you loud and clear, Da. They picked that planet deliberately, materiel for repairs. More importantly, an ecoforming planet infers a complex socioeconomic infrastructure. An infrastructure based on organic intelligence. They will think they found us!"

"Exactly! With all those Serrll regional factions playing power games, they'd fold up in a day if the Krans were to come in force."

"I wouldn't sell them short, Karhide."

Arlon smiled at his executive officer. "I hope we don't have to find out the hard way."

"The Krans will have to get past us first."

"For sure. Our repairs completed?"

"The ship is ready in all respects, Da."

"Very well. Got anything else?"

"An advisory is being prepared for Karhide Zor-Ell on Captal."

"Very well. Keep me posted."

* * *

The combie banked and gradually lost height. Terr felt his palms go suddenly clammy. He wiped them against his thighs and cursed himself for a fool. This was not going at all as he planned.

Rit!

The dunes flattened and gave way to gently rolling slopes. Dust devils swirled the sand into playful funnels. Thin patches of brown tarad grass rippled and swayed with the breeze. Scattered oark browsed in the distance. Clumps of peelath clung stubbornly to the sides of a shallow gorge. Their broad flat branches hung limp in the heat. Children looked up from their play. They waved excitedly and ran after him as the combie swooped over them. The peelath grew thicker as the gorge opened, its sides falling away into a shallow valley. The rounded mud huts of the village lay amongst the shadows of tall peelath.

Poultry fluttered in alarm, scurrying toward the protection of the scrub as Terr descended. A lone combie sat parked beside a solitary peelath. Terr didn't have to ask who owned the machine. He drifted down and parked beside it. Hovering a few tetalans above the packed ground, the combie spooled down into silence. He shut down and rested his hands on top of the control panel. Sitting there, he took a few deep breaths and looked around.

Thin gray smoke curled lazily above some of the huts. It twisted and swayed as it followed the wind. Young unpaired girls, their brown hoods pushed back, clustered around a trough near the well. A thin ribbon of red cloth bound around their foreheads kept the long hair in check and proclaimed their unpaired status. The sleeves of their robes were rolled up, the washing forgotten as they regarded him with open curiosity. Small hands held over their mouths, they talked and giggled, upraising him with bold frankness.

Clothing hung limp on oark-hair lines. One girl paused, peg in hand, a brown surtaf in another waiting to be hung. She peeped at him shyly before turning away. The youngsters never hesitated. After a cautious scrutiny, they resolutely prodded each other toward the combie. There was always the possibility of a ride.

Older paired women emerged from the huts, some clutching babies on hip. An old matriarch, staff in hand, appeared on the steps of the women's communal hut and looked about her imperiously. She said something and the other women resumed their work. Paired, it was unseemly for them to stare at a male so openly, even an alien like Terr. They trailed slowly after the men making their way toward him.

The memories flooded him, some painful, some sweet. He desperately wanted to abandon himself among these people and push away everything else, if but for a moment. They had a deceptive simplicity to their lives he found compelling. Nevertheless, he could not forget the hard labor underlining their harsh existence. Still, the elemental struggle of their lives brought things into perspective and stripped away the veneer of artificiality and a clutter of complexity that tended to accumulate during the normal course of what others saw as contemporary urbane living.

He considered himself cultured, lacking in nothing a modern society and its technology could not provide. Contact with the Wanderers made him realize he bought his veneer of material and technological comforts at an unreasonable price—the pollution of his spirit. That is why the density and texture of their lives held so much appeal for him. They were not touched by the need to conquer others or their world, only themselves.

And he had been away from this basic living for too long. Yet they do toil, the cynical part of him observed.

Gathered around him they waited, chattering expectantly.

"Well," he muttered. "Might as well get on with it."

The bubble slid back with a hiss.

"Sankri! Sankri!" they broke into a chant, arms held high as they laughed. It surprised the hell out of him. It wasn't the reception he expected.

Smells and sounds, familiar and pleasant, assailed him. The burnt odor of rock and sand, mingled with the faint musty reek of oark. There was also the sharper smell of smoke-stained tarad grass covering the huts, the subdued voices of women doing women things, the sober voices of men, the splash of water being drawn from the well, and the shrill cries of children. They all pulled at his memories.

He accepted them, letting them sweep over him.

These were his people, even though their lives were so different, and he belonged in this land. He felt a lump grow in his throat. Blinking, he dragged himself out of the combie and the bubble slid shut behind him

"Sankri…Sankri!" they chanted and crowded around him, the children timidly touching him. They did not judge or expect anything. They were simply happy he was here, one of their own, even though alien.

He stood among them in helpless confusion. He wanted to join in their laughter, to feel their simple pleasure, to share in their contentment, if for but a moment. He wanted to tell them that he belonged, that he understood, but the words failed him. Unaccountably, he felt his skin start to prickle and a hot flush rushed through his body. His right hand twitched and he knew what was about to happen. A rumble of thunder rolled across the dunes as the god of Death touched him. Suddenly silent, they fell back and waited. He blinked back the sting in his eyes and raised his arms toward an amber sky. Blue lightnings played between them. He tilted back his head and a peal of thunder echoed his cry.

Their shouts followed the echoes of dying thunder as the children pressed around him. A rush of genuine affection made him shudder and he gathered them about him. His cares dropped away and he at last laughed freely with them.

A tall youth pushed his way through and stepped up to him. His orange hair was short, allowed to grow only after he completed the first spiritual test of Athal Than. Staff in hand, he covered his eyes with his right hand and knelt before Terr. The children looked on expectantly.

"Master, I crave your blessing," he murmured in a deep voice. He bowed until his head stroked Terr's boots. The older men nodded to one another and murmured approval.

With the power coiled in his hands, Terr touched the youth's head. A small blue spark arced between them. The young man stood and beamed with pleasure.

"Tabe. I welcome you home, Terr." He could not say Terr's warrior name until he underwent the trial himself.

They surged around Terr and pressed against him. A wave of emotion swept through him and he welcomed their touch. Wearing a stupid grin, he doubted he could have been capable of saying anything just then.

Some of the bolder boys tugged at his shirt, demanding he take them for a ride in the combie. In their simple lives, a combie represented a truly magical alien machine. With an impatient gesture, the young Wanderer struck his staff into the ground and glared kindly at them. Amid murmurings of keen disappointment, they drifted away, casting longing glances over their shoulders. They knew there would be another time. With a shriek of glee, they raced down the slope toward the corrals. The men shook their heads in amusement after them.

"I beg that you excuse them, Terr," the youth offered seriously.

"It is the joy of children that brings laughter to our souls, my brother," Terr said.

Murmuring approval the villagers started breaking away. They did not want to intrude on him now. Later, during the evening meal, they would share with him that which he was willing to give.

"Come," the youth began then stopped to follow Terr's gaze.

Teena emerged from behind one of the huts, frowning anxiously at the dispersing villagers. Her long black curls hung loose across her shoulders. The sleeves of her surtaf were rolled up exposing sunburned arms. Fingers splayed, she placed one hand across her heaving chest and paused. With the other, she absently pushed back a rebellious lock of hair.

Standing there, she looked small and slender, but even the shapeless robe could not hide her fine figure. Her face oval, marked with a slightly upturned nose. She had pale green eyes slightly too far apart, large and captivating. He easily got lost in those eyes, knowing from thrilling experience. Her high cheekbones gave her a fragile haunting beauty, which had enchanted him from the beginning. He traced every line of her face with longing and aching hunger. She had a small, but full and generous mouth. Her red lips were open, showing even white teeth. Her skin glowed a healthy pink, touching her cheeks with color. To him, she was gorgeous.

Something squeezed his chest as he stood there staring at her, not daring to breathe.

"Teena," he whispered brokenly and something tore deep within him.

She was real, not some ghostly image conjured by his mind. He wanted to rush to her, embrace her, hold her, touch her, but his feet were rooted to the ground. All he could do was gaze at her with a deep, urgent need.

"Later then, master," the young Wanderer said beside him, bemused and walked off. Terr just nodded, hardly hearing him. The other villagers chuckled among themselves knowingly and left him alone.

Then she saw him.

Her small fists flew to her mouth and she held them there until the knuckles showed white. Her eyes were bright as they stared at each other. Something flowed between them, an understanding, a bond and they were one again. He took a hesitant step toward her and she was running, hands fluttering.

"Oh, Terr!" With a squeal of joy, she stretched out her arms and flung herself at him.

He caught her about the waist and swung her around him. When he set her down, she buried her head in his shoulder and sobbed. He closed his eyes and held her tight, afraid this was all a dream and she would fade into nothing when he opened his eyes to find himself alone in their house.

"There, there. It's all right, pet," he whispered hoarsely into her hair. "I'm here now."

They rocked gently. She wept and laughed against him and he kept whispering things to her. Her heart a soft flutter, and he never wanted to let go of her again. Gods, how he loved this woman. The thought of losing her churned his insides into mush.

After a while, he lifted her face and she nuzzled the palm of his hand. Her cheeks were wet, eyes swimming, but happy and sparkling. He reached down and kissed away her tears, tasting the saltiness. Moaning, his lips found hers. She squirmed in his arms and her mouth opened and he felt the warm, velvet touch of her tongue.

After a timeless moment, he pulled back and smiled into her eyes.

"You feel so good."

She purred and snuggled against him. "You beast. What took you so long? I thought you would never come."

Tenderly, he drew her to him and buried his face in her black curls. His arms around her, she sighed contentedly.

"I was delayed," he murmured after a time.

"When I heard the thunder…"

He didn't know how long they stood there, muttering little nothings to each other, content to be close. Time did not matter. Nothing mattered then. Finally at peace, he did not want the moment to end.

Suddenly, she pulled back and her hand flew to her hair. "Oh, no!" she wailed, looking stricken. "Look at me!"

"I'm looking. You're the most beautiful thing I have ever seen."

"My hair! And you let me see you like this. I hate you." She pouted and punched him on the shoulder.

"Nothing wrong with your hair."

"I must look a torrid mess."

He fumbled in the pocket of his trousers until he touched the yielding softness of her scarf. The sheer material glittered in the sun as he held it up, the colors melting and flowing liquid into each other. She caught her breath and stared at it. He slowly pushed back her robe and tied the scarf around her slender neck.

Through the Valley of Shadow

"Oh, you wonderful man," she whispered huskily, fondling the soft material with nervous fingers.

"You don't know how hard it's been without you," he said softly and brushed her cheek. "When things were blackest, I kept seeing your face. On Earth, when they were after me, I thought of you. Back on Taltair and alone, I thought of you. That's all that kept me going. When Anabb told me you were gone, that they've taken you, that *he* took you…" The pain came rushing back and he swallowed hard. "At the house, with its hollow echoes and empty rooms, they were cold without you to make them alive and warm. I thought I would die. The scarf was a part of you and it kept me sane. I don't want to live if it means being without you, Teena."

"How did you know I was here?" she whispered, eyes radiant.

"When I called you to me, I saw the desert around you and I knew."

"It's true, then. It wasn't just a dream. And I am glad you're not a dream now either." She pressed herself against him, content. After a time, she pulled back, her eyes troubled. "But you didn't come here just for me, did you?"

"Where is he, Teena?" he demanded, his voice suddenly cold.

"Terr! I know what you're thinking—"

"No, you don't."

"But you're wrong! He rescued me."

"Rescued you from those Servatory Party thugs, right?" He gripped her shoulders and stared hard into her eyes, wanting her to understand. "That SP cell, Teena. He's the one *running* it!"

"But…"

"We'll talk about this later. I must pay my respects to the Rahtir. I must see my old master."

"What are you going to do?" she demanded and saw Death reflected in his eyes.

121

Stefan Vučak

* * *

Beneath a starry sky, the desert waited as the dunes whispered among themselves. A dark purple blotch smeared the western horizon where the sun sank beneath the sands. Although cooler, the air still smelled burnt and dry. In the darkness the wind rasped across the dune tops and swept fine sand after it. The broad peelath leaves rustled in understanding.

The young girls were clearing the long tables after the main meal. A special treat in Terr's honor and everyone relished the rare delicacies. The day's work done, loud talk and laughter mixed cheerfully with the snap and crackle of the small bonfire. Free from the stern presence of their parents, the children ran screeching in pursuit of their games. The elders talked solemnly among themselves and occasionally smiled at the exuberant antics of the young. A matron would sometimes frown pointedly at an unpaired maiden they felt was getting overly familiar with one of the youths. It was impossible to rein in the wild spirits.

Sidhara looked approvingly at Terr and Teena, their heads close together in animated conversation. When Terr smiled or laughed, Sidhara felt happy, but others could not see the darkness that hung about his adopted son, troubling the old Wanderer. The futile foolish impetuousness of the young...

Some of the youths brought out small drums, flutes and leetas to a general roar of hooting approval. Immediately the young men scampered and jostled for front positions and sat in the sand at one side of the bonfire. The unpaired girls hurried to the opposite side, leaving a small clearing between them. The older men and paired women nodded indulgently.

Beating in slow time the drums and the flutes tugged the air to the haunting strands of the leetas. The men around the tables slowly tapped the ground in time with the melody and the youths clapped. Occasionally a faster tempo and drumbeat brought with it shouts of encouragement and a furious round of feet pounding.

Through the Valley of Shadow

The drums faded and a hush fell as the leetas led into a slow tune. Then the drums began to throb again. Three young girls suddenly jumped to their feet and began a sinuous dance before the fire, to the delight and appreciative comments from the youths. The flickering light of the flames revealed their laughing faces. The girls moved their feet in slow circles, bodies swaying knowingly to a timeless rhythm. Arms held high they weaved slow patterns in the air. Occasionally, they would stomp their feet and dust would swirl around their legs. The drums quickened their beat.

Two of the girls drew away and danced toward the young men sitting on the opposite side of the fire. Others shouted with glee and much ribald commentary when the two girls stopped and tapped the ground before the chosen youths. With pushing and good-natured suggestions from the others, the two chosen youths stood and raised their arms. Weaving their hips to the music, they moved easily around the girls.

Teena sat beside Terr, watching with fixed fascination as the dance progressed. For the first time since her arrival, she saw the villagers in any kind of festive mood and she relished the joyous sensation. The dancers seemed almost oblivious to those around them, their eyes riveted on each other. The movements had a hypnotic, compelling quality to it and her feet involuntarily tapped the ground. Gradually the tempo of the movements increased to the urgency of the flutes and the drums. The dance ended with a final stomping of feet and the boom of drums. Chests heaving, the dancer's eyes held each other and the watchers shouted their enthusiasm.

Teena laughed and clapped her hands with open delight. The two girls bowed their heads, smiled coyly at the youths, and moved back to their side of the fire.

Teena tugged at Terr's shoulder. "Wasn't that wonderful?"

He looked down at her and grinned. "They are good. I've seen them dance before, but there is an almost electric quality about them tonight."

Sitting with her now, he was almost happy. It would not take much to immerse himself completely into this life. Not yet, his darker self told him.

The drums began their beat again and the girls resumed their solitary dance. Gradually the haunting tugs of the flutes and the leetas joined and whispered their magic. One of the girls broke away. Crouching, she hurried over to Teena. The two spoke quickly and giggled. Teena nodded and stood up. With a conspiratorial grin at Terr, she followed the girl to the circle and began to dance beside her. The youths roared their approval and clapped loudly. At first, Teena's movements were awkward and tentative, but she quickly fell into step with the others.

The drums picked up their tempo that added urgency to the leetas. A sudden hush fell when the other girls suddenly fell back, leaving Teena alone in the circle. Terr stared in rapt fascination, his mouth suddenly dry as she moved in graceful, mincing steps toward him. Her body seemed to glow against the backdrop of the bonfire. Her hands weaved delicately, winding seductively above her head. Her swaying hips beckoned with promise and he gulped. She stopped before him and tapped her feet against the sand, waiting.

"Sankri!" they shouted around him. "Sankri!"

He realized he'd been set up, but it was custom and he had no choice. The youths broke into another wave of roaring when he stood up.

Teena looked at him with consuming intensity. Something of a challenge also shone in her bold green eyes. Small red blushes colored her cheeks, partly hidden by long hair, only added to her mystery. Moving with her steps, he gazed hungrily at her, consumed by her presence, oblivious to everyone around him. The music merged with the dance and he surrendered himself to it. Their bodies twined and touched, her skin velvety and cool, and the tapping of their feet were the tugs of his heartstrings.

Through the Valley of Shadow

Their movements became more intense. She was his whole world and he fell completely under her spell. He could not say how long they danced. It took him a moment to realize the music had stopped and she stood pressed against him, one small hand splayed across her chest, her breathing ragged. Breathing a little hard himself and feeling somewhat awkward, he dropped his arms. The villagers crowded around them and shouted his name.

"Sankri! Sankri!"

He tore his eyes away from her and smiled at them.

Teena reached for his hand and pulled urgently.

* * *

Terr hesitated before the low entrance.

It was quiet outside. The walls of the mud huts, with their faded straw roofs, glowed dull orange from the dying ambers of the evening fire. A robed figure hurried past. Terr could hear snatches of solemn conversation in the shadows around him. Inside the huts, they would retell the events of the evening. It would make for happy telling. Oark snorted, stomping contentedly.

He stooped and walked into the gloomy interior, his mouth a hard line. The smell of smoke, dried meat, and fresh straw lingered in the air. A strong smell, but not unpleasant, and invoked memories from another time, a carefree time. He moved slowly down the short, narrow corridor. After a few paces it opened into the main room. Curving up into the ceiling smoke hole, the far wall revealed its mud-covered wooden frame. Tarad grass mats hid the entrance to the sleeping quarters.

A low fire flickered and crackled softly in a narrow stone hearth. The yellow flames leaped and twisted, yet it wasn't hot inside. Steam rose slowly from a small, blackened cauldron suspended above the flames by a sooty chain. The aroma of boiling peelath flowers clean and pervasive. Two tiny brass lamps filled with oark oil gave off a steady yellow flame. Shadows lurked in the corners.

Sidhara sat cross-legged on sprawled cushions, hands folded in his lap. His narrow head bent, showing long, snowy hair that glittered with rust. He appeared to be studying the flames in the hearth. Terr shook off his slippers and padded softly over the spread carpets, paused and sank soundlessly before his master. He covered his eyes with his right hand in a moment of respect. Sidhara did not seem to acknowledge his presence. Terr folded his hands in his lap and watched the fire. He could feel its warmth on his cheeks like a gentle caress as the fires leaped and danced. The peelath tea bubbled soothingly. He drank in the fragrant redolence, sharp and hauntingly sweet.

Time slowed and stopped, and he sank deeper into himself. A calm and an uncertain peace steeled over him, like a film of oil keeping down a stormy sea. He could not cross the chasm of rage and hatred warring within him. The lightnings leaped from the depths of his soul and he shrank back, feeling icy beads of sweat break on his forehead. With a groan of torment, he shuddered. His eyes snapped open when the touch came.

Sidhara's right hand, gnarled like the bark of an ancient peelath trunk, rested lightly on Terr's shoulder. Deep red, the slits of his eyes were searching. It was too much. Unable to contain the flow of emotion, Terr reached for the hand and grasped it with desperation.

"Master, I am lost," he said with a dry, wrenching sob.

All the pain, anger, uncertainty, and sorrow came boiling out. All Sidhara needed to do was will it and the anguish would be gone. He would be free, but he had chosen to walk the road of revenge. To his horror, he found himself afraid of what he contemplated.

"I know, my son," the ancient Wanderer murmured softly, his voice filled with understanding and compassion.

He turned away and reached for the steaming cauldron. He

poured tea into two small enameled cups. With deft economical movements, he set the cups on a round wooden tray. He held each one momentarily between his hands. Almost absently, he picked up a thin carved bone and carefully stirred the tea in each cup. Slowly, he took the cup closest to him and offered it to Terr. A wan smile touched his venerable face, wrinkling it into a thousand little scars.

Terr waited a moment before closing his hands around the cup. He felt the heat diffuse and spread through his hands, and he allowed it to warm him. Bringing the cup to his lips, he breathed deeply of the aroma and sipped. The taste slightly bitter and smelled of open sands and burnt rock. It cooled where it touched.

Only once before they permitted him to participate in a tea-drinking ceremony. That had been with the Rahtir after he had walked in the shadow of Athal Than. To sit here with his old master, drinking with him, he felt humbled and honored. They sat in silence, understanding without words having to be spoken. In the silence, his thoughts stilled.

"Teena, your loved, seems to have flowered among the sands of the Saffal," Sidhara commented gently after a time without breaking the harmony of the moment.

"I hope her transgressions have been overlooked, master," Terr responded gravely.

"As are the children's. We could not be offended."

"As the Saffal is not offended by the howl of the wind."

"Just so. Tell me, my son from the stars. Have you found contentment?"

Terr looked at him. It was a strange question, especially now. He certainly wasn't content now. *Had* he known contentment? How does one measure a mood? Such a transitory and fleeting thing, a shadow, and just as illusory. Sidhara must know why he came, what he intended to do. Obviously, the question had a deeper meaning. The power glowed about the old Wanderer like a cloak, almost palpable.

"There were moments, master, when I thought I was content. This evening, with Teena beside me, I felt content. Watching the unpaired maidens dance, the friendly taunting of the youths, the solemn dignity of the elders, I did not feel the burden of my guilt or the fires of my hate. But it was a stolen moment."

"That is not what I asked you," the old man admonished gently.

Terr faced the scrutiny of his master without flinching.

"I know. Over the years, I have learned a lot about myself and the power that lies in my hands. Did it give me contentment? Far from making me happy, it left me torn and stranded between two realities. That's been as much my fault as the circumstances within which I used, or abused, the god's gift. I guess in the end, it all comes down to a matter of perspective. In striving for some imagined perfection, I have overlooked the obvious that lay at my feet. I am still struggling to come to terms with the strange heritage the gods of the Saffal have chosen to bestow on me, and I fear that I have failed. Maybe being content was never part of the bargain."

"You must know by now, my son, the use of power is not to dominate or to wield it in the name of some illusory cause. The gods gave you power to control your excesses. It is a contradiction of sorts, and in their own way, they have thus expressed faith in their children. Unchecked, indulgence also leads to chaos and destruction, and the need to walk cloaked in your aspect can become its own reason. You have strayed down that path, my son, and tasted the exercise of raw power. You need not feel the guilt of your trespass, for each of us needs to venture into darkness to appreciate the light."

"Give of yourself and peace and contentment shall follow in your footsteps," Terr quoted from the *Saftara* and smiled. "Yesterday, in the deep of the Saffal, lying in the shadow of Athal Than, I felt a measure of peace, but out there among the stars of the Serrll, there are many temptations. Too many, perhaps."

"You have felt the call." Sidhara made it a statement. His eyes glittered as they bored relentlessly into Terr.

Last night, Terr thought about the judgment awaiting him there, a judgment he would have to face if he survived the encounter with his brother.

"I'm not ready," he said more harshly than he intended.

"You do not decide these things, foolish creature."

Terr's mouth twitched in a stillborn smile. Then his face grew hard.

"When I have found Nightwings," he whispered and met Sidhara's eyes with defiance.

The old man nodded gravely and sipped his tea. "When the hand of Death touched you, I called you Sankri, the strange one. Indeed, the road you walk is a strange one. It is alien and beyond reason, far removed from the calling of the Discipline. Yet I see in you a purpose and a purity of conviction, telling me that your spirit has met life's challenges with honor, misguided though those challenges have been. Now I sense in you this conflict that is tearing you apart. Why do you then refuse the call? The gods will overlook your transgressions and heal your soul."

"But I cannot be so generous, master, and you need not be so kind. I know I have soiled the teachings and betrayed not only your trust, but also the trust of the gods. I can at least be honest with myself."

"*Are* you being honest with yourself, my son?"

Terr felt a tug of guilt and refused to look his master in the eye.

Sidhara slowly reached behind him for a charred stick. He stirred the small flames until the sparks danced and the fire spat. He held the stick in the fire and the flames climbed, licking eagerly around his open hand. Terr stared in fascination.

Slowly, Sidhara lifted his unmarked hand and turned it before Terr. "What do you see, Sankri?"

"I…"

"You sit before me and refuse to acknowledge what you see written?" Sidhara demanded sternly.

Angrily, Terr thrust his fist into the fire and the flames leaped, but did not burn.

"This is not a lesson, master."

It was Sidhara's turn to stare as Terr lifted his hand. The image from a dream long ago came to haunt him then, of an alien, hands upraised with two stars adorning his feet; Sarumajan…the destroyer of worlds.

"You should not be able to do that. Not yet," he whispered uncertainly and looked deep into Terr's eyes. "The god of Death burns bright in you tonight, but it is a dangerous plaything you trifle with."

"I know what you're trying to tell me. By deceiving myself, the fires of Death wielded in my hand can destroy more than the object of my hate."

"Knowing that, you would risk obliteration for a misguided gesture?"

"I am prepared to face that to see his treachery avenged. The fire burning within me can only be quenched by the rite of his blood, or…" he hesitated, his throat suddenly tight. "Or the tears of my soul," he whispered and his hand fell limp beside him.

Sidhara nodded, his face sad. "Your hurt is deep and I feel your pain, but he's your brother and therefore is incapable of harming you."

"I *have* no brother and he *has* harmed me," Terr grated through clenched teeth, seeing the flames dance in Sidhara's eyes. "Don't you understand? Or maybe you refuse to see it. When he reached into me, he took everything I was, including the dark shadow of my base self. That part of me would not hesitate to kill or stoop to treachery. I know, for I have done it before and have done it since. You should have left me to die in the desert, master, for you knew what would happen when you allowed Nightwings to awaken me and the god of Death he left in me. When I walked out of Athal Than, the gods restored me, but I also cast two shadows. The power was mine to use and my dark side used it. And when I did use it, I felt immortal and I have been burning in a hell of my creation ever since. When Nightwings reached into me, he contaminated himself. For his own ends and those of the Unified Independent Front, and I really don't give a damn which, he has forsaken the purity of his teachings and used the dark side I helped waken in him to betray me. So don't tell me he is incapable of harming me."

Sidhara did not flinch from the harshness of Sankri's words, for there was much truth in them. And for his strange son to have said them implied a depth of understanding and perceptiveness of the Discipline and the *Saftara* was indeed profound, even if Sankri did not realize it consciously. Or perhaps he did realize it and the conflict tore him apart because he felt trapped, betrayed not only by his brother, but by the god of Death who had restored him.

Sankri knew what he had to do—*Give of yourself and peace and contentment shall follow in your footsteps*—but he needed to be shocked into acting on the words.

"No matter how real your hurt, it is pride clouding your judgment, my son. So blinded by revenge you are that you have forgotten everything you had learned. Your whole course of action is based on the single assumption that Nightwings has prosecuted you willingly. What if that is not the case?"

"He could have confided in me!"

"Foolish creature." Sidhara shook his head and grunted in exasperation. "Is that why you are fighting yourself so hard to believe?"

Terr gaped at him, feeling himself go pale. With mounting horror, he pulled back.

"No!" he cried in agony and scrambled to his feet. "It can't be!"

Wounded pride, was that his nemesis?

It wasn't pride, but betrayal.

Chapter Six

Crowded against a backdrop of dazzling stars the crescents of Devon 3-VL4 and its moon glowed with harsh brilliance. Ragged bands of swirling clouds stained the planet's equatorial belt with white that softened the blue of the small narrow seas and smeared the browns and the greens of the landmasses. The southern icecap glared with brittle radiance, its jagged fingers extending tentatively toward the equator.

Primary Flight Control felt eerily quiet. Connected to the central computer through the VI coupling, there was limited need for verbal commands. Nevertheless, soft talk among the watchstanders broke the pervasive silence.

Arlon Dee shifted in his seat as he studied the sharp gray columns of data marching in one corner of the virtual image in his mind. A bright pulsing blue dot hovered above the edge of Devon's moon. Two smaller orange points crawled slowly across the planet's surface.

He issued a mental command and the image zoomed, exploding the view of one of the small points. Two shield envelopes surrounded the stubby shape, presumably a navigation and primary defense net. A single bulbous pod flared at the base of the ship housing the power plant, a standard Kran scout craft configuration.

His tongue licked quickly around fleshy lips. He absently tapped the front of his teeth with one finger and shifted his view to the Kran *Daktar*. A typical module of two elongated sections. The first some five hundred kanampirs long, and the trailing pod around seven hundred. Both sections were two hundred kanampirs in diameter. It was a large and powerful vessel.

His attention wandered, preoccupied with the tactical situation he faced. While the thing remained on Devon's moon, he had a relatively simple set-piece scenario. He did not relish the prospect of engaging the vessel in Devon's atmosphere with all the environmental and political problems such an action would create. Orieli relations with the Serrll were delicate enough without having a devastated planet to worry about, no matter what the reason.

The strategic disposition, on the other hand, was more difficult to evaluate and far more serious in its implication. The mere presence of a Kran vessel this far from the Karina suggested an expansion of their search for the Orieli worlds on a much broader front than OSCOM had anticipated. For the Krans to be able to engage the Orieli as well as push beyond their normal tactical objectives implied a command and control network far greater than previously assumed.

Complex statistical modeling of all recorded contacts only added weight to the theory that the Krans originated from the inner hub of the opposite galactic arm. If the Krans had entered this arm some 9,000 light-years closer to the hub than they actually did, they would have avoided the barrier of the Karina Shield, and all the hundreds of Orieli systems there would have been exposed and vulnerable.

Sooner or later, though, the Kran primary nexus would deduce the location of the Orieli systems simply on the basis that there were no inhabited worlds on this side of the Karina capable of supporting a complex organizational infrastructure exhibited by the Orieli.

With the exception of the Serrll, of course.

The central nexus core in the crippled Kran cruiser sitting on that moon would have scanned Devon and its ecoforming stations. Arlon could almost picture its thought processes. The Krans had encountered superior opposition on this side of the Karina. The logic of the situation would be inescapable if inaccurate—they have found the outer limits of that opposition.

Through the Valley of Shadow

Zor-Ell's orders to Arlon on this point were quite blunt. The Krans must not be allowed to communicate their discovery back to the primary nexus, no matter what the cost. He pressed his mouth and detached himself from the VI coupling. For the moment, he was happy to leave grand strategy to Space Command.

"Target energy anomaly track positive, Karhide. Maintaining EMCON. Range to Devon 3-VL4 is forty-two million ampirs," Opturkarh Tavac announced quietly.

"Cent Comp, stabilize at quarter boost and maintain relativity."

"Stabilizing at quarter boost relative," came the acknowledgment from the housekeeping computer.

Tavac turned to Arlon. "Karhide, ship is ready."

"Very well. Cent Comp copy?"

"Ready, Karhide," the computer responded deliberately.

"Secure from condition one. Execute condition two."

The ceiling above the PFC changed from soft blue-gray to pulsing green, followed by a brief increase in inter-deck comms tests. Additional operators materialized in the PT, personal transport alcove, and took up their stations on the command level and the operations platform below.

"Condition two commencing," the computer said. "All decks at level two alert. Primary fire control on active standby. Auxiliary flight control passive. Interceptor net now at level three. Secondary net now at level one with level two on active standby. Status. Primary unit active. Tactical control in PFC. Condition two active." The ceiling stopped pulsing and faded to dull green.

Tavac cast a glance around the command level and nodded with grudging satisfaction. In a flash of amusement, he realized that crew performance was never likely to reach his demanded level of perfection. But what he saw was close enough. He issued a mental command to the computer, detached himself from the VI coupling and looked at his commander.

"Karhide, the *Daktar* is holed up on Devon's moon like it's planning to stay. Its shields are down and they are maintaining minimum power status. You've seen the two scout-size craft that overflew Devon 3-VL4. It is almost a certainty that we've been detected as we dropped normal. Target has not attempted fire control acquisition, yet. They're bound to do so when we get closer."

Arlon sat unmoving, pursed his mouth and his pale pink tongue licked delicately. "Any sign of Serrll activity?"

"Nothing within immediate tactical range. However, we show a positive track from a medium vessel identified as a K/11 M-3 sweeper, probably acting as point for a larger force. Expected vectored position on the M-3 in seventy-eight minutes at present closure rate."

"Devon?"

"We picked up minimal surface energy readings, but there is no way to tell whether they are from the ecoforming stations or the Krans. One site does show a signature consistent with Kran worker units."

"They have probably started ripping one of those stations apart," Arlon muttered and tilted his head at Tavac. "Comments?"

"We're too far from Devon or its moon to be of much use to anyone, Da. Suggest we move in and interdict Devon."

"Explain," Arlon demanded sharply.

"If the Krans are attempting to draw supplies from Devon, our presence will disrupt that, enabling us—"

"To give our undivided attention to the mother ship," Arlon finished for him. "Right?"

"That's it," Tavac said with a grin.

"Okay, then. Stop the ship when we're within effective acquisition."

Tapal moved deliberately toward Devon 3-VL4. The tactical mainframe plot holoview showed two orange points lifting out of the atmosphere envelope. Without pausing they fanned out and picked up speed, away from the Orieli ship.

But they had left their run a bit late.

"Cent Comp, fire status?" Tavac inquired.

"Primary fire control active, Opturkarh. Targets acquired and on positive lock. Effective firing solution in four seconds at present closure rate. Interceptor net active at your command."

"Permission to fire for effect, Karhide?" Tavac glanced at Arlon who nodded.

"You have weapons free."

"Cent Comp, engage at your discretion," Tavac said immediately.

With the Kran units acquired, *Tapal* slowed and stopped. Energy surged from one of the regenerating twin quantum point locus pods and flooded the ship's secondary net matrix. The field lines quickly saturated as power swamped the interceptor net rings. The energy overload rippled along the flux lines and formed a locus funnel where it quickly grew into a node. The matrix dissolved at the locus point and a pale blue lance of secondary ionization stabbed at one of the Kran scouts, enveloping it in cold radiance.

The Sardan-built 1704/SL Orieli survey cruiser had an effective acquisition range of almost 250,000 ampirs. The Kran scouts were well within it. The ship could project a maximum of 282 TeV in single or twin variable bursts of up to twenty-four milliseconds. Saturated with that much energy, matter literally tore apart into its constituent quarks as the binding forces were released.

The Kran ship seemed to stagger as though it hit a wall, which in a sense it did. Its shield net flared yellow and orange as it broke up from the overloading surge of energy. Backsurges arced along the hull, burning away plating. The hull began to glow and the ship immediately lost attitude before it vanished in a brilliant sphere of white light as the power core collapsed. Another blue track licked delicately at the remaining Kran scout. Its shields pulsed, arced wildly before fading, and left the ship drifting.

"Cent Comp?"

"Ready, Karhide."

"Tactical status."

"Target disabled, all shield envelopes down. Energy output configuration minimal, indicating power plant function in a dampening oscillation mode. Deactivation imminent."

"Any comms?"

"No communication detected on any bands."

Arlon studied the plot and nodded with satisfaction. "Have that thing brought into Hangar Bay Two, Tavac. Maybe we'll get lucky and find a central nexus core in there."

"Sure. And I just made karhide rank," Tavac said with a wry grin and stood up.

He walked to the PT alcove and issued a mental command. His form turned two-dimensional and he vanished. Arlon smiled after him. Tavac was a very good officer. He would hate to lose him when he came up for his command slot, which should be soon. With Kran activity on the increase, there were likely to be more slots than qualified personnel available to fill them.

"Cent Comp? Put us on an intercept course with Devon's moon and execute as soon as Opturkarh Tavac has the Kran vessel aboard."

"Course plotted and standing by," the computer acknowledged.

Tapal slowed as it neared the drifting hull of the Kran scout. A sphere of pale yellow energy enveloped the scout and drew it inexorably toward the cruiser. Arlon watched the evolution in one of the holoview repeater windows. Slowly the Kran scout vanished beneath the bulk of his ship.

The comms holoview cleared and Tavac's face came into view. "Karhide, the Kran scout is aboard and secured. I'm returning to PFC."

"What's its condition?" Arlon demanded and his tongue made a quick circuit around his lips.

"Deactivated. We made sure. The hull is mostly intact, but there is major circuitry damage as you can expect."

"Any of the units active?"

"Except for the control node, there were no other units on board."

"Hmm. Must have left them on Devon. Very well. Get back up here. We're about to overfly the Kran position."

Arlon sat back in his seat and watched the grid pattern of Devon's moon grow in the operational plot holoview. The *Daktar's* central nexus had made a rare tactical error in attacking his ship. Instead of consolidating its position on Devon 3-VL4 where it would have been more difficult to dislodge, it left Devon unsupported. An unusual mistake, and may indicate damage to the nexus core. Whatever the reason, he would make sure he exploited the mistake fully.

The mainframe holoview plot showed the moon sliding beneath them, a bleak pattern of sharp grays and browns. A jagged range of towering cliffs rose to meet them. As they neared the terminator the tactical overlay blinked and locked on the shield energy rings around the Kran ship hiding somewhere among the cliffs.

"Tactical caution," the housekeeping computer announced suddenly. "Energy anomaly track has shifted to active phase. Target confirmed as a Celi-Kran *Daktar* configuration attack cruiser. The unit is powering up to weapons status."

"Status fire control?" Arlon asked quietly.

"Primary fire control active. Condition two active. Initiating condition three to active standby. Secondary shields now at level two. Interceptor net active."

Tavac materialized in the PT alcove and quickly took in the tactical situation with one glance. He looked away from the mainframe plot at the comms operator.

"Anything?"

The watchstander shook his head. "They are quiet on all bands, Da."

Tavac nodded, took his seat and faced Arlon. "Karhide, what is our intention?"

Arlon's forehead creased in concentration. He tapped the armrest and pointed at the plot. "I would love to take a look inside that thing. We could learn a lot."

"So could they if we got careless," Tavac pointed out, the warning in his voice clear.

During the five years of engagements, the Krans had never managed to capture any of the Orieli ships, despite a few close calls. It did not include ships destroyed in place. However powerful, the Krans learned slowly, adapting to Orieli's tactics in predictable moves. Lately, those tactics had changed, evolved. They now used two cruisers to go after a lone Orieli vessel, OSCOM having learned about that move the hard way. Tavac didn't relish the thought of becoming a subject in another Kran experiment. He advised OSCOM of the Serrll tactic to tandem their fire control, something the Orieli might emulate against the Krans.

The tactical plot swamped the outside display to show a single energy band pulsing toward them. The communications operator studied his displays and looked up.

"We're absorbing a low-powered omnidirectional signal, Karhide. Very complex and modulated way out of shape. Looks like K or H band stuff we were getting prior to our first engagement."

"Recognition interrogation?" Tavac glanced at Arlon.

"Probably. It has the same signature. I suspect they know who we are. At least they are conforming to their standard operational pattern."

"Makes me wonder whether the signal could be something other than an interrogative," Tavac mused. "They must know it means nothing to us."

"Tactical caution," the computer warned. "Target has engaged active scan and acquired positive lock. Shields pulsing in preparatory firing phase. Status. Condition three is now active."

"All stop," Arlon ordered. "Clear tactical."

The mainframe plot dissolved, showing the Kran vessel nestled in the shadow of a craggy peak. Its shields were pulsing from pale red to orange from sublimating ionization as the shields charged. Arlon's lips pulled back into a faint snarl as he surveyed the odd bulbous shapes of the alien ship. He sensed something cold and menacing in those insect shapes even from here. When the orange beam leaped at them, he felt *Tapal* tremble, but the shields held steady. The beam reached for them again, this time visibly weaker. Clearly, the Krans still had power troubles or their firing would have been much stronger.

"All right. Let's rattle their cage a little. Give them a twin pulse, hard!"

Twin tracks of blue stabbed at the Kran ship. Its shields flared. The surrounding area glowed from arcing discharges that bled into the ground. There didn't appear to be any direct damage.

"Cute," Arlon muttered under his breath.

The *Daktar* had set up arrestors to bleed any overload energy from their shield net to the ground. The technique effective, but limited. The arrestors drew power directly from the ship's quantum point singularity core, albeit a mere trickle compared to what it took to support layered shield net envelopes. However, this tactic would protect the ship indefinitely. Still, it would demand larger pulse surges to penetrate the Kran shields.

"Do we finish them off?" Tavac demanded.

"With those damned arrestors, if we punch through, there won't be anything left but a puddle of slag," Arlon growled in irritation.

"We could also set off a singularity reaction," Tavac warned. In open space under normal battle conditions the Krans didn't have to worry if their power core containment field failed. Freed, the point singularity would flare in a millisecond burst of life, devouring everything around it before it evaporated. With the *Daktar* on the surface, a real danger, however remote, existed that a naked singularity could reach a sustained reaction using the moon's mass as fuel. It was a situation to be avoided.

Arlon was as aware of the danger. "What is the ETA on the Serrll M-3?"

"It should be breaking out of subspace in two minutes," Tavac said. "We're getting search band frequencies in regular pulses. They know we're here."

"Keep firing and see if we can collapse the Kran's shield net. I want this finished before that M-3 gets here."

Under increasingly concentrated fire the rock around the Kran vessel began to glow and melt, unfortunately, without any visible damage to the shields or the ship. Arlon studied the flowing slag with grim interest.

"We'll have to up our emission strength, Da," Tavac pointed out diffidently.

"Observational caution," the computer announced. "Secondary plotted anomaly track has shifted phase and is about to transit into normal space. Positive identification of track as a Serrll Scout Fleet K/11 type M-3 sweeper. Belligerency status unknown."

"Cease firing," Arlon ordered, looking disgusted. Although inevitable, the last thing he wanted now was to get entangled in a bureaucratic web of protocol. "The *Daktar* isn't about to lift soon and we can finish it off once we find out what our Serrll friend wants. Get some Burlig scanners into orbit and blanket the area. I don't want any comms, not one peep, to get through from that ship. Got it?"

"Copy that."

"I want a message to OSCOM relayed through LTN-9 advising them of our status. Send two RV/4 darts to check out Devon 3-VL4."

Through the Valley of Shadow

"Shouldn't we wait for the Serrll before taking further action?" Tavac asked.

"We need to know the disposition of the remaining Kran units down there. If there are Serrll ecoforming engineers holed up somewhere, they might need urgent help. The M-3 isn't equipped for it."

Tavac nodded and began issuing orders.

* * *

Se Kinai stared moodily at the tactical plate. His long snake-like fingers twined in agitation as he tried to stop his hands from twitching in frustration. His thin dark lips were an uncompromising line. He watched with growing misgivings the energy blooms of two small ships as they detached from the Orieli cruiser and headed side-by-side for Devon.

The maneuver only added fuel to his mounting anger. He didn't believe those ships were likely to attack Devon, but he couldn't take the chance. If he followed them down, it left the Orieli cruiser to do whatever it wanted. Then again, if he were perfectly blunt about it, the Orieli could damn well do whatever they wanted anyway. Was sending those scouts a move deliberately designed to confuse him?

He snorted in exasperation.

He wasn't angry with the Orieli. He'd been angry ever since the news of Ti Adi's death reached him. Ti Adi had been a good friend and his untimely death had shot their plans for a holiday in Orgomy, all to pieces. What a waste. Now, Sector TACOPSCOM compounded the problem by sending him to possibly share the same fate. He did not relish such an opportunity for glory. An M-3 was a scout, not a line fighting platform. But would TACOPSCOM listen? Their cold response; in case of trouble, withdraw and wait for support.

Great!

Once in trouble, it would probably mean he wouldn't be

able to withdraw. The two M-4s wallowing behind him might as well be on Captal for all the good they were. His small triangular face burned with pique at the stupidity of high command.

Unable to stop them, his fingers twined. "Plot? What's our status?"

"Range to Orieli cruiser is over eight billion talans," the tactical officer responded coolly. "Effective firing solution in fourteen seconds at present one-fifth boost."

"Go to initial alert and prepare to drop normal at one million talans." There was no point in getting any closer. What would he do if he were the Orieli commander? Se Kinai had monitored the cruiser's projector fire at the Kran ship. He could hardly believe the energy readings. If the Orieli commander chose to ignore him, there was very little he could do about it. Send a terse note to Captal in protest? The thought forced from him a wry smile of amusement.

Kopan's precursor field depolarized and the M-3 dropped into normal space and moved slowly toward Devon. On this course, he could at least position himself between Devon 3-VL4 and the Orieli ship. He felt confident in his ability to take out the two scouts before the Orieli could react, if that became necessary.

He watched with detached interest as the computer rotated the profile of the Orieli ship and the two RV/4 darts on the secondary plate. The specs matched, but he would not take anything for granted. He had his orders from Sector TACOPSCOM. If the worst happened, even negative information would be useful.

"We're being scanned, sir."

"Weapons lock?"

"Negative. Nav checks only."

With a curt order, Se Kinai set primary alert.

* * *

Through the Valley of Shadow

Arlon Dee watched the Serrll ship materialize out of subspace. Cent Comp immediately engaged the tactical plot.

"Observational caution. Energy anomaly track confirmed as an M-3 sweeper. Tactical caution. Target has initiated active scan and is attempting an acquisition lock on the patrolling RV/4s. The M-3's shield grid is assuming standby fire lock."

"Holy Master of Sin!" Tavac growled in frustration. "What in blazes do they think they're doing?"

"Just being cautious," Arlon mused. "Cent Comp? Open a channel to the M-3. Instruct the RV/4s to drop their shields and maintain neutral status."

"Acknowledged."

* * *

Se Kinai saw the shields drop around the two scouts and frowned. This was either an elaborate trap or…When the comms plate cleared, still suspicious of the alien's intentions, he felt secretly relieved. He had no desire to test his strength against the larger ship, or initiate something everyone might regret later, especially him. In a diplomatic screw-up, all too often the point guy found himself in a situation not exactly career-enhancing, no matter who's fault.

"First Scout Se Kinai, Serrll Scout Fleet, Palean Tactical Command. Please identify yourself," he requested politely, intently watching the image in the plate as he tried to gauge the alien's mood.

* * *

Arlon studied the young Palean with interest while attempting to suppress his annoyance.

"I am Karhide Arlon Dee of the Orieli Technic Union's ship *Tapal*. Before we proceed First Scout, I suggest you power down before you're tempted to do something rash."

Se Kinai blinked hard and nodded at the reasonable request.

"Very well, sir. I am standing down and maintaining neutral status."

Arlon glanced at the tactical holoview plot showing energy rings around the M-3 fade. Only the nav screen net remained. Cent Comp confirmed the M-3 had stood down, but still continued active scans. Well, he couldn't fault the Palean for his procedures.

"Thank you, Da Kinai." Arlon allowed himself a thin smile. "I would not be so eager to start shooting just yet," he remarked sardonically.

Se Kinai stared at Arlon and relaxed. "My orders were to investigate an attack on Devon 3-VL4, sir. Apparently by a large Kran vessel. TACOPSCOM had no specifics. When I detected your ship, I—"

"Came prepared," Arlon finished for him.

Se Kinai bobbed his head. "Thank you for understanding, sir. However, I'm still required to investigate the situation here, Karhide."

"Of course." Arlon nodded and his tongue made a quick circuit around his lips. "May I ask, Da Kinai, whether additional units of the Serrll Scout Fleet are expected in the area?"

Se Kinai frowned and his fingers twisted in agitation. *Damn command!*

Why the crap didn't they brief him on how to handle the Orieli? He fumed, more than a little peeved. Above a pointed chin, enormous morose black eyes protruded beneath a high rectangular forehead. The eyes were cloudy as he wrestled with the problem he suspected a little beyond him.

In the end, he could not see any harm telling the Orieli support was on its way. Maybe they would all need it, and the move would be expected. His head bobbed and his hands twined.

"Two M-4s are expected within five hours, sir," he said and

watched Arlon for any sign of reaction. He did not see any point in telling Arlon about the M-6 which COMPALOPS, Commander Palean Operations, was getting ready. The move could be misinterpreted.

Arlon nodded with satisfaction. "In that case, Da Kinai, before they get here, we need to determine our plan of action."

Se Kinai shrugged and his head bobbed. "What do you suggest, sir?" he asked diffidently, suddenly realizing he had lost the initiative. *He* should be the one making demands and asking questions. After all, this happened to be Serrll space! Before he could act on this revelation, Arlon began to speak.

"I have temporarily neutralized the Kran vessel on Devon's moon. The two support craft that presumably attacked Devon were destroyed." A subtle inaccuracy, but Arlon didn't feel it necessary to burden the Serrll with the knowledge of an intact Kran scout. Even inactive the thing was extremely dangerous. If ineptly handled, it could still bite.

"Our darts have identified some ground movement at one of your stations. The structures are partially destroyed. It may have been the planetary control complex and the only one with subspace comms capability. Tactically the Krans would ensure to neutralize it first, and the Kran units are probably dismantling it right now. I suggest the most likely objective is materiel acquisition for repair of their mother ship."

"What about the other stations?" Se Kinai demanded.

Arlon shrugged. "We have picked up energy emissions from three other sites. They are intact, but apparently subjected to massive power overload surges, which would have disabled their systems. That's standard Kran procedure."

Se Kinai stared hard at Arlon, inclined to believe the report, as TACOPSCOM had been unable to raise Devon 3-VL4 Center since the initial attack. What of the settlement crews and their families? He silently cursed the fool who ordered him here without adequate support to initiate appropriate action.

"Karhide, you stated there was Kran activity at one of the

ground stations?"

"That is correct."

"Do they constitute an active threat to the other stations?"

"Hard to say at this moment, Da Kinai. We don't know if they have long-range surface craft in place or whether it's a local operation only. That's what my RV/4s were tasked to find out when you appeared."

"Can support reach them from the mother ship?"

"Negative, First Scout. If they have additional scout ships the Krans will not risk them being destroyed. I will be here to make sure of that."

"Very well, sir." Se Kinai bobbed his head. "I need to contact TACOPSCOM and advise them of the tactical situation and request further instructions. In the meantime, sir, I must ask you to withdraw your patrol craft and maintain current status."

"Da Kinai," Arlon spoke softly, his whole attitude deadly serious. "I strongly urge you to reconsider. For the moment, the Kran cruiser is disabled and vulnerable. Any delay in its destruction only gives them time to make repairs. As for the darts, I suggest we both need a sitrep."

"Sir," Se Kinai wrung his hands in desperation, torn between orders and Arlon's common sense appraisal, "I must respectfully point out that Devon is outside your jurisdiction. You have no authority to take unilateral action, however sound." Looking at the massive shape of the Orieli survey cruiser, Se Kinai was painfully conscious of the vulnerability of his M-3. If Arlon refused? Worse, what if the Orieli left the system altogether?

Arlon nodded with apparent good grace. "I acknowledge that, First Scout. However, I would still recommend that you permit my darts to complete a survey of Devon."

"Very well. But you, sir, will stand down."

"As you wish, Da Kinai." The comms plate faded and Se Kinai wondered which of the ten things he should start first.

Through the Valley of Shadow

Pits!

* * *

Hands clasped behind his head, Terr lay staring into the gloom of shifting shadows and strange shapes that seemed to stalk the inside of the dwelling. His breathing slow and even. Embers from a dying fire shifted and stirred, keeping the murkiness at bay. Muffled spasms of racked coughing from the next room broke the small sounds of the night. He heard oark move on their broad-padded feet, snorting, grunting contentedly amid the soft cackling of poultry. Thin, sharp wailing of a hungry infant shattered the silence. Somebody shifted and a bed creaked, followed by comforting whispers and stifled slurps as an eager searching mouth sought a warm breast.

He turned his head slightly and traced the soft outline of Teena's face, slender neck and body. She had one arm flung out that hung limp beside the bed. The other curled beneath her head, clenched lightly in a small fist. Her hair hid the curve of her smooth shoulder to spill in a black veil across the pillow. Slowly, he reached out and his fingers disappeared into the soft velvet of her hair. She stirred and moaned softly. It would have been easy to touch her, to run a probing finger gently over the sheen of her skin, exploring the hidden curves, the cool softness of her flesh, and the trembling flutter of her heart.

He felt huge hunger deep within him as he lay staring at her, longing to hold her in his arms, to whisper the words he could not say aloud. Trapped behind a barrier he had thrown up, the cold calculating part of himself did nothing to help him climb it. He could not let go, not yet, and he would not steal his pleasure like a thief in the night.

Slowly, he swung his legs out and stood up, tensing as the bed creaked. He held his breath and watched her, but she didn't move. Like another shadow, he drifted soundlessly across the room. In bare feet, he padded to the doorway and eased back the heavy oark blanket. Donning slippers, he strode down the narrow corridor toward the outline of a low entrance. Outside, he straightened and looked around quickly, imprinting everything at a glance. Near the well, washing stirred weakly on a shifting line. On the sweeping dune slopes beyond, tarad grass shimmered like fields of ice; white, silent and ghostlike. All around, tall peelath stood watch in the darkness.

With a blinding slash a meteor tore through the sky in a voiceless scream, trailing an orange-white wound that left a vivid memory. Blinking solemnly, cold and remote, the veil of stars was a frozen sweep of a giant's hand through a glittering cascade of crystals suspended in eternity.

Touching the horizon the hand of Amulran the Damned lay outstretched, supporting himself as he knelt, bent, bolstering the bridge of the gods, preventing it from sinking into the eternal night. Above him, reaching across the sky, bow held stretched taut, the Stalker stood locked in his moment of revenge as he prepared to loose the arrow which would have killed Amulran and allowed the bridge of the gods to tumble into the lake of night. The gods had touched the Stalker and hurled him into heaven to stare at his enemy for all eternity, unable to loose the arrow of doom.

After the heat of the day, the air was deliciously cool. The sand beneath him still chill as he stared at the constellation of Amulran, doomed to stand beneath the weight of time. He shook his head thinking how cruel the gods were even toward one of their own. What then the pain of a mere mortal?

He climbed the shifting side of the dune and sat down. Absently, he picked up a handful of cold sand and allowed it to slip between his fingers. Knowing what he was about to do, he became resigned, his spirit heavy. He might have doubts, but the fates were carrying him toward a destiny he did not want to change even if he were able, which he didn't. The realization left him unmoved. It was all too late anyway.

Her footfalls were hesitant and mincing as she climbed the

dune behind him, the sand hissing beneath her feet. He waited for her until she stood beside him.

"Terr?" she whispered uncertainly and touched his shoulder. With a muffled rustle of robes, she sank down beside him. Hesitating, she leaned and rested her head against his shoulder.

"What are you doing up so early, Sankri, my god of Death?" she husked dreamily, her mind still foggy with sleep.

He smiled and laid a protective arm around her shoulders. "I had some thinking to do, pet," he murmured into her hair.

She burrowed her face into his chest and made soft growling noises as he pulled her against him. Content, they sat beneath the cloak of night as his hand moved slowly over her body, searching, remembering. He looked down and her eyes were black pools into which he sank gratefully. Her chest heaved and her breath came in short warm gasps, smelling sweet as he leaned over her face. His lips touched hers in a fleeting caress. She moaned and pressed herself into him. He kissed her cheeks, forehead and the tip of her nose before their lips met and her pointed tongue touched his, and he crushed his mouth against hers. The fires of love burned hot and roared in his ears as his tongue explored hers, twisting in a frenzy of desire, tenderness, and smoldering passion.

He pulled away and stared at the brightness of her eyes. With his finger, he slowly traced the outline of her lips.

"When I was on Earth, how I longed to touch your hair, touch your cheeks, see your smile, taste the sweetness of your kiss," he mumbled as he held her close. "I died a little each day I was without you. When I saw you again dressed in a surtaf, I felt some black chasm within me filled and I wanted to live again."

"You were always good at making pretty speeches," she murmured dreamily and he drew back.

"Is that all I'm good for?"

"Oh, you have one or two other uses."

"But not enough sense to keep what I have."

"Let's leave. This is our time and I need you with me."

"I have to finish this."

Her troubled eyes searched his. "Why? Why must you go on? Why do you torture yourself like this? I told you what happened."

"What *he* told you happened," he said harshly, convincing himself. "Why do you think he's running that Servatory Party cell on Taltair?"

"Anabb knows all about it. It's a cover for his work with the Unified Independent Front."

"Sure! If his work was so completely innocent, why didn't he just take you home or to the Center instead of bringing you here. Don't you see, Teena? He wants *me*! That's why you're here, to make sure I came, to finish what he started."

"But he's your brother, a part of you, and you want to kill him," she protested, exasperated. "Why? For what he did to you on the Moon? For bringing me here? For politics?" She reached up and her fingers brushed his cheek. "My love, if he wanted to harm me, I wouldn't be here now. Don't do something you know is wrong."

"How I want to believe you," he said, trying to keep the rage from consuming him. "Don't you think I don't know what this is doing to me? I would have forgiven him everything, even what I went through on Earth. When I got to the Serrll Moon Base, he only had to be there. Last night, my old master tried to tell me that I'm only fighting myself, afraid to believe that he had no choice and the realization holds me in terror."

"We are together now. That's all that matters. Isn't that enough?"

"I cannot leave it alone. I must confront him," he said brokenly, his voice full of anguish.

"It's only revenge then, to salve your pride?" She pulled away and looked at him, a stranger.

His laugh was hollow and bitter. "Perhaps. It's me and it's him and what I do for the Diplomatic Branch. I cannot tell you all of it and most of it I don't know myself. You can guess some of it. You worked with Anabb long enough to know what I do and you've seen some of my reports. Despite everything, I would have helped him, whatever he was doing. He only had to ask," he grated and flung a handful of sand into the night.

"And if he couldn't?"

Was she right and only wounded pride kept him going?

The stars were cold and indifferent. Then again, perhaps not. He looked at the Stalker and felt a pang of sorrow. The Stalker too had faced betrayal at the hand of a brother. Surely a god's suffering couldn't be greater than his. Would he be able to stay his hand when he faced his betrayer?

He stood and shook the sand off his surtaf.

"I must finish this, Teena. No matter what, remember always that I love you."

"Terr!" she cried after him as he walked toward the combie.

* * *

Terr felt suspended in a strange reality, hurtling toward blackness. On his left, blood smeared the horizon. The soft hum of the combie kept him company. The only company he needed right then. On his port quarter, the desert turned a blotchy mauve. Darkness lay thick about him. Above him, the stars began to die and the combie hummed to itself.

He tried to keep his mind frigid and remote, untouched by emotion or feeling. Yet beneath the brittle outward facade, it all threatened to burst through, to overwhelm and destroy him. Teeth clenched, he dared not think what lurked within the black corridors of his vengeance-filled mind. Hate had kept him going through it all and he needed its strength to finish it. He had to focus on that.

Gradually the rolling sands merged into pea-gravel and rocky flats. The jagged buttresses of Katai Than thrust themselves high into red cliffs, the wadi still shrouded in pre-dawn darkness. He sensed a burst of light on his cheek as the sun broke above the desert. Unconsciously, he banked the combie toward a familiar canyon opening and waited as the chiseled walls grew and closed around him with a rush. Heavy silence lay among the dark shadows. Even the power plant seemed to whisper more softly in the gloomy half-light, making the thunder of his heart loud in his ears.

In days now long gone, both of them had traveled this path many times. He'd been innocent then and the memories were happier. Now, he saw hate, bare rock, and sand. A place of death, nothing more. That other time did not belong to him anymore. In this reality the brother he thought he had became an enemy, and part of him grieved.

Patches of dry yellow tarad grass hugged the mute walls of the canyon. Muddy green shrub gave way to an occasional solitary peelath. Tall, its broad leaves limp, it too waited. The combie lost height, slowed, and glided silently above the twisting dry watercourse. The rough landscape's wild beauty and serenity tugged at him. He pushed the feeling away. He could not afford to be distracted now. After a time the dark cliffs opened to reveal a still pond surrounded by a wooded glade of gently swaying peelath. Taklan moss-palms leaned over dark, still waters, trailing long strands of moss from the branches, nodding at their reflection.

He touched a glowing pad on the console and the combie stopped. It hovered above the polished glint of brown water, the hum of the power plant a muted whisper. The soft white sand of the small beach slid into the still pool without a ripple. Dhar sat on a flat stone, his legs crossed, surrounded by shadows. His long thin hands rested on his knees palms up, spread in contemplation. The yellow skin drawn tight over his narrow face. The wide mouth with its dry lips was open slightly, revealing even brown teeth. He wore a traditional brown surtaf robe, the red hood pulled up, covering his head.

A tendril of thin dark smoke rose from the black embers

of a nearby campfire. In the predawn light, magic touched this place and reached out to him. At another time, Terr would have savored the quiet peace of the gorge. Now, he only wanted to reach out, to smash and destroy, to blot out the affront before him. He shuddered and his fingers clenched into fists to stop himself from crying out and unleashing the terrible forces stirring within him. With a trembling hand, he touched the controls. The combie moved slowly toward the beach, hesitated and sank. His eyes were fixed on Dhar's unmoving form. He wondered why Dhar didn't move. It would have taken just a token gesture and the fires inside him would spring forth to consume everything.

He didn't know how long he waited, watching, staring fixedly at the still form. Finally, he tapped a pad and the bubble slid back with a hiss. He stepped out and sand shifted beneath his feet. Then Dhar turned his head. The vertical red slits of his eyes were two expressionless lines. He reached up with both hands and pulled back the hood.

"My brother, I am happy to be in your shadow again," he rumbled softly, the words ripping Terr apart.

His mouth went suddenly dry and had a bitter metallic taste, and he felt his face drain.

"I have no brother," he choked back a broken sob. "Through your hand, that part of me died on Earth," he grated between clenched teeth.

Dhar looked stricken and slowly rose to his feet, his arms hanging beside him.

"If death will atone for my sins and your pain, then I welcome its embrace," he whispered, resigned to his fate.

"You won't have to wait long," Terr snarled and raised his arms. He had waited an eternity to drink from this cup and he found the taste suddenly harsh, but he could not turn back the furies of hate now.

"I shall walk in the shadow of Death," he intoned flatly, watching the acceptance on Dhar's face and part of him wept.

155

"And it shall be with me all the days of my life. With shadow shall I smite my enemies and with thunder shall I purge their land!" he cried out as the power flowed through him, surging, burning away his inhibitions. The hand of Death touched him and he welcomed the unholy joy of its deadly power. "And all who stand with me in the shadow of Death shall know my power and be comforted. With shadow and thunder shall I walk their land!"

The killing lust hot in his eyes, he savored its sweetness. He remembered the shooting pain in his back and the helpless flight as the dart cut through the atmosphere. He remembered the jagged wound in his side and the hot sands of the New Mexico desert. He remembered Morrow and the Larkins and the blood shed because of him. He leveled his arms. Bright blue lightnings danced between them, coiled and ready.

"Wait!" Dhar cried out, but Terr ignored him.

His eyes stung with regret and Dhar flinched as he reached for him. The lightning crash lit the gorge and thunder shook the ground between them. Blue light danced around Dhar like a halo, crackling and twisting and burning. He gasped and staggered, but remained standing. Agony contorted his face, but his eyes never left Terr. His robe smoldered where the lightnings had burned through.

"I called you a brother," Terr rasped savagely, relishing Dhar's pain. "But you betrayed that by knowingly sending me to my death. Now it's your turn."

Lightning cracked again and Dhar screamed in pain and shock of its touch. It coiled and flared around him before draining into the sand. The canyon walls echoed his cry. He lurched forward and groaned, clutched his chest and fell heavily.

Ignoring the sympathetic pain coursing through him, Terr trembled with the terrible joy of power and destruction, only mildly wondering why Dhar didn't fight back. It would have made his annihilation all the sweeter. No matter.

"I died the death of betrayal! I was alone and I didn't even know why you abandoned me." Terr's cries faded with the echoes.

Dhar struggled to his feet. When he finally managed to stand, he looked up, his distress mixed with tragic sadness.

"I die, forever your brother," he gasped, muscles contracting spasmodically as pain twisted his face.

"Then die!"

Nightwings!

Terr only had to will it, and this time, Dhar would not be rising. His hands were leveled, ready to pour forth his revenge, but he found himself unable to do it. He stared at Dhar in disbelief, feeling his resolve crumble. He could not bring himself to kill him. After everything he endured, all the agony and hurt, he discovered that he still loved him. Betrayed by his emotions. The irony of the moment was not lost on him.

Rit!

But Dhar *deserved* to die.

His arms trembled from the inner struggle to hold back his will. With a bellow of rage and frustrated bewilderment, he spread his arms and lashed out. Again and again, thunder crashed and lightning cracked until the rocks themselves cried in torment.

Dhar stood very still as Death raged around him. Sand glowed in fused, smoking puddles of yellow glass at his feet.

Spent, Terr let his arms drop.

"Damn you!" he croaked weakly. "I trusted you. I would have *died* for you."

For the second time, he placed himself in Dhar's hands. If his brother chose to finish what he began, Terr could not stop him. He felt the sting in his eyes and blinked back hot tears. Biting back a sob, he sank to his knees in helpless confusion.

"When the Orieli picked me up, I waited for you," he moaned and hugged himself, his eyes imploring. "You only had to be there. I would have forgiven you everything…everything. You only had to be there."

Tears streaming down his face, he waited for Dhar to end it. He didn't care anymore. Death would be a welcome release now and he was ready for its embrace. In a way, it would be a fitting punishment for his sins.

Dhar stood there frozen, trying to still the play of astonished emotions on his face. He fully expected to die then. That Sankri stayed his hand…It tore him apart to see his alien brother suffering and he cursed the fates that brought both of them to this state.

"My poor brother," he whispered brokenly as he searched for the right words. "There was no other way."

"You tried to kill me!" Terr sobbed in outrage. "And I don't even know why."

Dhar gave a tragic sigh and took the few steps separating them. Sankri looked up as he knelt. Eyes burning, Dhar reached for him.

His touch was like fire and Terr recoiled as blue sparks jumped between them. Firmly, Dhar's arms went around him and drew him close.

"I understand, my poor brother," Dhar whispered with infinite gentleness and sadness. "I understand."

With a soul-wrenching gasp, Terr pushed against him, trying to burrow into him, welcoming his strength. He wept unashamedly as Dhar held him.

* * *

Terr gazed vacantly at the reflections in the pool as they shifted and merged. Insects buzzed dreamily around him. Somewhere, there came a brief flurry of wings, a squawk, then stillness returned. The sun peeked above the lip of the cliffs and bathed the gorge with defused light. Everything was subdued, holding its breath, waiting. Moss hung limp in loose streamers from the palms beside him, brushing the water like spilled hair. He waited as he sat there, empty and drained, just another bit of flotsam cast upon the rocky beach of life.

An empty shell, content to gaze at nothing, he felt the sun's warmth caress his face. He was not ready to deal with the harsh reality waiting for him beyond those cliffs. Time enough for that later.

Dhar sat beside him in his shadow.

"Remember how we used to sit here like this and talk? It seems such a long time ago now," Terr said absently.

Dhar did not move or say anything, intensely aware of Terr's fragile mood and of the brittle calm within which they stood, still surrounded by chaos and death. A frail, tentative peace that bridged the chasm between them. He did not need to look at his brother to sense the coiled power ready to unleash Death's wrath again. And Dhar feared that power. He had seen Death's manifestation among the Saddish-aa, but in Terr, it held a qualitative difference that bordered on the religious.

He sought guidance in his master's words and did not find it. Chagrined, he realized he already held the answer, had it all along. Could he open himself to say the healing words?

Terr traced a pattern with his finger in the warm sand.

"There was one time…it the dark, and we had a fire going. I remember our shadows dancing in the pool. The air still with no wind. We talked…" He paused, lost in yesterday, trying to recapture the nostalgic mood and an innocence he left somewhere. Perhaps it was simply a process of healing. "We talked of life and love and death—"

"And glory and honor," Dhar added. "Warm memories…"

"Of a time long ago…" Terr trailed away. After a while, he looked up. "You walked here?"

"I didn't expect to be getting back."

Terr's mouth twitched. He threw another pebble into the glassy waters of the pond and steeled himself for another confrontation that had to be. The tranquility around them offered a moment of order, but it was a false thing.

"I woke up in the dart, controls locked, with Earth looming

before me. At that moment, I didn't expect to be getting back either, but I did, and in the process, I discovered disillusionment. After all the years working for Anabb, I should have known better, but I let myself be used by everyone. In the end, even you used me. That's what hurt, Nightwings, my brother of the night. I hated you then. On Taltair, when Anabb told me that Teena was gone, something died inside me. What did you expect me to think? Between you, you took everything I had and I vowed vengeance." Indignation and Death stirred within him. "Why didn't you just tell me what you were doing? Whatever your mission, I would have helped. Are we not one in spirit? Have we lost so much that you couldn't turn to me?"

Dhar's features were drawn and uncertain and Sankri's words cut savagely at his conscience.

"I could not tell you," he said lamely, unable to look at his brother, aware of his guilt.

"Orders!" Terr snorted and shook his head at the stupid futility of it all. "To think our work has reduced us to servile obedience. Is the Unified Independent Front so important that we need to sacrifice the very principles we're supposedly fighting for? If that's the case, the Rahtir Council has indeed lost its way and the words of the *Saftara* are nothing more than trite spouting."

Dhar ordered his thoughts. By trying to explain it to his brother, he was perhaps explaining to himself...or justifying?

"It is difficult to put into words—"

"Give it a go."

"Anar'on is not like other worlds, Sankri. And the Wanderers are not like other people, and you know why. For their whimsical reasons, we are favored by the gods, but that favor exacts its own price. The power we wield is a trust and a heavy responsibility. With the Discipline we could rule the Serrll, take of it what we wanted with no one to stop us. Yet that is not our way. The rage of the gods is too terrible to be unleashed on the worlds. Checks and balances."

Through the Valley of Shadow

"In the process, you learned political expediency," Terr accused him. "Enough to corrupt you and the teachings of the Discipline. Don't quote the *Saftara* to me, Nightwings."

Dhar winced, the remark hitting uncomfortably close to his own misgivings. In a flash of anger, he hit back.

"Would the gods approve of *your* deeds? At least, I had a cause to fight for!" Dismayed, he reached out and touched Terr's arm in contrition. "Forgive me. That was thoughtless of me."

Terr shrugged. "There is nothing to forgive. You spoke the truth. I'm not proud of what I did or why I did it, and I am ready to face the god's judgment. But who judges the Rahtir Council?"

"Sankri, with a multiplicity of choices, they were bound to make a mistake along the way. Don't think the moral dilemma was not realized. You know our history. On one border stands the Palean Union, always sly and scheming. Then there is the Deklan Republic with its cursed Ecumenical Order, ready to enslave the minds of its people with the doom of their Path. Over the centuries both have tried to absorb us. What should we have done? Let those sons of rock rays reduce our lives to religious serfdom, mere spectacles for outworlder curiosity seekers?"

"To avoid becoming prey, you don't necessarily have to become a hunter," Terr commented dryly.

"Indeed. But it helps to have sharp claws."

Terr's look was quizzical. "With the shadow of Death riding in your hand?"

It took Dhar a long time to reply. When he did, there was a hollowness and regret in his words.

"It happened before. There is something terrible watching a world die."

Terr's mind reeled. If pressed, would Anar'on be prepared to wield that power again? The image chilled him.

"That was a long time ago," Dhar added. "We use different

tools today, economics and interstellar diplomacy. Like all living organisms, political systems must grow and evolve or die. You know that. Anar'on and the Kaleen group face the same problem. We are caught between forces of evolutionary change and we had to adapt. It has taken us many decades of planning to overcome entrenched interests and establish a favorable climate within which the Unified Independent Front could deal with the Serrll powers."

"By infiltrating Captal's Councils?"

"Of course. We needed intelligence and a means of exerting influence on selected Assemblymen."

"You mean, sowing discord and confusion?" Terr suggested and Dhar grinned.

"Working for Anabb has corrupted you."

"I wallowed in it, happy to be one of his assassins."

"You judge yourself too harshly, my brother."

"I think not. I was merely being naive and idealistic. A freshly minted Wanderer, with Death in my hand, I became a perfect tool for Anabb." He trailed off and chuckled. "No, not Anabb at all, but Enllss. I knew, but refused to believe it. He's been playing both of us, hasn't he?"

Dhar felt unaccountably disturbed by the speed of Terr's reasoning. He picked up a pebble and threw it into the water. It made a soft plop and ripples shattered the mirror of the pond.

"Sofam wants to scuttle Sargon's merger with the Paleans. Formation of the Unified Independent Front would go a long way toward achieving that goal and will prevent skittish Kaleen systems from ceding to the Paleans, something not in the Provisional Committee's interest. Despite the Khiman-ra disaster, they still want those systems."

"How did all this maneuvering bring the two of us into the picture?"

"Ever since his ascension to the General Assembly, Ed-Kani Takao's efforts to secure the merger have been intense and disturbingly successful. You know how ruthless he and the

Committee are prepared to be." .

"Lemos."

"Just so, but they didn't stop there. They groomed selected planetary Controllers to appear sympathetic toward the Unified Independent Front. A newly cloaked Controller and, although a Servatory Party appointee, Gashkarali appeared to support the UIF. Being deep in Sargon space, Director Marrakan saw the Trillian system as an ideal staging point for gathering intelligence and a means to strengthen Sargon's opposition. He urged Sofam not to muddy the waters during Gashkarali's appointment."

Terr cocked an eyebrow. "I can imagine what Sofam wanted in return."

"To put us in bondage. Sofam would sanction the formation of the Unified Independent Front as a legitimate interstellar block in exchange for UIF's unconditional support in the Executive Council."

"Ah, and if Marrakan refused to cooperate?"

Dhar's smile was grim. "Sofam would dissolve the nonaligned independent's Executive seat."

"Wow. And Marrakan told them to shove it, right?"

"Something like that."

"I like it. Has the General Assembly met?"

"I don't know."

"But Gashkarali still ended up as Controller," Terr mused, then thought of something. "Wait a minute. If Sofam didn't support him to help the UIF, they must have done it to screw up the Servatory Party. But that means—"

"Gashkarali worked directly for Ed-Kani and the Provisional Committee, not the Servatory Party, and the Captal government knew it," Dhar said dryly. "At least the Sofam Executive Directors did. I exposed him."

"You?" Terr stared at him.

"We did not care who Gashkarali really worked for as long as he helped us. As it turned out, our trust was misplaced and it cost us several agents. We tried to have him removed through the Administrative Council, but Enllss blocked that and called for termination."

Terr blinked as the pieces clanged into place. "Let me guess. That's where I came in. Did Enllss suggest me for the assignment or—"

"You must understand his thinking, Sankri. He faced a difficult situation. On one hand, he did not want to stand in Anar'on's way, but he was still very much concerned about who the UIF would support."

"A power manipulator to the core. Your cell on Taltair…infiltration of both sides. To maintain your cover, you informed Terchran of my mission." Terr stopped, unable to put into words the obvious.

"And he ordered me, using their euphemism, to neutralize you in retaliation for sanctioning Gashkarali," Dhar finished for him. "Enllss counted on that to protect my cover as a double agent."

"Why am I not surprised?"

"Enllss who persuaded Anabb to include you in the Orieli Formal Mission to Salina. In theory, to get you out of Terchran's reach, I suppose."

"The communal gag on Taltair and the sabotage attempts on the Moon. It was you. Everything meant to fool Terchran that you were indeed trying to kill me."

"Partly true."

"We don't want to forget Anabb's game with the Orieli, but the dart? Why did you engineer that crash?"

Dhar felt himself getting boxed into a corner. "Remember the training flight on the platform? I did not set the Death Messenger for you, just as I told you, but for the Karkan crewman. If I could not kill you, it would have been his turn. It is quite probable he had orders to eliminate both of us. Something I did that annoyed Terchran. I knew by using my aspect, I would compromise myself. I was under orders not to tell you anything, and I did not know if Terchran had someone else ready to finish the job. I had to make your crash look real."

"So you chose to remove me from the picture altogether. Not quite kill me, but do enough to maintain your cover." Terr shook his head at the ironical twisting of events that inevitably unfolded. "Orders or not, you should have told me, Nightwings. It would have helped."

"In hindsight, all things considered, it would have been the wise thing to do."

"And Teena? Why her?"

"That is something I don't understand," Dhar said brooding. "Enllss leaked information to Terchran that Teena was somehow involved with the Gashkarali sanction. As one of Anabb's senior analysts, Terchran believed it and ordered my cell leader on Taltair to pick her up. Anabb made it easy for them."

"Enllss again. And I suppose Enllss ordered you to bring Teena here to ensure I would follow."

"That is correct."

"Enllss didn't tell you why?"

"I have given that some thought. Perhaps he wants all of us safe and out of Terchran's reach."

"Maybe. But if Terchran wants us, he'll find us. I think he sent Teena with you to make my exile more bearable."

"Exile?"

"Nightwings, what do we have in common?"

Dhar's eyes were expressionless, his red vertical slits a thin line. "We are both Wanderers."

"Next time you talk to Marrakan, ask him how many Wanderers have been removed from Captal's bureaus."

"Why would Enllss want to do that?"

"Think about it."

Dhar's narrow head, poised on a long neck, gave an impression of coiled strength.

"Because he wanted to limit the Unified Independent

Front's intelligence-gathering capability?" he said slowly and Terr smiled.

"Marrakan as much as spat into Sofam's eyes. This was their way of evening the score."

"A cynical, but perhaps accurate analysis."

Terr gazed at the still brown waters of the pool. Insects hovered above it. The sun had climbed high above the gorge and the heat warmed him. He kicked the sand at his feet.

"The other night, I looked at the face of Athal Than and wondered how I would face my judgment. Wrapped in my cloak of power, it was easy to see myself as the avenger, the destroyer of evil. Yet during all that time, I only fed my delusions and the need to wield the hand of Death. I understand now what our master once told me. The shield of righteousness can hide a lot of misery." He looked at Dhar, his cold scheming self not convinced. "Your commitment to the Unified Independent Front is total, isn't it?" he asked softly.

"Every Wanderer…" Dhar faltered, then paled, caught in a trap of his own making. How casually had *he* used the UIF's perceived high moral ground to justify his actions? A bitter realization to swallow. Stricken, he ripped open his zip-shirt. "If I ever wanted your death, Sankri, my brother, end this now! Let your touch cleanse away my transgressions and release me from my guilt."

Wanderers don't cry, but a tear glistened in Dhar's eye and slid down his drawn cheek. Terr felt ashamed that even now, he could feel anything but total loyalty to his brother. Both of them have suffered enough. He didn't believe his new calculating self was scoured, but maybe some of the wounds have scabbed over.

"Perhaps it is I who should be making the apologies, Nightwings," he said heavily. "I should have trusted you, believed in you, even when I did not understand. In that, I have failed and I crave your forgiveness," he growled and swallowed hard.

Dhar wiped his cheek and slowly raised his hand. "Sankri—"

"It's all right. I understand," Terr said and reached up with his hand.

When their palms touched, blue fires flowed between them and they were one. Terr felt cleansed, but empty.

Stefan Vučak

Chapter Seven

Illeran tilted back his head. Massaging his neck, he winced as sharp pain shot down his spine. His thin pointed tongue flicked quickly in annoyance. He should get out more often and exercise. In two years, he would be out, all right, permanently. His close-set black eyes lit with sardonic amusement.

Within the fish tank that formed most of one wall, dark shapes moved with slow deliberation. A sand groker drifted out of the gloom to stare myopically with bulging gray eyes at a world beyond its comprehension.

He pushed back his formchair, stood and walked slowly to the window screen. Thick green pile muffled his footsteps. The sky clear and the traffic light. The towers of the city stood out sharp and clean, aloof and indifferent to the joys and pains of its inhabitants. To rule, getting too close was to lose perspective.

Far below, Celean Park formed an oasis of greens, yellows and browns, changing and shifting as the shadows touched it, a point of stability surrounded by chaos. He wondered where he had lost *his* perspective. Bemused, he turned and surveyed the opulence of his office. Was this the only reward for almost thirty years of service? He knew it wasn't true, but the thought left him with an ashen taste in his mouth.

The comms alert gave a muted beep and his lips curled.

"What is it?" he hissed with frosty annoyance.

"Commissioner Katan, sir." Illeran noted the indifference and impatience in his aide's voice and frowned.

As a member of the General Assembly, perhaps his First Assistant thought that serving an Executive Director was too lowly a position for him. He allowed the horizontal slits of his eyes to close slightly and his tongue flicked quickly with grim humor.

"Very well." He reached across the desk and touched a small pad in the console array. The Wall cleared and he turned to face it.

"I have an update on Devon 3-VL4, Illeran," Katan said without preamble.

They might be both Karkans, but Illeran had never managed to warm to Katan. He did not deny Katan's efficiency and energy, and perhaps the problem. In Katan, he saw a new wave of policy-makers waiting for the coming elections to sweep out the old guard and bring them to power. Was he as transparent twenty-eight years ago? He frowned, trying to mask his dislike, annoyed that it wasn't working.

"This is direct from COMPALOPS," Katan said, smug at getting one up on Illeran's intelligence machinery. Still, as commissioner for the Bureau of Defense, Katan had better communication lines with the Serrll Scout Fleet.

"And what do they have to say?" Illeran demanded impatiently.

"Not all the facts are in, but it appears that a Celi-Kran ship, possibly equivalent to one of our M-6s, attacked Devon 3-VL4 in an attempt to obtain materials to affect repairs."

"Repairs?"

"Data from Devon suggests the Kran vessel may have had an engagement with an Orieli ship."

"How reliable is this?"

"*Kopan*, an M-3 sweeper, is on the scene babysitting an Orieli survey cruiser while waiting for supporting M-4s."

"That's not what I asked, Katan," Illeran hissed, his frown deepening.

Katan's black eyes disappeared within the horizontal slits and his tongue flicked in annoyance. What did the old fish-head want anyway?

"The evidence is conclusive. COMPALOPS has examined

Devon's telemetry sent by Controller Aill-Massai before he shut down, and Sector TACOPSCOM confirms that the M-3 picket *Valetta* was destroyed by the Kran ship. While still in transit, *Kopan* reported observing the Orieli cruiser firing on the Kran vessel that had camped itself on Devon's moon."

"Have the Orieli offered any explanation how a Kran ship managed to slip past their Line Tracking Net?"

"I don't see an issue here, Illeran. The M-4s will take out the Kran vessel and that will be the end of it."

Illeran looked coldly at Katan and gave a low hiss. "If you want that second term as Commissioner, you'll have to start using what little brains you've got. Tell me. Why are the Orieli here?"

Katan resented Illeran's patronizing tone, but he could not ignore the question.

"To prevent the Celi-Kran from finding us." Hiss.

"We've got a damaged Kran ship sitting on Devon's moon. What does that tell you?"

Katan's tongue flicked out quickly, his mind working furiously. "That they have now found us—"

"Not us, you fool! The Krans think they have found the Orieli!"

Katan frowned. "I'm not dumb, Illeran. The Orieli want to prevent the Krans from communicating that information and they suspect that the M-4s may not be up to the job."

"Excellent. And what should be our response?"

"I will instruct COMPALOPS that the M-4 force commander seek Orieli's assistance in neutralizing the Kran ship."

"Prima Scout In Tain is a good commander, Katan, and may have issued such instruction already. However, it won't do any harm if you talk to him."

"You realize, of course, the Orieli are in technical violation of our territory."

"It will be a moot point if that Kran ship gets away from us," Illeran said dryly. "What's your threat assessment?"

Through the Valley of Shadow

"My Bureau has worked the issue, but the bottom line is that we don't have much. The only thing I can give you is a comparative perspective. You have seen the brief regarding the unfortunate encounter recently between an Orieli survey cruiser and a linked triad of Master Scout Keller's M-4s off Sol. Tactically a disaster, but it gave us valuable information and the figures are bleak. A single Orieli ship probably has a four-to-one superiority over an M-4, and a Kran ship is supposed to be a comparable weapons platform. What's worse, the Orieli ship wasn't even a proper warship."

That got Illeran's attention.

"The implication is stark," Katan went on. "To honor the Kran threat, I will recommend that we release additional M-6 squadrons to Sargon and Palean Union commands. Getting a few more M-6s built would be prudent. I'll also look very closely at accelerating the new M-9 program, given the lead time for their construction."

Illeran pursed his lips and stared hard at the young Commissioner.

"What you're advocating will effectively put the Serrll on a war footing."

"That's right."

"Mmm. What about a potential *Orieli* threat?" Illeran demanded and his jaws worked quickly.

"It's a relevant point. The Orieli are almost as much a mystery as are the Krans. Their non-belligerency *appears* to be genuine. It could also be indifference on their part. To understand them, we should be looking at what they have done, not what they have said. Keep in mind, Illeran, that in the pursuit of their interests, they have brushed aside our protests regarding the protectorate status of the Sol system. LTN Station Twelve is now a reality. We can draw our own conclusions from that," Katan mused and gave a wry smile. So, the old fish-face could be rattled like anyone else.

"Keep me informed." Illeran cut contact and the Wall

broke into random color patterns.

He didn't like what Katan said, any of it. As Director of the Bureau of Colonial and Protectorate Affairs, incursion on an outpost or protectorate fell under his direct responsibility. Having Devon attacked was one thing. Outposts all around the Serrll Combine came in for a share of that from overzealous fringe groups, and the Paleans were particularly notorious. Their Alikan Union Party extremists held a dim view on interfering with the natural order of things. Religious groker shit! The fringe, he could handle. It was the strategic impact of two alien races on Serrll's doorstep that made him uneasy.

He reached with a long finger and touched pads on the comms console. When the Wall cleared, Terchran's scaly features focused into view.

"Fa'sure, you look like you're about to lay an egg," Terchran said, his face split in a humorless grin.

Illeran merely grunted at another one of Terchran's attempts at dry humor.

"I didn't call you to listen to your feeble wit."

"Then what is it?" Hiss.

"I think it's time that we had another long chat with our ambitious Sargon colleague."

"You mean, Ed-Kani?"

"Arrange a meeting," Illeran ordered. "Tonight, if possible."

"Why the rush?" Terchran asked, noting the deep concern on Illeran's face. "Has anything happened?"

"It's Devon 3-VL4."

"What about Devon?" Terchran demanded, suddenly alert. "What are you talking about?"

"An Orieli survey cruiser intercepted a Kran ship when it got too close to their Line Tracking Net. There was an engagement and the Kran ship sustained damage—"

"And it's holed up on Devon to affect repairs," Terchran finished for him.

"Exactly."

"What has this got to do with Ed-Kani?"

"Don't you see?" Illeran hissed with annoyance. "The Ori-eli LTN curves down from above the Palean Union and runs all the way past the Sargon Directorate. Palean and Sargon outposts will be first in line to be hit if the Krans decide to push toward us."

Terchran's fishy black eyes squinted and his long slender neck tilted slightly as he stared hard at Illeran. "It's not a pleasant scenario, but not exactly news either. His latest merger campaign strategy used that very fact to bolster support."

"An attack on Devon might be just the catalyst he and his AUP Provisional Committee need to sway the moderate elements within the Palean Congress, and the merger will be a done deal!" Illeran snarled and his tongue flicked out in a blur.

"Fa'sure. I'll speak to him. Do you want Ti Inai there?"

"No. He lusts after personal power. Ed-Kani is the visionary and therefore much more dangerous."

* * *

Smoke rose in gray tendrils toward a brittle blue sky, dissipating slowly in the frigid morning haze. Drifting banks of silent gray fog shrouded the blackened, twisted ruins of Devon's Center. Thick frost covered the steep foothills still lying deep in morning shadow. Beyond the valley the ice-covered peaks glittered like a giant's crown, trailing jagged streamers of cloud from high-velocity winds. Hugging the steep slopes, heavy dark bands of fog rolled ponderously through the shadowy ravines. Devon's sun, a sliver of yellow-white radiance, peeked above the valley's rim and flooded the hills with light.

Almost invisible, no larger than a water-worn pebble, the scanner probe drifted slowly toward the seared skeleton of the Center, its twin towers now nothing more than twisted frames. The subspace antenna array was a fused puddle of slag from which partially melted pieces of the grid protruded in frozen agony.

Detecting movement below it, the probe stopped and hovered, its electronic eyes rotated as they scanned the surface. Beside one of the intact wall frames of the tower complex, what looked like a squat bean pod, pale orange and smooth, shimmering a faint yellow from its protective shield, moved along a wall. As it moved a cut panel gaped like a black mouth drawn back in a thin grimace. The panel detached, held horizontal by a force beam and began to move. The oval orange shape drifted slowly after it toward an already cut stack of panels. The probe shifted its attention, noting the two neat rows of stacked panels and girders being added to by other silently moving orange shapes.

"What in the pits are those things?" Aill piped in high treble.

Mataeer shrugged as he watched the scanner trace with keen interest. "According to the Orieli, nanometric constructs," he said quietly. "Kran worker units, judging by their configuration."

"Ach!" Aill exhaled noisily through flared nostrils. "They make my skin crawl simply looking at them."

Mataeer nodded in silent agreement. There was something totally alien and menacing in those deceptively innocent shapes drifting silently through the frozen landscape. He had watched the Center since first light, careful to keep the scanner probe from getting too close. Even so, earlier in the morning the first probe detected the shadow of one of the patrolling bulbous scout craft and suddenly ceased transmission.

Aill was tired and irritable, his tunic looked like he felt, rumpled and dirty. Since the attack, he had been too busy coordinating activities between the shelters to afford the luxury of sleep. Some of his staff unexpectedly cracked under the strain and he replaced them. Most of those men had families, confirming his opinion that ecoforming was not a family job. If he

174

lived through this there would be some changes.

He took a deep breath, felt his barrel chest expand, and exhaled with a hiss. With one hand, he wiped oily sweat off his face and glanced at his exec with quiet satisfaction. He figured that after last night, Mataeer deserved command of his own project. It would have been impossible to coordinate the web of tasks between the stations and atmosphere processors without Mataeer's stolid support.

"Any sign of the two Kran scouts?" he demanded suddenly. "It's been over an hour since they took off."

"When they dropped out of scanner range, they were maintaining a heading for the moon," Mataeer replied absently. "None of the other shelters have reported seeing them."

"How long before that M-3 gets here?"

"*Kopan*?" Mataeer glanced at the chronometer trace. "Just under an hour."

"An hour," Aill repeated slowly. "Keep an eye on things, will you? I've got to talk to the others. Things are getting out of hand."

"They are just anxious, Aill."

"Ach! We're all anxious."

They carved the underground complex out of existing natural caverns. One hundred and sixty years ago, it served as the first ground station on the frozen world. It had never been completely abandoned, but its age showed in faded wall lining, hairline cracks that ran along pressure lines, and in the musty damp atmosphere whose smell the air purifiers were never quite able to remove.

With the imminent arrival of the M-3 sweeper, everyone expected that things would immediately return to normal. Some of the crew were getting impatient and annoyed at having to endure the sparse comforts of the old base. What did they expect, a going-home party? Walking along the lined tunnel, Aill knew that after this, Devon would never be the same. An increased Fleet presence was the least he could look forward to.

The unpaired professionals, most of them at any rate, had stood firm and calmly went about their duties. The men with families in tow were more worried about their partners and digits, understandably enough, than about their work. They had all gone soft, he mused bleakly, starting to take things for granted.

Holy worm shit!

He'd been telling the Bureau of Colonial and Protectorate Affairs for years that ecoforming and families wasn't a good combination. Taming a planet all too often made women widows and men left without a partner. But would the Bureau listen? Hah! Bureaucratic record shufflers and buck passers all of them. Blasphemers against the Path!

Still, he admitted grudgingly, no one could have predicted what happened. And Devon *was* a Class Five world, suitable for preliminary colonization.

To the pits with it! He was a planetary engineer, not a politician. Handling Krans did not fall under his terms of reference.

The cable-tube took him down to the recreation level where stragglers hurried to get to the main hall. Children ran screeching down the corridor, oblivious to the worried grownups. People moved out of his way as he strode purposefully past them. An excited buzz trailed in his wake.

Someone grabbed his arm and stopped him. "What's going on, Aill? When are we—"

Aill shook off the hand and glared at the man, who after a moment shrank back.

"Yeah! When is the Fleet going to—"

"Are we free to go back—"

"Quiet!" Aill bellowed, but his high treble voice didn't carry well. He clenched his hands and scowled at the faces pressed around him. "All of you! I'll tell you what I know. But not here! Ach!"

In the main hall the chatter died down as he appeared with a muttering crowd in tow. Everyone gradually found a seat or leaned against a wall. Aill walked to the podium with brisk strides, noting the worried looks from his senior assistants. He clasped his hands behind his back to stop them fluttering and faced the gathering.

"We've been here one night and you're already behaving like a disorganized mob," he chided them. His black eyebrows were drawn together in a frown and his pinched olive complexion flushed with genuine anger.

"As I explained already," he spoke quietly and pushed forward his massive barrel chest to full effect, "the Center has been attacked by two scout-like craft and we lost all subspace comms capability. Reports from the other ground stations show their facilities intact, but subjected to a massive EM surge. The electromagnetic energy pulse hasn't harmed our systems or the organic molecular chip circuitry, so we're effectively functional. However, with the loss of long-range space observation capability, we're deaf and blind.

"As you know, after the initial attack the alien scouts landed at the Center. What appear to be robot units are now dismantling the remaining structures. It's pretty obvious that materiel acquisition is their primary objective. As to what they are, I can only guess. It's likely we've been attacked by a Celi-Kran ship which sustained damage in some engagement, probably with an Orieli vessel."

"What's the Fleet doing about all this?" a shrill voice called out and a murmur rippled like a wave through the assembly.

"I am expecting an M-3 within the hour, with supporting units arriving sometime afterward."

"A sweeper against a Kran ship? We all saw what happened to *Valetta*," someone snorted derisively to a ripple of nervous titters.

"That's what the support units are for," Aill pointed out patiently. "*Kopan* is only supposed to scout the tactical situation and report. Any action that needs to be taken against the Krans will be left to the heavies."

"I'll tell you what the tactical situation is," another voice called out. "It sucks!"

Nasty chuckles and hollow laughter swept through the crowd.

"What about us?" a throaty voice rang out. "How long are we going to be stuck here?"

"Our shelters are not under any immediate threat," Aill said. "We're all safe. If you remain calm and do your jobs, we shall remain so. Ach!"

"And if those Kran things decide to come after us? We don't have weapons to defend ourselves. What then, Mr. Controller?"

An excited buzz rippled through the crowd. Aill waited for it to die down. "Firstly, I don't believe—"

"Hope more likely."

Aill paused until they settled down. When the silence began to get heavy, he took a deep breath and thrust out his chest.

"Now listen to me. All of you! Ach! None of the other ground stations have been occupied and they represent far softer targets. The Krans probably know that we're around somewhere. If not from random transmissions, then from the scanner probe they neutralized this morning. Given their apparent objective, attacking us would serve no tactical purpose. Now, I—"

One of the assistant controllers tapped his shoulder and pointed at the comms plate. "Urgent message from Executive Mataeer, sir."

Aill grunted. With a last glance at the assembly, he quickly walked to the plate. Mataeer nodded briefly and grinned broadly. "We had a flyby from two alien ships, Aill."

"Kran?"

"No." Mataeer shook his head. "These are larger, roughly saucer-shaped, approximately forty-five katalans in diameter. Tentative computer identification makes them out as Orieli RV/4 darts. Scout ships, Aill!"

Chapter Eight

The afternoon shadows slowly crept across the dunes. The desert shimmered and twisted from the day's relentless heat. On Terr's port quarter, a rolling brown wall of sand advanced remorselessly toward him. He could almost hear the thin shriek of tortured wind and the urgent hiss of tumbling sand. The marrakan storm front made the air lumpy and the combie shuddered and skidded as it punched through pockets of roiling air.

Thin ribbons of sand, dragged in the wake of high-velocity winds, streaked the amber sky overhead. Through the veil of scudding browns the sun's bloated orange disk glared white in the center. The wall of sand rolled and tumbled in slow motion like pipeline surf. The rounded bulges of the front glowed an eerie yellow, reflecting the hellfire rage that boiled within. An occasional electrical discharge flickered white inside the advancing wall.

He glanced at Dhar sitting beside him, then turned his head and watched the dunes grow and slip beneath him. The sands gave way to spreading patches of tarad grass, the leaves flashing, whipped by a frantic wind. The combie circled and came down in a low curving descent. Below, children urged restless oark toward the corrals. They waved as the combie flew over them.

Men were throwing extra lashing over thatched roofs of the mud huts and tied them to anchor stakes driven deep into the sand. Poultry fluttered in alarm as children, arms milling wildly, ran them down. Fine sand rolled through the village in gusts, melting outlines and blurring shapes.

The combie sank, rocked, then settled, and the plant whined down. Terr pulled back the bubble and sat there while the wind roared around him and tore through his hair. He blinked at its abrasive touch. Teena hurried toward them. Feeling empty and drained, he climbed out and the bubble closed behind him with a click. Dhar stood beside him, his cape fluttering and snapping in the wind. Terr touched his arm and nodded. Dhar looked at him, glanced at Teena, then turned abruptly and walked toward the huts.

She wiggled her fingers after him in greeting and looked searchingly at Terr, walked slowly toward him and stopped. One hand held across her chest, her clear gaze was questioning. Terr knew his face appeared an empty mask and only his eyes betrayed the churning emotions threatening to burst forth. The sand shifted beneath him as he reached for her and drew her against him, holding her fiercely. The wind whistled and howled around them. Her robes whipped about her legs and clapped like muted thunder. He stood over her, their foreheads touching.

Suddenly, she pulled away and grabbed his hand. Bracing herself against the wind, she picked her way toward one of the huts with him in tow. In the lee of the hut they shook off the sand and she gave him a flashing smile.

He crouched, pulled back the grass mat, and stepped quickly into the gloomy interior. The wind howled outside, swirling dust after them. He slid a peelath panel across the doorway, ushering in comparative silence.

"Ah, this sand," she mumbled and shrugged off the robe, leaving her in a brief tight shirt and oark skin shorts that revealed her fine figure. With a quick grin, she moved down the narrow corridor toward their room. Inside, oark oil lamps cast deep shadows among the corners and he breathed deeply of the smoke-tinged air and the faint mustiness from cushions lying on the carpeted floor.

She ran her hands through long black bangs, tilted her head, and shook out the last of the sand. "I wonder how long these storms last?" she demanded absently.

"The marrakan? Days," he said and grinned at her wickedly. Her head jerked and her pale green eyes widened in consternation. "Or it could blow itself out in an hour," he added with a chuckle. "This one, by the looks of it, is going to last a while. Time for us to snuggle up."

Her eyes softened into an impish grin. "Beast!" she murmured and rolled her hips.

He exhaled loudly and stretched his arms until the joints creaked. He sank to the waiting cushions and looked at her with tender longing.

"Come here," he said softly and opened his arms.

She knelt before him, hands in her lap, slender fingers working in agitation. The corners of her eyes were creased in puzzlement and her small mouth looked soft and vulnerable. He wanted so much to touch those lips and feel their taste.

"What happened out there, Terr?" she said, her voice breathless.

He brushed the softness of her cheek, not saying anything. She pulled back and went pale.

"You and Dhar—"

"Everything is all right, pet."

He was back at the oasis of Katai Than where the echoes of thunder he unleashed still rolled through the gorge. When he focused on her small oval face the thunder he heard reflected the hollow booming of the wind outside.

His anger and rage purged, left him satisfied and at peace, but feeling wrung out. He was a hollow shell yearning to have the emptiness in his soul filled. He felt the pull of Athal Than and did not fear the gods anymore. Judgment was upon him and his sins were many. He could now accept the release that surely awaited him. His only regret lay at leaving Teena.

Her small hand rested lightly in his. He gave it a gentle squeeze, then lifted it to his lips. Her skin soft and warm, he tugged and she was in his arms. He did not kiss her, content just to hold her. After a moment, he leaned back and sank to the cushions. They lay there, aware of each other and the hollow booming of the wind. Her head on his shoulder, he stroked her hair. He knew the questions she wanted to ask and he talked softly. He wanted to reassure himself as much as to answer her, or maybe he only wanted to share his release with her.

"I almost killed him," he said simply, seeing Dhar with Death coiled about him. "He just stood there looking at me. He didn't say anything, almost as if he expected to die. I didn't care. All I wanted was to lash out at him. When the lightning struck him and he fell, I fell with him and his cries of pain were mine." He shook his head in wonder.

"All I had to do was will it and he would have died. I wanted him dead and. Then, in all my rage and anger, I realized that he was still my brother and I couldn't bring myself to kill him. But anger and hate were the only things that kept me going. Without it, I was empty and I didn't want to live. Even having you wasn't enough." He brushed her cheek. "You see, my love, I walked in the shadow of Death and thought myself immortal. I believed to be beyond judgment, handing out justice, when in reality, I learned nothing from the teachings of the Discipline. When I confronted him, finally comprehending what I was about to do, everything crumbled around me. Suddenly, I didn't know what to do. To kill him, I had to be prepared to destroy myself and I came so close to doing it."

"Terr—"

"No, don't say anything. You're here with me now and that's enough. That's all I ever wanted." His arms went around her and her head rested against him.

* * *

When Terr opened his eyes, dawn struggled through the blanket of night. Gloom still shrouded the hut. Beside him, Teena breathed deeply, her head nestled in the hollow of his left arm, hair spilling in black waves across his chest. He thrust his right hand behind his head and stared vacantly at the ceiling.

Oark snorted outside, pacing restlessly around the corral. Muffled footfalls padded through the sand and the silence returned. He could not hear the wind. The storm must have either blown itself out or wandered deeper into the Saffal. He cleared his throat and she moaned softly and shifted beside him. She blinked, lifted her head, and stared at him, still asleep, before her eyes focused.

"Feel like going for a walk?" He looked at her, surprised at the urgency and intensity in his voice.

"You mean now?" she mumbled and he nodded.

Her eyes regarded him, doubting his sanity, then grunted in resignation and rolled away. They didn't pack anything. It wasn't that kind of walk.

Outside, the eastern sky was a sheet of crimson. The air crisp, his skin tingled. Untidy drifts of sand stood piled around the huts and fence posts. Silent hooded figures moved around the corral. The oark stomped restlessly.

"Terr! I'm freezing!" she protested and hugged herself. He gave her shoulders a quick squeeze.

"Come."

She cast a longing glance at the mud hut and its warmth, muttered something under her breath, and reluctantly padded after him.

Sand crunched and whispered beneath their sandaled feet. Above them, Aribus made a pale circle in the sky. The dunes and the drifts gradually gave way to rocky flats and clumps of strewn boulders. Their feet slapped noisily against the bare stone. In the predawn gloom the desert suddenly became empty and Teena felt very vulnerable. Not for the first time, she wondered how anyone could live here.

He stopped, looked around and spread his arms. "We're here," he said, wearing a smug look of satisfaction.

She placed her hands on her hips and stared at the bare rocks looming before them. A solitary dwarf peelath hung its branches over them.

"You dragged me away from a perfectly good, warm sleep to see this? A bunch of boulders?" she demanded in outrage. "If you don't explain this in the next minute, I'll…I'll never speak to you again!"

He smiled at her and laughed. "Feel this air. Isn't it great?" He took a deep breath, held it and exhaled noisily.

"Terr…"

He chuckled and cocked his head at the two needles of red rock guarding a gloomy passage.

"Over there. Go on, take a look."

Expecting a prank, she hesitated. Nothing there but a narrow cleft between two boulders. With a backward glance at him, she slowly walked into the dark narrows, almost like a tunnel. The deep gorge suddenly opened before her, falling away between torn cliffs.

She stood at the lip and looked down in amazement. A narrow path wound its way into a cutting full of gloom and shadow. Tall strands of tarad grass covered the steep slopes waiting for a breath of wind to get them whispering. Twisted peelath hugged the gorge walls, the branches limp and lifeless, tired from the whipping frenzy of the storm the night before. A sand drift, piled against a boulder near her, sent a thin stream into the gloom below. It hardly made a whisper. She fancied she could hear a trickle of running water, but that was impossible. She stepped through and found herself in a miniature wonderland. She gaped in awe, unable to believe that something like this could exist here. She clasped her hands, gave a small shout of glee, skipped down the rough path, and disappeared among the shadows.

Terr smiled indulgently after her. It was getting light quickly and the sky turned pale amber. On his right the horizon brightened and the desert stirred, becoming alive. He followed her, his descent more dignified.

Reaching the bottom, he looked around the rocky slabs,

the dark hollows and the twisted winding passage of the gorge. This used to be one his favorite hiding places, back when he couldn't talk, when he was mad, recovering from his crash. It had been a while and he had forgotten. He felt a breath of cold air brush past him and shivered. He found her sitting on bare sand, propped against a scaly peelath trunk, knees against her chest. She scowled at him, accusation and wonder sparkled in her eyes.

"Men! You're all the same." She shook her head in exasperation. "Dhar had me here for days and never thought to tell me about this place," she muttered darkly, her mouth set in a pout.

"It must have slipped his mind," he said easily and offered her his hand. "Come, we aren't there yet."

He led her down the winding, sandy floor. The steep walls leaned over them, keeping them in shadow. Gradually the walls fell away as they climbed, and the gorge widened into the open desert beyond. Directly ahead of them the sky changed, turning bright yellow.

"Terr—"

"Wait," he whispered urgently and pointed.

It happened so quickly that her breath caught and she gazed in wonder. The desert suddenly bloomed with light and the sky turned a rich amber. The sun made a yellow crack, forming a halo of rippling color around the gorge entrance that sent a shaft of golden light past them. She turned and pressed her knuckles against her mouth. The gloom and the shadows fled, leaving the gorge full of brightness and magic and warmth. The rocks were transformed into rich reds and browns, and the orange and yellow sands glittered and sparkled. The tarad grass made sharp shadows and the broad peelath branches looked welcoming and comforting.

"Oh my," she whispered, entranced. The light behind her softened and the magic faded. She gave a deep sigh and glanced over her shoulder at him, a mischievous smile playing at the corner of her mouth. "You wonderful man, you. Thank you for letting me see this."

"I wanted to share something of this land with you," he said awkwardly. "To show you some of its magic." A blue-gray haze mellowed the harsh colors of the gorge, adding to its mystery. He took her hand and led her back down among the shadows. They found a comfortable spot between two peelath. She sat on a boulder, her legs dangling, absently tapping against the stone. He stretched out his feet and played with a strand of grass.

"Dhar and I spent a lot of time here. Even before I regained my memory, I remember exploring this place. I guess it gave me a measure of peace and comfort. The kids play here all the time."

"Terr?" She placed a small hand on his shoulder. "Dhar, is he all right?"

"Everything is all right now."

Her eyes were deep pools of green and serious. In a characteristic gesture, she brushed away a rebellious lock of hair.

"What's wrong? You've been brooding and tossing all night." She shifted to face him fully and hugged her knees. The long, broad branches of the peelath hung above them in silent company, blotting out the sky.

He picked up a pebble and threw it against a boulder. It hit with a flat clang and bounced off its side. Sitting there beside her in the cool of the dawn, he felt himself standing in an eye of a storm where one step in any direction would fling him into chaos. A step he had to take and he felt forces shift around him, pulling at him, calling him. Shrouded in shadow, the towering escarpment of Athal Than lay brooding as it waited for him.

"When I crashed, not very far from here, as a matter of fact, I found myself in the deep desert. Alone, injured, and burning with thirst. I exchanged the fire of the survival blister for the inferno of the Saffal. At the time, I couldn't see any difference between the two. Still, I couldn't just give up and die.

Call it stubbornness, if you will. I guess that out there, I really did die in a way because what the Wanderers found wasn't me. They found an empty shell, a shadow of myself. The desert claimed the rest, or the gods did."

Teena sat there, tense, hardly daring to breathe. He had never spoken of his crash in any detail and she listened avidly.

"Did you know that not every Wanderer has the power? Fact. All male children undergo training in the Discipline, but it takes more than that to make a Wanderer."

"Why only men? It sounds somewhat chauvinistic." She grinned impishly and he chuckled.

"The gods feel threatened by women."

"So they should," she said archly. "Really, why only men?"

He shrugged. "Death is a destroyer and women are givers of life. There has always been conflict between the two. Study any religion with a supreme male deity."

She looked at him strangely. "You mean it, don't you?"

"Some women have tried to walk in the god's shadow. None have ever survived."

She pondered that. "Why did they permit you to take the trial? You were not a native-born of Anar'on and you knew nothing of the Discipline."

"That's the cruel irony of it. To pull me out of whatever hell I sunk to, Dhar had to go into my mind. He fused my psyche or soul, take your pick, back into my body and I was reborn. At that moment, we became one thought, one life, one existence. Part of him lives in me as I live in him. He became a brother I never had, more than a brother. He became my very shadow. I would gladly die to protect him and he would do the same for me, without question or hesitation. But I wasn't fully restored. For that, I had to face the gods of Death."

"The teachings of the Discipline, he left with you also," she added, understanding.

"As I left my heritage with him."

Her face was a pretty frown. "Ah, that's why you couldn't

187

understand how he could turn against you?"

"I understood, all right," he said bitterly. "You see, as a native-born Wanderer, Dhar would never resort to treachery or deceit. Unfortunately, my soul wasn't so pure. Whatever else he picked out of me, my darker side he took as well. And that part would resort to everything I believed Dhar had done. Everything I believed myself capable of doing."

"What happened on the Moon, Terr?"

"He didn't tell you?"

"Yes, but—"

"It's simple enough. He locked the controls of the dart computer which caused the ship to crash to Earth."

"But why?"

He dreaded the moment that had to come.

"It's Anabb and what I do for the Diplomatic Branch. Dhar was protecting me from something I had done on my last assignment. You don't know all of it, and perhaps you do if you've read my reports," he said and grinned at her.

She arched her neck and looked defiant. "Most of your assignments were above my clearance, which I thought unfair."

"I'm not surprised. You see, part of my job involves more than counterintelligence." He hesitated, not sure how to say it, then looked at her. "It also involved the removal of political undesirables."

She didn't immediately understand what he said. Then her eyes widened and her face drained in shock. She shrank from him.

"You killed using your power?"

She probably wasn't even aware of the accusation in her voice and the words cut savagely. Something had been destroyed between them and the world wasn't as innocent as she believed. It was a side of him she had always hesitated to explore, given the nature of his work. Back at the office, they would talk, but to have it revealed like this...

"That's right. I killed!" He stood and looked at her. "It

would be easy for me to say it was necessary, that integrity of the Serrll depended on it. Maybe it did. I don't know. I'm not going to try and make it noble. The truth is, I used the hand of Death to satisfy my need to exercise the power I had. You cannot know the keen thrill and feeling of invulnerability I feel when I take on my aspect." He clenched his fists as Death stirred within him.

"But to destroy?"

He heard the outrage in her voice and his shoulders sagged.

"Death has a hunger as well," he said wearily. Emotions chased each other across her face in confusion.

"I can see how Anabb would recognize your power and its value to him," she whispered at length.

"That came later—"

"I'll bet he didn't have to push hard to set you on the path of being his righteous avenger."

"No, he didn't, and I took the job gladly." He spread his hands in a helpless plea. "Teena, how can I explain it to you when it wasn't clear even to me. Idealistic and trusting, I thought that at last, I had the means to right some of the wrongs."

"By killing," she glared at him, her eyes cold and hostile.

"Don't you see? I believed in the need! Gods know they deserved to die," he snarled and kicked at the sand.

"And the morality of it?"

"Whose morality? Mine, Anabb's, the government's? Who makes the rules? You cannot be so naïve not to know how the system works."

"You had the Discipline."

"Yeah, I had the Discipline, and with it an arrogance that prevented me from appreciating its value or the responsibility its application demanded."

"You knew enough to use it to kill."

"But you knew that already," Terr shot back. "When we first met, I told you there might be a time when I would have to raise my hand against another."

"As an assassin?"

"All right! Perhaps my pang of conscience comes a bit late. If the gods can forgive me when I walk through the shadow of Athal Than, then…" He hesitated, knelt before her, and folded his hands in her lap. "Maybe you could too," he whispered, searching her face.

"What do you mean?" She looked at him in alarm and real fear clouded her eyes.

"I must face the god of Death again. Call it a test of faith, a judgment. It's calling me even now and I shall have no rest until I answer it. Twice more must I face him and each is a step into the unknown, a revelation of self and a glimpse beyond my mortal desires. It is a surrender and a readiness to face obliteration not only of body, but also of one's soul. The time for my second trial has come."

She shuddered, and he wanted to reach and draw her against him, but he couldn't move. A storm raged inside him, threatening to spill and destroy everything around him. He feared if he moved, she would be pulled into it. He lowered his head into her lap.

"I've been waiting for this release since the first time I allowed the shadow of Death to fall on another life. It takes years of intensive training to understand the Discipline and the cultural environment within which it's practiced. I missed out on all that, but I still thought I could wield Death with impunity. How was I to know that with power comes humility, not righteous arrogance." He lifted his head and smiled wanly. "Who knows? I might live through it. I haven't screwed up everything. Dhar and I are brothers again. You're here. Maybe that will help counterbalance some of my sins."

"Oh, Terr." Her eyes filled, glistening bright and clear. Fat tears spilled and ran down her cheeks. "Just when we're together again, when I thought everything was all right, you're telling me I might lose you?"

With a tender smile, he reached and brushed away what might have been his tears.

"Don't cry for me, Teena," he said lovingly. "This had to happen."

"What if you don't come back? I don't want to live without you."

Then she stepped into his arms and he whispered the soft, tender words as they came to him.

* * *

Beanab shifted uncomfortably in his formchair, angry and intimidated. Prime Director Kernami Asai Tainam's scrutinizing ebony eyes clouded and the narrow gaunt face twisted into a disapproving frown.

"Have you spoken to the Triumvirate about this?" Kernami demanded sharply and Beanab pulled back in alarm, imagining Kernami climbing through the Wall.

"No," he said sullenly, regretting his impulse to call the Prime Director. "Not yet. As head of the Triumvirate, I wanted you—"

"Spare me your excuses, Beanab," Kernami snapped irritably. "Can't you see that Ed-Kani and Ti Inai are using you for their own ends? And you would risk Pizgor's independence just to further your personal ambition?"

"I don't see anything of the sort," Beanab pouted, attempting to stare Kernami down and failed. "What have the Revisionists done for Pizgor?"

"They have given us freedom."

"Some freedom!" Beanab snorted in disdain. "Their Paravan Trading Association is squeezing our shipping markets and you talk about freedom."

"That's how business is done, Beanab."

"That's not how it's done on Captal. Listen to me. Pizgor is surrounded with nowhere to expand. While we maintain our nonaligned independent status, we're shunned by all, dismissed as irrelevant. Right now our five systems don't count for anything. But they could! Your support for the Unified Independent Front is ill-advised and your misguided action has damaged our interests and earned the enmity of our powerful neighbors."

"You mean Sargon and the Paleans?"

"Aligning ourselves with them will not mean the end of our identify, Kernami."

"You're talking of alignment and I'm talking about selling us out. You're a bigger fool than I thought if you believe that Sargon would hand over an Executive Council seat to someone like you if the Alikan Union Party absorbed Pizgor's systems."

"That was uncalled for," Beanab declared coldly and thrust out his chest. "I worked hard to reach the General Assembly, and even harder for my position as Secretary to the Moderator. I tell you that you're wrong, Kernami, blinded by your distrust of Ed-Kani and Ti Inai. You must convince the Triumvirate to join the Alikan Union Party. Pizgor will be in a position to hold the balance of power. The Karkans and their Servatory Party machine will be swept aside, making way for a new order." Beanab beamed triumphantly, already imagining himself a director in the Executive Council and a major player in the Serrll. "You and the rest of the Triumvirate are removed from the real flow of progressive political thought to realize what is going on in Captal. That's why I'm here to advise you. And I urge you to meet with Ed-Kani and Ti Inai and listen to what they have to say."

Watching Beanab remonstrate, completely carried away by his vision of power, Kernami wondered how the fool had managed to get himself into the General Assembly to begin with.

"You have learned nothing of the lesson five years ago when Ed-Kani and his Provisional Committee almost destroyed our commerce," Kernami said sadly and shook his head. "Two years later they tried to do the same thing to Kaleen. Your own intelligence sources have confirmed a deliberate policy by Sargon and the Paleans of sidelining our cargo handling facilities, thereby starving our carrier lines of business. There is nothing overtly illegal about it, as the action does not directly contravene the Trade Protection Act. However, the end result is the same, namely to bring pressure to bear on the Triumvirate to cede Pizgor to Sargon.

"There is one other thing that you have forgotten. Above all else, a political center must deliver good government. Government for all. When that is forgotten, it risks becoming irrelevant. Ask yourself this. Swept up in its dream of creating a Greater Sargon, will the Alikan Union Party bring good government for all? It's the one crucial difference between them and Sofam. Sofam understands well the working and application of force, otherwise they would have lost the ruling government majority a long time ago. I also understand the working and application of force, Beanab," Kernami said and his mouth firmed. "At my earliest convenience, I shall recommend to the Triumvirate that your position as member of the General Assembly be revoked. I shall also request that Moderator Torres suspends your duties as his secretary."

Beanab felt his face drain as he listened to Kernami's declaration, unable to believe the magnitude of the disaster about to overtake him.

"You…you cannot do that," he spluttered. "The elections! I still have two years of my term to serve."

"As you pointed out, being head of the Triumvirate carries with it some influence. I don't anticipate too many problems affecting your immediate removal. Instead of occupying a director's chair, you will be warming a Pizgor shuttle seat within a few days."

The Wall cleared and random color patterns swam in its depths, reflecting the chaos of Beanab's thoughts. He looked about him, at the expanse of his desk, the deep carpet pile beneath his feet, the expensive wall paneling, and his anger grew. To give up all he had fought to achieve? The years of minority interest struggles on Pizgor before reaching Captal and the Assembly, with its own battles, to be all swept into oblivion and anonymity by Kernami? He found it maddening. He could not allow that to happen, he would not.

With a look of grim determination, he reached for the console pad on his desk.

"Yes, sir?" his assistant replied.

"Get me Executive Director Ed-Kani Takao immediately."

"Yes, sir."

* * *

"You haven't spoken to your party leader, Tao Karam, yet, have you?" Ed-Kani hissed and his jaws snapped impatiently.

Ti Inai smiled oily and his hands twined. "I arranged a meeting with him for tomorrow, friend Ed-Kani. After the General Assembly session with the Orieli." His black eyes darted slyly as he bobbed his head.

"Good," Ed-Kani nodded with satisfaction. It was important that he brief Ti Inai alone before the fool spoiled everything.

"Why, what happened?"

"Terchran just called," Ed-Kani said with amusement. "It appears that Illeran is anxious to talk to me."

"Illeran!" Ti Inai started in alarm and his long hands twined in agitation. "Then he knows about Devon and the meeting with the Committee."

"Take it easy. It doesn't matter what he knows or suspects. This attack by the Celi-Kran is exactly what we needed. Tao Karam and his pacifists are in a corner with no way out. Just make sure you talk to me before you see him, understand?" He watched Ti Inai's eyes lose their panic. "It's imperative that you do."

"Don't underestimate the weight of his faction, friend Ed-Kani. This attack may help our cause, but the Committee should not see it as a winning tactic."

"We don't."

Ti Inai managed a weak smile and bobbed his head. "I will do as you ask."

Ed-Kani scowled as he cut contact. Ti Inai was a nervous woman and getting more nervous as the general elections drew nearer. The comms alert beeped immediately and he glared at it.

"What is it?" he hissed impatiently. "I said no calls."

"I'm sorry, sir, but Secretary Beanab Kari Anam insists."

Ed-Kani paused, wondering what the idiot wanted. Still, it might be amusing.

"Very well," he said. He touched a small pad on the table console and turned to the Wall. He watched with interest as Beanab fought to control his emotions. "Mr. Secretary," he hissed and bowed with mock formality.

"We have a problem," Beanab growled and his ebony eyes flashed angrily.

"You mean, you have a problem."

"Don't be flippant," Beanab snarled and clenched his fists over the table. "This is serious."

"I am out of time, Beanab," Ed-Kani said, suddenly tired of the game. "What do you want?"

"It's Prime Director Kernami Asai Tainam. He is threatening to have me removed from the General Assembly. What's more, he'll be recommending to the Pizgor Triumvirate to reject any talk of an alliance with Sargon or the Paleans."

Beanab's removal from the Assembly would be no loss, Ed-Kani reflected, but Kernami's action, although expected, still came as an unpleasant development.

"And when does he plan to do that?"

Beanab wiped his forehead. "Presumably after the Independent Representatives Conference convenes. He's on his way to Pizgor after visiting Anar'on, as you know, but it could be immediately."

"What do you want me to do about it?"

Beanab hesitated as he stared at Ed-Kani with mild distaste. He lifted his chin. "I want you to arrange it so that he doesn't talk to the Triumvirate, or anyone else."

"Do you know what you're asking?" Ed-Kani looked closely at Beanab, surprised he had overlooked the underlying resolve and strength in the man. Perhaps he'd been wrong in his estimate.

"You think me a fool to want to see Pizgor with its own independent voice," Beanab declared with a condescending sneer. "If Pizgor joins Sargon under the Alikan Union Party umbrella, you will carve up the third Executive Council seat with the Paleans. But I'll make sure that you'll not be pulling any double-crosses." Beanab grinned without humor and Ed-Kani saw something of Kernami's character in those eyes.

"Maybe I have underestimated you, Beanab," Ed-Kani admitted and his jaws worked quickly. "Still, there is a lot of work left to be done before we realize our ambitions."

"Wasted if Kernami convinces the Triumvirate to reject your offer. Remember, without Pizgor, you won't have enough systems to claim that third seat. Without it, the Sargon/Palean merger will be an impotent gesture."

Ed-Kani frowned. Did Beanab know about Devon? It didn't matter really, he would know soon enough. And he was right about Kernami. The Committee should have taken care of him years back. Well, it still wasn't too late to correct that oversight.

"Leave it with me. Tonight's Executive vote to sweep away the independent's seat may solve the problem for all of us. If not, Kernami will have an accident and I'll make sure the Karkans wear the blame."

Through the Valley of Shadow

"Play your games as long as Kernami dies."

When the Wall cleared, Ed-Kani stood, stretched his arms and headed for the cable-tube.

* * *

The two visitor gallery levels that ran beneath the main dome were filling fast with dignitaries from all over the Serrll. A sprinkling of ordinary Captal citizenry added local flavor. General Assembly sessions did not normally attract a packed house, but everyone wanted to see and hear just one thing—the Orieli. Government propaganda being what it was, many planetary heads had decided to come and judge the proceedings for themselves.

The Assembly representatives were slowly taking their seats or clustered in small groups along the aisles. The noise from hundreds of excited voices drifted and rolled like booming surf. Raised above the main chamber floor stood a three-tiered platform. The second one housed twelve seats reserved for the Executive Council Directors, arranged in a horn table, even though only ten positions were currently filled. The upper platform held a longer crescent table reserved for the senior commissioners. Behind an elegant transparent lectern, four exquisitely upholstered formchairs were laid out on the lower platform, reserved for visiting dignitaries. Above the platforms a giant Wall rippled with color.

They built the General Assembly chamber to house nine hundred delegate seats. It would be a long time before they were all occupied. An old building, round with a high domed roof, ancient Sofam cursive adorned the rim between the dome and the ornate walls. Debate still raged whether the edifice should be torn down to make way for more modern quarters, or to let it stand as a historical monument. Captal had its fill of historical monuments. Besides, the comfortable building lent a certain majesty to the assembly. Since no one could agree on the new design, it stood, venerated and hated.

When the dome dimmed and the chamber floor brightened, the gallery fell silent and the reps hurriedly took their seats. The nine Executive Directors emerged from a side doorway and took their positions with unhurried dignity. Torres strode after them and took his position as Moderator in the middle. Behind him came the commissioners, shuffling and jostling to their seats. The Zaronian and Cetan members of the Orieli delegation followed them. The aliens paused, looked around the chamber and unhurriedly took the two center visitor chairs.

On the floor between the platforms and the first row of seats stood a dark metallic square plate.

A soft chime reverberated through the chamber and broke the tense, expectant silence. Torres stood up and surveyed the floor, his image reflected in the Wall behind him, hugely magnified. He quietly introduced the special session of the General Assembly and the Orieli delegation.

"Executive Directors," he said and glanced briefly at his colleagues on either side of him, "Commissioners, Assembly Representatives, and honored guests." He spoke with quiet dignity demanded by the occasion, not having to shout. The chamber acoustics were perfect. "During the proceedings of this special session the usual protocols are waived. There will be ample opportunity for questions and discussion. This is not a partisan sitting, affecting as it does the whole Serrll Combine." Torres looked around the hushed chamber and nodded.

"Over the last few months there has been a lot of unfounded speculation regarding the Orieli Technic Union's incursion into Serrll space. In particular, their occupation of the Earth's Moon. You have all seen the briefs. To clarify the situation, the Executive Council has seen fit to grant the Orieli a hearing to personally explain their actions and the Celi-Kran threat which precipitated those actions." He swept a hand at the visitor chairs. "I want to introduce Karhide Zor-Ell, commander of the Orieli forces on this side of the Moanar, and Opturkarh Tremane."

Zor-Ell found the days passing slowly while he waited for the General Assembly session to be convened. He and his crew were kept busy with cultural exchange missions, but now, he was anxious to end it and head home. Serrll government maneuverings and the heavy smell of political intrigue hanging over Captal were getting stifling. He stood and clasped his hands behind his back as his eyes traveled slowly across the packed chamber. An undercurrent of hushed whispers rippled through the chamber as everyone waited expectantly. He could feel the tension in the small hall; small compared to the vast theater housing the Orieli Klanina assembly that housed over three thousand representatives.

He brought up his right hand and touched his forehead with the tips of his fingers. In perfect Serrll interlingua, his voice soft and even, he began speaking.

"Thank you Da Moderator. On behalf of the Orieli Technic Union, I wish to express my appreciation to the Serrll General Assembly for this opportunity to present our case. The Moanar Nebula lies two thousand light-years beyond the Palean Union. To you, it is but a yellow and orange smudge among the stars of The Arch, as you call the galaxy. To us the Moanar has loomed above our stars for millennia, ever since we ventured into this part of the galaxy. It's a wall 6,800 light-years long and four hundred deep. Five years ago, we managed to break through that barrier. Our journey of discovery eventually brought us to you. Beyond the nebula, our sphere of influence reaches along this galactic arm toward the hub. Our home space is a giant globular cluster more than 12,000 light-years above The Arch and contains some 1,900 inhabited systems."

He did not tell them anything new, but stated aloud it provoked an excited ripple of comment from the gallery. Ti Inai nodded thoughtfully and looked up from the repeater plate, carefully judging the mood of the chamber. The entire Serrll, even with its outposts and ecoforming planets, was only 321 systems. By comparison, the Serrll were small and vulnerable. It was important to keep that fact in mind, and to encourage it when speaking to Kaleen independents. His hands twined with pleasure. The Orieli were giving him everything he could have hoped for to counter Tao Karam's resistance to the merger. Much could depend on how these proceedings developed.

"Collectively the Orieli is a family of some 3,200 inhabited systems," Zor-Ell said. "We are not so much a unified political power as a loose association of regional and commercial conglomerates held together by mutual trade, exploration, and defense needs. This is an oversimplification, of course, but it serves to illustrate a philosophy based on economic expansion rather than political or military colonization. Conquest is easy. Peaceful coexistence takes work. In that, we share your philosophy. I don't pretend ours is a perfect society. In any pluralistic and free system, poverty, misery and strife do exist. During our fourteen-thousand-year history, we had our conflicts, but we managed to learn from past mistakes. We're still learning. Now, everything we have built, everything you have built, is threatened.

"We reached out beyond the Moanar with curiosity and met violence. The Celi-Kran are not organic lifeforms, but artificial constructs. There is empirical evidence to suggest they come from the adjacent galactic arm across the galaxy's core. We're endeavoring to prove that. However, all attempts at contacting them peacefully have failed. Pattern analysis of their responses suggests that they follow a single simple doctrine—destruction of all organic intelligence. To call them mindless or unreasoning would be a grave error. It takes a multi-faceted and complex culture to build and support starships." He paused, allowing a ripple of subdued commentary to pass through the chamber.

"We found worlds that faced the Krans and lost. There are

many such worlds, burned-out cinders. Our analysis indicates that some two thousand years ago or so, the Krans had an active presence near the Moanar. Why they withdrew, we cannot say, but they're back now. Our ships must have tripped some dormant sensor array that caused them to return. Whether the Krans of two thousand years ago are the Krans of today, we don't know. What is certain, they don't have knowledge of our systems, or yours. Powerful as their vessels are, even they find the Moanar impenetrable. Since making contact with our ships, they have mounted a systematic search for our worlds." Zor-Ell slowly swept his gaze across the gallery. "The only organized inhabited systems of any significance in this part of the galaxy are those of the Serrll Combine."

It took a moment of silence before the impact of that statement sank in. The gallery erupted with noise. Ti Inai cast a thoughtful glance at the other commissioners. They all appreciated the strategic implication.

Zor-Ell waited patiently for the inevitable ripple to subside.

"Accidental as it might be, you're involved in our struggle. The struggle may lay in your future, but it will be a struggle nonetheless. I don't stand here in apology for the Orieli Technic Union. We cannot undo the random factors that brought us together. However, recognizing the threat facing all of us, we took steps to minimize it. To prevent the Krans from attempting to traverse the Moanar, we have built a line of stations designed to track and limit their movements. Since our initial contact with the Serrll, we have extended the Line Tracking Net along the edge of Serrll space as far as the Sol system. In their search for us the Krans will encounter the LTN and will mount a concentrated effort to penetrate it. By taking the fight to them, we shall seek to deny them access to your space.

"Your worlds have not faced the ferocity of a Kran attack. I hope the LTN will maintain that ignorance. We are not unaware of the potential risk faced by the frontier worlds of the Sargon Directorate and the Palean Union. Some might view the

Line Tracking Net as an interdiction line limiting your expansion. Such concern is unwarranted. If you accept the risks, we won't stop you should you choose to expand as far as the Moanar Nebula. Two thousand light-years gives all of us ample opportunity for peaceful and mutually beneficial coexistence."

He raised his arm and pointed at the floor beside him. The PT plate scintillated briefly and on it lay a squat pale orange elongated shape looking something like a bean pod. The pod had a faint shimmer from the barely perceptible glow of its yellow containment shield.

An excited wave of voices moved through the chamber and the gallery as everyone stared in tense fascination at the captive alien object. The pod was totally smooth, but it did have odd dents and small rounded protrusions of unknown purpose and function. There were no visible sensor points, but everyone somehow felt it even now watched them with malevolent intent.

"This," Zor-Ell said and casually pointed at the pod, "is a captured specimen of one of the Celi-Kran configurations. This is an active unit kept immobile in a stasis field. Your scientists are welcome to study it. Be warned. This is a warrior command cell. It has sophisticated offensive and defensive capabilities and is extremely dangerous. Treat it with the utmost caution and respect. Allowed free, it could do untold damage. I give it to you without having neutralized it so you can see the naked face of the Celi-Kran for yourselves."

Illeran allowed his tongue to flick out and sneered disdainfully at the hovering pod.

"A nanometric construct! That thing is no match for the Serrll Scout Fleet, Karhide."

Zor-Ell turned and gravely studied the Karkan. "If you do not believe me, Da Director, you might be prepared to change your mind when you see the result of a Kran attack on one of your worlds, as happened to the Devon 3-VL4 ecoforming outpost in the Palean Union."

Through the Valley of Shadow

Ti Inai smiled sardonically as angry questions rose from the chamber. The fear had been ignited. All he and the Committee needed to do was fan the flames. He could not have conducted the proceedings better if he had orchestrated them himself. Judging by Ed-Kani's satisfied look in his repeater plate, his ally seemed in total agreement.

"Da Moderator." Zor-Ell nodded to Torres and faced the chamber. "Representatives. The Orieli extends its hand in friendship and trust to the Serrll Combine. If you reject it, we will respect your desire for self-determination and will not intrude in your affairs.

"Ask your questions."

* * *

Sipping his tea with soft slurps, Ti Inai darted glances around the executive lounge. Clustered in discrete groups about low tables, Assembly members savored their various brews or nibbled at sweet cakes. Conversation remained subdued, but the air was charged with an undercurrent of tension.

He picked up a nameless delicacy off a crystal tray and took an absent bite. A shadow fell across him. He looked up and wilted as he recognized the figure.

Tao Karam smiled oily and bobbed his head in amusement as Ti Inai's shoulders sagged in resignation. Tao Karam's small round face may have been pinched and wrinkled with age, the pale white complexion mottled with gray, but his darting black eyes were bright and still penetrating. His body no longer carried him straight and tall, but he wore his age with dignity and authority.

"May I?" Without waiting, he eased himself into the yielding formchair. A white-garbed waiter appeared instantly to take his order. "And what did you make of our Orieli visitors?" he asked pleasantly. After a brief scrutiny, he selected a morsel off the offered tray.

Ti Inai's smile was stilted as he shrugged, his long fingers twining. "A damned nuisance if you ask me. An added complication we could all have done without."

"Mmm, yes." Tao Karam nodded, his eyes darting as he watched Ti Inai's growing discomfort. "And you're lying through your teeth." A figure paused beside their table. Tao Karam looked up.

Ed-Kani snapped his jaws and his ice-cold, blue-white eyes pinned Ti Inai. He smiled frostily, nodded to Tao Karam and stalked away.

"The Orieli are certainly a complication." Tao Karam grinned broadly as he watched the retreating figure, his hands twining. "A complication which could spoil a lot of plans," he said expansively.

Ti Inai took a hurried sip of his tea and glared. "Or aid them. I know that you and your faction opposes our merger with Sargon. Despite vindictive rumors to the contrary, my interest is only to strengthen the Palean Union's position."

"So you said five years ago." Tao Karam nodded and gave a low chuckle. "Just after the Fleet uncovered Lemos, if I recall."

"We polished our act since then, friend Karam," Ti Inai said smoothly.

"And Khiman-ra was an example?"

Ti Inai suppressed a smirk at the reminder. Loss of that base had been inevitable, if costly. He considered his initial concept still sound: harass Kaleen shipping to the point where some of the independents would willingly cede to the Palean Union. After failing to bring Rolan over, the AUP Provisional Committee shifted its focus back to Pizgor, this time with more subtlety. Nevertheless, the merger timetable set by the Committee, or more accurately, by Ed-Kani Takao, was simply far too ambitious for Ti Inai and some members of the Palean Congress, no matter how much they supported the concept. Ti Inai had discussed options with Tao Karam to slow things down. He still wanted the merger, but not if it resulted in massive social dislocation, or disruption to his career.

Khiman-ra had a special purpose, though. Through its five-four majority, Sargon effectively controlled the Provisional Committee, pushing through policies not always in the best interest of the Palean Union. With the support of rogue elements within the Palean Alikan Union Party, Ti Inai had set up Khiman-ra to raid Kaleen systems, which effectively derailed Ed-Kani's program to have some of those systems cede to the Palean Union.

"Despite its loss, Khiman-ra was successful," Ti Inai countered. "It abolished the Committee Chairman's casting vote and brought the Palean members to an equal footing with Sargon. And you have the gall to throw it in my face now."

Tao Karam smiled knowingly and bobbed his head. "Yes, you achieved a measure of success, I'll grant you that. And I'm not walking away from my complicity in the carnage caused by Kai Tanard. I only question the loss of life paid for our so-called success."

"To the pits with you! They were a necessary sacrifice if we're not to lose what we gained. The Palean Union is evolving and a firm hand must guide us through this period of change. My hand! Before the next elections, I'll have the Executive Director nomination confirmed, despite your negative endorsement. After the elections, they'll relegate you to some sinecure post on Palea in recognition of your exemplary service on Capital, and the merger with Sargon will proceed on our terms."

"Grandstanding ill becomes you, friend Ti Inai," Tao Karam murmured. "You will get that nomination, but your drive to make the Alikan Union Party a new political force can only serve to split the Palean Union."

"The Union is already split." Ti Inai waved the matter aside. "We have been vacillating between the Sargon and Sofam camps for centuries. It is time that we made our power felt."

"Our power?" Tao Karam demanded and raised his eyebrows. "And what of the Kran threat?"

"That's why we have the Scout Fleet," Ti Inai snorted impatiently. "I don't deny that I'm ambitious, Karam. In the final analysis, that's why we're all here. And I have not forgotten my responsibility or duty to the Palean Union either. I am simply reflecting a growing weariness at having to bow and scrape before our Karkan and Sofam masters."

"But you're ready enough to bow to the Sargon master."

"What do you mean by that?" Ti Inai frowned suspiciously, his fingers working, twining.

Tao Karam smiled gently and shook his head. "Like me, my misguided friend, Ed-Kani Takao will lose his Executive seat, come the next elections. After serving on Captal for thirty years, I dare say that he'll be glad to leave. However, his power and influence within the Sargon Dumas or the Committee won't be diminished at all. In all likelihood, they'll make him a life Pro-Consul. If I may be permitted to remind you of a salient point? First and foremost, Sargon has always been a military power. Amalgamation into the Serrll Combine merely served to channel that talent into refined political and economic adventurism. From blunt application of brute force, they have mastered the deft moves of diplomatic counterthrust."

"Your talk is all nonsense, friend Karam," Ti Inai growled irritably.

"Indulge me. Five years ago, Sargon adroitly demonstrated their mastery of the political process by ensuring the Palean Union bore the full embarrassing brunt of the bungled attempt to force Pizgor to abandon its nonaligned status."

"You never tire at pointing out the obvious, do you?" Ti Inai growled savagely.

"Friend Inai, it is perhaps the obvious which you and your faction have never properly considered. But consider it now. Should the Palean Union split itself as a result of your maneuverings, who will benefit? We or Sargon?"

Through the Valley of Shadow

Ti Inai stared at the older man and chuckled. "You're asking me this now? I remember you as a young Assembly rep advocating immediate annexation of the Kaleen group and the abolishment of the independent's Executive seat. What were your arguments? Economic expansion, a greater political voice in the Assembly, establishment of new trade routes. Sounds familiar?"

"There is a qualitative difference to those demands that you overlooked," Karam said quietly.

"And that would be?"

"We were doing it for ourselves only."

"This merger will benefit the Union."

"Will it? With all your parliamentary skills, you still failed to resolve one critical question. If we designed the merger with Sargon merely to give the Alikan Union Party a third seat in the Executive Council, you could have achieved that by simply splitting the Palean Union into two blocks. Each would have held enough systems to warrant an Executive seat in its own right."

"That's an insane proposition, Karam. Even if we wanted to, the Articles of Association forbid such a maneuver."

"True. What if the maneuver was a forced one? Forced by factional instability that is even now threatening a genuine split. I ask you again. Who will benefit?"

Ti Inai stared at Karam in confusion, suddenly uncertain. Divide and conquer? Could it be as simple as that? The bright future he planned for himself under the banner of the Alikan Union Party was developing unexpected storm clouds.

"Sargon would never dare…" he trailed off uncertainly, attempting to put up a brave front. Would they?

"Remember this, friend Ti Inai. Sargon doesn't seek a merger with the Palean Union in order to create the Alikan Union of worlds. They want to create a Greater Sargon. That's the only thing they ever wanted. Everything else is mere rhetoric. Surely you must know that." A pleasant chime sounded through the lounge. Tao Karam smiled and stood up. "Come and see me tonight and we'll talk."

Ti Inai found himself deep in thought as he watched the bent figure of the old statesman shuffle away.

To the pits with him!

Chapter Nine

Cloaked in dawn's shadow, Terr sat cross-legged as he faced the black wall of the Athal Than escarpment. It towered before him, thrusting into a jagged sky, blotting out the stars. A heavy stillness waited for something to happen. Only the thin whisper of shifting sands and the echoes of his thoughts disturbed the silence. All around him the Saffal stretched into night where it merged with the blazing cradle of stars.

The desert landscape shimmered beneath the watchful gaze of Aribus and Rima. The moons cast thick shadows among the long shallow valleys between the dunes. The sand glittered and sparkled like fields of frost and just as cold. The shadows comforted him as he sat waiting for the dawn to touch the cliffs.

He experienced a strange flight across the Keep of Death, hurtling through a lonely night. The soft hum of the power plant and the whisper of rushing air kept him company. He had not said goodbye to Teena. All the goodbyes were already said. She pretended to be asleep when he rose and dressed quickly, but she could not strangle her sobs as he padded out of the room. That evening, she pleaded with him, trying to stop him. When that failed, she even went to Sidhara, but the old Wanderer would not see her. In the end, she accepted the inevitable in broken desperation, stricken, refusing to touch him. To her, he might as well be already dead.

It pained him to see her suffer like that, but the fates could not be denied.

The combie fled across the desert. There were no more questions to be asked and no need for answers. The uncertainty, the doubts and the dread of tomorrow, they all melted into the blackness of night, leaving him with only the dull throb of Athal Than's call. He did not want anything and he did not expect anything, prepared to receive the judgment of the gods. There were no regrets. He hadn't even told Dhar of his coming ordeal, or that he might never see him again. They were at peace with each other, which should suffice.

He landed in Athal Than's shadow, sat in the combie and waited for dawn.

Beyond the escarpment the sky turned a deep purple and the lesser stars fled. The cliffs would soon be bathed with blood spilled in the silent battle between darkness and light. The towering buttresses stood black and sharp against a torn sky.

Some inner sense told him he should greet the sun now in the shadow of the Keep of Death. He climbed out of the combie and breathed deeply of the crisp air.

There were no rules how to enter Athal Than. The Discipline had no rules, how deceptively complex. He only knew that when the sun touched the cliffs, he must stand within their shadow. He watched as the escarpment slowly emerged out of the night. He allowed himself a faint smile of amusement as he remembered, foolish and still raw with the power, studying the scientific and technical papers that tried to describe the phenomena of Athal Than.

The escarpment rocks supposedly had unusually strong magnetic properties. Within their influence, molecular circuits behaved erratically. They theorized that in some strange way the escarpment affected the electrical network of the brain, inducing hallucinations and an impression of godhood. He didn't know about that, but that Sargon archaeologist remained a block of stone when they brought him out. And the fires held in his hands were certainly no hallucination.

It seemed such a long time ago, a simpler time that happened to someone else.

None of it mattered now.

Overhead, the stars were fading and the sky gradually turned amber. He didn't hurry his strides, knowing he still had a few minutes before the sun touched the cliffs. The cold sand shifted beneath his feet, hissing in protest as he walked. The silent, towering walls loomed before him. The moving sand gave way to pea-gravel that crunched beneath his feet. The sharp cliff walls were beginning to lose their coat of black, melting into slabs of brown and washed ocher.

He stopped before the sheer walls. When he looked up they suddenly brightened and began to burn with gold and fire. The shadows stirred and swept over him, leaping far into the desert. Aribus and Rima paled, fading into gray smudges. Robbed of their night glory, they lingered like lost ghosts.

He shivered and approached the broken cliff wall cut by black crevices. The shadows lay thick among them, waiting. He turned and swept his gaze across the emptiness of the desert, perhaps for the last time.

Teena...

He took a deep breath and slowly walked toward one of the fissures. The shadows parted to let him through.

It would have been comforting to have his master with him now.

"The fear I feel is only what I bring with me," he chanted silently.

The path he found himself on this time different, unlike his first trial. It did not matter. They all led to the same destination. He walked slowly, but steadily through a maze of narrow clefts winding their way between cliffs polished smooth by wind and sand. The floor flat, and the sand packed hard, no doubt traveled by uncounted Wanderers before him. His footfalls made no sound. In the silence the very air did not dare move. He walked among dark shadows and felt his fear stirring. He realized how easily panic could swamp reason as terror barely suppressed, threatened to overwhelm him. He remembered his master's words the last time he trod this path and was mollified. He need not fear the gods, and what fear he felt, he brought in with him. He took comfort from those words and some of his dread receded.

As he made his way through the narrow canyon, he could feel the hand of Death hovering over him. He knew the inherent danger should he stop, but he stopped nonetheless, looked up at the amber sky, and raised his arms.

"Take me!" he cried, letting it all go, not caring anymore. He didn't deserve the god's blessing. Teena's face formed before him and he felt a poignant tug of loss. Prepared to give up his life for her, he waited for the god's judgment.

The cliffs were mute and silent around him. He dropped his arms and walked on.

He didn't know where he walked or why, but he didn't want to tempt the gods by lingering again. Between the walls and the branching trails, he felt compulsion to move in a particular direction, a compulsion not to be denied. The walls of Athal Than were all around him and he knew he was deep within the escarpment. It would have been very easy to get lost here.

As he walked, the peace he felt in the desert slowly faded, replaced by the turmoil of his thoughts and the boiling images of his yesterdays. He was drowning in a torrent of experiences as they flowed into each other in seemingly random confusion. The cliff walls faded as he hurtled through his yesterdays.

His whole life lay exposed; his hates and sorrows, joys, laughter and pain, betrayal and death. It all tumbled out of him like scenes in a Wall, cold and unemotional. He watched with detached fascination, beyond judgment, beyond feeling.

He knew the trial had begun, his soul and life as the price of oblivion. It did not seem to matter which, and the difference too moot to debate. He could feel the spirits of this place crowd him and he knew no fear. That, as with everything else, had been washed out of him. Detached, he regarded the tapestry of his life, fascinated by the patterns it formed and reality faded.

* * *

Through the Valley of Shadow

In the mud hut, Sidhara stood beside him. The shadows lifted and he saw a body lying on a mat of peelath leaves, sun-burned, naked beneath a rough blanket of oark hair. Shock made Terr stop and stare. He was gazing at his body, but that could not be. In a kind of duality, he saw the alien was of the Saddish-aa—an impossibility.

Fear and terror lurked in those eyes. The pale skin dry and cracked, drawn tight over a strong face. He whimpered, shaking his head at the torment within him. Terr stepped to the mat and the woman moved aside in the sudden quiet. He reached out and grasped the other's hand.

"Do not fear, my brother," he heard himself say and wished his strength to flow from his hand. "Rest, I am with you."

The dual stranger on the bed returned his grasp with surprising intensity. Then the alien's eyes began to change and expand. They were orange eyes with vertical red slits and he sank into them. Terr felt he should know him, but the knowledge eluded him.

He felt reality dissolve as he sank into those compelling eyes and everything exploded around him.

And a day came when he crossed the barrier of minds that separated him from the alien. A furtive breeze tugged at the cape of his brown surtaf. The whispering of the sands lost itself among the shifting dunes. Hot air burned beneath an amber sky. Peelath leaves hung limp in weary acceptance. The pecking poultry and the contented grunts from dozing oark intruded into drowsy silence.

Only the children moved about the village. In the heat of the day everyone rested in what shade they could find. If anyone did work, they did it in the cool gloom of the huts. The hut where the alien lay seemed to swim in the heat and Terr fancied the gods were waiting. Yet he hesitated. He had seen a joining done before and knew the forms dictated by the *Saftara*, but this was the first time he contemplated such an act. As a youth, he

213

flirted with a friend, as boys would, an innocent game that meant nothing. Later, older, the Rahtir allowed him to witness a real joining with another Wanderer, but for the solemnity of the ritual, the experience meant little to him.

He took a deep breath and went into the hut.

For a time, he watched the tortured lines on the drawn face. Gray eyes stared inward at some private hell. He hesitated when those eyes suddenly turned and sought him out without any light of intelligence in them. When he reached with his hand the alien moaned and returned his grip with a strength born of desperation.

They were alone, for this was not for women or children. He knelt beside the bed and closed his eyes. Still clasping the alien's hand, he allowed his mind to probe delicately along the barrier that lay between them. He felt a pulse of power in that mind unlike anything from another offworlder. Surface impressions of confusion, fear and terror coiled like angry lightnings.

He probed the barrier with delicate touches and recalled Sidhara's words of warning that both of them might be lost if he failed to control the joining. He hesitated, realizing he feared personal oblivion. Done hastily, he could be trapped, consumed by the torment of the alien's mind. For a moment, he was tempted to withdraw.

The searching grip of the other's hand decided him.

He moved gently along the surface. When he found a fissure, he paused, then thrust firmly and allowed the barrier to topple away. He felt resistance, then a tearing, and he almost pulled back. With a cry of pain, he felt himself swept among the whirlwind of shadows into the other mind.

Once past the barrier, he found it easy. His fear of insanity and endless torture, of losing himself, had held him back. It was an interesting insight. He had to be careful here lest he added his nightmares to the alien's horrors. The other mind lay open to him now and he took of it, and they merged.

His name was Dharaklin, known as Nightwings, the

shadow who walks at night, and he became Terr's brother. In him, Terr saw a reflection of a searching, wandering spirit, free, but filled with purpose. There was ambition and a drive to succeed, mixed with a certainty of destiny for his people. But beneath the disciplined order of his thoughts, there also lay a capacity for compassion, love, and a need for fulfillment that was not so different from his own. Terr sank deeper into the murky depths of Dhar's subconscious and he knew everything and understood everything.

It all came tumbling out and he struggled to keep the flood in check. It was impossible. Once the process began, the merging seemed to take on a purpose of its own. Only when he slammed into sudden darkness that he experienced genuine horror.

It was not horror of the desert, as Dhar saw the Saffal as his home. The duality shifted and Terr saw his brother standing on a dune, cape flying behind him, staring into the open vastness. Terr struggled to understand the images. What was happening to him? *He* was the alien, the hunted one, and his brother risked his sanity to save him.

Looking down at the peaceful face, Terr saw himself reflected in the large orange eyes. He also saw Death lurking there and the images were one. He felt bathed in the glow of pure energies as their personalities integrated. After a time, he withdrew and pondered at the heritage they both now shared.

The joining over, he sat beside his newfound brother. He sat there for a long time, holding the alien's hand. When Dhar finally slept, the nightmares did not return.

Before leaving, Terr looked down at the sleeping form.

"My brother, what have I done to you?" he heard himself say.

There was twisting and the images were wrenched into another reality.

Dhar nursed his drink and watched Sankri over the rim of his glass in a dive near Tal Field on Taltair his brother favored.

It amused him that Sankri would venture into such an establishment. Then again, Razzo's Corner wasn't exactly a normal dive. They were celebrating Dhar's temporary appointment to the Bureau of Cultural Affairs. It meant going to Captal where he would be in a position to gather valuable data for the Unified Independent Front. It also meant he would be leaving his brother, and he felt strangely disturbed.

He could feel the power around Sankri like a cloak of invulnerability, and he felt troubled. Sankri's affinity with Anar'on was one aspect of his transformation he had never been able to fully reconcile. Looking at his brother now, proud and arrogant, how could he tell him that the hand of Death, a destroyer, if unchecked devours all it touches. Yet Sankri was a child of the gods, innocent of the terrible forces unleashed within him, playing the immortal, and Dhar feared to follow the path upon which his alien brother so recklessly trod.

Sankri laughed, waved his glass and slapped Dhar on the shoulder. Dhar smiled, but his eyes were cold.

"Cheer up, my brother!" Sankri roared and slammed the glass against the bar top.

The Walls were pulsing with heavy colors in time with the loud music, merging into tortured patterns. The place smelled of cloying, noisy humanity and Dhar longed for the quiet solitude of open desert sands and clear skies.

"Why the gloom?" Sankri demanded and swayed against him. "You'd think this was a funeral or something." He took a pull from his tumbler and prodded Dhar on the chest with a stiff finger. "You know what your problem is?" he said, suddenly serious. "You never laugh. That's it. You have to laugh or the pain gets to be too much."

Dhar stared at him in shock, wondering whether Sankri realized the implication of what he just said. The moment passed and Sankri sagged against him.

"With you gone, who will guide my footsteps now,

Nightwings, my brother of the night?" he mumbled and collapsed into Dhar's arms.

Dhar held him, uncertain of his emotions, but somehow knowing that he failed him. Secure behind the power of the Discipline and a lifetime of ingrained habits, he judged his brother imperfect because he did not conform. Torn between two cultures, Sankri walked an emotional tightrope, fighting a growing conflict within him. And he had stood aloof, reproaching Sankri's transgressions.

"Forgive me, my brother. I did not know," Dhar whispered and reality toppled away.

When the images cleared, he found himself sitting on a flat stone, his legs crossed, surrounded by shadows. His long thin hands rested on his knees palms up, spread in contemplation, red hood pulled up.

A tendril of thin dark smoke rose from the black embers of the campfire. His walk to Katai Than a trek of personal revelation. Not expecting to live, he had been brutally honest with himself and could now see where he had strayed. Pride, the sin he leveled at his brother, had guided his footsteps and colored his thoughts. And how easily he slipped into its embrace, seduced by visions of a cause to which he magnified his contribution out of all proportion. As a consequence, he destroyed a friendship and a brother's bond.

He sensed the approaching combie moving slowly toward the small beach. It hesitated and sank. Finally, the bubble slid back and he heard Sankri step out. Dhar slowly turned his head. He reached up with both hands and pulled down the hood.

"My brother, I am happy to be in your shadow again," he rumbled softly and saw Sankri's face twist into a sneer.

"I have no brother. That part of me died on Earth. You saw to that!"

Dhar felt the stab of accusation tear through him and he slowly rose to his feet, his arms limp beside him.

"If death will atone for my sins and your pain, then I welcome its embrace," he whispered, resigned to his fate. The gods *had* warned him, but he had chosen to ignore their warning. Or did he have any choice?

"You won't have to wait long," Sankri snarled, raised his arms and began to chant the words to invoke his aspect. With Death in his hands, he leveled his arms. Bright blue lightnings danced between them, coiled and ready.

"Wait!" Dhar cried out and flinched as his brother reached for him. The lightning crash lit the gorge and thunder shook the ground between them. The lightning struck him and blue tongues danced around him like a halo, crackling and twisting and burning. He gasped and staggered at the searing pain coursing through him, but still managed to stand. In agony, his eyes remained fixed on his brother.

"I called you a brother," Sankri rasped savagely. "But you betrayed that by knowingly sending me to my death. Now it's your turn."

Lightning cracked again and Dhar screamed in pain and shock of its touch. It coiled and flared around him before draining into the sand. The canyon walls echoed his cry. He lurched forward and groaned, clutched his chest and fell heavily, not believing that such pain could exist.

"I died the death of betrayal!" Dhar heard the anguish in Sankri's words. "I was alone and I didn't even know why you abandoned me."

Dhar's breath a labored wheeze, he struggled to his feet. When he finally managed to stand, he looked at Sankri with tragic sadness. His only regret was that his brother would always believe himself betrayed.

"I die, forever your brother," he gasped, muscles contracting spasmodically as pain twisted his face.

"Then die!"

Sankri!

Dhar stood there waiting for it to end. It seemed like an

eternity as his brother held his hands leveled, ready to pour forth his revenge, but the lightnings did not reach for him. With a bellow of rage and frustrated bewilderment, Sankri spread his arms and lashed out. Again and again, thunder crashed and lightning cracked until the rocks themselves cried out in torment. Dhar stood very still as Death raged around him. Sand glowed in fused, smoking puddles of yellow glass at his feet.

Spent, Sankri let his arms drop.

"Damn you! I trusted you. I would have *died* for you." Biting back a sob, he sank to his knees in helpless confusion. "When the Orieli picked me up, I waited for you," he moaned and hugged himself. "You only had to be there. I would have forgiven you everything, everything. You only had to be there."

Tears streamed down his face and Dhar stood there, frozen, trying to still the play of astonished emotions on his face. He fully expected to die then. That Sankri stayed his hand…It tore him apart to see his alien brother suffering like that, and he cursed the fates that brought them both to this state.

"My poor brother," he whispered brokenly as he searched for the words. "There was no other way."

"You tried to kill me!" Sankri sobbed in outrage.

Dhar's face twisted with inner pain and he took the few steps separating them. Sankri looked up as Dhar knelt. Eyes burning with emotion, he reached for him. Blue sparks jumped between them. Firmly, his arms went around Sankri and drew him close.

"I understand, my poor brother," he whispered with infinite gentleness and sadness. "I understand."

With a soul-wrenching gasp, Sankri pushed against him, trying to burrow into him. He wept unashamedly as Dhar held him.

* * *

When Terr opened his eyes, bright sunlight bathed him in

light as he stood in the middle of a small clearing. Red cliffs towered around him, and sharp shadows etched the sands. He looked up and allowed the heat and the light to suffuse through him.

"Nightwings, the shadow who walks at night," he murmured in wonder. "I also understand now." The images of his trial were vivid in his mind, astonished to see everything from Dhar's perspective.

He should never have doubted, but looking back on events, being what he was, he could not see how he could have avoided the trap he had set for himself.

He reached with his arms toward an amber sky and began chanting.

"I shall walk in the shadow of Death," he quoted from the *Saftara*. "And it shall be with me all the days of my life. With shadow shall I smite my enemies and with thunder shall I purge their land!" The power surged through him, clean and pure and he felt a keen joy as it burned. "And all who stand with me in the shadow of Death shall know my power and be comforted. With shadow and thunder shall I walk their land!" he roared joyously and loosed the lightnings.

They sparkled bright blue, crackling between his hands. Thunder shook the ground and rumbled through the canyons. Death settled on his shoulders, a feathery touch and he welcomed its hand. He felt no guilt or burden. His sins were washed away and he laughed. His spirit soared and the gods echoed his laughter at his rebirth, innocent as on that fateful day the first time he walked the canyons of Athal Than.

Surrounded by radiance, he lowered his arms.

His steps were light as he rounded a wall. Beyond the fissure the desert lay open before him, swimming in the heat haze. On the dunes, he could see his combie as the sun glinted from its polished surface. He didn't know what happened to him in the Keep of Death, but understood the reason, and he felt he'd been given a second chance—the gods had put him on probation.

The bubble slid back with a hiss and cold air washed over him. He paused, turned and allowed his gaze to wander over the red cliffs of the escarpment. Slowly, he sank to one knee, bowed low, and felt that the gods approved. The power was strong within him and it would have been easy to allow pride and arrogance to rear their dark heads.

* * *

The combie banked and sank toward the sharp-edged dunes, the afternoon shadows filling the valleys between them. The villagers looked up and children waved. They began running toward the spot where he would land. Below him, Dhar's combie lay waiting and he settled beside it. With the power plant still spooling down, Terr opened the bubble, climbed out and breathed deeply of the hot dry air, allowing the smells of sand and burnt rock, the heavy musk of oark, and the charred odor of tarad grass to wash through him. Everything smelled fresh and new and all the colors seemed brighter as though a veil had lifted from his eyes. And perhaps it had.

A young Wanderer, wearing a brown hood, stopped in his walk. He held his staff straight and glanced curiously at Terr. Then his orange eyes grew round in surprise. The youth nodded to him and hurried toward the hut of the Rahtir.

Terr had not told anyone of his visit to Athal Than, except Teena and Sidhara, yet they all seemed to sense the change in him. The women paused in their work around the well to look at him and children gathered in small groups, whispering excitedly to each other. He stood there, confused and embarrassed to be the center of such scrutiny, uncertain what he should do. The young Wanderer strode purposefully toward him and glared kindly at the children, but did not say anything.

He stopped before Terr and slowly pulled back his hood.

He planted the staff into the sand with one thrust of his powerful arm. His orange eyes were searching and Terr returned his gaze frankly. Then the youth sank to one knee, head bowed, and stretched out his arms.

"Master," he rumbled and Terr's skin crawled.

He felt a kinship, a bond between them that filled his soul. He touched the youth's head and felt something flow between them.

"You have my blessing."

The youth stood up, towering over Terr, wearing a smile of contentment.

"Tabe," he said and the women and children pressed around them.

"Sankri! Sankri!" they chanted and laughed and Terr felt strangely moved by their open happiness at his return, for somehow they knew where he had been.

The children timidly touched his robes and fled with shouts of glee. Others only stared at him in wonder. A hush fell and they slowly parted as the solemn figure of his old master approached, his lined face wearing an expression of pride and gentle approval.

Sidhara's eyes were clear and bright and the love in them Terr returned fully, in awe of the old man. The power radiating from him almost palpable. Terr understood then something of what the young Wanderer must have felt. After the crash, in his naiveté, had Terr known Sidhara for what he was, he would never have dared approach him. The gods indeed protect the foolish.

He sank to his knees before the Rahtir and bowed until his head touched the Wanderer's feet. Trembling, he waited for the touch. When it came, he felt the old man's strength and was content.

"My son," Sidhara said gently, the sound coming from deep within his chest.

Terr looked at him. "My master, I am not a worthy disciple

of the Discipline and don't deserve your blessing."

"The gods have judged, my son," Sidhara said with a smile and lifted him up. "It be enough." Then his face hardened and his eyes were the amber of the sky. "You must come to me tonight," he commanded and Terr nodded.

The villagers crowded around them then, shouting their names and Terr smiled and laughed with them. Then murmuring approval, they slowly drifted away with an occasional backward glance. There would be time enough during the evening meal to talk. Gradually the normal sounds of the village returned: the stomping of the oark, the cackle of poultry, the screech of running children and the quiet dignity of the old.

When he turned, she stood there, wearing a faint quizzical smile.

"Teena," he moaned softly, hardly daring to breathe. Dhar stood beside her, dwarfing her, and fire blazed in his eyes.

Terr opened his arms and she was there, soft and warm, and he blinked hard as he held her tight. It felt good to feel her touch, feel her trembling warmth, breathe her smell when he fully expected never to see her again.

"I will never leave you," he murmured and he felt her shiver.

"If you do, you beast, I'll be coming after you," she mumbled against him.

Then he looked at Dhar and reached for his hand.

"My brother," Dhar murmured and Terr felt himself unable to swallow. Dhar nodded with understanding. "I shall see you before I leave," he said simply and walked away.

Terr watched him, still trying to understand the duality he had experienced at Athal Than.

"You love him very much, don't you?" Teena said in a small voice, and he looked down at the puzzlement in her eyes, and envy?

He smiled and brushed her cheek. "He is my shadow," he said simply. "But you're real and I'm so glad I found you again."

223

He held her head between his hands and their foreheads touched. He gazed deeply into the clear pools of her green eyes. "The love I have for you is not for brothers, my pet."

"Beast!" she said huskily and made a face. Then her eyes clouded with concern. "I was so afraid you wouldn't be coming back," she whispered fiercely and clung to him. "Don't ever do that to me again."

Later, they sat outside their mud hut and watched the afternoon claim the desert. Obscured in a cloud of dust, children ran shouting over the dunes, chasing an inflated oark bladder. The small village noises were all around them, but the two of them were alone with their thoughts.

She turned, her eyes searching. "You're different somehow. I don't know how…and yet you are the same."

He smiled and squeezed her hand. "I'm alive and free. The gods have spared me and given me a measure of peace and a second chance. Not many are so fortunate and I came so close to ruining everything." He shook his head in wonder. "I could have lost you and I wouldn't have even known why."

"What now?" she asked, leaning against him.

"I don't know, but we've got four months in which to find out," he said and her laugh was a pleasant tinkle.

* * *

Thick gray smoke rose from the tops of the mud huts, twisting and coiling toward a purple sky. The oily smell of peelath hung heavy in the cool of the evening.

The sand warm to the touch, it whispered as it ran between his outstretched fingers. Terr watched the blood fade out of the sky and darkness covered everything. Very conscious of Dhar's silent presence, of his strength, gentleness and humility, belying the terrible power lurking sheathed in his hand, they watched night claim the desert. Strange that he never recognized those qualities in him before, judging him through eyes more used to dealing with human frailty, treachery and violence—and his own failings.

Aribus stretched and touched the dunes with silver hands. The shadows lay thick and heavy about them. He turned and Dhar's eyes were black pools beneath his red hood.

"Nightwings," Terr said his name and held out his hands.

Slowly, Dhar's arms came up and they touched. "Sankri, the strange one," he said and his voice was the voice of the desert.

Terr could feel the heat of Dhar's touch and he struggled to still the whirlpool of his thoughts. "My brother of the night," he said simply, almost seeing the smile on Dhar's face.

"It has been a while since you called me by name, Sankri."

"I had forgotten it before."

"Why now?"

"I had wakened, my brother."

"Indeed." Dhar nodded and they were one with the night.

"I seem to have inherited your fascination for dawn's awakenings and the day's death battles," Terr said after a timeless moment, staring at a spot where the sun had sunk.

"Each is a struggle with the shadow of night. Yet each still remains to see another dawn."

It grew dark quickly and Dhar became a black outline. "Not a struggle then," Terr said slowly, trying to understand, "but two sides of the same face. A renewal."

"Just so," Dhar murmured, looking at the desert. "Struggle assumes dominance, but it is only our internal unrest that would impose the same need on the appearance of a dawn or the soft caress of night."

The shadows pressed around Terr and his thoughts soared. "And the Wanderers lay in the cradle of the Keep of Death and the shadow of the gods are upon them," he quoted from the *Saftara* and searched Dhar's face, but he only saw darkness. "What does that make us?"

"Children of the gods perhaps?" Dhar said softly.

Terr pointed at the stars of the Stalker. "They may have created the stars, but even the gods cry."

"It is only the hand of man you see, my brother, and thus we forget the beauty of the bridge of the gods."

The sky was thick with stars. Terr tried to look beyond the images of the constellations and he understood and felt sad. "They are but our reflections, and yet, it's tragic to realize that the Stalker will have to wait till the end of time for his release."

Dhar laughed softly. "My brother, if our eyes will it, he will be free."

The stars swam and the Stalker trembled and dissolved as reality shifted. When Terr looked again, they were only stars.

"Do not mistake the creation for the creator, my brother," Dhar murmured. "There lies the risk of self-worship."

"The gods *are* whimsical." Terr shook his head. "They give you the power, but not the wisdom to wield it. You have to learn that the hard way."

"I am pleased the gods have smiled on you, my brother," Dhar said seriously and touched Terr's shoulder. "I expected—"

"Yeah, I know. The bridge I crossed was narrow and the chasm deep. They must have seen something in me to spare me."

"I feared for you."

"Me too."

"I must go, Sankri." Dhar rose and shook the sand off his robe. "Kanarath is far and there is much to do before the Conference."

Terr stood beside him and the bond between them was almost tangible. He reached and grasped Dhar's hand. He could not see his face, but he knew the fire in Dhar's eyes reflected in his.

"I have doubted you, my brother, because the road we walk is strewn with suspicion and deceit. I remember what you said to me once, about a deck beneath my feet and the sight of strange skies. I want to travel that road again…with you."

"Our paths are one and we may travel it yet," Dhar said softly. After a time, he turned and the only sound was one of sand shifting beneath their feet as they walked down the dune's slope.

Terr leaned against the side of the combie and his foot idly stirred the sand.

"I wish you didn't have to go."

"I know. Orders. And you?"

Terr did not pretend not to understand. Since his return from Athal Than, his thoughts have been skirting that very question.

"I really don't know. Officially, I'm still on leave and the problem might resolve itself. Anabb can wait."

"Wise."

Terr cocked his head and chuckled. "Although I hope the rest of my leave will be less exciting than what it's been so far."

They laughed, sharing a secret joke.

The bubble opened with a hiss and Dhar climbed in. The power plant spooled up quietly. The bubble closed over him and his face became bathed by the cold radiance from the instrument plate. He looked at Terr and pressed an open palm against the bubble. Terr swallowed, brought up his hand and held it against the hand of his brother.

The breeze tugged at Terr's robe as he watched the combie climb and disappear into the night.

Stefan Vučak

Chapter Ten

"It's not working, Enllss," Anabb growled irritably. "You may have succeeded at removing almost every Wanderer from the Bureaus, but the Unified Independent Front is more than just Anar'on."

The late-night lights of the Center burned cold. Anabb hated these nightly sessions, but there was no overcoming the time differential between Captal and Taltair—at least not on this side of the planet, he mused wryly. Anyway, he did not get too many such calls.

"I understand all that." Enllss nodded and folded his arms over the desk. "I never intended to remove every intelligence asset Kaleen and Orgomy had in place. I merely issued a warning to Marrakan. You would be amazed the effect a little pressure on the throat has on the head."

"I know whose throat I would like to put a bit of pressure on," Anabb muttered sternly and the burn on his cheek began to color. Enllss only laughed. "This isn't funny. Despite the aborted maneuver at the Executive meeting to abolish the independent's seat, a foolish and dangerous gambit, your actions have done nothing to resolve the issue of UIF's position. What's more, they have seriously curtailed our intelligence-gathering capacity in vital areas at a time we can't afford. If you remember, Dhar operated in one of those areas. His loss will compromise our remaining agents."

Enllss did not particularly care to have his policies criticized, even by Anabb. But he was too good an administrator and politician, for that matter, to ignore it.

"You have something specific in mind or are you just venting spleen?" he asked offhandedly, slightly miffed.

Through the Valley of Shadow

Anabb noted the warning, but he'd had a long day and not about to finish anytime soon. His branch provided analyses and advice for Executive Council bureaus, and Enllss should have known better; worrying about politics and elections rather than issues, he decided uncharitably.

"Perhaps it's a bit of both," he acknowledged moodily. "I have information which is only hours old, Enllss. Ed-Kani and Ti Inai have been lobbying Tao Karam and select members of the Palean Congress. After Devon, the Paleans are taking the Celi-Kran threat very seriously, you know. Enough to listen to Ed-Kani and his vision of a united Alikan Union Party."

"And you see these developments as significant?" Enllss looked at him suspiciously.

"Of course not!" Anabb snorted and waved his hand in an impatient gesture. "The Paleans are well aware that all security postures are decided by the Executive Council. Ti Inai seeks to generate public sympathy for the merger, but you're missing the point. By depleting our assets within the Servatory Party, you have introduced choke points into our intelligence network. The data is hours old, but the event took place yesterday!"

"I evaluated all possible consequences before I took this action, Anabb. Including operational constraints. Sill-Anais should have briefed you more fully, and I'll have a word with him about it."

Anabb cleared his throat, feeling a sense of growing help-lessness. What annoyed him, Enllss still liked to play his games of intrigue after all the years away from his previous job running the Bureau of Cultural Affairs. Once a spymaster, always a spy-master.

"Do you think Marrakan is sitting on his hands while you sideline his men?" he demanded peevishly.

"I'm counting on the fact that he knows what I'm up to," Enllss said. "And I am *not* underestimating him. After all, we still want him on our side, and I haven't done anything to in-timidate him. Not really."

"I wouldn't be so sure," Anabb said darkly. "This business with Terr and Dhar came as a pretty low blow. The Wanderers take their commitment to the Discipline very seriously."

"Terr seemed to have contained his enthusiasm fairly well while eliminating our opposition," Enlls pointed out with a daunting smile.

Anabb frowned. "I wonder." Images of lightning crackling around him and the cold fire in Terr's eyes sent his skin crawling. "What about Sofam's attempt to remove the independent's Executive seat? It was intimidation, plain and simple."

"Also just a friendly warning, Anabb."

"Hah!"

"Have you decided what to do about Terr's resignation?" Enlls demanded, clearly wanting to get off a sensitive subject.

"As a matter of fact, I have," Anabb said and leaned forward over his desk. "Remember our negotiations with Karhide Zor-Ell about a cultural exchange Mission?"

Enlls stared at him in surprise, then nodded with satisfaction. "Yes, a very neat solution. And the Independent Representatives Conference?"

"The delegates are due to land on Anar'on tomorrow. Security is in place. However, I don't think it will be needed." Anabb smiled grimly and his eyes glittered.

"I know what you mean," Enlls said and thrust out his jaw. "I've been talking to Sill. It seems that Marrakan has his own ideas on what constitutes appropriate security."

Two of Terchran's and one of Sill's men simply disappeared without a trace. Then there was the case of a body found in a Kanarath hotel, believed to be one of Ed-Kani's creatures. It must have been left there as a warning to others, a block of gray-veined stone wearing a contorted expression of terror.

Evidently, Marrakan would not brook any interference, and Enlls suspected that more demonstrations might be necessary before the message sank home. To have such power at his disposal...

"While we're talking of security, what is Ed-Kani doing mousing around in Kanarath?"

Enllss grinned, but with little warmth in his gray eyes. "You're referring to that stone specimen, perhaps?"

"I know of a few bodies who would be better served if preserved for posterity like that," Anabb growled testily. "The idea of Ed-Kani's men crawling around there makes me nervous."

"You talked this over with Marrakan?"

"Yes, but that's not what's bothering me," Anabb said, suddenly seeing his body turn to stone under Terr's relentless gaze. "Ed-Kani would stoop to anything to see the Unified Independent Front fail. Even he wouldn't be so rash as to try something massive. It might be late in life, but he's learned subtlety. He could be after an individual."

"And you think it could be Marrakan?" Enllss asked.

"Perhaps, but I don't believe it. Eliminating Marrakan would certainly be disruptive, but counterproductive in the long run. The Unified Independent Front has too much support and momentum to be affected by removal of a single individual, no matter how important. I think he has his sight on other game."

"Who did you have in mind?"

Anabb pursed his lips. "Ed-Kani may have learned subtlety, but not patience. He's after the same prize—Pizgor. If I had to guess, Prime Director Kernami Asai Tainam could be his target."

Enllss pulled at his chin and nodded. "You might be right. Apart from the UIF, Ed-Kani and Ti Inai have two obstacles to their merger plans, Tao Karam and—"

"Kernami," Anabb finished for him. "We spoke of this earlier, didn't we? Without Kernami, Pizgor may succumb, especially if urged on by Beanab's vision of a seat on the Executive Council."

"Exactly." Enllss nodded with satisfaction. "Ed-Kani could be using the Independent Representatives Conference as a convenient smoke screen while he gets Kernami to quietly join his ancestors."

"I'll see to it if we can make life a little more difficult for him." Anabb grinned without humor.

"By the way, Anabb," Enllss said casually and leaned back into his formchair. "How would you like to be commissioner of my Bureau?"

Caught flatfooted, Anabb's eyes opened wide in astonishment. "Thunderation!" he said softly and Enllss laughed.

"We've been watching you closely. The Sofam Conservative Party believes that you would be an asset in the Revisionist camp. The nominations are being prepared now and all you have to do is say yes."

"That's a big step," Anabb murmured, uncertain at the prospect of immersing himself in Captal's bureaucracy again. "I'll think about it, Enllss, and thanks for considering me."

"Of course." Enllss nodded and smiled warmly. "It might not be my Bureau, you understand. Sill-Anais is due for reassignment and there could be a vacancy in the Bureau of Cultural Affairs."

Stepping into the Security Council? Anabb had been director of the Diplomatic Branch for seven years now and had the place working smoothly. At least two of his department heads were more than capable of heading the Branch until a suitable Assembly rep took the appointment. After bossing screwy agents and running covert operations, did he want to give all that up? But what the challenge to help shape Serrll policy!

"I'll let you know," he said and the Wall dissolved into a pool of flowing colors.

* * *

Marrakan stood before the open window, hands crossed before his chest, and watched the sun's last rays flare among the towers and the fluted spires of the Center. Not a large city, Kanarath nestled against the only major sea on the planet, large enough for its intended purpose as Anar'on's administrative center. He shunned the images of a sprawling metropolis the likes of which he'd seen on other worlds. The Wanderers were not city dwellers, preferring the clean winds and smells of the open desert. Gentle fingers of a wafting breeze stirred his hair.

An oasis, Kanarath's constituted a sprawling profusion of organized activity in a sandy sea of silence. Also something alien compared to the simple pattern of life in Wanderer villages. A necessary intrusion perhaps, and a price Anar'on paid for its interaction with the Serrll. He felt the desert calling him and he yearned for the haunting solitude beneath its star-filled skies where only the whisper of shifting sands or the sigh of a furtive wind would disturb his thoughts.

As Controller of Anar'on and Prime Director of the Kaleen group, he no longer had time for the wandering treks of his youth. Since his only loved died fourteen years ago, his world had become a political quest for Kaleen's security. In two short years, he would see the work of decades completed. Later, the gods would be waiting for him in the escarpment of Athal Than.

Pulling tight his jacket, he turned from the open window and regarded the composed features of the young Saddish-aa warrior sitting rigidly before him. The clear floor-to-ceiling panel closed behind him with a snick, shutting out the desert. As dusk settled the walls took on a soft sandy glow. To one side a low table held a bottle of prana water bound in soft oark-calf leather. Two leather-bound glasses faced each other across a small matt. To one side a small tray of delicacies stood almost empty, strewn with odd crumbs.

The ceiling was almost four katalans high and the room looked like any other modern office. A Wall communications station faced a wide working desk at one corner. Soft form-chairs surrounded a comfortable visitors couch. Weathered, polished peelath boards made the floor. The only real luxury Marrakan permitted himself; a small vanity no one minded.

Soft and haunting the Wall's fluted notes trembled in the room. The music shivered in gentle agitation to the slow pooling of colors.

"It is not the first time someone used the hand of Death against a brother, my son," Marrakan rumbled softly.

"Had he struck me the third time, master, I would not have risen," Dhar said and his eyes traveled past the venerable Rahtir to rest somewhere in the fading sky.

"You could have resisted," Marrakan suggested mildly.

"He was my brother," Dhar said simply, and Marrakan nodded gravely. "To him, my actions were those of a traitor. Given his emotional turmoil and the circumstances under which I had taken Teena, his loved one, it was predictable that he would focus his uncertainties and rage on me. What happened at Katai Than was unavoidable. I must confess, though, his survival at Athal Than was not, much as his loss would have pained me."

"No, my son," Marrakan said and gave a sad smile. "When he stayed his hand against you, he crossed that fine line between revenge and acceptance. To his alien thinking, even though you betrayed him, he could not betray himself and deny what he is. If he could forgive you, could the gods do less?"

"I have often wondered who stands more worthy in the shadow of Death, master. I, surrounded by the comfortable cloak of the Discipline, or Sankri, immersed as he was into a culture he still struggles to comprehend."

Marrakan strode across the room and sat behind his desk.

"The danger of falling into complacency and smugness is ever present, my son. Ever since the fall of Lemos and the work you two did to eliminate Khiman-ra, I wanted to meet this alien brother of yours. By all accounts, he is a mischievous rogue."

"He is all that," Dhar agreed with a chuckle.

"The exposure of those Palean bases was exceptional work. At any rate, he seems to have confirmed one piece of intelligence. Enllss has been reassigning our agents from sensitive areas, carried out with his usual subtlety, and we responded as soon as we confirmed the pattern. In your case, he showed considerable imagination," Marrakan said with a faint grin.

"Sankri as much told me the same thing."

"When Enllss ordered you to disclose your brother's assignment to Terchran, the rest took its inevitable course. Why do you think Enllss blocked the attempt by the Bureau of Administrative Affairs to have Gashkarali removed when you exposed his operation? It wasn't simple retaliation, but part of an overall plan to gradually starve the Unified Independent Front of information. He had this thought out even then."

"I should have seen it before, master. It could have averted much pain."

"Some things just have to happen, my son."

"That Commissioner Enllss-rr could be so ruthless…"

"Do not judge him too harshly. As a government representative, he could not afford to be sentimental. I know. In your case, it was never a question of loyalty to the Serrll, only your commitment to Anar'on and our Unified Independent Front."

"And Sankri?"

"Family or not, by linking your actions with his, both of you were effectively removed from any intelligence-gathering capacity, even though Sankri was not involved. When the Orieli showed up, it presented Enllss with an opportunity too good to miss. He got both of you out of the way in such a manner that the move could not be questioned." Marrakan nodded with amusement. "He makes a formidable opponent indeed. Faced with an unpredictable power block, he wasn't doing anything I would not have done in his place."

"Even the Executive Council's move to remove the independent's seat?"

"Even that. As a warning, it's been noted."

The comms alert beeped and Marrakan reached across his desk.

"Director Anabb Karr, sir," Ronowan said in a deep voice.

Dhar began to rise, but Marrakan motioned him to remain. He touched several pads on the inlaid console and turned to the Wall.

Anabb's chiseled narrow face looked strained. His white lips were pressed into a line and Dhar wondered what ghosts stalked his days. He nodded when Anabb's eyes briefly rested on him.

"Director, it is a pleasure to see you again," Marrakan said gravely as he watched the crease lines fade on Anabb's olive face. "And what can I do for the Diplomatic Branch?"

"Good evening, Mr. Controller," Anabb growled after glancing at the open window and the amber of the sky. Behind him the night lights of the Center stared back with bright harshness. "This time the Diplomatic Branch can do something for you."

"Indeed?" Marrakan said and his eyebrows climbed.

"You must be aware, sir, of the active interest displayed by the various factions in the outcome of the Independent Representatives Conference."

"Noted. Where that interest has become too active, we took the necessary steps. I shall not tolerate any interference in our affairs, and I have informed Commissioner Sill-Anais accordingly."

"Your privilege, sir. As a recognized independent, nonaligned system, your domestic affairs are not within my jurisdiction."

"On Anar'on at least, that will certainly remain the case. Now, what is it you wish to tell me?"

"As long as you conduct your affairs without affecting other systems, my interest is a passive one. However, by involving yourself with the Unified Independent Front, you changed the rules. Political reality makes it inevitable that any action taken by the UIF will bring opportunists sniffing for deals, something I am sure you already noted. And we found the result of one of your necessary steps, sir," Anabb said and passed a hand through his hair. "As a block of stone, perhaps he serves a more useful purpose. As one of Ed-Kani Takao's agents, I suspect I know why he came to Kanarath, You're no doubt aware, sir, Ed-Kani is not kindly disposed toward the UIF."

"You suspect a sabotage attempt of the Conference?" Marrakan studied Anabb with interest. "That thought had already occurred to us and we have taken steps."

"I suspect more than that, Mr. Controller. I suspect a murder attempt."

"Indeed? And you have a likely target in mind?"

"Prime Director Kernami Asai Tainam of the Pizgor Triumvirate."

Marrakan stared at Anabb with growing, if grudging respect. He did not care for the interwoven byplays of Captal politics and its intrigues. Within obvious limitations, he had found Anabb honest and impartial. This came as valuable intelligence, and in hindsight, predictable.

"I am aware of Ed-Kani's ambitions, Director, and of Pizgor's strategic relevance to those ambitions. Your warning is timely and received with thanks. Rest assured, Kernami will be protected."

"Anyone can be made to disappear if the will is there," Anabb said with an ironic smile and his eyes traveled to Dhar. "Your encounter with Terr, evidently not a fatal one."

"No, sir, but not altogether a pleasant one either."

"I don't doubt it." Anabb suddenly looked old and tired. "Some things you were told, by me and by others." His eyes flickered to Marrakan. "You are a fine and perceptive officer, Mr. Dharaklin, and I am sure you have appraised the situation for yourself. As your superior, I need not explain further. As someone sympathetic to some of your, ah, past difficulties, I wish to point out that we all carry out orders. Orders which sometimes go against the grain," Anabb growled and studied the impassive face in the Wall.

"I'm not in a position to disclose the motives and objectives of the various government Bureaus. Time will tell whether the gains have been worth the price. On a different, but equally important matter, I am pleased to tell you, your promotion to the rank of First Scout, third grade, is approved, effective immediately."

"Thank you, sir," Dhar said surprised. Marrakan nodded with obvious satisfaction.

"As a First Scout, you rate a personal M-1 while you don't hold a command, and one will be made available to you on your return to Taltair," Anabb said good-naturedly. "But first, I want you to bring Terr to Kanarath and get him to contact me." Anabb raised his hand to forestall Dhar's unspoken protest.

"I know what you're thinking. After what happened, he might be less than disposed to talk to me. Tell him that it's not going to cost him any leave, and he'll be able to take Teena with him. As a matter of fact, all three of you will be going."

"Going where, sir?"

Anabb glanced at Marrakan and nodded. "Mr. Controller," he said and the Wall rippled into flowing colors.

Chapter Eleven

A tendril of steam coiled and rose lazily above the cauldron to fade into the gloom of the mud hut. Beneath the cauldron the coals glowed dull red, flaring bright orange as a breath of cold air brushed them with a fleeting caress. The silence of the dawn, disturbed by the bubbling of peelath tea, became a moment of timeless peace, a moment between the memories of yesterday and the unknowns of tomorrow.

Propped against the rough wall of the mud hut, hands behind his head, Terr watched the small tongues of fire leap and dance among the coals. He had always been fascinated by the magic of fire, its healing comforting touch, benevolent in the confines of the hearth, underlying the terrible power and terror of a firestorm.

In the quiet of the hut, he drew comfort from the shadows that stubbornly clung to the walls, the snap of darting flames and the flicker of the oil lamp. Teena stirred beside him. Forces shifted within him and his eyes softened as he looked down at her. Her mouth slightly open, she looked vulnerable and defenseless, and his heart went out to her. Her black hair spilled in waves across her shoulders, one arm hung over the edge of the bunk, the other cradled her head. Her chest moved lightly as she breathed soundlessly. Yet beneath the delicate softness of her form and the curving planes of her face, there were lines of strength and confidence, lines of anger and pain, lines of character.

He stared at her in the gloom of the mud hut and listened to the dawn's small noises.

It was easy to forget that held in his hand, Death was a plaything of lightning and thunder. Unchecked, it is a gathering of forces, a conflagration. He came away from Sidhara's hut late that night badly shaken and disturbed. The desert sands whispered in the night and the stars spilled across the sky in a white blaze as they nestled against the horizon's rim. He paused beneath the bright canopy and stared momentarily at his hands, wondering not for the first time his right to walk in the shadow of the gods.

They finished the tea ceremony in silence without the need for words. Terr was content merely to bask in his master's presence, and he didn't concern himself with the whys. The delicate aroma of dried peelath flowers lingered in the air. After a time, Sidhara raised his head and his eyes regarded Terr with chilling, probing clarity.

"My son," he said and his voice was the voice of Death. "Tell me. Why have you spared Nightwings, your brother of the night?"

Such an unexpected question, Terr suddenly found himself back in the gorge of Katai Than. The anger and the pain came flooding back. With echoes of thunder loud in his ears, he confronted that part of himself that was the Saddish-aa Wanderer. Why did he spare him?

Because he was a brother? He rejected that. Brothers have killed for less than what Dhar had done to him. Because they were both Wanderers? That one sounded even shallower. The Discipline may provide the path, but it took an individual to walk it. Why then?

"A test of faith, master," he said after a timeless moment.

"Just so, my strange son from the skies." Sidhara nodded wisely, pleased at the boy's perceptiveness. His eyes were pools of fire that seemed to grow as Terr stared into them.

"But even I didn't know that I would stay my hand," Terr protested weakly.

Sidhara's eyebrows arched as he regarded his alien son. "You hide the truth even from yourself?" he admonished. "The last time we sat here, you spoke to me of your anguish and pain.

That pain came from within. You knew your path of vengeance was twisted and dark, but wounded pride would not release you. Hence your conflict. Remember how you fled from me?"

"Are you telling me that I became blinded by self-pity?"

"Not pity. Wounded arrogance, foolish creature! Your power has distracted you, giving you the illusion of immortality. You said it yourself. You confused the teachings of the Discipline with religion. Unlike a religion, whose purpose is to stifle free thought, replacing it with regimen and unquestioning dogma, the Discipline embodies harsh truths, asking nothing. Not even an acceptance. And the gods, if such they be, do not demand worship, only respect."

They sat in silence and the flames crackled softly to them. Terr's mind reeled from Sidhara's words. Even now, cleansed, had he failed to understand his relationship with the powers living in the Keep of Death? It appears he may have.

"And my trial?" Terr ventured, daring.

Sidhara smiled briefly then absently placed a gnarled piece of peelath root among the coals. He stirred gently until the small flames crackled in protest.

"As the shadow is not that which created it, each one of us is but an imperfect reflection of the god who chooses to touch us. You have undergone two of the three trials of the Discipline, Sankri. What have you learned from each?"

Thrown into confusion again, he struggled to comprehend not only the question, but also the Discipline that underpinned it. Faith in himself and Dhar? But Sidhara knew that already. He spoke of shadows and reflections and Terr knew.

"Arrogance and humility," he said softly.

"But which one is the shadow?" Sidhara demanded with satisfaction and leaned forward. Terr chuckled.

"They are both my reflections."

Sidhara smiled and patted Terr's hand. "Indeed. The fires in your soul burn bright tonight, but no longer with the consuming flames of destruction. My son, for you the Discipline has been a road of thorns, filled with pain and sorrow. Many would have fallen. Do not feel unworthy that you misused your power. As with all things, the spirit grows through trial and contest. Your trials may have been more difficult perhaps, set in turbulence of what is the Serrll. But they were appropriate, however unfair or demanding they may have seemed to you at the time.

"You are strong with the power and the hand of Death rests lightly on your shoulders now. Every time you walk in the shadow of Athal Than your power is magnified and each in his way is transformed by the experience, as you have been."

His eyes stung and Terr found himself unable to look away.

"Beware of temptation, Sankri, or the power lust will destroy you. Let me show you something." He reached out and grasped Terr's hand. The heat of his hand flowed, burning and Terr wanted to cry out in alarm.

"Watch," Sidhara commanded and stared at the flames, his dream from a time long ago came flooding back.

And Terr looked at himself suspended in space, arms upraised, two stars adorning his feet. Before him, a painted world hung against the tapestry of night and lightning flickered in his eyes. He leveled his arms and the lightning went forth and lashed at the world. He heard the cry of billions and laughed, his laughter shaking the heavens. When the world exploded around him, only the sound of thunder remained in his ears.

Terr was alone, suspended in night with two stars at his feet.

When he opened his eyes, they reflected the horror he felt. Sidhara watched him solemnly.

"I have seen this vision before, master," he whispered.

"I know," Sidhara said. *Sarumajan…the destroyer of worlds.* This strange alien represented a terrible future for many—a possible future, he reminded himself.

"And you think that I…" Terr managed to croak and

clenched his fists to stop himself from trembling at the frightening use of such power.

"We live with a duality," the old man said softly. "In one hand we give life. In the other, we can take it. It is only a matter of degree how."

"Where is justice in power capable of such destruction?"

"The gods do not demand justice, my son, only compassion. Even they refrain from judgment, for there are no absolutes, no laws. You know the Discipline has no laws, only teachings. To stand in judgment implies a position of moral superiority, and the gods have their own morals. Ours they leave to us."

Terr remembered his call and the confrontation, and shivered.

"The trials I have undergone. Was each not a judgment?"

"But did the gods do the judging?"

"If the gods don't stand in judgment, why then are we given the power?"

Sidhara's chuckle was dry and hollow. "You know the answer to that. It is to know and master yourself. It always comes to that. What else is there? When you stand in judgment of another, the question you must always ask yourself is: by whose rules are you passing that judgment?"

Terr stared at the fire and the flames danced. "Social symbiosis," he said at length and shook his head ruefully.

Sidhara's eyebrows climbed with respect in his eyes. "A formidable leap of understanding, my son. You're right, of course. Social symbiosis. There is a subtle, but clear difference between morality and custom, which in turn governs the right and the wrong in a given social context. And there lies our dilemma. With all its splinter factions the Serrll is an ecosystem subject to all the laws of such systems. Checks and balances. In nature the strong do not victimize the helpless, but eliminate the weak."

"Then we do nothing?" Terr stared at him and the old man smiled sadly.

"To what end do we act, my son? A transitory victory or an exercise in hubris? There is still one lesson you must yet learn. A stone cast into a still pond generates ripples, changing all it touches. A blade of grass sways and its seedpod is disturbed, spilling seed into the water. Some will survive, some will not. When the wave reaches the shore, moss is disturbed, exposing larvae to the hunting fish and an insect never takes flight. A chain of events in fractal progression is unleashed from the original, seemingly innocent act whose effects are impossible to predict.

"The power you hold in your hand can be like a stone cast into a pond, but the ripples it generates are far more powerful. Remember, the mere presence of power is an influence. You saw the vision, my son, and the danger."

"And the one who sets himself as the ultimate judge with the fate of worlds in his hands?"

Sidhara closed his eyes as if reliving a memory. "Having exercised the excesses of your power, you know the answer. When there is an affront, the call of Athal Than is irresistible and the affront is removed. As you feared, before that happens there is much suffering and death."

Terr looked at his hands, then at his master. "What then of the injustices we can right?"

Sidhara slowly nodded. "My son, when you reach a cusp, you will know how to act."

Terr left him in the small hours of the morning, old and wrinkled, hunched, staring at the small flames playing in the hearth. Outside the mud hut, he stared at his hands and felt fear.

Through a sleepless night, he wrestled with a torrent of deeply disturbing emotions, trying to understand his new heritage.

He felt Teena's hand brush his chest and her eyes regarded him quizzically. She had a disconcerting habit of suddenly being awake, watching him while exposed and defenseless.

Through the Valley of Shadow

She pulled herself up and curled her feet beneath her. The soft oark blanket slid off her shoulders. Without saying anything, he touched the softness of her neck. His hand moved up through her hair and brushed her cheek. His fingers traced the softness of her lips, moved down and gently tugged at the tie of her robe. It whispered as it fell away to reveal smooth skin and the gentle hollow between her breasts.

She waited, hardly daring to breathe, her eyes bright. He wanted to share with her something of his transformation and there was only one way that he could do that. Death settled about him like a shadow and tiny blue sparks danced silently between the fingers of his hands. This time they were warm with life, not the cold of destruction.

Teena gasped in alarm and he felt her tense. She had seen him take on his aspect before and knew what the blue fires meant, but never like this, with her. She paled and gulped in dismay.

He smiled gently and stroked her bare shoulder, leaving a trail of blue fire. She shivered at the prickly warmth of the sensation.

"Do not fear, my pet," he whispered. He brushed her lips with his to still her trembling. Her small pointed breasts quivered as his fingers stroked her nipples and felt them grow hard. The blue sparks in his hands softened and began to spread up his arms. His hands moved over her slender waist and the fires bloomed, pulsing, warming them both. Reaching up, he cupped her breasts and the fires followed. The glow defused around her and slowly enveloped her.

Her breathing shallow and rapid as she stared with round-eyed fascination at the fire consuming them. He leaned toward her, his mouth searching for her lips. Her cheek against his, he reached with both arms to draw her tight against him. With a strangled moan, she clung to him, her breasts crushed against his chest. They held each other, rocking slowly and he whispered soft words to her. When he laid her down, he looked into her eyes and the room glowed bright blue as they merged.

Afterward, she lay on top of him, chin resting on his chest, her eyes misty and soft. They were clad in shadow again and the cauldron bubbled and steamed. The fires of passion might have receded, but the magic still remained. Her fingers marched across his chest, her nails exquisite pinpricks of pain and pleasure. An impish smile twitched at the corner of her mouth. His hands folded across her bare back on the swell of her hips. She felt cool, satin-smooth beneath his touch.

"I never believed this could feel like that," she murmured huskily and her lips brushed his chest. "But when the sparks started crawling over me, I was terrified. I hate you," she growled deep in her throat and smiled wickedly.

"I wanted to share."

"By scaring me to death?" She sat up, supporting herself with one outstretched hand, suddenly serious. "Sankri, the strange one. The name fits you well. You're changed, my god of Death. I felt it yesterday. You seem to have this terrible calm about you, and yet there is power held in check, waiting to be unleashed. I don't know which is harder to take. Your rage or this."

"Have I really changed that much?" he asked gently, knowing it to be true.

She nodded, her mouth firm. "You are almost a stranger, living someone else's memories. You're like your shadow Dhar. He also has a terrible calm and wears it like some cloak." She shook her head and shuddered.

He chuckled, surprised at how close to the mark she came. "The gods saw fit to forgive me my transgressions. Like someone reborn, I savor the feel of every moment that passes. There is a lot I don't yet know or understand. If nothing else, I am learning patience."

Teena sighed and lay against him, her head on his chest.

"Talk to me?" she mumbled against him. "I want to understand."

He slowly stroked her back.

"An exercise of power is an exercise in patience," he said softly, stroking her. "Right and wrong is only a point of perspective, and few things are truly evil. It doesn't mean acquiescence or acceptance, but a process of understanding, often a painful one. Which in itself is a trial, for all of us are tainted by our environment and its modes of behavior. If an omnipotent god were to set foot on Captal, he would be at a loss to pass judgment, given free will and a multiplicity of norms. Only in a truly homogeneous culture is that possible, and that's why the Wanderers don't march among the stars with Death as the ultimate leveler."

"Then what's the purpose of the Discipline and the power it evokes?"

"Ah, my love, I almost killed a brother and stood before the gates of chaos, my soul as the price, before I learned the answer to that question."

"I'm not sure I believe in these gods of yours if transgression is rewarded with death," she said, her cheek against him.

"If it were only death." His chuckle rang hollow. "It's a loss of self which is far more terrible. And that's the purpose of the Discipline, understanding of self. I stood in judgment of others without having judged myself."

She looked at him. "You may have made a bargain with your god, but what of us? I have been flung into your world of intrigue and power and almost lost you to these gods I don't understand and fear. You seem to have achieved a measure of peace, but where does that leave me? Back to Taltair and the Center, and you off again on some mission? Days and weeks without seeing you, without knowing what's happening to you, wondering whether you'll ever come back, only to be greeted by a *Deeply Regret* from Anabb? No." She shook her head and he could see her eyes filling. "I couldn't take that anymore. Not after this."

His hand brushed her cheek, saddened to see her sorrow.

"It's been hard for you, my pet. I know. You were there when I needed you and I wasn't there when you needed me. I wish I could tell you that we shall never be apart again, but I cannot do that. I am a serving officer of the Serrll. Short of resigning, there will be moments of loneliness, for both of us."

"Then let us stay here," she said suddenly and he smiled.

"No. This is not our world. Neither of us belong here. For you, life here would be harsh and demanding. For me, at night, my eyes would turn to the stars and my spirit would roam among them. I must return, not to the Diplomatic Branch perhaps, but I must be out there. This time, though, it will be on my terms."

"And what of me?"

"You shall be with me," he said simply.

* * *

Hands clasped behind his back, Arlon Dee paced impatiently the length of his day quarters. Through the VI connection, he watched Devon's painted blue-white crescent hang above the brittle gray of the moon's terminator. A beautiful world, cold and hostile, but young and unspoiled. If the Serrll wants to keep it unspoiled, he mused bitterly, they better the hell start taking the Kran threat seriously. He licked his lips in irritation, frustrated at the Serrll commander's vacillation.

To him the tactical situation was simple. Destroy the Kran vessel in place. For the past nine hours, Taran had his two M-4s sitting there, exchanging messages. Arlon glanced at the repeater plot showing the two blue points still maintaining position between the moon and Devon. If the Serrll chose to sit and wait for inspiration, he was damned sure the *Daktar* central nexus had not been wasting *its* time. What if it had managed to complete sufficient repairs and decided to lift? He preferred not to think about that.

He urged Taran to take action, only to receive a cold reply

that, as an observer, his presence was barely tolerated, the situation no longer any of his business. Chagrined, Arlon had to accept the unpalatable truth, but he didn't have to like it. And he didn't. The problem, he admitted glumly, the Serrll did not appreciate or accept the severity of the threat facing them from a single Kran ship, no matter how alien or threatening its appearance. For that matter, they did not accept his judgment either. If the price for their acceptance was the loss of Serrll lives, so be it.

He only hoped the price would not be too excessive.

The bottom left corner of the image dissolved and he noticed one of the blue points representing an M-4 start to shift its position. An overlay image formed showing Tavac in Primary Flight Control.

"What's its heading?" Arlon demanded with a soft rasp.

"Present course indicates a flyby over the primary target area, Karhide," Tavac replied flatly, aware of his commander's inner turmoil. "I've been watching *Kopan* and I'm getting worried. It hasn't maintained strict relative position and drifted into the *Daktar's* secondary fire control envelope."

"If Se Kinai isn't careful, he'll never get out of it."

"Should we warn him?"

Arlon shook his head. "No. We're simply observers, remember? What's happening with the *Daktar*?"

"Burlig scans show intermittent power surges leaking through its primary shield net. No secondaries. Apart from that, it's just sitting there. If we don't do something soon, the thing is liable to suddenly lift and the *cheech* will really start to fly."

"Tell it to the Serrll commander," Arlon growled in disgust.

"The way that M-4 is moving in, I might not get a chance," Tavac said and pointed at the main repeater plot.

One energy ring surrounded the moving blue point. The M-4 hadn't even bothered to raise its secondary net, coming in on what the Scout Fleet called the primary shield grid. Acceptable, provided the grid was powerful enough to sustain the initial thrusts. If penetrated, nothing remained to protect the vulnerable hull. The Krans wouldn't be at all squeamish about exacting full toll for such an oversight.

"Observational caution," the housekeeping computer's softly modulated voice suddenly broke the momentary silence. "Energy anomaly track shifting to active phase. Target powering to weapons status."

"What's our condition?" Arlon snapped as he watched the tactical situation rapidly deteriorate. If anyone was going to get caught with his pants down, it would not be him.

"We're still maintaining condition two. Primary fire control is on standby. Interceptor net at condition two. Condition three on active standby."

"I'm coming to PFC, Tavac," Arlon said briskly and walked into the PT alcove. "Cent Comp, initiate transport."

He paused as the after-effect tingle faded. He swept his eyes quickly around the command level and the operations platform below. Tavac took no chances and had a full alert watch manned. Arlon approved heartily.

Without taking his eyes off the mainframe holoview plot, he settled into his seat and propped his chin with the palm of his hand. His tongue made a quick circuit around his lips as he watched the M-4 draw closer to the outer edge of the *Daktar's* acquisition envelope.

When the M-4 crossed the invisible boundary the computer's voice sounded startlingly loud. "Tactical caution. Target has engaged active scan and established a firing lock. Shield pulsing in preparatory firing phase."

"Stupid," Tavac muttered in impotent frustration. "Where in damnation are Serrll sensors? Can't they tell they're about to be hit?"

"Clear tactical and activate the Burlig scan uplink," Arlon ordered.

High above the moon's surface, the small scanners showed the Kran vessel nestling in the lee of a craggy peak, its shield pulsed weakly from pale yellow to orange. The view shifted slightly, showing the M-4 as a large white triangle moving slowly toward the moon. On its port quarter the smaller disk of the M-3 maintained its position beside it.

The Kran ship fired without warning, its beam trailing a solid line of yellow ionization. The shield on the M-4 flared and the ship staggered, slued around and lost attitude. Vivid yellow and white discharge lines coiled around the shield matrix lines. A shower of blue backsurges rippled along the hull. *Kopan* started to pull away. Before the M-4 could respond, the *Daktar* fired again in a wider pattern. The beam had penetrated the primary grid and sliced through the M-4's port side, exposing structural frames that vented atmosphere, wreckage, and bodies. Hanging optic wave-guide cables arced as the ship struggled to stabilize its defense net and regain attitude.

The M-3 was lucky. The beam had expended most of its energy on the M-4. When it struck the smaller ship, its shields flared and fluctuated wildly before collapsing. Arlon shook his head as he watched *Kopan*, its shields flickering, limp out of range. The M-4 began to move and the Kran ship fired again. The M-4's secondary shield grid came up and flared white under the impact, but held. As the M-4 crossed the acquisition envelope the *Daktar's* shields faded as it powered down.

Arlon nodded to himself, his face expressionless.

"Those were full-strength projections," Tavac said grimly.

"It would appear so," Arlon agreed thoughtfully. "The *cheech* has hit for sure, just as you said, and the Serrll got splattered. Damn Taran's arrogant stupidity," he added softly to no one in particular.

Tavac pointed at the mainframe plot. "The *Daktar* has regained full weapons capability, Da. I recommend that we destroy it in place, now! If it decides to lift, we risk compromising our integrity."

"I realize the gravity of the situation, Tavac," Arlon said, his voice gravelly.

"Once that thing starts rolling, it will go through the remaining M-4 like it wasn't there."

"*We'll* still be there."

"Sure. And if we're disabled? You know what will happen, don't you? The Krans will repeat the whole Devon sequence in another system as though nothing has happened. And this time, they won't be leaving anything behind."

"Opturkarh—"

"Just painting a possible scenario, Karhide," Tavac persisted and watched the anger fade in Arlon's eyes. He relaxed. He was a good exec and it wasn't always easy telling his commander what he didn't want to hear.

"You're right, of course," Arlon said wearily. "I bet that wiped some of Taran's arrogance. Send a sitrep to Zor-Ell advising him of the tactical situation. Tell him I won't be taking any unilateral action without the express authorization from the senior officer commanding the Serrll force now present in the tactical zone. Advise him that should the chain of command be broken, I shall take whatever steps are necessary to neutralize the Kran threat. Send a copy to the Bureau of Colonial and Protectorate Affairs."

* * *

Master Scout Taran tilted his long slender neck and his pointed tongue flicked quickly between the thin ridges of his mouth. The horizontal slits of his eyes were almost closed as he watched the repeater scan from *Kopan* circling the crippled M-4. The only sign of emotion Taran allowed himself came as a rumbling growl of displeasure trembling deep within his chest.

The M-4 6/A Sofam-built main battle cruiser constituted the mainstay of the Serrll Scout Fleet and a front-line presence of the General Assembly's authority. It had a better part of nine tetalans grade C composite armor on top of the four-tetalan-thick polymer hull construct. Even without secondary shields, it could withstand several twenty-four-millisecond bursts of up to 128 TeV at close range. Hopefully enough time for it to get away or press an attack.

It mounted two Koyami 3/C phased array generators channeled through a single projector dome beneath its belly, powered by an artificial antimatter convergence reactor. An M-4 could pour almost continuous twenty-millisecond 128 TeV bursts to a maximum range of 140,000 talans. With a crew of 240, formed into a triad with two other ships, it formed a formidable weapons platform.

Alone, the M-4 proved itself to be no match against the Kran ship. Taran suspected that even a triad would be just as ineffective.

Dark jagged holes gaped vacantly at him as the M-3 hovered near the M-4's ripped port side. Skeletal frames jutted from burnt hull plates like ribs from an ancient monster. He found it hard to accept the level of damage from only a single strike. Fortunately, it hadn't been a fatal one. However, with more than sixty of its complement dead or injured, the M-4 could not withstand another exchange.

A one-sided exchange, he reminded himself ruefully.

"I've seen enough," he grated and waved at the main plate. "Order it to detach and proceed to Kalakan for repairs. Have *Kopan* proceed to Devon as per instructions." With a last glance at the plot, he rose and headed for the cable-tube. "I shall be in my quarters," he said as the hatch closed after him with a soft hiss.

In the quiet cabin lounge the small ship noises seemed loud. He sat behind his desk contemplating the inlaid console pads. Hands resting on their surfaces, he fancied he could feel the gentle vibration of the ship through his arms. It was an illusion, of course. With a soft growl deep in his throat, ignoring the computer, he quickly set the comms codes and waited for the Wall to clear.

A young Palean Third Scout nodded politely and told him

that COMPALOPS would be with him momentarily. The Wall cycled through merging patterns of violent color as he waited.

He was still lost among the images when the Wall cleared and Prima Scout In Tain, Commander Palean Operations, bobbed his head, his hands twining. Taran's lips were set in a firm line as he studied the small triangular face, pale white complexion, and large eyes that now stared at him unwaveringly.

In Tain permitted himself an oily smile, the long snake-like fingers of his hands locked together.

"I have been expecting your call, friend Taran," he said easily, amused as he watched Taran's emotional struggle ripple across his fishy face.

"I have the information you wanted, sir," Taran said, his voice brittle. In Tain's bushy eyebrows lifted.

"Do I detect a note of resentment, Master Scout?"

"Regret, sir. Regret at the price that had to be paid for the knowledge we gained. You will have my full report in due course."

"Tell me what happened."

"Teklan went in with his primary grid only, as ordered, and got suckered by a preemptive strike which collapsed his grid as though it wasn't there. Before he could react, the *Daktar* struck again, partly shearing away his port side. If the Krans had not been trying to get *Kopan* with the same shot, Teklan might not have survived the hit. Se Kinai caught part of the blast and sustained major damage to his circuitry."

"Teklan knew the risk when he volunteered."

Taran glared at the Wall. "If we knew the risk, sir, why send him against the alien? The Kran vessel is supposed to be equivalent to an Orieli battlecruiser, and we know what those ships can do. Arlon Dee's ship isn't even a warship and it still managed to contain the Kran vessel during their initial encounter. This action only served to illustrate our inability to neutralize the Krans."

"What were the Orieli doing during that time?" In Tain demanded, ignoring Taran's outburst.

"Nothing. They just sat there. After all, they were not the ones fired upon," Taran said bitterly.

"At least they were carrying out your orders. We had to verify the Orieli data about the Kran ship, friend Taran. Teklan's sacrifice will not be in vain."

"The dead will appreciate that, I'm sure. I detached him to Kalakan for repairs. Without his support the tactical situation is suddenly very serious. I must advise you, sir, should the Kran vessel decide to lift, I won't be in a position to stop it. The sooner we get that M-6 here the better."

In Tain pursed his thin black lips and frowned. This was bad news, all of it, and likely more to come.

"The situation is more critical than you might think, friend Taran. Departure of the M-6 is delayed by at least one day and there are none available closer to you. At max boost, flight time from Kalakan to Devon is over one and a half days. That's a total delay of some three days. From what you tell me, you might not have three days."

"I may not have three hours! We've been keeping those M-6s in mothballs too long, sir," Taran hissed in exasperation. "When we want one they cannot deliver."

"The whole strategic disposition of the M-6s and the new M-9s is being evaluated by the Bureau of Defense right now."

"Bureaucrats!" Taran snorted in disgust. "Fleet dispositions should be made by operational commanders."

In Tain smiled briefly and raised a finger in admonishment. "A word to the wise. The Fleet should be above politics, but both of us know that's a load of worm crap. A Karkan voicing dissent in a Revisionist-dominated government will do nothing to further his career, my impulsive friend."

Taran's tongue flicked out in a blur. "As a serving Fleet officer—"

"Just be careful, all right?"

They stared at each other before Taran relaxed. "What are your orders, sir?"

"Should the situation deteriorate before the M-6 gets there, you're authorized to request Karhide Arlon Dee's assistance in destroying the Kran vessel."

"Karhide Dee has been quite patient with us. If his patience wears out, he could up and leave this whole mess in our laps."

"He won't." In Tain shook his head, his hands twining. "If he hasn't already, he'll be receiving orders to remain in the area. Something to do with a Diplomatic Branch matter. That's not important, however. What *is* important, Master Scout, in the event of a confrontation, Karhide Arlon Dee is to assume tactical command. Is that clear?"

"Relinquish my command?" Taran stared at In Tain in consternation. "Sir, may I respectfully point out that the Orieli are in *our* space!"

"I understand your confusion, Taran." In Tain shrugged and his hands twined. "But you said it yourself. If the Kran ship lifts and you offer it battle, you will be destroyed. I may be prepared to lose an M-4, but I'm not prepared to waste one of my best commanding officers in a futile gesture. Is that clear?"

"Clear enough, sir, but I don't have to like it," Taran growled.

"Your feelings in this are irrelevant. What is relevant is that the Kran vessel never gets off that moon."

* * *

Like a wandering ghost, *Kopan* glided silently between Devon's icy peaks, its primary dull yellow shield barely perceptible. In the valleys far below, torn clouds sulked in the shadows hugging the steep slopes. Around the jagged peaks the clouds lay bunched in balls of fluff, smeared in orange and reds from a sun struggling to rise above a distant horizon.

Se Kinai watched the valley expand as the M-3 sank. His

long snake-like fingers drummed against the armrest. On the navigation plate, energy rings emanating from what used to be the control Center were slowly increasing in frequency. His presence had been detected, but then, he never expected to come unannounced. His concern lay with the kind of reception he was likely to meet.

And talking of receptions…

"Channel open to Controller Aill-Massai?" he demanded, his black eyes darting quickly to his exec.

"Standing by."

"Hold present status. Right, let's get on with this."

He did not relish encounters with superiors, military or civilian; too many ways in which one could end up in a hole not of one's own making.

The comms plate shimmered and he nodded to the Deklan. "My apologies for the delay, Mr. Controller," Se Kinai began smoothly. "I was compelled to wait for support units before establishing contact."

"Support units?"

"Two M-4s, sir."

"What's going on, First Scout? Ach!" Aill barked and thrust out his barrel chest. "We detected Orieli darts two *days* ago! Then nothing. Those Kran things are still crawling all over my damned Center, pulling it apart plate by bloody plate. By the Path! If they decide to move in on us, I have no way of stopping them. After all, I thought I had the *Fleet* at my disposal for mopping up any disasters." Aill sneered with contempt. "I don't have to tell you, Mister, I'm getting a bit pissed at this cavalier treatment. There are lives at stake here."

Se Kinai maintained a straight face, sympathizing completely. After yesterday, facing an overrun complex would be an anticlimax. Still carrying out repairs, he shuddered at the thought of how close he came to losing it all.

"Yes, sir. Devon 3-VL4 is sanitized, and only your control

Center is occupied. I intend to remove the source of your annoyance as soon as I reach the datum point, sir, but I could use any tactical information you might have."

"Ach! The Kran heavy, boy! What about the Kran heavy?"

"It is interdicted on the moon and its scout ships have been neutralized."

"Holy worm shit! I don't believe it. Ach! Who is in command of your force, Mister? You had two M-4s prowling around for days without even bothering to establish contact? If the Krans were not so preoccupied with tearing down the Center, we might not be here right now."

"Sir," Se Kinai interrupted with weary resignation. "It's no use giving me a hard time. I'm only a dumb M-3 driver following orders."

"Don't contradict me! Ach!" Aill growled and pointed a long finger at him. "We've been cooped up in this ice hole for three days and I want to vent some frustration at the stupidity of Fleet command. You just happened to be handy."

Se Kinai couldn't argue with him there.

"Someone is going to hear about this," Aill went on. "Now, as I was saying, if the bonehead commanding your force had bothered to contact me, I could have saved you a whole lot of trouble, but Fleet high-handed tactics win the day again." Aill continued to rage and Se Kinai took it patiently. Senior officers and officials all had their ways, and this one was no exception.

When the barrage ended, Aill clasped his hands behind his back and his large liquid-gray eyes softened. "Ach! Okay, Mister, it wasn't your fault. Now, fill me in."

"We're standing off some nine talans from the Center, sir. The Krans know that we're here. We've been getting nav check scans ever since we crossed the terminator. Before I move in, I want to know what to expect."

"Ach! I don't have a tactical situation report for you, but our probes haven't shown any defensive placements. If they are there, we cannot recognize them as such. It's likely their scout ships controlled the operational mission. With them out of the picture, what's left appear to be some type of worker units."

"Well, I'll just have to wade in and see, then," Se Kinai mused wryly, his long fingers twining.

"What about us?" Aill demanded.

"COMPALOPS is sending an M-6, but I don't know its timetable. When I have sanitized the area, we'll resupply you and bring down new comms gear. In the meantime, sit tight."

"Ach! And what about the next time?"

"Like I said, sir, I'm only a dumb M-3 driver. Take it up with Sector TACOPSCOM."

When the plate cleared, his exec looked up and smiled sardonically. "I don't envy him. Stuck in the middle of an icy mountain."

"Yeah. Life is a bitch. Right, let's move in. Go to initial alert and clear tactical. No one is going to get caught napping around here, so there is no need to pretend."

Kopan descended farther as it glided up the narrow valley. Hanging motionless, heavy gray cloud shrouded the steep mountainsides. When the cultivated fields of the agricultural station appeared beneath them in checkered patterns, Se Kinai ordered the ship to pause as active scans probed the periphery of the Center.

"Picking up a modulated interrogative," the exec said quietly, studying Se Kinai's drawn face.

The same pattern as reported by the Orieli, Se Kinai mused. If the Krans were running true to form the next contact would be an acquisition lock. He doubted the Krans had time to set up a defensive perimeter. However, he did not have to rush in and risk an unpleasant surprise. He'd had one yesterday and it had been more than enough. Now that the Krans were cut off, the tactical situation should be simple. It would have been if he were operating within a conventional set-piece maneuver. Here, he didn't know what to expect. His thoughts wandered to Ti Adi blasted to dust.

The steep slopes fell away and the valley widened and flattened out. Nestled against an unbroken barrier of brooding mountains the burnt-out skeleton of the Center looked deserted. Tactical plot showed anomalous energy sources moving about the battered complex. Se Kinai couldn't see any other activity. He turned to his exec.

"Talk to me."

"Getting some movement on the fire control acquisition bands. Single point source, sir. Probably a field support projector on a fixed platform."

"Go to primary alert and extend secondary shield grid."

"Ship at primary alert, sir."

"Very Well. Move us in, slowly."

That's when *Kopan* took a hit. The pale orange beam lanced from the edge of the ruins and the ship staggered and lost attitude. Despite the restraining field, Se Kinai went flying to the deck. After shaking his head, he picked himself up and massaged his wrist. He looked at his hand and swore. The pain sharp, he hoped the damned thing wasn't broken. He climbed into his seat and stared accusingly at his exec.

"Some field support," he snarled and savagely stabbed at a pad on his armrest. "Status?"

"Partial secondary shield penetration along frames eighteen to thirty," the computer announced indifferently. "Hull integrity maintained with no residual radiation. Target on L-band lock, maintaining standby fire control."

"Fire control free. Two bursts."

Beneath *Kopan* the projector dome glowed white and bright orange tracks flared from the ship in quick succession. Ahead, the energy pattern from the Kran shield wavered and broke up momentarily before it reformed. The reply came immediately and *Kopan* shuddered again, its shields pulsing as the energy surge discharged into the atmosphere.

"Maintain fire until their shield collapses and acquisition lock is broken," Se Kinai ordered, staring hard at the Center.

Through the Valley of Shadow

Under sustained bombardment the Kran shield became a glowing dome of flowing white and yellow light. The outline blurred and shimmered just as it began to break up. Se Kinai threw up his hand before his eyes and squinted as the command bubble polarized, cutting out the glare from the flash. The intense light from the fireball turned a mottled red and the mushroom cloud coiled and twisted in silent agony as it reached slowly toward a cold blue sky.

The shockwave passed them and *Kopan* barely trembled. Se Kinai kept swearing softly as the devastated Center emerged out of the cloud and smoke. Most of the structures had disappeared in the inferno of the fireball. What remained were flattened beams, twisted into untidy piles of fused metal and slag.

He slammed the edge of the armrest in disgust. "Status?" he rasped irritably. The site clearly lost, he wasn't looking forward to the ensuing red tape.

"Picking up anomalous energy readings from the far side of the Center, sir," his exec announced, unable to hide his surprise. "I wouldn't have believed that anything could survive such a discharge. Otherwise, no emissions. There is residual radiation, most of it short half-life, clear in two days. Either way the place is a junkyard."

"Move us in and let's check out those readings."

Hovering near the smoking ruins, it became obvious what the anomalous readings were. Their shields shimmering pale yellow, two squat bean pods were slowly moving along an intact wall. As they moved a gaping cut opened. A rectangular panel slowly fell away. Se Kinai watched in fascination as the panel lifted beside the hovering robots. Holding the panel between them, both glided toward a twisted, partially melted pile of what had been neatly stacked metal panels. The robots continued their work, oblivious to the devastation around them.

Another robot, its shield down, emerged out of the twisted ruin. It paused, turned and glided slowly toward one of the units working near a wall. Without seeming to notice, a ripple of green flashed from the working unit and the approaching thing was suddenly riddled with holes. It staggered and crashed heavily into the rubble. The remaining two units continued their work.

"I figured on taking one back," Se Kinai mused. "But after that display, I think we better leave them here. Fire at any remaining units whether they appear inactive or not."

Chapter Twelve

Dawn had already broken and the sky became painted with amber. The sun glared through the haze, a merciless white ball. Low on the horizon, intertwined bands of brown smeared themselves in the distance as the jet stream dragged with it sand picked up from some far storm.

Quiet, only the whisper of the combie's power plant interrupted the silence. Around them the desert of the Saffal stretched unbroken, changing from rolling dunes to rocky flats and swaying fields of tarad grass. The reds and browns of the rock merged, pooling into yellows and whites of the sand.

Teena sat unmoving beside him, her hands clasped tight in her lap. Terr could sense her excitement as the torn buttresses of Katai Than grew before them. Last night, he shared something of himself with her. Now, he wanted to share this with her also, to replenish that indefinable quality holding them together which kept their love a smoldering passion. Unknowingly, they have been drifting apart. Belatedly, he realized that he'd been taking her for granted, a fixture that filled a part of his life, a part he had neglected. To have foregone the pain of that realization!

As with other things, the cup of love must also be replenished with tenderness, compassion, and understanding. He had left his dangerously low.

He turned his head and flashed her a smile. His eyes traced the outline of her forehead, the gentle curve of her small nose and fullness of her lips, refreshing the images in his mind. She wrinkled her nose and, with a characteristic gesture, swept away a rebellious lock of hair. Her smile questioning, but happy. Her pale green eyes were deep pools and he saw himself reflected in them.

"Gods, but it's beautiful here," she whispered breathlessly and reached to squeeze his arm.

He grunted in agreement and gently brushed her cheek with the back of his fingers.

"You and Dhar used to *walk* all the way here?" she demanded in amused outrage, watching the cliffs of Katai Than become something solid and massive.

He laughed and nodded. "It's not very far. We managed to do it in two nights."

"Two nights marching through this heat?" She stared at him in wonder and shook her head in disbelief.

"It's not so bad at night."

"What did you guys do here?"

"Oh, we talked mostly—"

"About?"

"Ourselves, of course. What do women clack about when they are alone, eh?"

"Clack? Not the same thing at all."

"Sure it is, except the topics are different. Essentially, it was a way to discover each other and what we were."

The cliffs suddenly loomed huge before them and the shadows of the canyon parted into a deep, narrow fissure. He steered the combie in and the smooth walls suddenly rushed by them. They were in another world where the desert did not belong.

Strands of tarad grass clung to the cliffs and the winding sands of the watercourse beneath them. Clumps of muddy green shrub clustered around an occasional peelath as if seeking protection. The cliffs shrank back and opened into a wooded glade of peelath and tarad grass. Terr remembered how the very walls of the canyon had cried out at his anger and his skin crawled, but only an echo of emptiness remained now.

The combie rounded a bend and the pool opened before

them. They glided above the still brown waters and the clustered moss-palms. Teena inhaled sharply and pointed at the broken glaze staining the white sands of the small beach. Terr didn't say anything as their eyes met. There wasn't anything that needed saying.

The combie sank and the power plant spooled down. He waited a moment, then touched a small pad and the bubble slid back. Still cool in the valley, the smells of burnt rock, the tang of tarad grass, and the aromatic oil of the peelath, mixed with the musty damp of Taklan moss, crowded the air around them.

He breathed deeply of the scented air. Later in the heat of the day the smells would change and become more subtle. With a quick glance at Teena, he climbed out. Sand crunched beneath his feet as he walked toward the edge of the pool. With a contented sigh, he picked a pebble, threw it and watched it skip to the far side. Hands crossed before his chest, he gazed absently at the fading rings of water and the play of shadows as the breeze stirred the branches of the palms. He turned at the sound of her footfalls. She stopped before a pile of molten glass and slag where Dhar had stood. Her head lifted and her eyes were dark as she looked at him, searching silently for an answer to some question.

He sat down, the sand already getting warm, and hugged his knees. Her footfalls were whispers of shifting sand as she came up behind him. After a moment, she sank beside him and curled her legs beneath her, one hand sifting absently through the sand. He reached for her and drew her against him, comforted by the warmth of her body. She allowed her head to touch his shoulder.

"It's incredible to think that something like this could exist in such wilderness."

He grunted in agreement.

"He must have hurt you terribly for you to do what you did," she whispered uncertainly.

He stroked her hair. "I hurt myself by not understanding."

"I am glad it ended the way it did."

Me too, he added silently.

Her gaze wandered around the steep walls, the still water of the pond, the stands of peelath, and shook her head.

"In a place like this," she murmured dreamily, "I could forget who I am, where I am or where I'm going. Time doesn't exist and there is no tomorrow. There is only the now."

They sat in a moment of peace and stillness and they were one with the gorge.

"We can make it last as long as you want," he said softly and ran his fingers gently down her back.

She lifted her head and her eyes were searching. "Why did you bring me here?"

"To share. To try and make you understand something of what draws me to this world."

"And tomorrow?"

"I thought you said there were no tomorrows," he teased her.

"Beast!" She fisted him in the ribs. He growled and leaned across her, forcing her back. She squealed and her small fists pounded against his chest. He nuzzled her neck and cheeks, searching for her soft mouth.

Her lips parted and her tongue was a touch of velvet fire. Lying across her, his fingers marched through her hair and he rested his head on her breasts.

"My randy lord of the desert," she purred softly and he chuckled.

"Tell me," he said, looking at her. "What was it like on Taltair when that Servatory Party cell took you?" he asked and she frowned prettily.

"Strange, but I cannot quite figure it," she replied after a moment, looking puzzled. "They treated me like a dignitary, all very polite, but distant. Why do you ask?"

"I don't know. Just wondering." Wondering whether he should tell her it was Enllss who engineered her capture. But what would be the point of doing that now?

"Terr?" she mumbled as her finger traced the outline of his nose.

"Mmm?" He relished the warmth of her breast against his cheek.

"I want to see Athal Than," she said in a small voice and he heard her heart flutter in agitation.

He lifted his head and stared at her. Her eyes were bright and mischievous. He had shared everything else with her and he cursed himself for a fool, not realizing right away what drew her to that place. The forces in that escarpment had molded everything about him. No wonder she was curious. Now, she had a chance to see it for herself, a chance not to be denied.

"I will not be able to take you inside," he warned her.

She didn't say anything, but her eyes thanked him. "I just have to see it," she murmured.

He nodded gently and felt all puffed up with virtue.

The sharp beep from the combie shattered the dreamy peace.

"Rit!" Half feigning annoyance, he gave her a quick smile. "It's Dhar," he growled, stood up and patted away sand from his trousers.

"Oh, Terr," she groaned, looking at him tragically. "I thought that out here we'd be alone."

"We are, my pet," he said as he marched to the combie. "No one else knows the comms code," he said grimly and leaned over the bubble sill. The comms plate cleared and Dhar nodded to him, looking apologetic.

"I thought it might be you," Terr said testily.

"My brother, I did not wish it, but I was ordered."

"One guess. Anabb?"

"He said it was important."

"I'll bet."

"You are to call him immediately."

"You have got to be kidding me, right? I'm on leave. Business can wait. And I'm not sure I want to talk to him anyway."

"That would be unwise."

"What does the old fart want?"

"He did not say, but I gather it's some sort of mission."

"A mission?" Terr laughed. "And you called me just to tell me that?"

Dhar gave a little shrug and Terr shook his head.

"I'll think about it, but don't hold your breath." He then noticed the new insignia on Dhar's working grays. "I'm happy for you, my brother." He grinned broadly. "It is no more than you deserve."

Dhar nodded with pleasure and smiled. "Anabb's guilty conscience, perhaps?"

"A promotion is a promotion," Terr said with mock severity. "You take it and run and hope there is time to enjoy it."

"Indeed. My shadow rests on both of you, my brother," he said and glanced at Teena standing beside Terr. The plate faded.

Terr looked at her and her mouth drooped. Helplessly, he spread his hands and shrugged. "Anabb is a low life, but I have to confront him sometime."

"And then you'll be gone again," she muttered bitterly and her eyes flashed. "I know how his mind works. He'll talk you into something and—"

"He won't talk me into anything!" he snapped, unsure of himself. He reached for her and grasped her arms. "We have four months, Teena. I'll not let anything come between us now. I have to call him, you know that, but not today. I have something more important in mind." He grinned wickedly and reached for her. She shrieked in alarm and ran off.

"I'm gonna get ya!" he growled and stomped after her.

* * *

Sitting before the Wall as it cycled through shifting color

patterns, Terr hesitated, uncertain whether he wanted to complete the connection. That he had to confront him was inevitable, but he preferred it to be later than sooner, and on his terms. He wasn't sure he was ready.

They spent the flight to Kanarath in silence. Teena was apprehensive and resentful and still in shock. He couldn't say he blamed her.

It might not have been the way they intended, but on the way back, he kept his promise to her. With the sun low in the sky, the shadows were long and the cliffs of the escarpment were walls of red stone. He slowed the combie and they drifted in silence above the flowing sands of the Saffal.

Teena sat beside him, staring avidly at the twisted buttresses as the combie circled, her hands clasped tight in her lap. He picked a spot and brought the craft down. When the combie sighed to a stop the cliffs towered before them and he felt their power. A comforting feeling and he felt warmed to be in the god's presence. The bubble slid back and hot air rushed into the cabin, bringing with it the familiar burnt smells of rock, sand and dried tarad grass.

He had an urge to raise his arms. When he clenched his fist, he imagined he could hear a low rumble of thunder somewhere among the cliffs. When he looked down, blue fire slithered over his hands. Teena looked at him, her eyes questioning. He nodded at the cliffs.

"There it is. That's where the gods restored me," he whispered and brushed her cheek, leaving a wake of fire.

"I can almost feel it," she said breathlessly. "Can I—"

"Go and look. Do not fear, I shall watch over you."

She gave him a tight little smile. After taking a deep breath, she stepped out of the combie. With barely a hesitation, she walked slowly across the stone flats, her shadow preceding her. Then she slowed and stopped to stand before the silent cliffs. Time seemed to melt into a slice of eternity. She stood there, taking it in, letting it wash through her.

He felt the pull and found himself looking through her eyes. Not the pull of a call, more like a yearning to see what lay beyond the forbidding cliffs—a dangerous curiosity. He felt her sway as she took the first tentative step toward one of the gaping cracks. With a wrenching effort of will, he jumped up in alarm.

"Teena!" he cried urgently. She paused, then took another step. "No!"

He didn't remember clambering out of the combie or running to her. When he stood before her, alarmed, she stared through him, her eyes glazed. He grasped her shoulders and shook her. Her eyes flickered and she seemed to notice him. With a strangled moan, she clung to him and broke into gasping sobs.

"I couldn't stop," she kept mumbling into his chest. "It was you walking and I felt its pull…"

"It's all right. It's over now," he whispered, badly frightened, cursing himself for a fool. He looked over the top of her head and stared at the silent walls.

He should have realized what was happening when he felt the urge to summon his aspect. Teena and he were bound together in flesh and spirit. In the sight of the gods, they were one. He should have been there with her to channel the power.

He held her as she clung to him shivering. Her sobs stopped, but her body trembled in his arms.

It took a while to calm her down and to calm himself. She didn't resist as they climbed back into the combie and took off. They didn't say much during the flight to Kanarath. Not in words, anyway. Each had a lot to think about and the experience had left them both badly shaken.

He leaned across the desk and tapped a pad on the small console. The Wall cycled through another pattern. Sitting there, he remembered how it had been. He remembered how Anabb stood, afraid yet defiant, the shattered remnants of his office around them, and the wind howling through the gaping hole that used to be the window screen.

The Wall cleared and they stared at each other in silence.

"It is good to see you again, my boy," Anabb said gruffly and his mouth twitched in an uncertain smile. There was nothing uncertain about his close-set oval eyes that regarded Terr beneath ridges of unruly black eyebrows.

"I wish I could say the same," Terr said after a timeless moment.

In the corners of Anabb's eyes and mouth, the folds seemed deeper and the skin drier, brittle looking. The lines of authority were etched deep, but he wore them with dignity.

"I imagine so," Anabb said with a nod and his eyes took on a faraway look.

Regarding him, old beneath the weight of responsibility, alone and friendless, Terr wanted to reach out his hand and…tell him everything turned out all right? That he understood? Tempted, but one thing stood between them he could not afford to forget.

Anabb was a cold-blooded, heartless bastard, and manipulating people his specialty. Still…

In a moment of reflection that comes unawares, he remembered standing in the LTN-12's Observation Deck with Mark Larkin as they stared at the fragile beauty of the Moon. He recalled Mark's words. They seemed to fit this moment rather well. He shook his head at the sweet irony.

"As someone once said to me, Anabb, in turn, I give you his words. I understand some things better and I'm not blaming you for what happened. If that means anything to you." A small load seemed to lift off his shoulders, and he watched as Anabb's eyes regained some of their sparkle.

"Thanks, boy," Anabb mumbled and the ragged blue-veined burn on his cheek turned a mottled red. The brown flecks in his eyes glittered. "Enjoying your leave?" he asked innocently and Terr couldn't help but laugh.

"I've had a hell of a start," he said and a smile twitched in the corner of Anabb's mouth.

"I can imagine, and I regret the pain it caused you."

"Yeah."

"You're different somehow. It's your eyes, cold and remote. Eyes of a Wanderer."

It all came flooding back, but the memories were only that, memories, and the pain belonged to somebody else. As with other things, he must have left that behind somewhere in the Keep of Death.

"You wouldn't even understand."

"Probably not," Anabb said. Regret maybe?

"Why didn't you tell me?" Terr asked.

"I couldn't, and now, it probably doesn't matter. Events have progressed beyond the point of effective termination and have a momentum of their own."

"Was it worth it?"

"It depends on how you look at these things, my boy. The pieces are still falling into place and it will take some time to count the returns."

"Ironic, isn't it? Faced with a possible Kran incursion, instead of facing up to the threat and taking advantage of the Orieli's strategic position, the Executive Council factions are busily jockeying for seats and personal power."

"There may be some justification for your cynicism, but you're judging us too harshly."

"I think not, Anabb. I wish I could say what Enllss did was completely altruistic, but I cannot. His primary concern was to maintain the Revisionist Party majority and dominance over the Executive Council. Even to the point of abolishing the independent's seat. To pretend otherwise would be naive."

Anabb regarded Terr with a quizzical smile. "I know how you feel, believe me. Idealism and reality, my boy, are two states constantly in conflict with self-interest. It doesn't matter whether that self-interest is personal or organizational. We can only hope the decisions we make don't end up too destructive.

Through the Valley of Shadow

"But I didn't call you to discuss political philosophy," Anabb said briskly and the official facade snapped back into place. "Or to make explanations, although, by thunder, you deserve one. I have an assignment for you," he said, eyes hard and uncompromising.

Terr was too amused to be annoyed. "Another body deal or a world-saving mission, perhaps?"

"You may have had a rough time and you feel somewhat used, but resignation or not, you're still one of my operatives. If you cannot cut the responsibility, I can relieve you of that burden right here and now. Sort out what you want, but don't cry on my shoulder because your sense of justice is offended."

"Yeah, life is hell," Terr agreed, Anabb's message still ringing in his ears. He played with the big boys now and they played the game for keeps. In an imperfect world, he could either learn to live with disappointment or crawl into a hole and slam the door.

What *did* he want?

Above all things, power demands humility and compassion, he heard his master's voice. He learned that one the hard way. He recalled a memory of himself, suspended in space, hands upraised with two stars adorning his feet. Before him, a world hung awaiting his judgment. When the lightning went forth, he heard his laughter as the world dissolved with the cry of billions.

Even a god can stand helpless before his creation, perplexed, shaking his head in wonder at the working of free will. But then, Terr was not a god, or immune to pain.

"You're a cold, heartless, calculating bastard, Anabb," Terr told him with relish. "And like you said, maybe that's what the job calls for."

"And you wear your cloak of morality like a convenient shield," Anabb pointed out with detached candor. "Rising and lowering it as you find convenient. For all your protestation, my boy, we all do what we want to do. I just want one word from

273

you. Yes or no."

Anabb had maneuvered him into a corner and they both knew it. Time to stop feeling sorry for himself and get on with the job. But what was the job? More of Anabb's murky deals? He rejected that one outright. And the alternative? Conning an M-4 perhaps, on endless patrols, dying of boredom and monotony? Not so long ago, he dreamed of commanding an M-4. Had he really changed that much?

"I hate you," he said and Anabb grinned broadly.

"Now that's the Terr I know and love."

"There is a small matter of my leave," Terr said in defiance, and to his amazement, relief. Anabb smiled warmly.

"A detail." He dismissed it with a wave of his hand. "You can consider this an extension."

"What did you have in mind?"

"I want you to go to the Orieli Cluster," Anabb said smoothly and watched Terr's reaction with unconcealed amusement.

Terr stared at his old boss in astonishment. The Orieli? It took him a while before he grasped the significance of what Anabb had said. While wrapped up in his problems, Anabb must have been negotiating with Karhide Zor-Ell for a cultural exchange mission.

"Surely, I'm not the only team going in?" Terr demanded in alarm.

"What's the matter? Cold feet already? Never mind. There are three teams going in, two specialist groups and you. You'll be briefed in detail, but essentially, you'll be operating under very few specific objectives. Your job is to provide an overall perspective, a feel, if you like, of the Orieli and what they're all about."

"By looking into odd places, right?"

Anabb grinned. "All of it will be odd, I should imagine."

"And how many teams are the Orieli sending in?"

"Two teams of four," Anabb said, looking puzzled.

Through the Valley of Shadow

Two teams of four the Serrll will see, Terr reflected sardonically, remembering what Zor-Ell had gone through on Earth. How many observers would they plant? He had a duty to reveal to Anabb the Orieli data-gathering technique, but he also had a moral obligation to Zor-Ell.

"What's the timeframe for all this?"

"Not longer than six months."

"And I suppose you want me to start right now, is that it?"

"Immediately. Karhide Arlon Dee is waiting—"

Terr shook his head. "In that case, I cannot do it."

"But—"

"Anabb, I almost killed a brother and lost Teena. That we're all still in one piece is due to luck rather than any planning on my part. I need time to pull it all together. I cannot leave Teena alone again. I won't. If I go now, I'll lose her."

"You won't lose her. I may be cold and calculating as you suggested, but I'm not insensitive. I know what you went through, or at least I can imagine it. You will take Teena and Dhar with you. Didn't he tell you?"

"I guess it slipped his mind. Why the sudden generosity?" Terr looked at him suspiciously.

"Thunderation! Have you forgotten that Terchran still wants your hide for a rug? Now that Dhar's cover is blown, he'll be after him as well."

"I'm relieved that your gush of generosity isn't based on any altruistic motive," Terr said sarcastically.

"I really don't know why I suffer your impertinence." Anabb glared and the burn on his cheek turned livid. "In case you harbor any misconceptions of self-grandeur, Master Scout, you should remember something. There are dozens of people far more qualified for this mission than you who would jump at a chance like this."

"I apologize," Terr said humbly and meant it. Anabb's motives may not have been completely altruistic, but the gesture was nevertheless sincere.

"Perhaps I should simply hand you over to Terchran. It would rid me of a major problem in my life," Anabb growled and ran a hand through his hair. "At least I'll have some peace and quiet with you gone."

"I apologized, didn't I?" Terr said and gave him his innocent look.

"The quicker you get out of my sight the better. I want you to take your M-1 to Devon 3-VL4, an ecoforming station in the Palean Union. You must be there in two days and you'll just about make it under full boost. Karhide Arlon Dee is expecting you, and has orders to await your arrival."

"What are the Orieli doing there?"

"They had an encounter with a Kran cruiser and damaged it. The Krans have holed up on Devon's moon and were raiding the ecoforming stations for repair materials."

"So, it's started." Maybe driving an M-4 on patrol would not be so boring after all. "What's been our response?"

"Well, it would be funny if it weren't so serious. The Orieli were ordered to stand off while two M-4s went in to take out the Kran heavy. One got shot up pretty badly and they're now waiting for an M-6 from Kalakan."

"Rit! Why the hell didn't COMPALOPS request Orieli's assistance in the first place?"

Anabb raised his eyebrows and shrugged. "In Tain wanted to verify the Kran ship's firepower."

"Great! At least the M-6 should be able to take it out."

"That's the funny part. Departure of the M-6 is delayed. In the meantime, you can be sure the Krans haven't been wasting time making repairs to their ship. If they decide to lift off that moon before the M-6 gets there, things could turn out to be rather unpleasant."

"Well, it will certainly provide COMPALOPS with an evaluation of Kran's firepower," Terr mused sarcastically when the awful implication dawned on him. "You're sending me right into the middle of that mess!"

Through the Valley of Shadow

"It cannot be helped. You should be safe, provided Karhide Dee doesn't take his ship into action."

"Oh, that's terrific! You won't need Terchran to finish me off. The Krans will do the job for him," Terr said bitterly, taking back all the kind thoughts. He had *known* that Anabb was a low, manipulating bastard!

* * *

It was a clear night and Ed-Kani Takao imagined he could see the stars through the curtain of light thrown up by the city. Instead of stars, he saw darkness that matched his mood.

After a lifetime of planning, intrigue and factional in-fighting the returns have slowly but steadily started to come in. In many ways the unification of the multi-faceted Sargon government machinery behind his policies had perhaps been his greatest achievement. Maintaining that momentum with the parochial Pro-Consuls had proven to be singularly difficult.

To his dismay, he found, as had many others before him, the power he represented in the General Assembly constantly undermined by factional byplays inside Sargon. Taking home support for granted had cost more than one Assembly rep his political head. Bad enough having to cope with the tangle of Captal duplicity without constantly looking over his shoulder for an aspiring delegate to drive a pike through his back.

He survived not only his party's circumspect attempts to truncate his tenure, but more significantly, Captal's own imper-sonal winnowing gambits. The process had hardened him, until now, he would not have recognized the idealistic man he was twenty-eight years ago. To be Sargon's most powerful Captal representative, and to a large degree, managing to control the unwieldy and disparate interests embodied in the Sargon Direc-torate machinery, demonstrated his single-minded determina-tion and ruthlessness.

Looking out the window screen, the scowl on his face grew

deeper. Despite his unwavering drive, it had not been enough. How far they had come, yet how little they learned. Sargon's history was a proud litany of expansion, conquest and military prowess earned over many centuries of refinement. With Karkan, they owned half the Serrll Combine. Somewhere along the line, the Karkan Federation had lost the edge. They had gone soft, preoccupied with Captal politics and elaborate schemes for gaining the Executive Council majority—a fool's pursuit.

What a waste, he thought.

And through the centuries, Sargon had allowed its military apparatus to be absorbed within the Serrll Scout Fleet, thereby losing its traditional means of implementing decisions and exercising its sovereign will.

With all its military might, the very pride in their ability blinded them, humbling them before their conquerors. Sargon never understood the forces arrayed against them. Or if it did, it refused to recognize what was happening. They were vanquished without a shot fired. For a culture schooled in harsh military philosophy and discipline, Sofam's merchants were seen as representatives of a weak, morally loose people, and were treated with contempt. Too late the economic weapons wielded by the Paravan Trading Association, backed by Sofam warships, were finally recognized for what they were.

The road back to independence and self-determination now narrow and rocky. With the Karkan Federation, they have achieved much. Now, Sargon needed to push out on its own if it is to achieve its former greatness. The problem, he admitted grudgingly, he lacked patience and a perspective that spanned centuries, a failing recognized by others. He was a fool to have tried to shift the inertia of dozens of planets. But how close he came!

Like a badly woven tapestry the strands were beginning to unravel along the edges. The Palean Congress failed to be moved despite the imminent Kran threat, and Ti Inai was getting cold feet. Why the rush, he protested weakly, assured of his power for another term. Did Ti Inai suspect Sargon's underlying motive for the merger? Unlikely, but possible. He remembered that Ti Inai could be clever when he chose to, and he didn't need to look farther than Khiman-ra.

Palean slime!

He realized he should have tackled Tao Karam personally. Too late now.

He hissed and snapped his jaws in irritation. He should not blame Ti Inai, he knew that. His thoughts turned to Prime Director Kernami Asai Tainam. Five lousy systems stood between him and total unification. No, just one man!

Beanab was right. The sooner Kernami returned to his ancestors the better. There were sure to be howls of indignation and protest, but none of that would bring Kernami back. Without his powerful influence in the Triumvirate, Pizgor would fall within Sargon's umbrella. His carefully built cells and Triumvirate appointees personally loyal to him would see to that.

A keen student of history, he was sensitive to momentous events caused or prevented by intervention of a single individual. His motivations were largely based on such effects. Focused on individuals, it was ironic how he managed to underestimate the unwieldy conglomerate of the Palean Union. Even with Pizgor secured, it was unlikely that enough Palean Congressmen would be swayed to change their allegiance. In time perhaps, but beyond the coming elections certainly.

Patience and perspective?

Bitter, he reflected that manipulating parts did not necessarily influence the whole. And that could be a costly lesson, for him and Sargon. It really was too bad that his plan five years ago to have Rolan cede their systems to Sargon never came off. It would have been such a neat solution. In that, the Provisional Committee had to carry part of the blame. They squandered their chance to secure Rolan before the cursed Orieli showed up. When that happened, everything piled up in an unmanageable rush. Sargon and the Paleans supposedly united in a common cause, but in reality, still pursuing expedient short-term advantages. That's how everybody played the game, even at the cost of damaging long-term objectives.

The comms alert beeped softly and he snapped his jaws in annoyance. He was tired, tired of Ti Inai, of Illeran and the whole tangled merger mess. He'd had a long day and should have retired hours ago. What did they think he was, he reflected peevishly, a bloody fixture? There was only so much he was prepared to give.

Wearing a stormy frown, he walked to his desk and tapped the comms pad. "What is it?"

"Prime Director Marrakan, sir," came the surprised voice of his first assistant.

Marrakan? Puzzled and suspicious, he wondered what in slime that desert creature wanted? One thing he felt certain about. It would not be a social call.

"Very well. Put him through." Another singular identity he could have done without at this particular time. The whole Unified Independent Front movement had become one monumental pain, and he had no trouble identifying Marrakan with it.

The Wall cleared and the Wanderer stood outlined against an office backdrop that could easily have been Ed-Kani's own. Instead of traditional brown robes affected by the nomads, Marrakan wore a suit that would not have excited comment on any planetary executive. And that's exactly what he was, Ed-Kani reminded himself.

Except for the eyes.

They seemed to burn through the Wall and Ed-Kani felt himself going on the defensive. It felt uncomfortably like having his soul bared. He held too many secrets and dark memories to face those eyes without a qualm. He never feared any man, faced every challenge, feeling himself superior, but he feared the unknown of this Wanderer.

Through the Valley of Shadow

He could not afford to underestimate this man.

"Executive Director," Marrakan said with a deep rumble and inclined his head briefly. "I appreciate you taking my call without prior notice."

The heat of the desert seemed to drift out of the Wall and Ed-Kani felt himself grow warm.

"What can I do for you, Mr. Controller?" he hissed, demoting him from his rightful title of Prime Director as he stared intently at the Wanderer.

"I shall keep this short, sir." Marrakan folded his hands and turned slightly to bring the orange hues of a late afternoon within range of the Wall. As the silence grew, Ed-Kani became more uncomfortable and angry.

The Wanderer appeared to be deliberately trying to unnerve him, he thought furiously. To his chagrin, he realized it was working.

Those eyes…

"Then keep it short."

Marrakan merely nodded. "I wanted to see the face of my enemy, albeit a political one only," he said easily, noting Ed-Kani's discomfort with amusement. "You need not bother denying it."

"Why should I deny it?" Ed-Kani scowled at the Wall. The power of the man tangible and disconcerting. He pondered whether some truth lay behind those outlandish tales about the Wanderers. "There is nothing personal in this, you understand. The Unified Independent Front is a momentary inconvenience, that's all."

"It might be an inconvenience, Mr. Director, but it is certainly not momentary. As for it being personal, you made it so when you decided to take a life," Marrakan said and his voice was suddenly cold and gravelly.

Ed-Kani understood immediately and didn't bother with histrionic denials, allowing himself a thin smile as he studied the Wanderer with grudging admiration.

"Like the Unified Independent Front, Pizgor is strategically critical to my plans. However, unlike the UIF, Pizgor is more amenable to manipulation. The Triumvirate could have been reasonable, but Prime Director Kernami Asai Tainam chose otherwise. I would have respected their independence and self-determination. Sargon has no interest plundering their worlds. We're already prosperous. It's the numerical value of those systems that's important."

"That is altogether quite clear to me," Marrakan said. "With Pizgor, Sargon, and the Paleans, under the banner of the Alikan Union Party, would have almost enough systems to hold three Executive Council seats. Your plan is bold, Mr. Director. With those three seats, you would assume dominance of the Servatory Party, presupposing that the Paleans would be withdrawing their support from the Revisionists. In short, Pizgor, or more correctly Kernami, is all that stands between you and a third Executive seat. Having failed twice through covert manipulation, you reverted to form and now seek to accomplish your objective more directly."

Ed-Kani laughed in appreciation, a prolonged hiss that revealed small, sharp teeth.

"Obviously, living in a desert hasn't filled your head with sand. And you're quite correct in your analysis. It's unfortunate that I relied too heavily on Beanab's compliance, thereby underestimating Kernami's influence and power. A mistake, but one that is not beyond retrieval."

Marrakan breathed deeply of the burnt air, savoring the smell of flowing sands. The alien before him totally ruthless, above morals in his struggle for power, but he refrained from judgment, aware of Sargon's history and military discipline. The centuries of stifled, controlled existence imposed by Sofam and its traders must be an enduring humiliation for them. Nevertheless, he could not allow the deed to take place.

"You may conduct your political intrigues as you please, Mr. Director. Kaleen systems have seen many conquerors, and the Serrll is merely the last in a long line. We don't seek to hold the stars, but we will act to protect ourselves and those we hold in trust."

"And what will you do? Make a strongly worded protest to the General Assembly?"

Marrakan smiled and shook his head. "I seek your assurance, Mr. Director, that Kernami Asai Tainam will not be harmed."

"I'm sorry, but the course I have chosen, no, which Sargon has chosen, is too important to be deflected by concern for the life of one man."

"I am tempted to argue the value of one life, sir, but I suspect it would be a futile gesture."

"Make your point, Mr. Controller," Ed-Kani demanded, suddenly impatient to end this charade. The man was naive if he thought to sway him with emotion.

"I intend to. You already surmised that the power balance has been gradually shifting from the Karkan Federation to Sargon. Otherwise, your whole course of action would mean little. The merger with the Paleans might be achieved in time and is perhaps inevitable, but not now. You're risking a premature confrontation, when with a little patience all the pieces will eventually fall into place."

"You may be right," Ed-Kani acknowledged reluctantly. "However, events have taken their course and I cannot change them now even if I was predisposed to do so."

"Does personal glory and a place in history mean so much to you?"

Ed-Kani keenly studied the Wanderer, impressed by the other's sensitivity. A redoubtable enemy indeed. And Marrakan was right, of course, given another reminder of the virtue of patience.

"I'm out of time, Mr. Controller. What is it you want?"

"I am asking you one last time—"

"And I have said no."

Marrakan pressed his lips and nodded. "Very well, then. I shall make my point in a more personal way."

Ed-Kani frowned in puzzlement, then involuntarily stepped back against his desk as Marrakan raised his arm. Blue sparks arced between his fingers. When the lightning struck, Ed-Kani screamed and fell, clutching his left wrist. The pain seared through his body in a burning wave. He groaned and looked at his left hand, his eyes growing wide in horror.

Below his wrist, his hand was a sculptured piece of veined gray stone.

"No!" he screeched in terror. Cradling his hand, his eyes remained fixed on the Wall. The yellow face there stared at him, eyes cold as his hand.

"You have been warned, Mr. Director. Should Kernami die, you and Sargon will have more than your hand to contend with."

When the Wall faded and began to cycle, Ed-Kani pressed his hand against his body and moaned. He knelt and rocked slowly from side to side.

* * *

The warm desert breeze barely stirred the shrubbery of the hanging garden. The slatted lattice softened some of the harsh glare from the amber sky and cast sharp angular shadows among the tables. In the middle of the garden, surrounded by pale yellow taslexia orchids, a small fountain gurgled and hissed, glowing with shifting colors from a hidden light source below.

Most of the tables were empty. Still too early in the day for that kind of action. Those occupied were mostly by offworlders or anonymously garbed executives from one of the various civilian buildings near the Center. Two attendants stood unobtrusively beneath a shrouded arch, waiting patiently, unmoving.

There were no Wanderers in the place, this being strictly a tourist trap. A Wanderer wouldn't be caught dead dining at one of the hanging gardens. Such profusion of greenery and water reeked of decadent opulence—something almost sinful.

Terr took a long pull from his tumbler and absently twirled the crushed ice inside. Frosted beads of dew slid gently down the glass.

After glancing at a pair of civil servant types, he caught Dhar's eye.

"Life doesn't seem such a burden for them. What do you think?" he said easily and sucked on a tooth, enjoying a perverse sense of pleasure at Dhar's unease.

"We should not have come here," Dhar growled, glaring at him with mock severity.

"Maybe not, but I always wanted to find out what one of these places looked like from the inside. And this might be our last chance for quite a while."

"Never mind all that," Teena said impatiently. "Mind telling us what this is all about? You've been wearing that smug satisfied expression ever since you came back from your talk with Anabb. He hasn't talked you into anything, has he?" She glared at Terr with sudden suspicion.

"Now, you know me better than that, my pet."

"I certainly do. He *has* talked you into something, hasn't he?"

"It's not what you think."

"Meeting like this is most irregular, my brother," Dhar said.

"I simply wanted to share an interesting piece of news. What's wrong with that?"

Teena scowled and shot Dhar a quick look. "Let me handle this. I know how a one-tracked mind works." She pulled back a rebellious lock of hair. "It has to be something big or you wouldn't have fallen for it. You always had a weakness for grand schemes," she added with cutting perceptiveness. That one stung a bit, but Terr let it ride.

"All right. As soon as we finish up here, we're off. All of us," he said.

"Off? Off where?"

"The Orieli Cluster."

She gaped at him and Dhar leaned back in his seat. "The Orieli, of course."

"Wait a minute!" Teena pulled urgently at Terr's arm. "Aren't they supposed to be at war or something?"

"Nothing to worry about. We'll not be going anywhere hot."

"That's comforting to know," she said tartly and Terr shot her a sharp look.

Dhar watched them for a moment before discreetly clearing his throat. "I assume that this is part of a cultural exchange mission? What are our terms of reference?"

Terr scowled, his enthusiasm somewhat cooled by their reaction.

"The official chapter and verse is in the computer aboard *Sheeva*," he told them. "It boils down to mousing around trying to capture the feel of the Orieli culture, their social structures, formal and informal institutions. Stuff like that."

Dhar raised an eyebrow. "A tall order. How long do we have?"

"Not longer than six months."

"Six months!" Teena pulled back in alarm. "What about us? We were supposed to have four months together, you said. And my job? I cannot just up and…" she slowed and stopped in confusion.

The whisper of the fountain suddenly loud and Terr set his tumbler down with a sharp click. He didn't say anything as he looked at her. Her eyes turned dark green, her mouth firmed and her cheeks colored. She stared at him in defiance, regretting the words, but they could not be unsaid.

She looked so beautiful sitting there, watching him, body tense, her pert little nose turned up in a challenge, fire lighting her eyes. He appreciated her concern. She wanted him near her, but on her terms. Perhaps fair, he didn't know, but he couldn't do that. After everything they had gone through, he thought she understood.

"This is important, Teena, and I want you with me," he said softly, watching her chest rise and fall in agitation. "But you can go back to Taltair if you want. I would hate that, though."

"You said you wanted to share. Now this." She glared at him, her eyes clouding as the fires faded. "I want to be with you," she whispered uncertainly and hung her head. "It is just—"

"I know," he said and squeezed her hand. He placed a finger under her chin and lifted her head. "I took this assignment because I do want to share, to show you something of what I do, so we can be together. If this is going to come between us, I'll turn it down. I don't want to lose you."

"It's a tremendous opportunity for you, isn't it?"

"It's not worth our happiness."

She looked at him steadily, then slowly reached with her hand and placed it in his. "I guess I'm afraid to leave what I know. I am not a field agent and the Orieli Cluster—"

"Is like another galaxy," he said. "Teena, after all that happened to us, will your old job be enough now?"

She bit her lip. "We were just getting close again…" she managed in a tight whisper.

"This won't take us apart."

"Why the urgency, Sankri?" Dhar put in when the silence began to get uncomfortable.

Terr cleared his throat. This is where the situation got challenging.

"Anabb made a deal with the Orieli. He's got Karhide Arlon Dee waiting for us at Devon 3-VL4."

"Devon? That's an ecoforming station somewhere off the Palean Union, if my memory serves me."

"Nothing wrong with your memory."

"What are the Orieli doing there? It seems somewhat out

of their way," Teena observed, still stunned by the news and unsure of her feelings.

Terr braced himself. "It is, but it looks like they've got a Kran cruiser bottled up on Devon's moon and are babysitting it until heavy Scout Fleet units get there."

"I thought you said we weren't going anywhere hot," she remarked darkly.

"Nothing to worry about, my pet," he said comfortably and stroked her hand. She pouted and pulled it away.

Rit!

"You are not telling us everything, my brother. Such as, what is a Kran cruiser doing off Devon? That is far beyond their normal operating area. I thought the Orieli Line Tracking Net was supposed to prevent that very thing from happening. More importantly, why Karhide Arlon Dee? Sending us into a tactical zone always carries with it some risk. It would have made more sense to have arranged a rendezvous at one of their LTN stations."

Terr picked up his tumbler. After giving it a quick twirl, he took a sip and collected his thoughts.

"All right then. I'll try and explain it, but there is one thing that must be clearly understood." He gave each of them a hard look. "If anybody wants to back out after I've had my say, I'll scrub the whole thing."

"Now, just—" Teena started but Terr held up his hand.

"Let me finish before you start protesting, all right?"

She glared at him.

"Good. Two days ago, Karhide Zor-Ell presented to the General Assembly an assessment of the Celi-Kran threat and brought the house down. Damn near caused a riot. While the Orieli told us the truth about the Krans, they haven't told us everything. Not altogether surprising. Kran efforts to find the Orieli have landed them in Serrll space much sooner than anyone expected. As a result, the Serrll have to honor the threat."

"Is that the reason for the cultural exchange?" Teena demanded.

"Of course not, but we also have to know who we're dealing with. That goes for the Orieli as well as the Krans."

"Why should the Orieli bother?" Teena asked. "If what you say is true, we're hardly of any consequence to them."

"You've done the analysis. I guess it all comes down to security. The Orieli may be benevolent, but as Arlon Dee pointed out, they're not altruistic. Over time, probability becomes almost a certainty that some Kran prowler would stumble onto us."

"As has apparently happened at Devon," Dhar pointed out.

"That's right. The Orieli want to make sure the Serrll take the threat seriously and prepare for a possible conflict. Anyone still wants to back out?"

* * *

In the quiet afternoon, strands of mist were gathering among the lengthening shadows of Celean Park, the avenues already bathed in light. There were no clouds to mar the pristine sky and the early mist promised a crisp night. Along the western horizon, orange and red hues were broken by an occasional cluster of towers, black outlines reaching toward a purple sky.

The last rays of the sun faded and the internal lighting system compensated automatically. Enllss canceled the response with a soft growl. As the lights dimmed, shadows crept into the office. In the background the Wall cycled through gyrating color patterns, filling the room with delicate unobtrusive music. This high up the Security Council tower was almost within reach of the lower flight bands filled with streaming lines of combies, private sled-pads, and communals, all moving in radiating lines toward outlying residential and industrial centers.

He leaned back in his formchair, sipped tea, and allowed

his eyes to wander aimlessly along the shifting colors of the sunset. The Wall never got them quite right, he mused absently as he followed a line of traffic disappearing from view. He had two or three minutes before his visitor arrived and he wanted to savor them. It was like standing in the calm of a storm's eye before being plunged back into peril. Holding the cup, he candidly admitted to himself that twenty years ago, had he known the price of his ambition, he might have thought twice about setting foot on the political trek. But the load was lighter then, and he was younger then.

Power and responsibility had toughened him and made him old. Like an invidious decease creeping on him unawares the addiction was now complete, his commitment total. Even if he wanted to, he could not see himself languishing in some sinecure post back on Kaplan. He had become a power mover. Knew it and liked it that way.

Still, it had been a beautiful sunset.

With it, another of his worries faded. Earlier that day, part of a troupe of dignitaries, he watched with mixed emotions the Orieli ship lift off Sal Field. Media coverage was heavy, with dozens of lights from every corner of the Serrll espousing their own interpretation of events. Even now, he did not feel at all certain the Serrll had made tangible gains in their complex relationship with the Orieli.

He remembered clearly part of a conversation he'd had with Zor-Ell yesterday evening. It had been a small gathering of executive directors with a sprinkling of senior commissioners and Assembly reps for flavor. The significance of his inclusion wasn't lost on him. Conversation flew back and forth easily, both parties glad to discard formalities. All seemingly innocent enough, but Enllss did not forget his first encounter with the karhide above the Moon. The Zaronian belittled his skills as a diplomat.

The large brown eyes of the alien fixed on him as Zor-Ell sipped tentatively at his wine. With a dismissive shrug, he said,

Through the Valley of Shadow

"Within three years, Da Commissioner, the Serrll Combine will either be actively involved repelling a Kran incursion, or by the time your term as director in the Executive Council expires, the Serrll shall be overrun."

The sip of fragrant wine caught in Enllss' throat and he had to fight to prevent himself from spluttering. With a strangled gasp, eyes swimming, he hurriedly composed his features into a semblance of normality. With masterful tact, Zor-Ell pretended not to notice.

"That's quite a statement, Karhide," Enllss said in a choked voice. "With many underlying assumptions."

"Granted, Da. However, not an unrealistic one."

"Even with your LTN to protect us?"

Zor-Ell lifted an eyebrow. "Da Commissioner, please understand. The LTN is not there to protect you, but to protect *us.*"

"But—"

Zor-Ell raised his hand. "Permit me to give you a piece of cold reality, Da. We have almost one thousand three hundred inhabited systems in The Arch. You must appreciate then how we view the two hundred and fifty-odd Serrll systems, not counting your outposts and protectorates. By that, I don't mean to devalue your strategic relevance, only to correct a point of perspective."

Enllss relaxed in his formchair, the words still ringing in his mind.

What had Zor-Ell said the first time they met? Points of incompatibility? Now it was a point of perspective. Enllss took a sip of tea and shook his head. It seemed that his Orieli friend had a penchant for delivering poignant points.

Has the Serrll lost the edge? The driving vitality that marked a period of unparalleled expansion some two thousand years ago seems to have foundered in a morass of consolidation and bureaucratic red tape. Have the interstellar blocks become too intent on devouring each other politically and economically to realize that their outlook had shifted inward rather than outward? If that were the case, it would go a long way toward explaining the growing unrest among the nonaligned independent systems and the psychology behind the formation of the Unified Independent Front. In a stagnating environment it was always the aggressive fringe that abandoned a decaying corpse first.

He made a mental note to check some Central Planning Council's 'what if' models. If he remembered correctly, the rate of expansion over the last two or three centuries had declined in a straight-line projection. He recalled that during his term as a BCPA commissioner, only three ecoforming projects were started, and two planets opened for colonization in two different systems.

It took the Orieli five years to span more than three thousand light-years with twelve outposts. Enllss wondered whether the Serrll could have mounted two over the same period. He did not count the galaxy core exploration ships, a special once-off deal. Anabb's comments back at the Serrll Moon Base suddenly became very relevant.

If his nomination to the Executive was confirmed, he would see to this problem personally, he promised himself with grim resolve. Nonetheless, there were things he could do now.

Absently, he laid the empty cup on the table with a soft click. Outside, remnants of dusk still lingered, but the shadows in his office had grown deeper, cradling him in their own way. When the comms alert beeped, the window screen polarized and the walls brightened automatically.

It had been a lovely sunset.

He touched a pad on his inlaid console and waited. His aide responded immediately.

"Executive Director Illeran is here to see you, sir," she announced in a low contralto. She knew her voice disturbed him and that's why she played the game.

Through the Valley of Shadow

"Show him in, will you?" he growled, allowing himself momentary images of temptation.

The translucent panels slid away and Illeran walked in with his familiar purposeful stride. Despite the crowding years, he still held his wide, flat head high on a slender neck. The close-set black eyes were clear and searching as ever. The scales on his head may have faded from their deep green, but it would be a mistake to underestimate the Karkan maluran solely by his appearance, as many have found to their cost.

With a subtle flick of a thin pointed tongue, Illeran nodded his greeting as Enllss casually waved at a spare formchair.

"Tea? A drink?" Enllss asked. Illeran shook his head and hissed with a sigh of pleasure as he sank into the formchair and stretched his long legs before him. A side Illeran few ever saw, Enllss mused wryly. Behind the facade of deadly political rivalry, in the final analysis, both of them were dedicated to serving the Serrll, or ruling it. The point moot. The reality was that both were power movers. In the privacy of their offices at least, the mask could be lowered guardedly, but lowered nonetheless.

"I wanted to congratulate you personally on your nomination to a seat on the Executive, Enllss," Illeran said, the horizontal slits of his eyes hardly visible.

Enllss gave a wry grin. "Bit early for celebrations, but thanks."

"Tell me." Illeran cocked his head and crossed his hands before his chest. "Your protégé, Anabb. Has he accepted?"

"Not yet. But I think he will."

"He is a good man," Illeran admitted grudgingly and his tongue flicked quickly. "We will not stand in his way, even if he's a Sofam Confederacy appointed slime."

"You're not usually so generous with your praise," Enllss remarked dryly. "Not getting sentimental in your old age, are you?"

Illeran shot him a pointed look and snorted. "In two years, you'll probably be running one of the Security Council Bureaus.

293

Until then, allow me one of the few privileges of my office. Because by then, my friend, whatever fate has in store for us, you'll be the one having to deal with it. Until that happens, I still set policy for your Bureau."

"What's the matter, Illeran? Some of your schemes beginning to smell?"

Illeran chuckled and inclined his head slightly. "We all have our moments. Your office seems to have a faint whiff about it as well."

"You're right there, by damn!" Enllss agreed and laughed. "Your visit here wouldn't have anything to do with that, by any chance. Would it?"

"In a way, but I'm glad to see you're still able to laugh at it," Illeran hissed with amusement.

Enllss shrugged. "Nothing else I can do. You told me yourself often enough. We must keep our attention focused on the broader objectives."

"Indeed. The Unified Independent Front is a pointed failure for both of us. And for the Servatory Party, more than you realize. That's only a personal disappointment, and not necessarily such a bad thing for the Serrll as a whole, given the current situation."

"You wouldn't be referring to Sargon and the Paleans, would you?"

"They do come to mind. The Provisional Committee of theirs, a very disturbing organization, my friend. Perhaps something drastic should be done about them. I don't suppose Sill-Anais managed to establish a link between them and the raiders, has he?"

"Afraid not, but he's still looking into it."

Illeran sighed and shook his head. "A waste of time, but we must go through the motions, I guess. You won't catch me saying that in public, mind you," he hissed and raised a finger in warning.

"Someone will make a mistake."

"I wouldn't count on it."

"They made one with Khiman-ra."

Illeran slowly nodded. "Point taken."

"Getting back to our Wanderer friends, you must admit that with a bit of finesse the Unified Independent Front could have been yours," Enllss said candidly. "But we aren't taking any bows either."

"Yes, it's a mess for everyone. Still, it would have been very interesting to be around if the recent Executive Council vote had abolished the independent's seat. Marrakan seems to be a singularly unique individual, all right. Beyond reproach like all the Wanderers. Do not disturb me, I am sleeping. Yes?"

Enllss stared at Illeran then leaned toward him. "Are you telling me that removing the Wanderers from the Councils was a mistake?"

"Not at all. A wise precaution and it had my approval, but a futile gesture nonetheless."

"Why do you say that?"

"Your thinking is still mission-oriented, Enllss," Illeran chided him. "When the Unified Independent Front announced its intention to formally form a political block, all our subsequent efforts have merely served to delay the inevitable. From a strategic point of view, we should have been directing our attention toward preventing them from ever making the announcement in the first place. Once made, the announcement merely capped a decision already reached, and set events into motion we could no longer control. We were blinded by our individual parochial interests."

Enllss thought that one over for a few minutes, not liking its taste. "I have been thinking along similar lines before you came. What you're saying is that as a government, Captal has failed."

"Somewhat simplistic, but in this instance, essentially true," Illeran growled and his tongue flicked in a blur. "Tell me. What would you say constitutes a greater threat to the stability of the

Serrll? Merger between Sargon and the Paleans or the Unified Independent Front?"

"The merger, without a doubt," Enllss said without hesitation.

"Indeed." Illeran nodded with satisfaction. "In this at least, the Revisionists and the Servatory Party are in agreement. The objectives of our respective pursuits may differ, but the bottom line is that neither of our parties wants to disrupt the stability of the Serrll Combine. In this important respect the aims of the new Alikan Union would differ. The elements within it are after personal power, regardless of the social cost."

"But so is the Servatory Party," Enllss pointed out evenly.

"That's true only at a party level, and certainly not by risking massive social dislocation. As individual politicians, most of us have never used the party machinery as a vehicle merely to pursue personal power." Illeran unfolded his hands and cracked his knuckles. "By the way, have you noted the absence of Ed-Kani from last night's reception?"

"I wasn't particularly interested in finding him."

"I noticed. The reason for our colleague's absence is that he's a sudden owner of a stone hand. Interesting, don't you think?"

"Stone hand?"

"Sill-Anais tells me of a better specimen found on Anar'on. A whole body, to be precise. One of Ed-Kani's operatives, I believe."

"It's Prime Director Kernami Asai Tainam. Ed-Kani has been threatening his removal for reasons I am sure you're aware of. Marrakan must have taken steps."

"Formidable indeed," Illeran hissed. "I have taken pains to learn something of the Wanderer Discipline and I can imagine what it cost Marrakan to do what he did. I can only hope that this represented an isolated incident and not a precedent. Apparently, he realizes the consequences equally well. A few hours ago, Moderator Torres received Marrakan's offer of resignation as Prime Director of the Kaleen group and Controller of Anar'on."

"Has it been accepted?"

"No, of course not, but a masterful tactical stroke, though. Torres could not accept the resignation even though every Executive Director voted for it. Including me. You see, by accepting, it would have salved our pride, but it would also have hardened the independent systems against Captal. Besides, it wouldn't have done anything to stop the Unified Independent Front. On the contrary, the resultant publicity would have undermined whatever tactics Ed-Kani and Ti Inai may have had in mind for the unification. Ed-Kani would also have found it difficult to survive an attempt to remove the head of a legitimate government.

"No, Marrakan knew what he was doing. His apology and intent might have been sincere, but his warning was unmistakable. Ed-Kani overreached himself and paid the price. The Provisional Committee will know better next time," Illeran said with quiet satisfaction.

"Why are you telling me all this, Illeran?" Enllss asked pointedly, wary of anything free from his political opponent. "You want something, don't you?"

"That's obvious, isn't it?" Illeran said with a predatory smile. "Karhide Zor-Ell seems to have monopolized you for most of last night. I want to know what went on between the two of you."

"What if I just tell you to go to the pit?"

"You could, but you won't. And what's more, I'll tell you why. Whatever the Orieli say could be significant. That kind of information cannot be evaluated by any single individual. It's too important and the consequences of a misunderstanding too serious to worry about personal pride or ambition.

"While Zor-Ell monopolized you, I had a chat with his sidekick, Opturkarh Tremane. He reminded me somewhat of your nephew and that Wanderer shadow of his, Dharaklin. Cast from the same mold, all of them. Now, about your conversation."

"The Bureau of Central Planning has it all," Enllss said and Illeran laughed with a prolonged hiss.

"You're a sly fish, Enllss. I could use you in the Party."

Enllss pulled back with a scowl. "I will not be insulted in my own office!" he said severely, but a conspiratorial twinkle lit his eyes.

"Hah!"

"If I interpreted what he said correctly," Enllss ventured, "Zor-Ell gave us a warning. He said the Serrll has three years within which to prepare to face the Krans or we shall be overrun. And the Orieli won't be doing anything about it."

"I doubt that very much," Illeran mused. "The message being, if they get too involved with their problems, they'll throw us to the Krans and withdraw beyond the Moanar, right?"

"That's the picture."

"Definitely needs looking into. Still, I wonder if the situation is really so desperate."

"What do you mean?"

"Anar'on. Would the Wanderers really sit still if the Krans attacked?"

Enllss stared thoughtfully at his mentor. "Khiman-ra—"

"While Kai Tanard remained busy harassing Naurun and Omiron, the Deklans though to profit from the confusion by starting some raids of their own. We all know what happened then."

"Marrakan placed third-level adepts in their ships. They destroyed three raiders before the message got home. I remember. And you think Anar'on would do it again?"

"To save themselves, if not the Serrll? Yes."

"Given what's happened on Devon, perhaps I should have a quiet talk with Director Marrakan."

"You do that, and I'll have that drink now, Enllss," Illeran said musingly and his tongue flicked quickly across his lips.

Chapter Thirteen

Sprawled in the contoured hug of the couch, Terr felt wonderfully relaxed and at ease. Content for the ship to simply keep going without end. They had a quick, but intense flight to the far edge of Palean space. He repaired and renewed the depth of bonds that held Teena to him. Both had rediscovered each other during periods of long talks, warm silences and moments of feverish passion. And he came so close to losing her. There had been an awful lot of blue glow in their quarters…

Sometimes tentative and awkward, he also reached out to Dhar. Laying himself open and vulnerable, he shared his secret fears, prejudices, dreams and failures, until both transcended mere understanding, becoming one again. A disturbing and healing experience.

The command deck almost silent, a cocoon of warmth and security. Even the management system had stopped its muted commentary. Color-reactive control consoles winked to themselves. Through the transparent nav bubble the gravity waves snaked around the ship in brown lines, growing denser as they neared Devon 3-VL4.

Terr glanced at Teena sitting beside him. He gave her a slow smile, reached out and brushed her shoulder.

"It won't be long now," he murmured and gestured at a yellow star swelling before them.

"Is that Devon's sun?" she chirped, obviously enjoying herself, and Terr nodded.

"Crossing IP," the computer announced, startlingly loud, shattering the mood. "Transition available at your discretion."

"Time to closest transition?" Terr requested.

"Four minutes thirty-seven seconds."

"Tactical."

The nav bubble and the main plate dissolved into a positional grid showing the Devon system, his interest held by the highlighted disposition of ships around Devon's moon.

The hatch opened behind him and he heard Dhar's heavy footsteps.

"Are we transiting?" Dhar said and nodded to Teena. She flashed him a smile as he lowered himself into the remaining couch with a satisfied grunt.

"Just about there," Terr said, studying the main plate.

"Look at all those ships!" Teena frowned and pointed at the tactical display grid.

"The large white blip hanging above the moon is an M-4. The blue one is the Orieli cruiser."

"And the small one?"

"That's an M-3 sweeper. Probably a surveillance picket."

"What's that?" Teena demanded, indicating an area of pulsing brown on the moon's surface. Terr exchanged a glance with Dhar.

"That's an emission trace from the Kran vessel's power core. It's below the terminator, otherwise we would be getting a direct signature."

She looked fully at Terr. "Can it tell that we're here?"

"Probably, but I wouldn't worry about it, my pet. The whole mass of the moon is between that ship and us. It's not a threat," he said—unless it lifted.

"Hmm," Teena said.

Looking at the tactical display and the set pieces, the situation seemed almost tranquil. Terr wasn't fooled. Judging by his stern expression, neither was Dhar.

Teena shot both of them a dark scowl. "You two are having me on," she declared firmly.

"Receiving an interrogative from Master Scout Taran," the computer announced, saving Terr from an impossible reply.

"Transmit IFF and open a channel."

Through the Valley of Shadow

A small window cleared in the tactical display and Taran's fishy features rippled into view. Cold black eyes stared through the plate. Terr returned the gaze without flinching.

"Master Scout Terrllss-rr, on route to rendezvous with Karhide Arlon Dee."

"I presume that you're the mysterious reason why the Orieli are still here, Master Scout?" Taran hissed and Terr grinned.

"I'm afraid so."

"Well, I can certainly use you," Taran said briskly.

Terr sensed the tension and the strain in the Karkan's voice. He did not relish the other's tactical position. If things got hot, he wanted to be somewhere else. Taran's casual inclusion of *Sheeva* into his command did not fit into Terr's mission plan. As the site commander, Taran was nominally his superior, but Terr wasn't part of Taran's chain of command, and Taran had no authority to issue him tactical or operational orders.

"You might be able to use me," Terr said firmly, "but I'm not available."

"What's that?" Taran hissed and his eyes glittered with anger. "Did I hear you right?"

"My orders are clear, Master Scout. You can confirm them through COMPALOPS."

"I don't give a worm's shit about your orders. As soon as you break normal, you fall under my authority."

"Negative! I am on a diplomatic mission."

"I know all about your mission. Cultural manure raking." Taran's internal struggle all too evident. "Damn it, man. I *need* you," he snapped, eyes pleading.

Terr was not impressed. "What you need is an M-6, not a gnat M-1. Even if I were in a position to do so, I can't help you."

"I am about to engage a superior enemy asset and you are refusing your duty, sir!" Taran thundered and his tongue flicked in a blur. "You can be assured that your cowardice will be brought to the attention of COMPALOPS." Any sympathy

Stefan Vučak

Terr may have felt for the Karkan disappeared.

"Your tactical situation is untenable, Taran, and you know it. You're in no position to confront the Kran ship with only an M-4 and an M-3 sweeper. Consider what happened to your other M-4 and the lost lives of its crew."

"To the slime with you! The Scout Fleet has never retreated before an enemy and I'm not about to be the first!" Taran snarled and the plate rippled as he cut contact.

"A proud man," Dhar commented with a sad shake of his head.

"Proud and foolish," Terr rasped. "He's not only risking his ship, but Devon and the whole ecoforming project. He *must* realize that."

"Terr?" Teena placed her hand on his shoulder. "You're not exactly calming me down, you know."

He smiled and patted her hand. "Sorry, pet. Just voicing my pique at the stupidity of high command."

"Surely COMPALOPS must know that Taran's position is a hopeless one?"

"You would think so. What I don't understand is why Arlon Dee doesn't simply wade in and clean up the mess?"

Teena raised an eyebrow. "Why don't you ask him?" she said primly.

Terr grinned broadly and chuckled. "Why not? Let's do that." He glanced at Dhar and nodded.

"Approaching closest transition point," the computer announced.

"Noted. Open a channel to the Orieli cruiser."

The tactical display cleared and Arlon Dee studied them with keen interest.

"Master Scout Terrllss-rr. It appears that our paths have crossed yet again," he said easily and his tongue slid over his lips.

"Strange crossroads this time, Karhide," Terr said with a smile.

"Not by choice, Da Terr. I can assure you of that. As soon as you dock, I am pulling out. I don't intend to linger here longer than is absolutely necessary."

Terr was appalled. "You cannot mean that, Karhide?"

"Oh? And why wouldn't I mean it?"

"The Kran vessel. What's its status?"

Arlon remained silent for a moment. "It has regained full weapons capability. Over the last two days, there has been a marked increase in power emission levels and its defense net is now stable. I wouldn't be surprised if it lifted."

"Is Master Scout Taran aware of this?"

"He is."

Terr didn't have to have the consequences of a marauding Kran vessel rampaging through Palean space sketched out for him. He felt equally certain Arlon Dee was painfully aware of the consequences.

"Then you have answered my question, Karhide," Terr said. Arlon smiled ruefully and nodded.

"I look forward to taking this up with you personally, Da Terr," he said and his image faded.

Sheeva dropped into normal space and immediately initiated a status sweep of the area. Terr had brought the M-1 much closer into the tactical area than he intended, but it wasn't a serious oversight. After all, no one was shooting at each other—yet.

On the tactical display a web of complex energy readings covered much of the area around the Kran's position. It did not register as a shield matrix, looking more like an interference pattern. An Orieli sensor grid? The whole tactical situation gave him the creeps. He silently cursed Anabb for sending him here and potentially endangering Teena. He also cursed himself for accepting this screwy assignment so glibly. During their transit from Anar'on, he pondered why Anabb had arranged for Karhide Arlon Dee to take them to LTN-3 where they were supposed to join up with Zor-Ell for their final transit into Ori-eli space. He could have met Zor-Ell on Captal just as easily.

Was Anabb once again spinning his web of intrigue?

Terr docked *Sheeva* into the Orieli's cavernous Hangar Bay Two. Arlon Dee and Tavac were there to meet them personally. Dhar, Teena, and Terr stood clustered around the landing ramp, gaping with undisguised curiosity at the charred wreck of the Kran scout. Terr had seen strange ships and fought them, but this bulbous, twisted insect-shaped thing made his skin go cold. Inactive, it still looked deadly and menacing. Crewmen worked around it, moving in and out of its interior. He looked at Arlon and hooked a thumb over his shoulder.

"Does Taran know about that thing?"

"Master Scout Taran has a lot on his mind right now." Arlon's tongue flashed around his lips. "I didn't want to add to his problems."

Terr's grin didn't touch his eyes as he glanced at Dhar in an unspoken sharing of unease.

"This is an affront. An evil," Dhar muttered darkly.

"I cannot argue with you there, First Scout," Tavac mused, gazing at the alien craft. After a moment, he turned and nodded at the insignia on Dhar's uniform. "And congratulations on your promotion."

"Undeserved," Dhar said and Tavac grinned wryly, noting Terr's plain working grays. "And yours."

Terr shrugged. "A dubious honor, Karhide," he said and took Teena's hand. "Allow me to present Teena-raye, my part-ner. Teena, this is Karhide Arlon Dee, commander of this ves-sel, and Opturkarh Tavac, his first officer."

Arlon smiled broadly and bowed. "Honored, Dapata."

Teena blushed and gave a small curtsy. "The honor is mine, sir. Terr told me a lot about both of you."

Arlon chuckled. "I trust it made for interesting listening," he said and turned to Terr. "You may indulge your curiosity about the Kran ship at a later time. Right now, we have a situation to address."

Terr nodded. "By all means."

Arlon gathered them with a glance. "This way to the PT alcoves."

Teena cooed with delight after experiencing transport.

The Observation Deck gloomy and deserted, Devon's moon glared bright and full above them. They made themselves comfortable in wide contoured couches, separated from the main viewing area by a discrete partition. Looking at the moon, Terr could forget that Death waited to be unleashed there. Arlon was right. There would be time for sightseeing later.

Arlon sat back, his gaze direct and penetrating. Making up his mind, he looked directly at Teena.

"I don't know what Terr may have told you about us, Dapata—"

"Must we be so formal?" she inquired in a small voice. Arlon gave a small bow.

"Thank you—Teena. I want you to make up your own mind as to who and what we are. After all, that's the purpose of the Cultural Exchange Mission. Once we're underway to LTN-3, you will undergo cultural orientation and environmental assimilation. This is not only for your protection, but ours as well. Terr will fill you in on the procedure. You've been assigned quarters, which I trust will be satisfactory. Cent Comp is instructed to recognize you and accept your non-tactical mental and verbal commands. Make use of the computer's extensive library and VI entertainment facilities. You will find it stimulating, and another window into what we are. You have the freedom of the ship and may go anywhere you wish. That includes Primary Flight Control. Cent Comp will caution you if you approach a restricted area. The crew is briefed of your presence and will offer any assistance consistent with your personal and Mission-oriented duties. Opturkarh Tavac will be at your disposal at any time to address specific problems and requests."

A professional, Teena took the information in stride. "Thank you, sir. I shall try not to be too much trouble."

"Karhide, may I ask how long it will take to reach LTN-3?" Terr inquired softly, suspecting the information just given was as much for his benefit as it was for Teena's. He had to admire Arlon's tact.

"Fourteen days at maximum boost."

Terr almost gaped. Two thousand light-years in fourteen days? It took fourteen days just to reach Anar'on from Captal, a mere three hundred and sixty light-years.

"About the Krans. Something just occurred to me."

"Yes?"

"The Moanar Nebula breach. I wondered why the Krans haven't found it. Pattern analysis of your ship movements should have identified a concentration of vessels around LTN-3."

"We don't allow Kran ships to come close enough to do pattern analysis, Terr," Arlon said with a thin smile. "And LTN-3 is not exactly near the breach."

Terr did not return Arlon's smile. Being of such critical strategic importance, he felt certain the breach warranted special security arrangements. He looked forward to seeing them.

"Should that breach close, the Orieli would be in some difficulty."

Arlon smiled. "We took steps not to become stranded on this side."

Terr nodded and smiled in return. "Like installing a transport portal?"

"Very good, Terr. That is exactly what we have done."

Terr smiled as another thought popped to the surface. "You already closed the entrance to the breach."

Arlon reflected his smile. "Not yet, but it's one option we're considering."

"Right. Now that we're all on board, I would like to reopen the matter of your intentions regarding the Kran vessel."

Arlon looked frustrated, his frustration directed squarely at Taran and COMPALOPS. Terr didn't have to have it explained.

"As much as I would like to, I am unable to do anything until Master Scout Taran specifically requests my assistance," Arlon said. "This is Serrll space and I have no authority here."

"If Taran takes his M-4 into combat, he won't have a chance, will he?"

"The Kran vessel can discharge almost continuous multiple bursts of up to two hundred and forty TeV. The M-4's shield grid cannot withstand such pulses," Arlon said flatly.

"And you're still going to do nothing?"

"If I take unilateral action, I'll be flaunting Serrll's sovereign integrity and setting a bad precedent. Until the Serrll request our help, my hands are tied."

Intellectually, Terr understood very well the broader ramifications of this confrontation, but emotionally, he rebelled.

"Even if it costs lives?"

Arlon towered over him, two katalans of sheer muscle and power. The Cetan was an imposing presence, red eyes glittering like chipped ice.

"It might not come to that. I surmise Master Scout Taran is waiting for reinforcements and is confident in his ability to contain the situation."

"There aren't any reinforcements!" Terr snapped and heard Dhar clear his throat in disapproval. Terr ignored him. He wasn't in violation of Serrll security saying that. "The M-6 he was expecting is delayed. It won't be here for another fifteen hours."

Arlon accepted this without reaction. "Then Taran intends to confront the Kran cruiser alone."

"As you knew he would."

"I can only act within the guidelines you yourselves have set," Arlon answered with heavy weariness.

Terr wondered how true that really was.

* * *

Taran closed his eyes and got pleasantly drowsy when the comms alert beeped. He hissed in annoyance and struggled out of bed. This better be important, he fumed, or someone would be very, very sorry.

Rubbing his eyes, he touched the comms pad and turned to the Wall. His Deklan exec looked apologetic.

"I didn't want to call you, sir, but we have a situation. Ach!"

Taran bit back a blast and gave a tired sigh. "Talk to me."

"*Kopan* has picked up anomalous energy readings from the Kran ship. What we read as their primary shield grid just went up several quantum levels. Ach! Before that happened their power core emissions spiked."

Taran digested the information, not liking any of it. They have been monitoring an increased level of Kran activity over the last forty-six hours. Could the infernal thing be getting ready to lift? He was only surprised that it hadn't done so already.

"Where is *Kopan* now?"

"I ordered it to fall back beyond the Kran's acquisition horizon."

"Ship status?"

"We're at initial alert."

"Go to primary alert and prepare to move us in."

"Ach! May I point out, sir, the M-6—"

"Just do it, okay?"

The exec did not relish the idea of confronting the Kran vessel alone, but orders were orders, no matter how crazy.

Taran dressed quickly. Sipping leaf tea, he instructed the Wall to show him a real-time scan of the Kran vessel.

The alien ship nestled in a hollow between steep crags, deep in shadow, its two bulbous shapes almost invisible. Detectable leakage came from its shields. The enhanced image showed business-like patches along its blackened hull. They may not look pretty, but they apparently did the job. He wondered how much time he had. Probably not enough.

He tapped in the comms codes and waited for the Wall to clear. His connection to COMPALOPS came through immediately.

In Tain twined his fingers and sat back into his formchair.

"I have been expecting your call, friend Taran."

"The tactical situation has crystallized, sir," Taran started without preamble. "The Kran vessel is about to lift and I intend to take my command and offer it battle. We must neutralize it before it's able to maneuver. With the M-6 still eleven hours away, I've run out of options."

In Tain studied his impetuous protégé with a mixture of irritation and fondness. His irritation directed at Taran's recklessness, while secretly admiring the Karkan's courage in the face of such heavy odds. But he had to concern himself with broader issues. Nevertheless, however brave, Taran's misplaced zeal was a futile gesture.

"You are aware of my previous orders on this issue, Master Scout?" he asked softly.

Taran flared, resenting the implication that he was incapable of carrying out his duty. He didn't want to admit it even to himself that perhaps pride clouded his better judgment. He knew that a more humble man would have swallowed his resentment and called for help. He may well be placing his ship and the lives of his crew at needles risk. He also had to consider the strategic implication of a Kran ship loose in Serrll space.

It was a calculated gamble.

"The tactical situation has not deteriorated to a point where I need or want to call for Orieli assistance. I also want to point out, Prima Scout, that it's a sad day for the Serrll Scout Fleet when we're incapable of protecting our own space."

In Tain bridled, but secretly agreed with Taran's assessment. In this instance the Fleet's response time woefully inadequate, something CAPFLTCOM was even now evaluating. If this had been a Kran penetration in force, he suspected the Ser-rll would have been rolled, suffering horrifying losses in the process.

"You are the tactical area commander Taran, and it's your call," he said sternly. "Just make sure you make the right one."

* * *

Getting used to being hooked into the VI coupling again, Terr liked the godlike perspective it offered. The Serrll used holographic imagery extensively, and although prevalent in commercial networks, only dabbled at the application of virtual technology in its military ships. Being able to experience the full range of ship's activities and sensor capabilities instead of hav-ing them machine interpreted, had obvious tactical and opera-tional advantages. Something to be noted in his report to Anabb.

Devon's moon glared in shades of whites and grays; close enough to touch. He could have been in open space protected by a personal shield. The experience complete and utterly real. He issued a mental command asking the housekeeping com-puter to show him the existing tactical disposition. Cent Comp hesitated, probably clearing the request through Tavac. Then, two transparent spheres, the outer yellow and the inner green, sprang around the blue points of the two Serrll ships, indicating the primary and secondary shield grids. A dull pulsing orange dome appeared above the Kran vessel's position—what the Orieli classified as a *Daktar*-class heavy cruiser—hidden below the moon's horizon. The M-4's power bloom brightened and its secondary shield grid extended as it began to move.

Terr deactivated the VI coupling and looked searchingly at Arlon sitting in his command couch.

"I know, Terr. I know," Arlon said softly. "Cent Comp?"

"Ready, Karhide."

"Status?"

"Condition three on active standby. Tactical control in PFC."

"Terr?" Teena queried softly.

He turned to look at her sitting beside him.

"Taran is going to attack, isn't he?" she asked.

"I'm afraid so."

"But...he'll be destroyed!"

"Karhide!" Terr said urgently and pointed at the main repeater holoview plot. "You must warn him!"

"He has already been warned," Arlon said heavily.

Terr fumed. Damn the man's pride! He bit his lip and watched the tactical situation develop to its inevitable conclusion.

The M-4 crossed the *Daktar's* acquisition envelope and moved steadily in. As it sank below the moon's horizon, the view switched to the orbiting Burlig scanners. Two shield rings sprang around the Kran ship.

"Tactical caution," the computer announced immediately. "Target has powered up and acquired a weapons lock on the Serrll vessel. The M-4's shield grid is pulsing in preparatory firing phase."

As the M-4 cleared the craggy peaks around the stationary Kran vessel, both ships fired. A solid line of yellow ionization stabbed at the M-4. Its secondary shield flared and collapsed. The primary shield arced in twisted discharges, but held. A bright yellow sword sheared through the Kran's outer shield grid and dissipated in a spectacular flare of orange fire. The M-4 fired again, the beam worrying the same impact point. It maintained a sustained fire for another four seconds without any visible effect on the Kran ship.

The *Daktar's* outer shield grid faded. Another lance of yellow light, this time more intense, stabbed from the ship. The M-4 staggered and its shields flared, collapsed and reformed. It stopped its advance and maintained a steady return fire.

Teena gasped as the Kran ship slowly rose a few katalans,

righted itself and maintained hover. A circle of white light rippled around its forward section and drained into its shield grid. A searing blue point formed, from which a brilliant bolt of pale blue reached for the M-4. The M-4 staggered as the beam bored through the secondary and primary shields, rippling along the ship's starboard side. The hull appeared not to have been penetrated, but Terr knew that there would be massive circuit and system damage to Taran's ship.

"Terr!" Teena gasped and clutched his arm. He took her hand and squeezed gently.

Shields flaring, the M-4 limped below the moon's horizon. The Kran vessel maintained its hover.

"Why doesn't the *Daktar* close?" Terr asked Arlon.

"It's probably carrying out diagnostic self-checks. That won't take them long."

"And you still won't do anything?"

"Karhide, we have a comms link from the Serrll M-4," Tavac announced quietly.

"Very well."

The Kran vessel rose clear off the moon's peaks and fired two quick bursts. The first completely collapsed the M-4's shield grid. The second traversed along the bottom of the hull and sliced through the projector dome. Secondary explosions rippled along the M-4's hull and blew away huge sections of plating, exposing the naked frames beneath. The M-4 shook, canted and wallowed, completely helpless.

Terr watched in horror as the once proud ship was reduced to a wreck. If the Krans fired again, the M-4 wasn't even in a position to protect itself. He felt Death stir in his hands, but checked the impulse.

When the holoview window opened, Taran staggered into view. A wide cut on his scaly head oozed blood, but his eyes were bright and alive. Behind him the command deck was a shambles of broken equipment and live conduit cables. Bodies lay on the deck and smoke obscured some of the control panels.

"Karhide," Taran hissed, obviously in pain. He coughed and winced before looking up. "Proud I may be, but not so stupid as to recognize a hopeless cause."

"Can you maneuver, Master Scout?" Arlon asked, his tongue moving around his lips.

Taran shook his head. "Main and secondary reactors are down. I cannot even raise a nav grid."

"You should not have gone in alone, Master Scout," Arlon admonished him with more than a trace of irony.

"I had my duty, sir," Taran hissed.

Arlon nodded. "I understand, Da. I'm assuming command of the tactical area. The Kran central nexus core will ignore you as long as you don't attempt to raise your defensive screens or maneuver. Do nothing, Master Scout."

"I wish you better success, Karhide," Taran managed a gruff growl and cut contact.

"Cent Comp? Bring the ship into line-of-sight with the target and set condition three."

Tapal shifted position and moved deliberately toward the moon, changing its attitude to take it above the Kran vessel as they sighted each other. Terr understood the logic of the maneuver. The problem was, it took time, and nothing could stop the *Daktar* from firing at the helpless M-4 if it wanted to. He watched impatiently as they maneuvered, mentally urging Arlon to hurry up.

"Tactical caution. Target is ranging in an attempt to acquire a firing lock," the computer advised.

"Fire maximum twin bursts at designated bearings," Arlon commanded quietly as the Kran ship became visible.

Power surged through the interceptor net rings. The energy overload twisted along the flux lines and formed two locus nodes. The interceptor net matrix dissolved at the node points and two lances of vivid blue-white ionization stabbed at the

Kran vessel. Its shields flared, then stabilized. A pale blue spear reached for the Orieli ship. Terr felt a sharp jolt and the deck shuddered. In the mainframe repeater plot, he saw the shield lines twist and fade before they reconstituted. Arlon maintained steady fire. When the *Daktar* responded, *Tapal* trembled more violently, but the shields held. Under *Tapal's* fire, the Kran's shield grid flared in a rippling cascade of yellow and orange discharges, collapsing and reforming, while backsurges licked along the hull in sheets of fire. Plating deformed and debris shot from the torn frames.

The M-4 managed to bring up its nav shield and began to slowly drift away from the fire zone. Arlon ground his teeth in impotent frustration.

"I told him not to move!"

The Kran ship stabilized its attitude and a single traversing beam ripped along the M-4's hull. The collapsed shield lines arced in a brilliant display of white and yellow lightning as they drained. The hull began to glow and plating sheared away, tumbling around the ship. Most of the command bubble simply vanished, vaporized, exposing the main structural frames beneath. The ship began to tumble.

Teena sobbed quietly beside him, her hands covering her cheeks.

Tapal fired a burst and the Kran ship lurched as its outer shield grid collapsed. Terr stood up, his eyes fixed on the drifting M-4. He clenched his fists and the words from the *Saftara* came unbidden. Death settled on his shoulders and he felt comforted by its touch. The *Daktar* fired a twin pulse directly at the M-4. The ship shimmered and swam as its structure deformed and twisted, literally melting away. The overstressed main reactor containment field failed, followed by a blinding flash, and the ship vanished in a brilliant sphere of white light. When it cooled to orange, then dull red, nothing remained of the M-4 but a cloud of expanding wreckage. He could hardly believe what he had seen.

Through the Valley of Shadow

Terr glanced at Teena, his horror reflected in her eyes. It was wanton destruction. The Kran ship's sensors must have told it that the M-4 was no longer a tactical threat, but it chose to destroy a helpless vessel anyway.

Tapal staggered heavily under Kran fire and its interceptor net arced as point collapses reformed. Damage reports were coming in. Terr's reaction became automatic. He fixed his eyes on the Kran vessel and Death stirred in his hands.

Dhar felt the god's presence and turned to Terr. The aura of power surrounded Sankri like a cloak and Dhar flinched at its intensity. He sprang out of his couch, his arm reaching.

"Sankri! Don't!"

Arlon jerked and gaped at Terr in astonishment.

Terr pointed at the fading red sphere of light where the M-4 had been, blue sparks licking his fingers.

"This evil must be burned away, my brother," he grated and lightning crackled between his hands. Tavac stared at him, then slowly stood and stepped back.

"Terr, what are you doing?" Teena demanded in alarm. He grasped her shoulders and looked into her eyes.

"What must be done."

Arlon shouted something, but Terr didn't hear him. There was only a burning desire to blot out the evil alien presence before him.

He leveled his arms at the image in the holoview plot and bellowed his anger. Thunder cracked in the PFC and a solid bar of golden light speared through the hull toward the Kran ship. Its shield grid hardly had time to register the incoming surge as they collapsed along the entry point of the beam. The golden lance lit the hull, splashing it with white fire before it tore through the center of the ship to emerge in a burst of flying melted hull material from the other side. A ripple of arcing discharges danced along the shield force lines before they vanished, leaving a blackened, jagged hole in the ship. From the rear module of the ship, a pencil-thin yellow-white spear shot through opposite sides of the hull as the quantum point singularity discharged.

Terr maintained his rage, ready to stab at the alien again, but sensed it wasn't necessary. The *Daktar* slowly tilted, rotated in place and began to sink toward the moon. It struck a broken peak that sent shards of rock cascading down in a cloud of dust. In slow motion the ship plowed into the valley bottom and its side split along the hull breach sustained in its previous encounter. Plating and frame beams flew in all directions. Dust slowly settled around the wreck.

Terr slowed his breathing, shuddered in a long exhale, and lowered his arms. Death lingered for a moment, then faded, leaving him drained, but satisfied. This felt right. This time, he used his power to save life, not take it, and the realization sobered him. In that moment, he finally understood the qualitative duality in the use of his gift. And he loosed Death through *Tapal's* hull without damaging it! He would have to think about that. Something else occurred to him.

It might not have been wise to expose himself to the Orieli, and he would have to live with the consequences. For all he knew, Arlon may have dealt capably with the Kran vessel, but the cost could have been high, not only to his ship, but to Devon and this whole part of Palean space. Taran failed to see that and paid a costly price for his mistake.

Dhar stared at Sankri in awe and disbelief. Only a third-level Discipline initiate could direct the path of Death through a solid object without damaging it. His brother should not have been able to do that. He was tempted to kneel before him and seek absolution.

Terr cleared his throat and smiled sheepishly. Teena's eyes were wide in shock as she stared at him, one small fist pressed white against her mouth. Display of this kind of power had shaken her badly. He reached for her, but she shrank back as fat tears slid down her cheeks. He looked at her in helpless confusion, not knowing how to reach her.

Arlon, his face serious and uncertain, studied him, undecided what to do.

Looking about the command level and the operations platform below, Terr saw tense faces, wary eyes, and fear. Most of them were still not sure what had happened exactly, but they had seen the lightning in his hands and heard the thunder. The section of hull where the bolt had gone through was unmarked. He turned to Dhar and saw the same wary look.

"Nightwings…"

He strode into the PT alcove, issued a mental command and the housekeeping computer transported him to the Observations Deck. The moon filled half the sky and Devon was a fat blue-white crescent hanging beneath it. The sheet of stars that was The Arch stretched in a torn, brilliant backdrop. Above him, the few visible stars burned harsh white. He sprawled into one of the comfortable couches and plunged his face between his hands.

Reaction set in and a cold shiver ran through his body. He could still see the fires devouring the M-4. He could imagine the chaos and the crew's terror as energies tore the ship apart around them, but the sight of the dead Kran ship left him satisfied. And also sobering to see Death unleashed on such scale…and surprising. He had not thought himself capable of controlling such an outpouring. The image of a dead Kran ship left him with a cold, burning hatred for the aliens. No, not hatred, more a desire to wipe away an infestation.

The soft hum of the personal transport transceiver faded behind him, followed by a sound of firm footsteps. He didn't bother looking up. In silence, they watched the stars, each absorbed in their thoughts.

"So much is hidden by those stars," Arlon Dee said absently and settled himself into a couch. The material squirmed around him.

"And much that we need to be prepared for," Terr agreed.

The stars shifted. The moon swung beneath them and fell

away as *Tapal* began to move, its mission in Serrll space completed.

"The Kran vessel is disabled and its systems are inactive," Arlon said. "The Serrll will learn a lot about their new enemy from the central nexus core, and we have a rendezvous to keep."

Terr sensed Arlon's hesitation, but did nothing to lighten it.

"Da Terr—"

Terr winced. "Must we?"

Arlon smiled and nodded. "Terr…I'm not certain a being with your power should be allowed into our space."

"The Orieli have some formidable powers of their own," Terr pointed out, hinting at, but not revealing Zor-Ell's secret.

Arlon digested that for a moment. "Dharaklin, is he—"

"We both walk in the shadow of Death," Terr said simply.

"In the shadow of Death…A lyrical way of putting it. How many—"

"How many of us are there?" Terr smiled as the image of Anar'on firmed in his mind and warmed him. "A whole world."

"I will have to report this incident to OSCOM," Arlon said after a time.

"Of course, I understand." Terr saw no need to pretend.

With their observer techniques, the Orieli were bound to find out about Anar'on and the Wanderers. It might have been better not to reveal the power of the Discipline before he reached the Orieli Cluster, and certainly not in such spectacular fashion, but he suspected that Arlon had no authority to amend any aspect of the Cultural Exchange Mission. He was curious to see what Zor-Ell would do.

When he turned, Arlon Dee had left and Teena stood in the shadows. Her eyes were troubled as they regarded him.

"Who are you?" she whispered, face lost and tragic.

"I am the harbinger of eternity," Terr said as he rose, but the god of Death provided the words.

She bit her lip, trying hard not to cry as his words tore her heart open.

"And can I love you, Lord of Death, as much as I love him?" she choked softly, almost too low to hear.

Unbidden, like invisible gossamer, Death settled about Terr and he stood in its shadow. The lightnings did not writhe in anger in his hands. A blue softness began to envelope him as he opened his arms to her. Her steps were hesitant and she stopped just out of reach of the aura surrounding him.

Terr did not move. He wanted her to make the choice, wanted her to cross the barrier that would otherwise always separate them. Then she was in his arms, her heart beating fast against him.

"There has always been only me to love, my pet," he murmured tenderly into her hair and held her tight. "Only me."

About the author

Stefan Vučak has written twenty-one novels, which include eight SF books in the Shadow Gods Saga. His *Cry of Eagles* won the coveted Readers' Favorite silver medal award, and his *All the Evils* was the prestigious Eric Hoffer contest finalist and Readers' Favorite silver medal winner. *Strike for Honor* won the gold medal.

Stefan leveraged a successful career in the Information Technology industry, which took him to the Middle East working on cellphone systems. Writing has been a road of discovery, helping him broaden his horizons. He also spends time as an editor and book reviewer. Stefan lives in Melbourne, Australia.

To learn more about Stefan Vučak, visit his:
Website: www.stefanvucak.com
Facebook: www.facebook.com/StefanVucakAuthor
Twitter: @stefanvucak

More Books by Stefan Vučak

https://www.stefanvucak.com/Books/

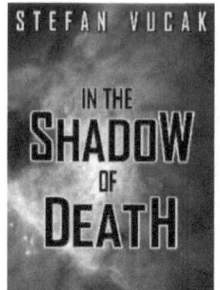  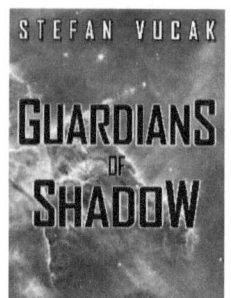